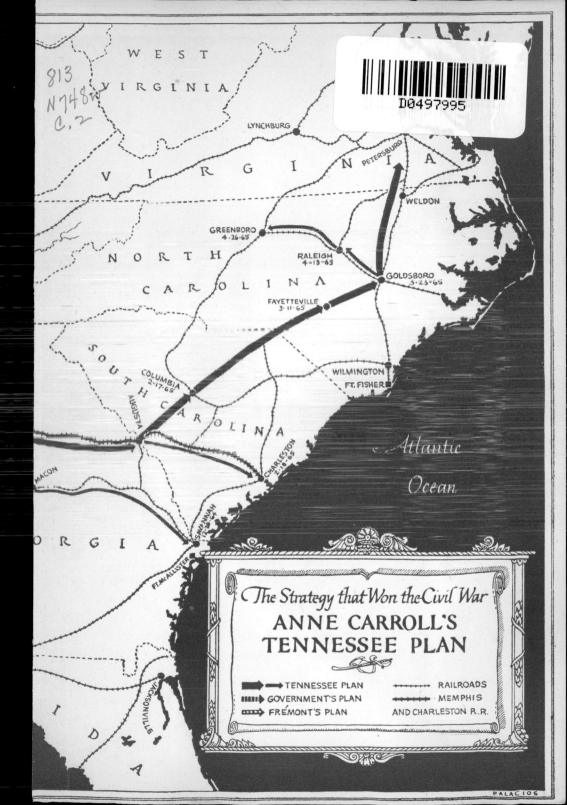

The Strategy that Won the Civil War

ANNE CARROLL'S
TENNESSEE PLAN

→ TENNESSEE PLAN   ┅┅┅ RAILROADS
▮▮▮▮▷ GOVERNMENT'S PLAN   ┿┿┿┿ MEMPHIS
┉┉┉▷ FRÉMONT'S PLAN   AND CHARLESTON R.R.

WOMAN WITH A SWORD

IN FIDE ET IN BELLO FORTE

THE CARROLL COAT OF ARMS

Arms of Carroll, Chiefs of Ely,
King's County, Ireland

WOMAN
WITH A SWORD

THE BIOGRAPHICAL NOVEL

OF ANNA ELLA CARROLL OF MARYLAND

BY HOLLISTER NOBLE 1900 -

> Hers was the greatest course
> in the war. She found herself,
> got no pay, and did the great
> work that made others famous.
>
> —Edwin M. Stanton,
> Secretary of War

DOUBLEDAY & COMPANY, INC.
GARDEN CITY, NEW YORK, 1948

FOR IRIS

ACKNOWLEDGMENTS

ALL OF THE CHARACTERS IN THIS BOOK WERE LIVING persons, with one exception. Harry Heyward is a fictional dramatization of several of Anne Carroll's Southern suitors.

All of the major military and political events took place very much in the order in which they are related. The opinions, military and political, expressed by the principal characters in *Woman with a Sword* were taken directly from their public documents and personal letters. A great deal of the historical material in this book may be found in the files of the National Archives at Washington and in the records, documents, and letters in possession of the Library of Congress; also in a valuable collection of Miss Carroll's papers in the Maryland Historical Society files at Baltimore, and in certain private collections to which I had access.

I wish to thank the many individuals and institutions who were most helpful in the preparation of this book. Among these are Mrs. Blair Cameron and the personnel of the William Wyles Lincoln Library at Santa Barbara College, University of California, Santa Barbara; officials of the Los Angeles Public Library, the St. Louis Public Library, the St. Louis Mercantile Library, the Texas State Library, and the library of the University of Texas; officials of the National Military Parks at Fort Donelson, Shiloh, and Vicksburg; Mrs. Guy Blount of Nacogdoches, Texas, a grand-niece of Judge Evans; and two nieces of Miss Carroll, Miss Nellie Calvert Carroll of Walnut Landing, Cambridge, Maryland, and Miss Katharine Cradock of Pikesville, Maryland.

I particularly wish to express my deep appreciation for their unflagging interest and invaluable editorial assistance in the final preparation of this book to Lee Barker, Executive Editor of Doubleday and Company, and to his wife, Eileen Lange.

I also wish to express my gratitude to Mr. William H. Seward, grandson of Secretary Seward, for his kind permission to examine certain documents in the Seward home at Auburn, New York.

For important suggestions and criticisms incorporated in this book, grateful thanks are due the following: my wife, Iris Noble; John Howard Lawson, Barthold Fles, Sidney Harmon, and John Weber, with appreciation to Mrs. Jean Kovner for valuable clerical assistance.

Woman with a Sword owes a special and obvious debt in both content and spirit to four unusual volumes: Sarah Ellen Blackwell's *A Military Genius: A Life of Anna Ella Carroll of Maryland,* published by the Women's Suffrage Association in 1891; *My Dear Lady,* a biography of Miss Carroll by Marjorie Barstow Greenbie, Whittlesey House, 1940; *The Novel and the People,* International Publishers, 1945, by the brilliant young English critic, Ralph Fox, killed fighting Fascist forces in Spain in 1937; and to Carl Sandburg's great volumes on Lincoln, an inexhaustible source of information and inspiration.

HOLLISTER NOBLE

DRAMATIS PERSONAE

Abraham Lincoln, *President of the United States*

Anne Carroll, *prominent author and political writer of Baltimore*

Lemuel Dale Evans, *special agent of the State Department for Mexico and Texas*

Harry Heyward, *lawyer and soldier of Charleston, S.C.*

Benjamin Franklin Wade, *senator from Ohio. Chairman of the Committee on the Conduct of the War*

Caroline Wade, *wife of Senator Wade*

Edwin McMasters Stanton, *Secretary of War, 1862–68*

Colonel Thomas A. Scott, *Assistant Secretary of War*

William H. Seward, *Secretary of State*

Judge Edward Bates, *United States Attorney General*

Captain Charles M. Scott, *chief river pilot for General Grant*

Ulysses S. Grant, *General, U. S. Army. Lieutenant General, 1864–65*

William T. Sherman, *General, U. S. Army*

Cabinet officers, senators, representatives, generals, officials and their families, members of the Carroll family, and various individuals, civil and military, of both North and South.

TIME—1860–65

WOMAN WITH A SWORD

1

A RAW NORTHEAST WIND DROVE GUSTS OF COLD RAIN across the tawdry, confused, and thoroughly frightened capital of the nation.

Georgetown busses and a few funereal hacks, their drivers huddled and bent against the wind, plowed through seas of mud in the unpaved streets. Here and there hardy pedestrians hugged store fronts under flapping awnings that made passage a little easier along the built-up portions of Pennsylvania Avenue, or scurried past interminable vacant lots piled with cordwood and filled with rain-soaked garbage and debris.

Acrid wood smoke from thousands of chimney pots swirled in gray clouds across the rooftops; eddied in long streamers in the empty streets.

But in the comfortable rooms of Senator Benjamin Franklin Wade of Ohio, at Number Six 4½ Street, a few blocks from the Capitol, the Senator and Mrs. Wade, with Judge Edward Bates of St. Louis, sat cozily before a brisk fire with curtains drawn and a great rose-shaded lamp warming the scene. It was December 29, 1860, and the little group had just finished dinner.

Judge Bates, who had been in town only two days, leaned back in his big chair with a sigh of satisfaction and prepared to light a vicious-looking cigar. He was a well-preserved man in his sixties with strong features and a calm, almost gentle expression. Bates was a Virginia-born gentleman who had moved to Missouri in early manhood and had since enjoyed a colorful political career as state attorney general, state senator, and Whig congressman. Eight months ago, before the Chicago Republican Convention, he had been a presidential possibility.

"You haven't lost your touch, Caroline," he remarked, smiling at

1

his hostess, who was seated on the sofa with her sewing. "The finest beef I've tasted this side of St. Joe."

Caroline Wade smiled with pleasure. She shook her blond hair with its almost invisible strands of gray.

"I was trained very early, Judge. In a New York State village. Cooking went hand in hand with my schooling. And besides, I love to cook."

Ben Wade, who sat as firmly in every chair he occupied as if carved from part of its frame, grinned at Judge Bates.

"Years ago, sir, Caroline fell in love with my speeches. I fell in love with her cooking." He winked slyly and his dark eyes seemed to caress Caroline. "There were other factors, as you can see, Judge."

He laughed, got up, and moved quickly across the room to the decanters on the buffet. He was a vigorously handsome, defiant-looking man in his prime, whose appearance reflected his personal history. He had had a varied career—as day laborer, farm hand, teacher, and prosecuting attorney—before he became what he was now, one of the ablest and most popular men in the Senate, and one of the first Northern senators to challenge the South's control of the Senate. There was definitely an inexplicable touch of the actor in his manner.

Studying his old friend, Judge Bates recalled Wade as he had first seen him a year or two earlier from a gallery seat in the Senate. In considerable alarm he had watched Wade's entrance as the senior senator from Ohio, wearing a conspicuously flowered vest and form-fitting frock coat, strode down the center aisle of the Senate chamber, unbuttoning his well-cut coat, and calmly laid two huge and handsomely silvered navy pistols on his desk, the muzzles parallel and pointing unmistakably at the desks of Senator Toombs of Georgia and his Southern colleagues a few feet away.

An open riot in the Senate chamber such as had occurred in the House that very day was narrowly averted.

But Wade could also raise a laugh in exposing the pretensions of his Southern foes; and Judge Bates smiled as he remembered Wade's famous reply to Senator Badger of North Carolina who had pleaded with bathos and outraged Southern pride that he should not be prevented from taking his beloved old black mammy to Kansas with him if he chose to do so. Wade had instantly shouted, "We haven't the least objection to the senator's migrating to Kansas and taking his dear old mammy with him. We only insist he shan't sell her after he's taken her there."

Tonight Bates sensed a touch of unusual tension behind Wade's geniality.

2

"I got you here tonight for a purpose, Edward," Wade said. "The new Attorney General, Mr. Stanton, and a young Texas judge will be here in a few minutes to discuss the crisis we are facing in Maryland. Since South Carolina seceded nine days ago, Stanton has been wild about the situation there. If that state secedes anything can happen. Lincoln's inauguration, the security of the nation itself, may depend upon Maryland's remaining loyal. Stanton is most pessimistic, but I hope to reassure him a bit. You know him, don't you?"

"Slightly. I met him in Chicago several times," said Bates non-committally.

"Well," continued Wade, "when we put him in as Attorney General less than two weeks ago we hoped to stop the collapse of this government. But we may have been too late. At any event, I want you to discuss the situation with him. It's pretty generally known, isn't it, that you're to have the same place in Mr. Lincoln's Cabinet?"

Bates nodded. "I've been very much honored, Ben. Mr. Lincoln will announce the appointment in a few days. I saw him in Springfield last week. Seward is set for the State Department, but Lincoln is having a fit over Cameron and would like to scalp Judge Davis, his manager."

"What's he got against Cameron?" snapped Wade, who was a friend and mild admirer of the Pennsylvania leader.

"Judge Davis made a deal in Chicago," retorted Wade, "and never said a word to Lincoln about it. He got Pennsylvania in return for Cameron in the Cabinet—and now there's the devil to pay. Cameron wants the Treasury or the War Department."

Wade laughed.

"Modest Simon! He'd probably like 'em both."

"Lincoln's got to take him," agreed Bates. "But tell me something—before the others get here. How in the devil did you get Stanton in Buchanan's Cabinet? I thought Stanton had washed his hands of politics. He was enraged by Lincoln's election."

"He was. But Stanton can't stand the treason he smells on all sides. And when Seward and I saw what Buchanan was up to—that he was a conscious party to the whole Southern conspiracy—we ran a fort-night ago to Judge Black, Old Buck's Attorney General, who was about to shift over and become Secretary of State. Black, thank God, is devoted to the Union. He suggested that Stanton, who was both loyal and an old friend of the President, step into his shoes. Seward and I then rushed to the White House and so frightened Old Buck that he sent Stanton's nomination to the Senate the very next day."

"But what's Stanton been able to do in so short a time?" demanded

3

Bates. "The situation is shocking. I doubt very much if Mr. Lincoln will ever be inaugurated here in Washington."

"We'll soon find out," retorted Wade. "Speaking for myself, I'd like to see Buchanan taken out and shot. The man's a traitor. And he's President of these United States."

The doorbell tinkled lightly in the hall and Caroline arose.

"That must be Stanton," exclaimed Wade. He glanced at Bates. "You'd better brace yourself, Judge."

Caroline opened the front door. A stocky figure shook a dripping umbrella on the porch, stood it there, and then came into the house in a flurry of driven rain. Behind him towered a second man wearing a long military poncho which made him look unnaturally tall. The two men entered the Wades' parlor. Stanton looked like some battered smoking volcano. Wade helped him off with his streaming coat and after brief greetings Stanton, breathing heavily, seated himself in a mahogany rocking chair close to the fire. Caroline quickly poured out half a tumblerful of port.

"Will you have some wine, Mr. Stanton?"

He nodded, took the glass, and tossed off half of its contents. His hands were visibly shaking. Then, recollecting himself, he turned and addressed the Wades.

"I beg your pardon, friends, for appearing like this, but I've had to take more than I can stand. I should like to introduce a very good friend of mine, Judge Lemuel Dale Evans of Marshall, Texas. Mrs. Wade, Judge Evans; the senator, whom I believe you've met, and Judge Bates of St. Louis."

The gentleman whom Stanton introduced was a striking individual. He had hung his poncho in the hall and returned to the parlor with long, deliberate strides. Well over six feet tall, he was large-boned and large-framed, with a military set to his wide broadcloth-covered shoulders. His head was the head of a frontiersman, but his expression and his high forehead under curling brown hair gave an impression of great intellectual force. Something of the soldier, too, was suggested by his strong deeply tanned face. Although he was at ease, there was a glint in his wide-set brown eyes which hinted that he could be quick to anger.

An almost beautiful face—and a rather fanatical one, Caroline thought. Having greeted each of them in turn, the Texan folded himself neatly into one of Wade's deep leather chairs. He was obviously playing the role of spectator at this little gathering, but his eyes, alive and curious, seemed to probe each of them in turn. The bold handsome face, for the moment, conveyed nothing at all.

4

Judge Bates, in an instant of intuition, wondered if Mr. Evans had not had to deal all his life with a great majority of individuals with whom he rather violently disagreed.

Wade, meanwhile, wasted little time in pleasantries. He addressed Stanton at once.

"Well, sir, have you been able to make the President stand his ground anywhere?"

Stanton stiffened. His face grew crimson.

"Buchanan? That windbag, that idiot, that mealymouthed, spineless, abject wraith of a man! Never in my wildest dreams could I have imagined the incredible crisis into which this mass of collapsing jelly, misnamed the President, has now placed us. By God, it's a damnable outrage!"

The volcano began to rumble and spit forth fire and smoke. As Stanton's energies began to reassert themselves, Caroline was amazed at his never-ending fascination for her. She knew him well, but each time she saw him he seemed more remarkable.

Stanton's eyes in his heavily bearded face were very striking, large and liquid, almost womanly at times, and she, like many others who met him, had commented that they always seemed to convey in their depths some mysterious message, some veiled reproach, as if for a remote and ancient injury. This singular man had a driving inflexible will, a frightening capacity for hard work, and a sweet and exasperating voice that became positively silky when his temper caught fire. But when this temper exploded, as it often did, Stanton could bellow, curse, and outscream any brass-voiced maniac.

"I've got to speak my mind," he was exclaiming. "I've played diplomat to the last degree of my endurance. I worship the law. But there is no law in this land today. Nothing but the design of traitors, nothing but the stink of treason, nothing but the actions of scoundrels—and every damn one of them a member of this government under oath of office. Let me review for you the insane events of this past month. Listen!"

He hitched himself to the edge of his chair as if he would hurl himself at them bodily.

"On the ninth of this month," he said slowly in his repressed smooth voice, "Buchanan, our President, wrote to the South Carolina congressmen that he would personally see to it that everything was held in check while the South prepared for disunion! A few days later Jacob Thompson, our Secretary of the Interior, told Old Buck that he wanted to go to Raleigh in order to induce North Carolina to leave the Union at once! What did the President do but give him his blessing and say that he hoped he'd succeed! So Thompson held a public

5

reception before the North Carolina legislature, delivered a fiery speech urging immediate secession, and then calmly resumed his place in the national Cabinet! Ye gods!"

Bates was incredulous. "Can't you arrest him?" he asked.

"Every damn one of them should be shot, sir. But my hands are tied by the Constitution. I suppose the nation may be destroyed, but at least we shall retain that revered document in our empty hands to remember it by! I was sworn in as Attorney General just nine days ago—on the twentieth, the very day South Carolina seceded. On examining the situation I felt like calling for ten thousand dung forks! Why, Trescott, the Assistant Secretary of State, resigned one day and showed up the following morning as the official agent of South Carolina in Washington! Think of it!"

Stanton stopped a moment, looked fiercely at each of them, and then went on.

"This milksop of a President doesn't even deign to sell the nation. He's *giving* it away, piece by piece, and signing on the dotted line wherever some traitor guides his trembling fingers."

Stanton gulped more wine. Judge Bates addressed him cautiously.

"Do you think this avalanche can be halted, sir?"

"I doubt it," retorted Stanton. "I think it's too late. Floyd—Secretary of War, mind you, for these United States—has stripped the *North* of troops, sent 'em to Western outposts, and manned *Southern* ports for war. Yesterday I learned that Colonel Maynardier, Chief of Ordnance, had ordered the commandant of the Allegheny Arsenal at Pittsburgh to ship to Gulf ports no less than one hundred and thirteen Columbiads and eleven thirty-two-pounders for the *Southern* defenses. By God, I've stopped that. But I can't do everything.

"And Louis Wigfall, a sneaking, conniving senator from Texas, threatens to resign and recruit a rebel force in this very city if anyone, meaning me, tries to tie Old Buck's hands. And when Major Anderson moved into Fort Sumter three weeks ago, the only sensible thing he *could* do, the President raged and fumed—told Jefferson Davis it was a calamity, done against *his* wishes, *his* policy!"

"What have you said to Buchanan about all this?" demanded Wade.

"Yesterday I had to stand in the Green Room and shake my fist in his face—the President of this country! I got Judge Black and Ben Butler of Massachusetts to back me up. I terrorized Buck. I told him that if he continued to deal in any way with the South Carolina commissioners—Barnwell, Adams, and James Orr—we would arrest them at once and Butler would prosecute them without fees. I told Buck he would find himself hanging from the highest scaffold in Washington if he continued his treasonable path."

6

"My God!" breathed Wade. "What happened?"

"He began to cry," said Stanton softly. "He began to weep. He was clad in an old worn dressing gown. He sat down, trembling, white as a sheet, directly beneath that full-length portrait of Andrew Jackson —was ever a more tragic contrast?—and moaned that he didn't know what to do any more. He said over and over, 'Stanton, it's too late. We are helpless.' I lost my temper. I cursed him, reviled him, told him it was never too late to save the nation."

Stanton stopped. His eyes filled with bitter tears. Wade put an arm about Stanton's shoulders.

"At least, old friend, you've got your foot in the door. They haven't closed it—and we won't let 'em."

But Stanton shook his head.

"We're too late, Ben. The most we can do is to hold Maryland— and we can't. If Maryland goes South we are lost indeed. And the governor of Maryland sits quaking in Annapolis under demands of the legislature that he convene them so they can vote secession at once. This man Hicks is a coward. He hates Lincoln. He's hand in glove with Maryland slaveowners—and he'll do their bidding. His silence proves it. I'm informed Hicks is resigned to secession and will not lift a finger against it."

"I'm informed differently," said Wade, and something in his tone made Stanton look up at him.

"You've heard from Governor Hicks?" he asked.

"Not directly. But I'm reliably informed that Hicks will *not* convene the Maryland legislature, that he's thoroughly loyal to the Union."

"I don't believe it——" began Stanton.

"And furthermore," continued Wade smoothly, "Hicks will make a public address in a very few days pledging Maryland's loyalty to the Union. He will *not* convene the legislature, Edwin."

Stanton was obviously startled. His eyes widened in astonishment.

"That's glorious news, Ben. But it doesn't fit the facts. Where did you get this information?"

Caroline glanced at her husband, a slight smile on her lips. The others were alert and curious. Wade walked over to his desk, picked up a sheaf of papers, and sat down again.

"I had a caller the other night who gave me written proof of Hicks's intentions. Here's an advance copy of the speech to be delivered in Baltimore next week. Maryland will never secede after that address."

"You haven't answered my question," snapped Stanton. "Who was your informant?"

"Miss Carroll of Maryland," said Wade mildly. "She's a close friend

7

of the governor's and reviewed with me thoroughly the whole situation in Annapolis. Do you know her?"

Wade was puzzled by Stanton's ludicrous expression of astonishment and outrage and by a startled exclamation from the hitherto silent Texan.

"Miss Carroll of Maryland!" bellowed Stanton. "Do you mean to tell me you are relying upon any suggestions or information passed along by that female schemer in petticoats? She's nothing but a rebel agent, Ben. I thought you knew that."

"See here," protested Wade, surprised in turn by Stanton's violent reaction. "That's a pretty strong statement, Edwin. I didn't know you knew her."

"I don't—and I don't want to," retorted Stanton. "But I know all about her. I made it my business to."

Color crept into Caroline's cheeks. She saw that the young Texas judge was leaning forward, watching Stanton intently. Wade was nonplused.

"Let's back-water a bit," he said slowly. "This is important. I've known Miss Carroll only a few months. But she impressed me as being a very talented and brilliant woman. Moreover, I soon discovered she has considerable influence with Hicks. From the nature of her information I've never had any reason to doubt her loyalty."

"I can give you a number of reasons," said Stanton grimly. "And what's all this nonsense about her influence with Hicks?" he added sarcastically. "Don't tell me Miss Carroll is governor of Maryland."

Wade laughed shortly.

"Unofficially, she's mighty close to it. Hicks owes his office to Miss Carroll's press campaigns in Maryland. He's said so publicly. The man won't move without her."

Stanton slowly removed his spectacles and looked with sudden gravity about the little group.

"We had better clear up Miss Carroll's status at once before we go any further. If you are accepting in good faith any information from this woman, Ben, then the situation is even more serious than I feared. This woman is nothing but a Southern informant. I'm shocked to find that a mere female can pull the wool over your eyes. Wait a minute," he exclaimed as Wade started to protest again, "I think it necessary to inform you all in strict confidence that I've had Miss Carroll under investigation for weeks, ever since the election. And Judge Evans, here, has been my investigator. Evans, this is all among friends. Suppose you tell us the results of your observations."

There was an angry exclamation from Caroline, now sitting very erect on the edge of the sofa, and Judge Bates was plainly startled by the turn their conversation was taking. Wade raised a hand to silence them. He looked very solemn.

"By all means let's hear what Judge Evans has to report." He turned to Evans. "Go ahead, Judge. What's this all about?"

The Texan leaned back, leisurely crossed his legs, and looked inquiringly at Stanton. Then he finally began to speak in a soft, resonant drawl, addressing Wade.

"Senator, I haven't seen your exhibits from Miss Carroll. I'd like to. But first of all, I reckon I'd better explain my own part in all this. Six months ago I sniffed the wind in Texas and decided I'd better get out. I was all Union and that's a mighty small minority in Harrison County. I came here, went to Judge Black, and told him my situation. The judge introduced me to Mr. Stanton. I was engaged by both men in legal research and in time this led to a quiet investigation of a number of prominent people in and about Washington whose loyalty was questioned. One of them was Miss Carroll of Baltimore."

The Texan paused long enough to become uncomfortably aware of Caroline's bright eyes fixed unwaveringly upon him.

"I had," went on Evans, "already become acquainted with Miss Carroll five years ago when I was elected to Congress from east Texas on the American ticket. I'd been impressed with some able campaign material signed 'A. E. C.' At that time I discovered to my surprise that the author was a woman, Anna Ella Carroll, living in Baltimore. Shortly after entering the House I met her at a political rally in Baltimore. I was mighty impressed with her. I was also astonished to discover she was one of the organizers of the American party in Maryland and quite a political power in the state. Five years ago she was battling Buchanan's political machine and determined to get Tom Hicks in the governor's chair, which, as the senator has just pointed out, she eventually did."

Evans smiled reminiscently. "Miss Carroll was also a charmer. Very dainty, very blond, an excellent talker, and she seemed to know everyone. Her social affairs on Mount Vernon Place were real events."

Stanton snorted contemptuously.

"Judge, you're young and too damn impressionable. Get to the point."

Evans grinned but kept his eyes on Wade.

"I'm of two minds about this woman, Senator. I'm not quite so certain as Mr. Stanton about her game—but it looks bad." His voice hardened, took on a professional tone. "Following Mr. Lincoln's election, Miss Carroll gave up her profitable business connections in Baltimore, at once established herself here in the Washington House, the only Southerner in a boardinghouse exclusively occupied by Northern

9

senators and their wives. Her family, I understand, are all rebel sympathizers."

"I beg your pardon," interrupted Caroline forcefully, "but Miss Carroll told me herself that she freed all her slaves on Election Day."

Evans appeared surprised. "I didn't know that," he said slowly.

Judge Bates interrupted them both. "I had a brief correspondence with Miss Carroll last year and certainly thought she was loyal at that time. But her relatives in St. Louis—her uncle Charles Cecelius Carroll is an able lawyer out there—are all rabidly Southern."

Wade said harshly, "This is all guesswork, Judge. Let's have some evidence, Mr. Evans. What did you find?"

"Well, sir," continued Evans thoughtfully, "here you have a Southern woman living in a house full of Northern senators. But for a solid month she's done nothing but lavishly entertain every important Southerner, in or out of the government, at expensive levees, receptions, and what not. There were all sorts of rumors about her. Judge Black and Stanton, in mid-November, asked me to keep an eye on her."

"Indeed," said Caroline in a challenging voice.

Evans looked ill at ease.

"Understand, ma'am, I was not too happy over such an assignment. But the loyalty of certain persons is crucial at this time. I—I found Miss Carroll a most intriguing and confusing person."

Caroline suspected that under the concealing tan his color had deepened a little. Her eyes never left his face.

"The facts are these," said Evans with emphasis, "Miss Carroll's closest friends in this city are Jefferson and Varina Davis and the Vice-President, John C. Breckinridge. In recent weeks she has conferred repeatedly with every prominent Southerner in town. She is close to them all—to Senator Toombs of Georgia, Wigfall of Texas, Alex Stephens, Rhett, Iverson, and all the Richmond crowd. Until recently she was close to the President himself, a constant caller at the White House. Moreover, a number of Baltimore ladies told me it was common knowledge there that Mr. Buchanan had twice proposed marriage to her." The Texan paused and glanced at Stanton's grim face. "I formed the definite impression that Miss Carroll was conveying information, documents, and letters from Northern editors and politicians to her Southern friends."

"Might it not have been the other way around?" suggested Wade quietly.

Evans shook his head. "I don't think so. I'll tell you why. A month ago, Senator Davis gave a large ball to which I secured an invitation. Miss Carroll was a guest of honor. There was a great deal of champagne and oysters—and I had quite a talk with the senator. I delib-

10

erately introduced the subject of Miss Carroll. Jefferson Davis told me that she was one of his family's closest friends, that she had given him more accurate information on Maryland than anyone else. He idolizes her, and Davis is no fool regarding politics or women.

"He finally told me in confidence that through Miss Carroll he was about to offer her father any position in the South that he might desire, the vice-presidency if need be. Miss Carroll's father, Thomas King Carroll, was once governor of Maryland. He is still a power in that state. If he chose to do so, he could swing Maryland out of the Union. At least that's what Davis believes. The senator told me in his own words, 'I've been working on Miss Carroll for a month. I'm prepared to offer her father anything he wants. And I'm convinced Miss Carroll can bring him into our camp.' " Evans paused and then added with a trace of reluctance that only Caroline noticed, "There's another and a more personal matter that I feel clinches the case against her."

Wade was looking most unhappy. Caroline, pale and tense, gazed at Evans with an inscrutable expression.

"The fact is," said Evans, "for two or three years Miss Carroll has been pretty thick with a Charleston lawyer named Harry Heyward. He's a handsome bright young fellow—I've run up against him in more than one Southern court. His family are close friends of the Calhouns, and young Heyward when a boy was quite a pet of the old man. A week ago this chap moved into Willard's and has frankly told a number of his friends he's here to take Miss Carroll off to Charleston 'where she belongs,' as he puts it, and before actual war breaks out. It seems to me this finishes the case against Miss Carroll. On the other hand" Evans shrugged—"I guess I vote with Mr. Stanton," he concluded.

"You said earlier, Mr. Evans," remarked Caroline, "that you were still of two minds about Miss Carroll. Why?"

Evans looked thoughtful and slightly embarrassed.

"Because I can't square her actions now with what I first knew of her in Baltimore. It doesn't make sense. But," he added simply, "I could guess Mr. Lincoln's election was just too much for her, as it was for others. All of her actions, as I've observed them since the election, proclaim her a rebel agent."

Wade turned a bit belligerently to Stanton.

"Anything else, Edwin?"

"I'm afraid our young friend," barked Stanton, "is too susceptible to feminine charms. He's stated this case much too mildly. A clerk in the Senate told Evans that the Vice-President has given Miss Carroll both written and verbal reports concerning rebel conspiracies hatched in the very committee rooms of the Capitol itself, secret meet-

11

ings at which this traitor Breckinridge himself presided. There's no doubt about her at all, in my opinion. She's a female meddler, a damned nuisance, and possibly dangerous. She's pumping you, Ben. I wouldn't touch her with a ten-foot pole. She's hypnotized a lot of able men. But for God's sake, don't be one of them."

Wade rubbed his chin reflectively. But there was an angry glint in his dark eyes.

"You and Judge Evans make out quite a case," he said. "Do you mind if I take the floor for a few moments?"

Stanton laughed shortly.

"If you want to testify to her charms, Ben, go ahead. But don't tell me you still repose confidence in this female!"

"It's possible Miss Carroll *has* taken me in," said Wade. "And it's just possible she's taken *you* in, Edwin, and your young investigator into the bargain, begging your pardon, Mr. Evans." Wade leaned forward and added vehemently, "This woman is loyal. I can prove it. She's married to her country in this crisis."

"You'd better begin at the beginning," suggested Caroline. "Tell them about your first encounter with—with Mr. Stanton's rebel agent," she finished a little acidly. Wade nodded.

"Last September I dined in Baltimore with Governor Hicks and Senator Reverdy Johnson of Maryland. In discussing the Maryland legislature Hicks kept referring me to Miss Carroll. Said she had more knowledge of the situation than anyone else. I thought this mere gallantry until Hicks insisted on taking me to her home that very afternoon. Well, sir, Hicks and I drove up Charles Street to Mount Vernon Place and rang the bell of a charming little gray two-and-a-half story structure. We had a glimpse of a small garden and fountain in the rear. Miss Carroll, very animated, was in her drawing room surrounded by milliners and dressmakers, with hats and gowns flung everywhere."

Wade smiled in retrospect before he continued.

"I didn't get out of her charming clutches until early evening. That young lady, once my own sentiments were well established, proceeded to show me a powder magazine in her possession that could blow some of our Southern brethren to smithereens."

"I suppose she offered to turn it over to you, gratis," observed Stanton contemptuously.

"She damn near did," retorted Wade. "She showed me the first written constitution of a Southern confederacy I'd ever seen. It was dated at Jackson, Mississippi, in 1849. This young lady, then scarcely out of her teens, got it from Jefferson Davis himself and she gave it at once to Henry Clay. I'd never heard of the transaction. But Miss Carroll told me Clay used this document repeatedly in the great debates

12

of 1850 as a club over Davis. Clay's obvious possession of the document alarmed Davis and greatly smoothed the passage of the Compromise Act of 1850."

"Tell me," Bates asked, amazed by the whole discussion, "how can any young female achieve weight in political matters? It sounds preposterous."

"You must remember," Wade reminded him, "that the Carrolls are one of the first families in Maryland. Miss Carroll is not a Catholic herself, but her kinsman, John Carroll, was the first Catholic bishop on this continent and founded Georgetown College. She's also a blood relative of Charles Carroll of Carrollton, the signer of the Declaration of Independence, who died in '32. Her father was governor of Maryland. All this prestige gets her everywhere."

"Social prestige don't make a politician," protested Bates.

"It helps," Stanton interrupted impatiently. "But let's get to your evidence, Ben. What have you got?"

"A number of exhibits," snapped Wade, picking up the papers in his lap. "Here is Governor Hicks's speech to be delivered in Baltimore next week. In it he takes an unequivocal stand for the Union. Miss Carroll told me she helped him prepare this speech. Here is a note to her from John Gilmer of North Carolina who has just refused an offer to join Mr. Lincoln's Cabinet. Mr. Gilmer writes: 'Dear Miss Carroll, I have just read the planned address of Governor Hicks, which you sent me, with great pleasure. I have been overwhelmed with work and anxiety for North Carolina. It is a great matter that you hold Maryland *now*.' "

"May I see that?" demanded Evans sharply.

"Certainly." Wade handed him the letter and continued. "Here's a similar note from former Governor Corwin of Ohio—now in the House—which says, 'Your advice to your friends is wise. I believe you will succeed in saving Maryland.' As for the offer Judge Evans reports that Davis made to her father—Miss Carroll herself mentioned it."

For the first time Stanton looked taken aback.

"She did? What did she say?"

"She told me she had used her father's name to secure a great deal of valuable information from Davis and many others and that when the senator renewed his offer to her in writing last week she promptly replied, 'Not if you give him the whole South.' "

Stanton snorted. "Go on, sir."

"Here is written proof—from Miss Carroll—that on Tuesday afternoon last both Jefferson Davis and Jacob Thompson, Secretary of the Interior, personally subscribed twenty-four thousand dollars in this city for the purchase of *Confederate arms*."

13

"I'd heard the rumor," Evans commented. "I was unable to confirm it."

"There's your confirmation," said Wade, passing over several papers. "But here's the clincher. Here's the private correspondence of one Thomas Drayton of Charleston with Governor Gist of South Carolina and John B. Floyd, our Secretary of War. Drayton proposes to Floyd and Gist, who agree in writing, you'll notice, that *everything for the South be purchased from the War Department through New York bankers!* How in God's name Miss Carroll got these letters I don't know. They aren't eight weeks old."

Judge Evans stifled an exclamation. Stanton, scowling fiercely, impatiently reached for the letters, but Wade waved him off. "It's still my turn, Edwin." He sorted over several documents and then said explosively, "These damned rebels haven't the consciences of pickpockets! Here's Floyd proposing to Drayton that these arms purchases be made through G. B. Lamar, president of the Bank of the Republic in New York, with a list of ten other Northern bankers to deal with—all traitors!"

"In short," added Wade angrily, "Cabinet officers, through Northern bankers, are ransacking the North for the very munitions they need to wreck this Union! Well, sir, all these documents came from Miss Carroll. You think these voluntary contributions are the work of a rebel agent?"

"They could be," said Stanton stubbornly. "After all, Ben, they'd be a small price to pay if this female could lull you and your committees to inaction in the face of a planned secession by Maryland and other moves of which we may know nothing."

"Well, it's just contrary to all logic and reason," exclaimed Wade in exasperation. "Miss Carroll even gave me inventories of arms and details of a proposed assault upon the capital in early February intended to prevent the counting of the electoral vote."

"A proposed what?" Stanton almost shouted the words.

"Edwin," said Wade firmly, "you and I are looking at two sides of the same coin. Suppose the current of information this woman has set in motion is flowing from South to North—instead of the other way. I think my evidence proves my point a lot better than Mr. Evans's statements prove yours."

Stanton ignored this line of attack.

"What's this nonsense about an assault on the capital?" he demanded again.

Wade tossed a whole sheaf of papers in his lap.

"That information shows that two thousand rooms have been engaged in this city for armed rebels in civilian clothes. Here are plans

14

for a military force near Alexandria, to be commanded by Major Ben McCulloch of Texas, to march on Washington, seize the national archives, and force the secession of Maryland, if that's not yet a fact. This data, may I remind you, was also gathered by Miss Carroll."

The Texan fairly jumped from his chair and leaned over Stanton, who was obviously staggered by these revelations. Wade shot home another bolt. His voice was tinged with irony.

"Your own investigator don't seem too sure of his own convictions, sir. Judge Evans is a Southerner. So is Miss Carroll. Another thing, she's a conservative by principle and a radical by instinct. That always leads to unpredictable fireworks." Wade winked at Caroline. "I always bet on instinct. Anyway, I think Mr. Evans must appreciate the difficult position this woman is in, whichever way she's jumped."

Caroline saw the confusion on the Texan's face.

"What do you really think, Mr. Evans?"

"Ma'am, I don't rightly know. After these broadsides from the senator, I'm more at sea than ever. I still think Miss Carroll leans to the South. But what her real game is I don't know."

"Well, I know," broke in Stanton angrily. "She's feeding us all opium. While we're in a trance these Maryland traitors will vote secession and jump out of the Union before we can say Jack Robinson —and probably take the country with 'em. Miss Carroll and her young rebel lawyer will be safe in Charleston. Bah! Why anyone has anything to do with a female in politics is beyond me."

Judge Bates appeared baffled. Caroline was about to retort angrily when Bates spoke.

"I agree with the Attorney General," he said in an exasperated tone. "It all goes to show the chaos and confusion that result when any woman, charming or otherwise, gets out of her element. Will someone kindly inform me *how* this young female has come to be taken so seriously? I never heard of anything like this in Missouri. And what you've told me, Wade, still doesn't explain how Miss Carroll got the ear of Governor Hicks in the first place. The man must be daft."

"I can explain that quite simply," said Caroline sharply, though trying to control her rising irritation. "To begin with, she's known Governor Hicks all her life; he's an old family friend. He was sheriff of Somerset County, or something of the sort, when her father was governor. I know Miss Carroll. Like Ben, I believe in her. Miss Carroll told me that right after Mr. Lincoln's unexpected election she had a long talk with Hicks. She had been working for Senator Seward's cause—and the senator is certainly not a rebel sympathizer, Mr. Stanton. She said Hicks was badly frightened by Lincoln's election but that she made the governor see that, much as he might detest Mr. Lincoln, he *had* to recognize that Mr. Lincoln was constitutionally elected, and that his inauguration in Washington depended largely on Hicks's standing firm. Hicks finally agreed to hold out against secession."

"The gospel according to Miss Carroll," said Stanton in a disagreeable voice. He got up and looked at them with ill-concealed impatience and hostility.

"I've had my say, friends. I'm afraid it's had little effect. Come along, Evans. I think we'll still keep an eye on Miss Carroll. Ben, I beg of you not to have anything more to do with this woman. Beyond that, I'll say no more."

Evans, looking quite unhappy, joined him and they bundled themselves into their rubber coats. Stanton turned in the doorway and surveyed the three who remained.

"Good night, friends. This has not been a very fruitful evening, though I thank you for your hospitality, Caroline. The fact of the matter is," he ended bitterly, "we are living in the midst of a wreck."

The front door slammed and a moment later they heard his carriage drive rapidly away.

2

THERE WAS ONLY ONE CUSTOMER BROWSING IN THE
back of Mr. Shillington's bookstore on the Avenue early the next
morning. Joe Shillington, the genial, gray-haired proprietor, who knew
a great deal more about everybody in Washington than most people
suspected, had fired up the round-bellied little stove in the center of
his shop, and the place was rapidly acquiring its characteristic pleasant
aroma of pine knots, oiled leather bindings, rag paper, and ink. The
leisurely atmosphere, combined with Shillington's penchant for gossip
and his rare understanding of his customers' problems, both professional and private, had made the shop a social and political center
for legislators living near the Hill.

Mr. Shillington was dusting off a handsome London edition of
Vattel's *Commentaries* in the front window when he paused to watch
his second customer walking rapidly with an easy swinging gait toward
his establishment.

She was a blond woman, perhaps thirty-five or -six, who always
carried herself very erect and dressed in exquisite taste. Today she was
wearing a soft blue wool cloak and a bonnet the same color trimmed
with rose-colored flowers. With one hand she held the cloak about her
closely against the chill wind, and Mr. Shillington noted with approval
that this gesture accentuated the trimness of her rounded little figure.
As she turned the handle of his door and came in, Mr. Shillington
stepped forward to greet her.

There was a pertness about her bright face with its deep blue long-
lashed eyes, regular features, and generous mouth which always
delighted him. This morning even more than usual he was pleasurably
aware of her vitality and charm and her air of confident competence.

"Good morning, Miss Carroll." He watched her place a small

17

traveling bag on the floor and asked approvingly, "Off to the country for a bit?" Miss Carroll was quite a favorite of his and he was accustomed to her week-end trips to Maryland.

"For a long time, I hope, Mr. Shillington," she replied, and asked for a number of books she had ordered. As he wrapped her books, Mr. Shillington quietly studied her from the corners of his shrewd gray eyes, noting an unusual tenseness about her.

"I haven't been feeling at all well," she volunteered. "I'm going to spend New Year's with the family and take a long rest." Her high color had faded so that she looked almost pale.

"There's many in this town would like to do the same. Do give my regards to your father—and how is he?"

"Very worried but quite well," she answered mechanically and then stiffened a little as she caught sight of a tall man in the rear of the bookstalls reaching for a volume on the highest shelf. Mr. Evans deftly picked out his book, turned and looked directly at Miss Carroll, then raised his free hand to his hat.

"Good morning, ma'am," he said without any expression.

She acknowledged his greeting, tucked her volumes under her arm, picked up her bag, and walked slowly to the door under Mr. Shillington's watchful eyes. As she reached the street she heard the voice of Mr. Evans just over her right shoulder.

"You're pretty well loaded down, ma'am. Let me carry that bag at least. Have you a carriage here?"

"I'm only walking to the depot, Mr. Evans."

"Well, ma'am, that's two long blocks. I'll gladly put these on the cars for you. Are you off to Baltimore?"

She nodded and smiled gratefully at him. He had even curbed his long strides and was trying gallantly but rather unsuccessfully to keep step with her as they walked toward the Baltimore and Ohio depot at New Jersey Avenue and Third Street. The hour was early and she wondered a little at his presence in Mr. Shillington's bookstore. It vaguely occurred to her that Mr. Evans had popped up on numerous occasions lately.

Evans was silent for so long that she finally said, "I have a confession to make, Mr. Evans. I'm running away—to my family. And for a long time, I hope."

Evans glanced at her quickly, noting the slight violet shadows under her eyes and also the graceful firm set of her chin.

"Well," he said briefly, "that's a good place to run to with a new year in the offing." He added a bit ruefully, "It looks as though I'm going to have the town to myself."

At the depot she was surprised to see that she had forty minutes

18

before the Baltimore train left and the cars had not yet been backed into the station. She had intended spending more time in Mr. Shillington's store and now realized that the appearance of Evans had put her to flight. She walked to a vacant bench.

"I'll sit right here until the cars are ready," she announced. "You've been most kind. I do appreciate it. I hope to see you again when I return in a few weeks—if I decide to do so. Are you spending the holidays with friends?"

He stood before her, his dark eyes boldly surveying her face. He was disturbed by her pallor and tense expression, but nothing in his demeanor said as much. All at once he seemed quite solitary, standing there beside her. He said rather plaintively, "Hardly, ma'am. My friends and family are in Texas—and I doubt if they'd welcome me home just now. I aim to commune with myself a bit. It will be a welcome change."

Something in his words puzzled her. But before she could reply he went on, "I'd never say you were running away, ma'am. Judging from the papers, you've enjoyed quite a social whirl. Let's put it you're simply retiring for a spell to regroup your forces."

She laughed.

"Social whirl? In these times, social war would be a better term. You're putting it most optimistically, Mr. Evans. We'll see. And now good morning."

It was almost a curt dismissal. But he smiled warmly at her, tipped his wide-brimmed hat, and walked away. He was really a curious creature, she thought, always alone and turning up at unpredictable moments. To her surprise she felt a little bereft and solitary herself as his tall figure crossed the almost empty waiting room. An impulse from some remote recess of her mind made her speak words she was sure she had never intended to say.

"Mr. Evans——" she began, and then hoped that he could not hear her. But he turned at once and walked toward her.

"Yes, Miss Carroll?"

She had her eyes on the clock and was delighted to see there really wasn't time to carry out the absurd purpose that had entered her mind quite unbidden. But to her surprise she found herself saying, "Mr. Evans, you've never met my father or my family, have you? You mentioned you had no plans for the holidays and I wonder if you'd care to join us. I'm meeting Father in Baltimore and we're taking the afternoon boat to Cambridge. Would you be interested at all in accompanying us? I warn you, the Eastern Shore is quite another world. But you'd really be most welcome."

It was preposterous and due solely, she told herself, to her casual

19

sympathy for anyone forced to remain in the almost deserted capital over the holidays. She wasn't sincere or honest about this impulsive invitation and she was quite aware he knew it. But to her horror he pulled out a large silver watch and solemnly compared it with the station clock.

"What time does your train leave?" he asked almost indifferently.

"Ten o'clock," she said faintly.

His face brightened. There was just a hint of warm mockery in his voice.

"Miss Carroll, I'm going to accept your invitation. I thank you most kindly for taking pity on a lone Texan. There's nothing I'd enjoy more than dodging the politicians for a day and seeing an honest-to-goodness family sit down together." He added a bit enigmatically, "I've more than one good reason for entertaining your offer. And all my life I've wanted to see that Eastern Shore of yours. I'll tell you why sometime. I'll pack a bag and be back here in a jiffy. You just get on the cars and I'll join you."

She was astonished by the fervor with which he mentioned the Eastern Shore. She was also annoyed at herself. She had been counting on the fact that there was hardly time for him to get to the Ebbitt House, where she knew he lived, and back again. The color rushed to her cheeks. She said stiffly, "If you really think there's time——"

"Loads of time," said Evans confidently. "I'll take a hack. You're a mighty good Samaritan, Miss Carroll. I do appreciate this."

And then he was gone. Good Samaritan! That was intended irony, surely. It reminded her of her first casual meetings with this young lawyer, then in Congress, at gatherings in Baltimore several years ago, when his careless self-assurance, his blunt manners, and an occasional hint of indifferent impudence had piqued her more than once.

The cars were backed into the station; she found a seat and took out one of the books she had just bought, confident that she would be making the trip alone after all. But when the departure bell rang Evans was standing beside her thrusting a battered carpetbag into the overhead rack. He picked up two well-thumbed books he had thrown on the seat and sat down. To her further irritation he seemed completely unhurried, completely composed, and almost disturbingly at home.

They chatted politely like two people who have just been introduced, until they arrived at Camden Station. Ten minutes later, on the Light Street wharf, they found her father, a tall, rather delicate, kindly-looking patrician in his early sixties who instantly concealed his surprise that Anne had brought an unexpected guest.

"Father," she said rapidly after a warm embrace, "I've brought someone I've long wanted you to meet. This is Judge Evans of Marshall, Texas, whom I've mentioned on several occasions. He's to be with us for a few days. Judge Evans, my father, Governor Carroll."

Her father repressed a smile. He was quite used to Anne's surprises and always amused that she persisted in calling him by his former title. He greeted Evans cordially and they made their way to the main saloon of the old side-wheeler *Columbia*. By the time the vessel had thumped past Seven Foot Knoll her father and Evans were getting along famously.

Later, when Evans left them to buy some cigars, she said almost shyly, "I—I invited him down on the spur of the moment, Father. What do you think of him?"

He looked at her closely and then laughed softly. "Upon my soul, what a little provincial you're turning out to be! You sound as if some trussed-up frontiersman had been placed on your doorstep and you're wondering what the family will think of him. I like him very much. He's intelligent and he's certainly a most striking-looking man. Those eyes are remarkable. I wouldn't care to oppose him in any decision he had finally taken. And, my dear girl, if Mr. Evans is your friend we shall all accept him as such. Isn't that quite enough?"

She was somewhat annoyed at herself. Of course her family would be hospitable to Evans. What surprised her was her unexpected desire to have them really like him.

"Don't tease me, Papa. He is *so* different. And his manners are sometimes abrupt. But I'm told he has a remarkable mind." She added lightly, with a trace of her usual confidence, "I hardly know him personally. Just consider him a political protégé of mine."

"I've never known a Texan to be a protégé of anyone," was her father's good-humored thrust. She blushed but laughed with him.

The midwinter afternoon had turned unusually mild and a light haze clinging to the calm water gave the low shores the look of Indian summer. With a long mournful blast from her whistle the *Columbia* turned to port and headed into LeCompte's Bay and the channel to Cambridge. Off Castle Haven the paddles stopped and the ship slid quietly through the smooth water. The Carrolls' cutter, waiting for them, came alongside and they were rowed ashore by four blacks while the *Columbia* puffed leisurely away toward Cambridge, the steam from her pipes rising straight up in the motionless air like two triumphant white banners.

Castle Haven was a picturesque old Huguenot home standing near a sandy spit where the Choptank River widened into LeCompte's Bay. As the cutter rounded the spit and moved across the cove and they saw the spacious grounds of Castle Haven and the gay group moving toward them from the little dock, Anne wanted to hug this pleasant shore. Evans, she noted gratefully, was delighted by the scene. He turned to her father.

"This is—yours, sir?"

"Ours, Mr. Evans," Carroll said proudly. "And these are my youngsters with their husbands and a few young friends. Anne," he added with an amused look, "I'll leave the honors to you, my dear."

"I should have warned you, Mr. Evans," she said, suddenly shy, "I have two brothers and several sisters, to say nothing of their beaux. And here they all are!"

There was a chorus of excited greetings and cries of welcome as the cutter glided up to the dock. It died away when the younger girls, embarrassed, saw that the third passenger was a stranger. Anne could have shaken them for their frank stares. But there was something incongruously alien about Evans as he towered among them in his unmistakably Western clothes and military greatcoat. It was a little like having Daniel Boone lead off the Bachelors' Cotillion, Carroll thought, thoroughly enjoying the whole situation, especially the expression on Anne's face.

The family had advanced with a rush and smothered Anne in warm embraces. When she had disentangled herself she began somewhat breathlessly to introduce all the young Carrolls.

"My family—Mr. Evans," she said, her blue eyes flashing with affection and excitement. "This is Sallie and her husband, Mr. Thomas Cradock, of Pikesville. This is my sister Henrietta and her husband, Dr. John Chew Gibson, of Talbot County, and my young sister Ada and *her* husband—another doctor too—Dr. William Bowdle, of Dorchester County. This is Mary and young Mr. Dennis. And my brother, Dr. Thomas Carroll, of Walnut Landing, a few miles away. And my younger brother, Harry—and the Handy girls, Miss Evelyn and Julia, who's married to Mr. Brady, the photographer. There!" she finished triumphantly.

Other guests were introduced and they all trooped up to the manor house. Anne saw that in spite of their renewed chatter the girls were fascinated by Evans—his height, his outdoor look, and his laconic, though friendly comments.

As soon as he had been taken to the guest room they began.

"Pet, *where* did you find him?" . . . "That ridiculous hat! It could cover four men." . . . "How will he ever get through the doors?" . . . "But he *is* handsome." . . . "What are you going to do with him, Anne?"

Sallie stayed after the others had gone.

"Well, I declare," she said. "No wonder we can't keep up with you. I read in the Washington *Star* that Mr. Breckinridge has been taking you to a number of affairs. Where is the Vice-President's charming wife, by the way? And now you appear, looking quite worn out, if I may say so, with Daniel Boone's younger brother in tow. Where did you capture *this* one?"

"How does he impress you?" Anne asked lightly.

Sallie, with the privilege of a young sister, looked at Anne suspiciously.

"Oh—so he's down for approval, then?" She considered her verdict a moment. "I've never seen anything quite like him, pet, but——" She looked at Anne inquiringly.

"But what, dear?" asked Anne disarmingly.

"I don't know," Sallie said candidly. "There's something about him that puzzles me." She frowned, searching for words. "He—he seems to have good manners, but he acts as if he didn't care whether he had or not. And his face, with those bold eyes and clear-cut features, is remarkable. He's like a rather docile but untamed eagle, isn't he? Am I wrong?"

"You're very observing," Anne replied, surprised by Sallie's appraisal on short acquaintance. "He puzzles me too. Not so much his manners as his manner."

"Then he *must* be extraordinary." Sallie dismissed the subject of Evans and sat down. The north light was on Anne's face and Sallie looked at her sharply. "And now will you kindly tell your country sister what you've been up to to make you look so terribly tired?"

Anne was silent and Sallie was suddenly aware that her sister was not only tired but depressed.

"What's troubling you, pet? Tell me."

Anne sighed. "I've been working very hard, for one thing. Yes, I am tired. I'm rather discouraged too." She paused. "You aren't very interested in politics, Sallie, but I want you to know that I did everything I could to help elect Seward—and now that man from Illinois is going to be our next President. I don't like him, even though I've never met him, and I think he's a shockingly bad man for the position. I have a notion to give up politics altogether and come back here and live."

"But what about Harry?" Sallie asked. "I thought you were going to be married this spring."

Anne wondered again at the directness with which her younger sister arrived at conclusions about personal relationships. She herself lacked this quick intuitive understanding.

"Oh, Sallie, you know what Harry is like—the gallant Southern

23

gentleman who thinks a woman in business and politics is unladylike and one who has been a success is a positive freak. He's never taken my work seriously. I've known that for some time, but I wouldn't face it. I'm sure he thought I was showing off and I have the idea he's been waiting for me to outgrow it. He's a very patient—and stubborn —man, Sallie, sometimes frighteningly so."

"But if you're thinking of giving up your career anyway, why does Harry's feeling about it matter?" Sallie asked.

"It's part of a lot of things," Anne tried to explain. "I really can't marry a man who doesn't understand me any better than Harry does, although I suppose I'm still in love with him, and right now a home like yours, Sallie, especially appeals to me. But besides that, Harry and I think completely differently about what's happening to this country." She sighed again and rubbed her cheek in worried perplexity. "Sallie, you must have guessed how fervently I've been working for the Union cause. I know you don't approve, but I've had to do what I believe in. But you haven't guessed how many dear Southern friends I have alienated in these past few months. It's very hard. . . ."

Sallie, who had always possessed a shrewd understanding of her sister, saw again the two opposing sides of Anne's character—the hard driving will and intellectual purpose in conflict with a certain emotional confusion, an openhearted blindness of affection and an almost girlish indecision where her heart was concerned.

"I don't want to hurt Harry," Anne was saying with a look of tenderness and pity. "And I must do something very soon. He's in Washington now, expecting me to marry him at once and go back to Charleston with him. . . . Sallie, there are so many things I must decide in the next few days."

Sallie's eyes were dark with affectionate concern. She was startled that Anne had spoken so frankly of her Union sympathies, knowing that Sallie's were intensely Southern. She was even dismayed to learn how far this confident, independent sister had carried them. Still she managed to say quietly, "If you'll forgive me, dear, I must say it. You haven't been fair to Harry. You will have to——"

"I know, Sallie. I know. There he is without the slightest idea of what I've been doing lately. I'll have to explain."

"Wouldn't it be better to keep it on personal grounds, Anne? That is, if you're sure you don't love him enough. *Are* you sure?" she said gently.

There were unaccustomed tears in Anne's eyes. "I don't know, I just don't know."

24

3

BY DINNERTIME THE NEXT EVENING ANNE WAS FEEL-
ing much restored. She had slept late, taken a long walk during the
afternoon, and enjoyed hearing the family news at tea. As she went
in to dinner at eight, dressed in a favorite green moiré dress, she not
only looked rested but had regained some of her usual composure.

Dinner was a gay and ample affair, with roasts, jellied meats, wine,
and, awaiting them on the buffet laden with silver gleaming resplendently in the light of a huge fire, cream punches and liqueurs.

Everyone was in a holiday mood. As Anne glanced around the
table she thought how happy and carefree and handsome they all
looked, the girls in their bright party dresses, the men, except for
Evans, in black with a profusion of fine ruffled linen. Evans was an
exotic note. He had changed to a striking pearl-gray coat, with wide
lapels setting off his broad shoulders, and beneath it, in honor of
the formality of the occasion, a black twill waistcoat heavily em-
broidered in silver thread in an intricate pattern of Spanish design.

Toward the end of the dinner Evans provided another surprise.
He and the elder Carroll had been discussing the Eastern Shore and the
families who lived there. Carroll suddenly put down his napkin
and looked hard at the other man.

"Your middle name, you say, is Dale, sir? There are many Dales
in Worcester County and many Evanses in Somerset County and
Sussex. Am I wrong in assuming that you may possibly be connected
with them?"

Anne thought from Evans's broad grin that he must have been
well aware of the effect of his costume and the effect to be expected
from his next words. "I reckon, Governor, I'm trapped. I've never

been on this Eastern Shore in my life, but my family lived for generations in Somerset and Worcester counties."

In spite of herself, Anne was amused at the respect with which her family greeted this news. They had found him engaging and likable, but there had been a slight reserve, which was fast vanishing.

"But you must remember, sir," Evans continued. "I'm a native of Tennessee myself. My father moved there at the turn of the century. I can't even rightly claim to being a Tennessean any more, either, since I left there when I was a young man with a cousin of mine and settled in Marshall, Texas. There was plenty of excitement there in those days, sir," Evans added, his eyes reflecting it. "I got mixed up in a long feud between the Regulators and Moderators, served in the Mexican War as captain, and then jumped into politics."

It was Anne's turn to look at him with new respect and interest. These were facts about him she had not known before.

After dinner as they sat before the fire and the great brass fire rail and towering andirons the King family had brought from England to Kingston Hall two centuries before, Evans completed his conquest. Seeing in the corner a guitar that had belonged to Mingo, Anne's former servant, now freed, he unself-consciously picked it up and tuned it. Then in a few minutes, during a lull in the conversation, he began to play and hum a plaintive theme in a minor key. The others were silent and he began to sing in Spanish.

"Why didn't you tell me he sang?" Sallie whispered to Anne. But Anne shook her head, surprised herself.

In a rich baritone voice Evans sang a song that rose to a gentle climax, then slowly faded away with a dozen soft phrases repeated over and over. There was pleased silence, broken at last by Anne's father.

"Thank you, sir. We've heard nothing like that since my wife used to sing for us. That is a magnificent song. What is it?"

"It's called 'Nina,' sir," Evans replied. "It's an old Mexican lullaby I first heard during the war in Sonora and the Rio Grande country. Perhaps you'd like to hear a new Foster song—'Oh! Lemuel!' My friends claim it's named for me." He looked around the room at them smilingly. "Here it is."

Evans sang with gusto:

> *"Oh! Lemuel my lark,*
> *Oh! Lemuel my beau,*
> *I'se guine to gib a ball tonight,*
> *I'd hab you for to know;*

26

> *But if you want to dance,*
> *Just dance outside de door;*
> *Becayse your feet so berry large*
> *Dey'll cover all de floor."*

They all laughed and Evans made an exaggerated bow and plunged into a new steamboat song they had never heard—"The Glendy Burk."

> *"My lady love is pretty as a pink,*
> *I'll meet her on de way;*
> *I'll take her back to de sunny old south*
> *And dah I'll make her stay.*
> *So don't you fret my honey, dear*
> *Oh! don't you fret Miss Brown;*
> *I'll take you back 'fore de middle of de week*
> *When de Glendy Burk comes down."*

This time as he sang he looked at Anne and she was glad of the firelight which hid the color that came unexpectedly to her face. He *was* impudent.

As the year neared its end, gay groups from neighboring manor houses joined the Carrolls, while the punch continued to flow and many of the girls and their beaux gathered around the piano.

A little after ten, Governor Carroll invited the Texan into his study for brandy and a cigar.

"I'm glad Anne brought you down, Mr. Evans," he said with unusual cordiality. "I haven't seen her as gay as this in months. I suspect that's your doing."

Evans laughed. "I doubt if I can claim the credit, sir. I think there's a simpler answer. She's home."

Carroll looked at him closely. "You've known her long, Mr. Evans?"

"Only most casually," replied Evans. "I first met her in Baltimore five years ago. But I saw very little of her until she moved to Washington recently."

There was more than a shade of disappointment in Carroll's voice.

"Well, sir," he said frankly, "I was going to try to enlist your services in persuading my daughter to stay with us at Castle Haven for a time. I'm worried about her, sir."

The Texan chose his words carefully. "I'm afraid, Guv'nor, I'm hardly in a position to influence Miss Carroll's decisions at this point.

27

But she seems to enjoy a remarkable prestige in Washington among important folks of all political complexions."

Evans was astonished by the expression of sharp anxiety, and something more, that flashed across Carroll's patrician features. The older man said abruptly, "There's no time for pretense or deceit these days, sir. My daughter and I are Union to the core. With my son, Dr. Carroll of Cambridge, we stand alone among our family and friends. I think you should know this. Are you familiar with my daughter's activities in Washington?"

Evans studied Carroll a moment, astonished by the trend of these remarks. At last he said simply, "Guv'nor, I'm a Texas Unionist myself. You know what that means. I know many things are said of Miss Carroll's activities. I should like to ask you one question, sir——"
He hesitated and Carroll nodded encouragingly. "I wish you'd tell me a bit of your daughter's story. How on earth did she reach the—the unique position she seems to occupy today?"

For a brief moment Carroll looked immensely relieved over Evans's confession of faith, but then his expression of anxiety increased. "I appreciate your confidence, sir, and I'll gladly answer your question. At Kingston Hall, when Anne was three, I——"

And Carroll launched himself with almost painful precision on a detailed account of Anne's early life, the precocious training in her father's study, and many details of the Carrolls' pleasant family life at Kingston Hall, Warwick Fort Manor, and Castle Haven that held Evans spellbound.

"Education is my hobby," said Carroll with great emphasis. "I detest the nonsense females are exposed to in the name of education these days. I determined my daughter should be the peer of any man she met. I trained her, too, for leadership—and that is now a most painful responsibility I continually face. Anne is capable of many things—but I ask you, sir, where can any woman so trained find a place in our prejudiced society today? And what has made me most fearful is the fact that my daughter has now flung herself into the very heart of this great storm that threatens to break at any moment. Mr. Evans, I'm worried about her. If you find any proper opportunity to persuade her to step out of this storm—I'll be everlastingly in your debt."

Carroll talked a great deal more while Evans listened in attentive silence. The hour was late when he left Carroll's study.

Long after midnight, when many of the household had retired, Evans made his way to the now deserted library and found Anne sitting before the fire, absorbed in her own thoughts. Unobserved, he watched her for a moment. Many things were clear to him now that had either been concealed or that he had misinterpreted.

"Ma'am, may I speak to you for a moment?" he said gravely.

She looked up at him, startled, but smiled pleasantly.

"Of course, Mr. Evans. I wondered what had happened to you."

The Texan's easy composure had vanished. He seated himself in a large leather chair and sat for a moment almost tongue-tied. With an effort he finally spoke.

"Miss Carroll, I've something most painful to say. A mighty unpleasant confession to make. And I must make it or I cannot remain here as your guest. I—I wonder if——" He actually stammered. What ails the man? she thought. Evans drove on: "I wonder if you've been aware, ma'am, that your activities have been under investigation for a number of weeks—and I've been the investigator."

Her astonishment was convincingly genuine.

"That's preposterous, Mr. Evans. Are you serious? I can't believe——"

"Miss Carroll," he interrupted almost harshly, "I was detailed to investigate you some eight weeks ago. I did so, most reluctantly, until today. Thank God it's no longer necessary."

Anne had stiffened. There was an angry light in her eyes.

"Investigated me? For what purpose? Is this some practical joke of yours, Mr. Evans?"

"On my honor, ma'am, I never felt worse about anything in my life. It is my business in Washington to observe many people. Your loyalty, after Mr. Lincoln's election, was questioned by certain prominent men for whom I was working. But I saw Senator Wade the other night, and I've just talked to your father. Now I've made my decision and I wish to confess and apologize—and to ask you to accept my friendship as sincerely as it's offered."

But gathering anger and resentment were obvious in every taut line of Anne's face and figure.

"You accepted my invitation and came here in this role?" she demanded incredulously. "That's unforgivable, Mr. Evans. Who are these men? Why didn't you come to me directly instead of pursuing such shabby tactics?"

"Forgive me, ma'am," said Evans. "I didn't know you as I do now. And treason in town, treason in high places, as you well know, is incredibly widespread. I myself, as a Texan, have been under heavy suspicion at times. We all——"

To his huge relief her anger suddenly vanished. She laughed.

"Well, I never! I ought to be furious with you. But you've placed me in an impossible situation. I, too, Mr. Evans, have been expos-

29

ing some very dear friends of mine whose loyalty I question. But to find myself, an investigator, being investigated! Good heavens, is that why you've popped up so often in recent weeks—at the Davis home, in Gadsby's last week? In Mr. Shillington's store yesterday morning?"

Evans, looking embarrassed, nodded mutely.

"And who questions my loyalty?" she asked, watching him intently.

"That, ma'am, I am simply not at liberty to divulge. But they are loyal men high in government councils."

Anne was practically openmouthed.

"But, whoever they are, they should know that I'm a close friend of Senator Seward. Why didn't they go to him? Why didn't *you* go to him?"

"Ma'am, you know the insufferable atmosphere in town. Not a man trusts his neighbor there today. But," he added with expressive irony, "it will be my great pleasure to inform certain people in Washington what I think of their unfounded suspicions—and what I think of you."

"And what *do* you think of me, Mr. Evans?" she asked boldly.

"Senator Wade put it a great deal better than I ever could, ma'am." He proceeded to tell her something of what had taken place in Wade's home.

"But I would add a word of warning, ma'am. I would be most careful in your further operations in Washington. You are engaged in dangerous work. A number of people are interested in your activities."

"You can rest your mind, Mr. Evans. I have no intention of returning to Washington for a long time."

Evans eyed her warily. But there was a hint of a smile on his lips. He even shook his head.

"Ma'am, I reckon I'll have to contradict you. You know you can't stay down here long, lovely as it is. You'll have to come back to Washington. You belong there."

"If Seward had been elected," she replied, "I'd go back to Washington at once and fight secession with every power I possess. But now I don't know."

"You don't think much of Mr. Lincoln, ma'am?" Evans replied, and the impudent light was back in his eyes.

"I certainly do not."

"Well," Evans drawled, "you and a lot of other people are going to be mighty surprised about Mr. Lincoln."

He paused and studied the carpet. For the second time that evening he shocked her when he said hesitantly, "It's none of my affair,

30

ma'am, but young Mr. Heyward is hand in glove with the Richmond folk. Under certain conditions he could be dangerous. And now I guess I've said more than enough."

"You know Mr. Heyward?"

"Fairly well, ma'am," said Evans in his most impersonal tone. "We've appeared as opposing counsel several times in Southern courts. A very gallant and able man in many ways—but dangerous in these times, in my humble opinion."

She was so taken aback by these unexpected observations that she could find nothing whatever to say. And Evans's whole manner made her understand he did not wish to pursue the subject. But his words jarred her, made her most curious as to his own role in Washington. Evans, noting her pallor and fatigue, came to a quick decision.

"Ma'am, I'll be quite rude. You need rest—and I've upset you. You're going to bed. Tomorrow we can talk of more pleasant things."

He did not tell her she looked utterly exhausted, but the tone of his voice conveyed a great deal. He could be very disconcerting, and she was irritated that he brought the evening to a close so abruptly and without even allowing her to make the first move to leave. She decided she had no wish to go to bed. But now the wretch actually turned down the lamp before she could think of a suitable retort. He even picked up some papers he had left on the table and escorted her to the wide staircase.

"Good night, Miss Carroll," he said warmly, and pressed several pamphlets into her hand. "I wish you'd look these over at your leisure."

"What on earth are they?" she asked frigidly.

"I promised myself not to talk politics down here," said Evans casually. "But you don't like Mr. Lincoln. And I believe you're coming back to Washington sooner than you think. These are some of Mr. Lincoln's recent speeches. I wish you'd read 'em. They'll tell you a lot about him that may be useful. Good night again, Miss Carroll. And sleep well."

The man was impossible. Confessing his shabby role, telling her she was tired—and then sending her off to bed with a parcel of political speeches! She made some choked reply and tried to stalk upstairs, an impossible feat. She felt like a truant child admonished by an elder. But on the landing she quickly turned, looked down, and surprised him. He was standing looking up at her, his tall figure aglow with reflected firelight that cast a tall silhouette of him across the parlor wall.

There was an expression on his face that startled her. It was at once solemn, thoughtful, and surprisingly tender.

31

4

━━━⌁⌁━━━

A LITTLE MORE THAN A WEEK LATER ANNE RETURNED
to Washington. As she stepped off the cars onto the familiar depot
platform, she remembered Evans's prediction with a shock of surprise at the accuracy of his judgment of her. Evans himself had returned to town several days ahead of her.

Walking briskly toward the Washington House, she knew that
her vacation had been most useful and that most of her doubts and
decisions had at least been carefully appraised if not resolved.

And then she saw him.

He was seated quite comfortably on the steps of a private house a
few doors from her boardinghouse, his face almost hidden behind
the outspread pages of a morning paper. His whole presence reminded her entirely too much of his uncomfortable disclosures to
her at Castle Haven. Evans, seeming to catch sight of her accidentally,
got to his feet as if enjoying a morning stretch, leisurely folded his
paper, tipped his hat a little too jauntily, and gave her a warm smile.

"Well, ma'am, welcome to Washington again. And I'm delighted to
see you looking so rested and well."

She responded warily.

"Good morning, Mr. Evans. I'm sure my arrival here confirms
your gift of prophecy. Have you been calling on Senator Wade?"
Wade's home was only a block distant.

Evans descended from three freshly scrubbed steps and joined her
on the sidewalk.

"No, ma'am," he said firmly. "The fact is"—the clear brown eyes
were mildly amused, but his expression was almost stern—"though
I assure you I've tossed away my old role, I guess I have been am-
bushing you. Senator Wade told me you indicated in a letter you'd

32

be coming back this morning. I hope you don't mind my waylaying you."

She did mind. She had decided the morning was to be her own.

"I think you're still spying on me," she began, irritation apparent in her tone.

"I told you at Castle Haven," Evans replied impatiently, "and I'll tell you again that you've utterly convinced me of your loyalty to the Union. In fact, after I made my report the investigation was dropped."

"I still want to know who started it. And if it has been dropped why you're here now."

"The answer to the first question, ma'am, I'm now at liberty to reveal. I was working directly for the Attorney General, Mr. Stanton. Judge Bates, who will succeed him, was also interested. They are both now convinced of your value to the Union cause."

"That's very good of them," Anne said with a trace of sarcasm, "but why have you been waiting——"

"Because I have a request to make," Evans said quickly.

"Yes?"

He was looking straight down the Avenue.

"Miss Carroll, I'm a poor diplomat and my request is not a personal one. But after my confession a few days ago and the understanding you gave me of many matters that had not been clear, I've looked over the ground here carefully, and I wish you wouldn't go to the Washington House for a few days. Couldn't you arrange to stay with Mrs. Wade until the end of the week?"

"Why, Mr. Evans?"

When he did not reply at once she was startled and bewildered. What was wrong with her rooms at the Washington House? She suddenly remembered Evans's earlier warning. He now appeared most uncomfortable, but his expression was also dogged.

"Ma'am, I'll not say a word more on these matters after this morning. But I now believe your personal situation is far more serious than you or I had realized. A certain party is in possession of evidence against you, from his point of view. That individual is now in the Washington House waiting for you. A personal encounter at this time would gain nothing—and might be dangerous."

"And who is this party?" she asked sharply.

"You should know, Miss Carroll," he said gravely.

Then it came to her.

"Do you mean to imply that Mr. Heyward—or any of his friends—has this evidence, or has had me under surveillance?"

"Exactly, ma'am," said Evans in gloomy relief, as if spared the unpleasant duty of making this revelation himself. "I've discovered

33

since returning to town that your activities have alarmed several of your Southern friends, particularly Mr. Heyward. He has practically haunted the Washington House these past few days. And I think I know why—because he's found out you've been passing important information to Wade."

Evans paused, then added quickly, "He's there now, waiting for you."

He saw anger cross the vivid face of the woman standing beside him.

"And why is all this any further concern of yours?" she demanded, exasperated by a sense of interference and an awareness of an increasingly threatening situation which she could not fully command. "Mr. Heyward is no assassin! He's an old friend of mine—of my family. If he's there, as you seem to have made it your business to discover, he's simply waiting to see me on personal matters of concern only to him and to me."

In the face of this outburst Evans simply tipped his hat.

"I'm sorry I stepped into this, ma'am. I beg your pardon. Good day."

Before she could say a word he turned and walked rapidly away.

The pleasant peace of a sunny morning had vanished. Her anger swept her along to the Washington House and into the wide front hall. She was relieved to catch a glimpse of Leah polishing the parlor lamp and to see Mrs. Prescott, the cheerfully plump proprietress, rocking gently over the morning paper. Mrs. Prescott jumped up with a little cry of pleasure.

"My dear Miss Carroll, I'm so glad you're back. You look quite like your old self. And we've some lovely fine chickens for dinner that George brought in from Alexandria."

Anne was greatly reassured by this familiar reception. And there was no sign of Harry or anyone else in the parlors.

"Bless you, Edith, I've had a marvelous rest. Is there any mail?"

"Several letters I placed on your desk, dear." Mrs. Prescott added coyly, "You've had a visitor too. Mr. Heyward called early this morning."

"Mr. Heyward was here?" asked Anne faintly. She felt as if the sharp brown eyes of Evans were again boring into her own.

"He *is* here," replied Mrs. Prescott, puzzled by her expression. "I sent him up to your parlor to wait for you. Leah's been cleaning here all morning. You'll find your young man upstairs safe and sound, Miss Carroll. You go right up."

Mrs. Prescott, who had often wondered why Anne hadn't married long before this, had followed Harry Heyward's suit with avid interest.

34

But to her now obvious astonishment Anne said nothing. Lifting her skirt in a tightly clenched hand, she slowly ascended the stairs and turned the knob of her parlor door, leaving Mrs. Prescott disconcertedly staring after her.

Anne swung open the door reluctantly and saw a man's figure standing before one of the long french windows. There was a tense air about Harry Heyward as he turned and walked toward her.

"Hello, Anne. I thought you'd never come."

The words were cool, a little too casual, and revealed nothing of Harry's mood. But as his face caught the full light from the windows she was reminded sharply of each word of warning Evans had spoken. In the strong light she saw every sign of a gathering storm in Harry. All at once her calm assumption that she could break their engagement without hurting them both grievously appeared utterly childish. Harry, alien as he seemed now, was the man with whom she had fallen in love as unexpectedly and completely as he had with her. He was a man to make decisions—not merely to accept them. And she saw that he, too, had made one.

He was a graceful, slender man of impeccable manners, with a taut dash in his gestures and an assurance in his bearing that just missed arrogance. His ash-blond hair, high cheekbones, and finely sculptured features—a little too fine, she sometimes thought—had appealed to many women besides her. Looking at him, she felt less strongly, but still unmistakably, the old familiar tide of warmth rising within her.

"Anne dear," he went on in the new impersonal voice which alarmed her more than his expression, "would you mind making yourself comfortable in that chair over there? I think we have something to talk over."

She sat down, very erect, on the edge of a small rosewood chair. Harry half leaned on the corner of the big mahogany table covered with her papers and books. A panorama of little scenes from the past flashed through her mind as she waited—her first glimpse of Harry, on his fourteenth birthday, resplendent in a bright blue suit with brass buttons, standing behind his mother and peering in at her as she sat in her father's study at Kingston Hall, long before they had had to give up the old manor house and move to Castle Haven. She was just nine then. And she remembered Harry, when she was at boarding school near Annapolis, riding with her up West River and the Severn, or over to Tulip Hall, dancing with her at the Brice and Carroll mansions, and sailing with gay groups to Kent Island on Saturday afternoons.

Years of absence had followed and then Harry had appeared in Baltimore, handsome, serious, and all at once in love with her. In

35

love with her he might be, but now she flinched as she saw the look of harshness tinged with incredulity on his suddenly unfamiliar face. How long, she wondered, had she taken Harry for granted? How could she have taken such a man for granted?

"What on earth is the matter, Harry?" she asked as calmly as she could.

He smiled rather woodenly.

"I was going to ask you that. I've been very curious to know what your connection is with Senator Wade."

She tried to conceal her shock at his directness by saying stiffly, "You seem quite familiar with my social calls."

Harry waved his right hand impatiently.

"Social calls? For heaven's sake, Anne, let's not pretend today. Let me review what's happened these past few weeks and then if you can, and I hope you can, tell me it's all nonsense. A month ago Clarkson, Senator Toombs's chief clerk, came over to Willard's and had a long talk with me. At first I wouldn't even listen to him. Then he showed me some interesting exhibits——"

Clarkson had been startled that a speech of Wade's before the Senate had revealed confidential material from a memorandum to Toombs from Jefferson Davis. Only two people had seen that memorandum—Anne and a representative from Alabama. Twice such a thing had happened. Harry went on to other leaks, other activities traced unmistakably to Anne alone. It was a devastating broadside, and Harry's evident determination not to believe it was a tribute to his strained faith in Anne. She was quite pale when he had finished.

"Anne," he added, "there's nothing wrong in seeing all these people. I know they've been your friends for years." For an instant the voice was tender, excusing. "I won't believe all these charges of betrayals of confidence until I hear you say they're true. But Clarkson insists, and Toombs now agrees with him, that you are responsible for Hicks's idiotic stand. And, furthermore, that over half the advance information the damn Yankee radicals possess comes through you. Now tell me it's all pure fantasy and I'll tell Clarkson to go to the devil."

Leaning toward her, desperately pleading, he mistook the reason for her sudden pallor.

"Anne, there's never been anyone else for me. There never will be. For God's sake, let me take you out of this storm. Let's get away from this damnable town and go South, where we belong. I've respected your professional life, although I've never approved of it. Still I've respected it and you. But you must see it's at an end in this crisis. Let's get out—together. There's not much time and I've waited so long—so terribly long."

36

Harry was studying her as if weighing a choice of weapons for a possible attack which he dreaded to make and which he was praying she would make unnecessary. He had had a severe shock. All his passion for Anne had been formed and colored by the demands of his own nature. The time had now come when he was obliged to face qualities in Anne that he had either discounted or refused to recognize at all. He had always believed that once Anne gave up her ridiculous professional life, once they were safely married, he would soon arouse those dormant forces of affection in her that must exist. He had blamed her career for her lack of the ardent romanticism, the flowery warmth, the extravagant allusions, however careless or superficial, which were his measure of affection. He had missed them, without ever realizing that Anne's feelings were nonetheless passionate and sincere for being revealed in ways quite different from his own.

Anne sat stunned before him, stunned and silent. Looking into his hurt but eloquent eyes, she wanted nothing but to fling herself into his arms, forget all her—suddenly silly—ambitious plans, and cry out: "Yes, Harry, yes! For God's sake, take me, and love me, and shelter me, and care for me all the days of my life!"

But the ancient alarm bells destiny had fashioned for her clamored faintly and then rose in a crescendo of conviction that she felt would tear her flesh apart. Guilt, too, overwhelmed her. She *had* kept him waiting. He was waiting now.

"I've behaved thoughtlessly, Harry, perhaps even badly, toward you. But I—I'm afraid the trouble is we've each been trying to change the other. And it cannot be done."

"What is it you think I want to change in you?" he asked with an unexpected gentleness that made her feeling of guilt almost unbearable.

She said, with a note of desperation in her voice, "I can't make even one man I know understand the simplest fact about me—that I'm fascinated by people, not men but people; by what they plan and do, most of all by what they think, and why. And I have to have a part in all this or die. It's not something I chose, Harry. It's the way I am. Dearest, suppose I agreed to marry you tomorrow, to go with you and live wherever you wish—Charleston, Savannah, New Orleans. Would you really like to have me go on writing or taking part in commerce, or politics, or law? *Would you?* For that much of my own life I would have to preserve."

Harry started to speak, to sweep aside these questions. But he could not. After a moment he said in a metallic voice she hardly recognized, "No, I wouldn't. I can't stand to see you sully yourself in trade. You have nothing in common with vulgar tradesmen, traffickers in votes,

37

rabble-rousers. Yet you mix with them constantly. And you're a woman of the South. How can you stand these Yankees who take such damned pride in being busy? Busy about what? Trade is for white trash. Work is for niggers. That's the kind of world I believe in—and in the South it exists. The South, thank God, is my home. And while values are being destroyed right and left, you demean yourself by rushing about among those who have *no* values—and not the slightest idea of how to live."

All feeling seemed to have left her as she listened to this tirade. This was not the man she loved. Had Harry really believed all this during the years she had known him? She thought incredulously, Harry really loathes the people I love. He will fight anyone who tries to change his conceptions of life. He hates business because business is conflict and requires hard work, decision, and risk—and not because he believes it's beneath him. The knowledge that she had been so mistaken in him was like a blow.

Harry's aristocracy, she thought, his love of leisure, his art of living, is pure laziness. He hates rivalry in any man, doubly so in any woman. And the idea that a mere woman can successfully invade this alien world and formulate her own decisions . . . !

At least his words were making her decisions much easier to bear.

She said sadly, "What curious times we live in. First you plead with me to marry you, then in a few moments we're quarreling about your ideas of women and the South. But perhaps it isn't so ridiculous, Harry. I've seen your South—a drop of clear water in an ocean of muddy misery. I've also seen another South and studied it—to my eternal discomfort. Are you blind to it? Look at your ragged, slovenly, ignorant South as it really is, at the unpainted houses, the uncared-for barns, the fanatics, the poverty and violence, the miles of ragged rail fence on worn-out soil, the millions of miserable, undernourished blacks and whites. Oh, Harry, don't you see! Look where Southern hypocrisy has led us all. No, thank you. I don't want to share in it. I have my own work to do. And, thank heavens, I know what it is!"

Harry could no longer escape the terrible conviction that what Clarkson had implied was so.

He said savagely, "Then these charges *are* true? You haven't answered my questions, you know."

It suddenly seemed to Anne that there was little to salvage from their relationship and she spoke recklessly.

"Certainly. In the sense that I won't stand idly by and watch traitors wreck everything old Charles Carroll and my father taught me to hold dear. This storm you talk of is nothing but the result of a deliberate conspiracy planned years ago by a handful of fanatics.

There's no mystery in it. Every step is known to me and others. I not only understand what these tyrants are up to—I know exactly what they intend to do. I found out ten years ago and told Henry Clay; I got the information directly from Jefferson Davis. Ever since then, whenever I could lay my hands on any treasonable information, I have given it to patriotic men who knew what to do with it. And I am doing it today."

She drew a deep breath and thought, This is insane, I must stop—and she went right on. Under the strain of the moment she rose quickly and walked over to Harry. Seizing his coat in both hands, she shook him. He leaped to his feet.

"I'm not through," she cried. "I want you to understand me. We may be finished, but before you go I want you to understand *who* I am, and *what* I am, and why I can't bear to see every decent freedom my fathers fought for destroyed. I want you to know that——"

She took a deep breath and fought down her temper. Her fury fled —but it fled to Harry, for now he loomed over her, his face white with sudden rage.

"Why, God damn it," he shouted, *"you* dare to talk of traitors! You dare to make a fool of me! If you were a man I'd horsewhip you. I didn't believe Clarkson. I almost called him a liar. But to hear all this from your own lips! *You* speak of traitors! Why, you betray yourself, your family, your friends—day after day. Well, from now on, my girl, I'm going to expose you and ridicule you and I'll run you out of Baltimore or Washington or anywhere else you dare force a foot inside a door!"

His voice, raised in fury, seemed to reverberate through the whole house. She faced him, white-faced and frightened.

"Harry! Stop this. Stop it at once."

It was too late. All the pent-up passion of his months of waiting to marry her, all the bitter knowledge that at the end of this futile siege he had lost her, all the blinding insight he had obtained so swiftly rushed over him in a wave of hot fury.

"I could stand anything from you but the dirty prostitution of everything you represent," he shouted. "I'd rather see you walk down Gay Street working at a real trade—at least my friends would know what you are. But, my God, Davis still admires you. Buchanan remains your friend. The others all trust you. And I thought I loved you! I thought I *loved* you! What kind of disloyal, cold-blooded woman are you? You would suck us all dry and sell us and everything we hold dear to the first filthy Yankee blackmailer who comes down from the North with your price!"

At that, her eyes blazing, she drew her arm far back and struck

39

him in the face as hard as she could. She was horrified to see a thin trickle of blood start from the corner of his mouth. Harry neither stepped back nor raised his hand to his face. Without expression he took out his handkerchief, unfolded it deliberately, and wiped the blood away. Then he turned and left the room.

His footsteps on the stairs died away. She stood in the center of her parlor, appalled by what had happened. Like some shaken somnambulist, she walked to the sofa and flung herself face down.

Waves of shame and grief swept over her. Harry was gone—the one man she had cared for. She had not been able to make even this one man who had known her so long, so well, understand her.

A few moments later Mrs. Prescott found her. The landlady's usually carefree face filled with concern as she caught sight of the crumpled figure on the couch. She rushed to Anne and sat beside her, chafing her hands, frightened by what she had overheard, shocked by what she saw.

"Don't talk to me," Anne said tonelessly. "Just stay here beside me. But please don't talk to me." Her voice rose. "Oh God, I want to die."

5

IN THE WEEKS THAT FOLLOWED HER QUARREL WITH Harry, Anne turned to her work with desperate relief. Several times she had dined with Evans, and when John Breckinridge gave her seats in the House gallery for the sixteenth of February, she had asked Evans to accompany her. They sat there now, leaning forward, absorbed in the drama below them.

The electoral vote was to be counted at noon before both chambers of Congress. The atmosphere was electric. Every senator and representative who came onto the floor was scanned closely by the galleries. Holsters, derringers, heavy Colts, and Navy pistols bulged under armpits or coattails. It was as tense a moment as that when a hunter sights his prey.

Shortly after twelve Vice-President Breckinridge rose. His sullen gaze swept the packed chamber. He rapped twice with his gavel and called out in a clear, strong voice, "It is my duty to open the certificates of election in the presence of the two houses, and I now proceed to the performance of that duty."

A Southern senator vigorously signaled the Speaker's rostrum and then pointed to the armed guards in Union blue stationed in solid ranks across the rear of the chamber. The galleries hummed.

Breckinridge saw the senator, stiffened, and said loudly, "Except questions of order, no motions can be entertained."

The senator's face purpled. He shouted, "This *is* a point of order. Is the count of the electoral vote to proceed under menace? Shall members be required to perform a constitutional duty before the Janizaries of General Scott are withdrawn from the hall?"

"The point of order is not sustained," shouted Breckinridge savagely. "Proceed with the count."

A member behind the senator tugged at his coat. The senator struck aside his hand. But he sat down, his eyes fixed on the uniformed riflemen.

The long sealed envelopes were opened one by one.

In the midst of tremendous tension Breckinridge advanced a step, glanced at a sheet of paper in his hand, looked out over the chamber, and said in a loud, clear voice, "Abraham Lincoln, having received a majority of the whole number of electoral votes, is duly elected President of the United States for four years beginning on the fourth of March, 1861."

The ceremony was over in a patter of formal applause. But a deep undercurrent of feeling had been released, and men and women rose slowly and streamed wordlessly out of the chamber, out of the Capitol itself, as if a profound change had been wrought most suddenly and everything that was familiar half an hour ago was familiar no longer, had changed subtly but irrevocably, and would never in all the land be the same again.

In the darkness of her rooms, very early one morning a week later, Anne heard the first uneasy rumblings of an awakening city.

Downstairs the night clerk dozed, one hand still curled about an empty coffee cup perched on a deal table beside him. In the doorway a sleepy Negro wrung out his mop as a figure brushed past him and flipped an envelope in the face of the sleeping clerk.

"Wake up, man, wake up!"

A moment later the sharp pounding on her door brought Anne to her feet. Tossing a dressing gown around her shoulders, she stumbled over a small stool at the foot of the bed and awakened Milly in the next room. She went to the door and called through it, "Who is it?"

"Paul Randolph from Mr. Pinkerton's office, ma'am."

Anne opened the door a few inches.

"For you, ma'am."

The man in the hallway handed her the envelope and stood there. Milly was lighting a small night lamp. Anne went to it and tore open the envelope. The message, on a Pennsylvania Central telegraph blank, was addressed to Randolph, 21 I Street, Washington, D.C. It read:

INFORM MISS CARROLL ON SAFE ARRIVAL OF PACKAGE FROM THE WEST. ESCORT HER TO WILLARD'S AT ONCE. BREAKFAST AND FURTHER ORDERS TO BE HAD THERE. T. A. SCOTT, VICE-PRESIDENT, PENNSYLVANIA R.R.

"I'll be with you in five minutes, Mr. Randolph."

"I have a carriage, ma'am. I'll be in the lobby," he replied, and went downstairs.

Twenty minutes later, in a mud-spattered hack, they reached the side entrance of Willard's. The raw darkness was only just broken by a dirty streak of dull light in the east. Two army wagons laden with work details clattered past on the rough cobblestones. Far up the Avenue, out of a light mist that prophesied a fair day, the gaunt base and skeleton of the Capitol's unfinished dome, with booms, hoists, rigging, and tackle, rose like bare ribs silhouetted against a gray-black sky.

There was sudden life inside Willard's, an air of concealed excitement. Blazing gas globes threw a ghastly white light on the dusty-flowered carpet. She saw several friends standing about, all of them with expectant expressions on their faces, but Randolph led her past them. Halfway down the carpeted corridor they met a stocky open-faced man with small alert eyes and a short beard. Holsters bulged under his long linen coat. He was unsmiling and looked as if he needed sleep. But his voice was pleasant, unhurried, and he walked along with them in a curiously smooth, swinging gait. He was Allan Pinkerton, an able detective employed by the government.

"In half an hour—in Parlor Six," he said shortly as he left them at the dining-room door.

In the long, gloomy, almost empty room Judge Bates sat at one of the tables waiting for her. He rose at once and walked over to her

"My dear lady, good morning. Can we breakfast at once?" His matter-of-fact tone almost hid his excitement.

Not until they were seated did she dare ask *the* question. She said in a low voice, "Then he's actually here?"

"Certainly," replied Bates.

"I'm not in favor of this meeting, Judge," she said slowly. "You know I don't particularly want to meet the man. You know my opinion of his capacities, or rather lack of them. Do you really think this is wise?"

Bates studied her a moment, almost coldly.

"I'm surprised to hear you talk like that, ma'am. This occasion has nothing to do with your feelings—or mine. The problem of Hicks and Maryland is paramount. And you know Tom Scott insists on this meeting. You're to have five minutes with him."

Willard's was famous for its huge breakfasts, and Willard's great bar was the political nerve center of the city. The shrewd Willard brothers from Vermont had provided plushy parlors ideal for small political conferences. Their expansive dining rooms poured forth, for

43

breakfast alone, mountains of fried oysters, steak and onions, blanc-mange, pâté de foie gras, eggs, bacon and ham, robins on toast, pheasant, quail, sausage, pancakes, half a dozen varieties of rolls and muffins, and coffee cups that looked like punch bowls with great monogrammed handles.

But Anne could hardly force down half a cup of coffee and a small portion of the season's first run of shad. This meeting might well be a most important turning point in her career.

"I'm nervous," she confessed to Bates. "Have you seen him?"

"No—and I'm not going to," replied Bates. "Lamon wrote me the man was exhausted. Be as concise and emphatic as you can. Lamon says it has been most difficult to convince him of the violence of the situation."

Judge Bates hastily swallowed some coffee and exclaimed, "Do you know what happened? Scott rushed him out of Harrisburg in the greatest secrecy last night on a special train. He made the night express wait at Baltimore for his prize package. Curtin and Lamon came along with him. Scott restored his wire circuits at dawn this morning and Pinkerton sent him an unsigned message already agreed upon—'Plums Delivered Nuts Safely.' Whew, what a night!"

Anne pushed back her cup and nervously wiped her lips. She saw Pinkerton standing by the door. She rose reluctantly.

"Will I see you later, Judge?" she asked, a note of entreaty in her voice.

He nodded reassuringly. "I'll wait for you and drive you home. Later we can lunch together."

She joined Pinkerton, who led her down a long corridor, up a flight of carpeted stairs, and knocked on a door with a white enamel marker: 'Parlor No. 6. Private.'

A deep voice called out, "Come right in."

Pinkerton held the door open while Anne walked slowly into the room. As it clicked shut, a tall athletic man with sweeping black mustaches and clear piercing eyes came toward her.

"Miss Carroll? I'm Colonel Lamon, ma'am. I want to thank you for coming over at this early hour."

She greeted him almost without being aware of it. Where, she wondered, was the man she had come to see? Then she saw him.

The President-elect, his gleaming new black broadcloth coat badly wrinkled, sat half reclining on a shabby horsehair sofa in a far corner of the parlor. His head, a dark shadow in the poor light, was turned toward them. He was absently creasing a morning paper and prepar-ing to get to his feet. She was fascinated by the slow unfoldment of

44

his tall rawboned figure. In a series of deliberate, almost calculated moves he rose impressively to his full height of six feet four and a half inches and advanced awkwardly to meet her. Lamon's introduction was brief.

"Mr. Lincoln—this is Miss Carroll of Maryland, sir."

Lord, he's just as homely as everyone says he is, was her first impression as Lincoln's shaggy head and gaunt features came into the full glare of a wall lamp. He gave her a friendly nod.

"How do you do, Miss Carroll. You're a brave young lady to come out so early. I hope you've had breakfast?"

It was a rather high, queerly cadenced voice, full of curious ups and downs. The minute you were sure it was too high, Anne thought, you heard hints of depth and resonance and richness. Then all at once it was just a homely, high Western voice again. He was obviously tired, but there was a friendly smile on his face as he towered over her, quietly surveying her with frank curiosity. She thought in dismay, Good lord, I don't even come up to his shoulders, and to her surprise found herself curtsying lightly.

As if reading her thoughts and being himself amused by the marked discrepancy in their statures, he laughed.

"Well, ma'am, you and I seem to be the long and the short of it this morning."

"Good morning, Mr. Pres——" She caught herself and smiled. "Good morning, Mr. Lincoln, and welcome to Washington where you belong. We are all delighted to see you here."

"About five people have seen me here," he said solemnly, and then broke into a sunny mischievous smile. "They've smuggled me into town like an old carpet," he said. His gray eyes sparkled with life that as suddenly died away. "I don't like it."

She watched the quick play of expression on a face that seemed cast in rigid melancholy and yet rippled like the surface of a deep stream with little cat's paws of humor and amusement.

"Nevertheless, Mr. Lincoln," she said boldly, "they were right."

"Well, please sit down here, ma'am." He indicated the sofa and tossed his newspaper to Colonel Lamon. "Here's your paper, Ward. And please stay—we'll be but a few moments."

He sat down in a low chair that raised his knees almost as high as his chest, and looked at her quizzically.

"You're much younger than I'd judged, ma'am," he said frankly. "McClure and Governor Curtin told me a good deal about you in Philadelphia." There was the hint of a smile on his lips. "Tell me, ma'am, how do you do it?"

Again the white flaring gaslight made him look tired, worried, thin.

45

His question took her aback, but she was becoming aware of a warmth, a magnetism in him of which his appearance gave no hint, and her nervousness disappeared. She answered laughingly, "Do what, Mr. Lincoln? I don't know——"

"Oh, come now, ma'am. Judge Bates wrote me you have one of the most promising legal minds in Washington. In New York last week Mr. Seward showed me some reports of yours on the South American trade crisis. In Harrisburg last night Tom Scott told me you know as much about the Pacific Railroad problem as Grenville Dodge— and that's a great plenty. And Curtin told me any communications from Governor Hicks should be referred to you for advice." There was gentle mockery in his eyes, now alight again with humor. "I repeat, ma'am, as a struggling lawyer who's had enough difficulties following a single profession, I'll pay you handsomely for the recipe to your fourfold career." He repeated again, "How do you do it?"

Both of them were laughing now and taking stock of each other. Anne shrugged her shoulders almost imperceptibly and said, "Surely, Mr. Lincoln, you must be familiar with flattery. I've made my own living for a number of years. I'm afraid I've had to play jack-of-all-trades to do it."

Again his expression changed, leaving her a little bewildered at the rapid and scarcely concealed parade of emotions that passed through his mind and was so magically reflected in his features. His voice, too, changed with his thoughts.

"Well," he said abruptly, as if humor were over and done with, "Curtin insisted I question you about Governor Hicks. Tell me"— he studied her intently with the eyes of a lawyer—"how did you happen to get mixed up with these Know-Nothings who elected Hicks?" He added emphatically, "I never cared for them. You don't get rid of one prejudice by fighting it with two others."

"What do you mean, Mr. Lincoln?" she asked tartly. She did not care at all for the expression she saw now in his deep-set eyes. He said testily, "Well, ma'am, as a nation we began by declaring that 'all men are created equal' except Negroes. If the Know-Nothings had got control it would have been 'all men are created equal except Negroes and foreigners and Catholics.' When it comes to that I shall prefer emigrating to some country where they make no pretense of loving liberty."

"Mr. Lincoln," she said earnestly, trying to repress her anger, "let me tell you the facts at least so far as Maryland and Baltimore are concerned. For years there has been a terrible alliance between Southern slaveholders and Northern business interests, with James Buchanan as their hired agent, to handle the illegal votes of thousands

46

of newly arrived immigrants, as well as, in many cases, their forced labor. The sole purpose of this alliance has been to keep the slave-holders in power. Since every free laborer in Baltimore was impressed with that fact, he voted for Hicks and our ticket. In attacking tyranny like that, I would use *any* and *all* weapons at hand. At least the Know-Nothings stood for Union. And we smashed Buchanan's machine in Maryland, a feat accomplished nowhere else."

There was a deep silence. She was conscious of her rapid breathing. She was also aware that an unpleasant light had come into Mr. Lincoln's eyes. He said harshly, "I see. I think, ma'am, you greatly misconstrue or localize most narrowly the purpose of the Know-Nothings. Your situation in Baltimore, I admit, may have been unique. But in a land at least professing equality, the Know-Nothings stood for the exclusion of foreigners and Catholics in a democratic way of life. I think no one can gainsay that. You believe in deals, I take it, to gain your immediate ends."

His face had flushed a little. Colonel Lamon was looking at her sharply, trying to catch her eye. For a moment panic swept Anne and her too ready tongue threatened to run away with her. But a sudden inspiration seized her. She managed a wintry smile and said as lightly as she could, "I was at the Republican convention in Chicago, Mr. Lincoln. It seemed to me that Judge Davis was very fond of deals —especially in Indiana and Pennsylvania."

She heard a smothered exclamation from Lamon. And Mr. Lincoln was angry, quite angry. There was no doubt about it. He looked at her, his gray-blue eyes flickering and the flush on his sallow face deepening. But just as suddenly his mood changed again, his tension vanished, and he laughed heartily, although his eyes still smoldered with fading irritation.

"Not another word, ma'am. We'll declare this a draw right now. And what I've said to Judge Davis in private won't bear repeating. He sewed me up in a gunny sack. Now then—what about Hicks? Will he stick with the Union? And what about that confounded Maryland legislature?"

Her voice rose, clear and emphatic, and Lamon looked up over his paper at her flashing eyes and animated face.

"I'll make him stick, Mr. Lincoln. The man is crushed with private troubles and bad health. But if all possible encouragement is given him—Governor Hicks will stick. He won't convene the legislature."

"All right. But suppose the legislature convenes without his authority and votes secession," he said sharply, almost rudely, and she bridled at his tone. "Tell me, ma'am, what would *you* do in such a case?"

"I'd arrest them, Mr. Lincoln, just arrest them. You can't bargain

47

or compromise with pirates. If they make a move to convene, pack them off to jail."

Lincoln's lips were thinner than she had seen them.

"Indeed, ma'am. By armed force and the suspension of habeas corpus proceedings?"

"Absolutely. You have the authority."

Mr. Lincoln regarded her rather grimly.

"You seem to believe in pretty direct action, ma'am. Do you want the whole of Maryland invested by armed force?"

"That's not necessary, sir," she said quickly. "Most of the people are loyal to the Union. I know that. All that's necessary is to bag the traitors in the legislature."

She was aware that his attitude toward her had stiffened again. But his eyes were inscrutable and studied her so long that she became embarrassed. At last he sighed.

"So that's your opinion, is it? And you urge all possible moral support for Hicks under this pressure, I take it."

"Yes. He wants not only moral support but public evidences of support. He wants the feeling not only that there is a strong national government but that it is backing him."

Something in her voice, some veiled criticism, aroused Mr. Lincoln.

"I take it you are not satisfied with these public evidences so far. What is your own idea of the present situation, Miss Carroll?"

This was, in fact, the very kind of opening she had longed for. But now that it had been offered she was frightened at her temerity. She was alarmingly aware that this meeting was not at all what it had been planned to be. Moreover, there was a quality in Mr. Lincoln that completely baffled her. Noting her hesitation, he smiled reassuringly.

"Come, come, ma'am. We're all entitled to our opinions. I'm interested in yours."

"Then I'll be completely frank with you, Mr. Lincoln," she said a little breathlessly. "My belief is that the split in the Republican party, the struggle between Conservatives and Abolitionists, has nearly destroyed the hopes of Southern Unionists, and there are thousands of them. What is now merely a rebellion of traitors, a deliberate but limited conspiracy on the part of a few, may soon, if the Southern Unionists are abandoned, become a revolution in fact."

"You think I have abandoned them, ma'am?"

She hesitated only a fraction of a second before she answered boldly, "Yes, I do, Mr. Lincoln. That is my whole quarrel with the incoming administration. The Southern people have not been heard. They are being abandoned at this crucial moment. And yet these many friends of the Union in the South are ready to start a counterrevolu-

48

tion at a single sign from you. But you have given none. Those responsible for secession don't represent a tithe of the people in the seceded states. And yet——"

Again she paused, then went stubbornly on: "Yet the new Cabinet has been formed purely on partisan grounds—that is what I cannot endure—to unite the Republican party *in the North*. I think it is a fatal blunder. If this crisis were being met in a *national* spirit, if a number of constitutional advisers in the Cabinet and high government places were taken from the loyal South and the people of the South were rallied to the Union, you would see a counterrevolution that would sweep away this insolent little group of fanatical aristocrats like chaff in the wind."

Mr. Lincoln was regarding her very soberly.

"Miss Carroll," he said earnestly, "I *have* tried to reach these men you speak of. I pleaded with John Gilmer of North Carolina, a friend of yours, I believe, to join my Cabinet. He refused. Certain overtures were made to Henry Winter Davis, from your own city of Baltimore, to be my Attorney General. He's a cousin of my campaign manager, Judge Davis. But Winter, too, refused. Informal but definite advances *have* been made to other Union leaders in the South. For one reason or another all these attempts failed. And you have forgotten something. A counterrevolution requires force. The national government has no force at its disposal with which to commence such operations as you seem to recommend. We have, in fact, no army at all. This man Floyd who's been running the War Department for Buchanan has disposed such troops as we have in far Western posts. If you'll pardon me, I think you are looking at this upheaval with a lawyer's mind."

"I just don't believe," she argued stubbornly, "that wholehearted attempts have been made to reach the loyal forces there are in the South. I know Southerners. I am one of them. Every progressive cause in the South will be doomed for years if present policies are adhered to."

"What present policies?" asked Mr. Lincoln testily.

"Why," she said angrily, "this policy of treating all Southerners as rebels, of lumping the people with their traitors, these—these policies of yours as President-elect," she exclaimed in sudden confusion.

"Miss Carroll," he said solemnly and a little sadly, "I give you my word I have no such policies. In fact, I have *no policy at all* at the present moment. That is one reason I am listening to your point of view and that of many others."

She was horrified by this confession from the tall gaunt man before her.

"Do you mean, Mr. Lincoln, that you actually have no definite program to place before the nation at your inauguration?"

49

"Just that," said Mr. Lincoln grimly. "None at all. So many things have to ripen, so many forces crystallize, so many voices have to be heard, and weighed, and understood, before we can see where we are and what we have to do."

She was stunned by these words, words which ordinarily she would have taken as confessions of weakness, fear, and sheer indecision. But there was nothing weak, fearful, or indecisive in the face and figure of this compelling man from Illinois.

"You see, ma'am," he said patiently, "I would try to realize that no crisis of this nature has ever before confronted the nation. I understand your point of view. You see a simple, deliberately planned conspiracy allowed to ripen. You cannot understand the paralysis that grips the North. But behind all this, Miss Carroll, is a truly vast seething of human forces no man can assay at present. It is all hot molten metal and nothing solid a man can cling to. It will have to cool. I don't yet believe there must be a war. I am inclined to think, in some ways, that the fire can be allowed to burn itself out. I think, ma'am," he added with a fleeting smile, "we'll manage to keep house. What you've suggested as a way of dealing with Maryland, ma'am, seems too drastic to me. But it will give Judge Bates something to chew on."

Again his mood changed. His features relaxed.

"Tell me, ma'am," he said curiously, obviously wishing to change the subject, "were you born in Baltimore?"

"I'm from the Eastern Shore, Mr. Lincoln. I was born in Somerset County, at Kingston Hall."

To her amazement Mr. Lincoln laughed heartily.

"The Eastern Shore!" he exclaimed. "Don't tell me!"

She was blushing furiously, completely confused by these lightning-like shifts in his moods.

"I don't understand——" she began.

But his laugh disappeared and he seemed embarrassed. "I beg your pardon, Miss Carroll. I really do. But you reminded me of a yarn I told Weed the other day. The fact is, ma'am, Weed and I were discussing this very problem and Weed told me in times like these Maryland must be a good place to be *from*." He hesitated and looked pleadingly at Anne, as if to be let off.

She managed to say "Yes?" as lightly as possible, and Lincoln had to go on.

"I guess I've got to deliver," he said gloomily. "Well, I told Weed the situation reminded me of a witness I examined in court once who was asked his age and said, 'Fifty.' 'Now look here, Ben,' I said, 'the Court knows you're a whole lot older than that.' 'Oh,' said Ben, 'I know what you're driving at. You're thinkin' of those fifteen years I

50

spent on the Eastern Shore of Maryland. That's jest so much time lost, Mr. Lincoln, and don't count at all.' "

Anne laughed as much at his expression as at the anecdote, and Lincoln added gallantly, "But on seeing you, Miss Carroll, I guess that story hasn't the ghost of a point."

Over his shoulder Anne caught an impatient expression on Lamon's face. She got up, smiling.

Mr. Lincoln unfolded himself from his incongruous chair and walked to the door with her. Again she sensed that he was weighing her with a decided measure of disapproval. A mood of violent depression swept over her. Rebuffs, direct or implied, had a painful and immediate effect on her energies. Curiously enough, much of her antagonism toward Mr. Lincoln was now directed at herself. To increase her chagrin, he opened the door for her and again that sunny smile illumined his face.

"When Mrs. Lincoln and I are settled, Miss Carroll, come and see us. Meanwhile"—the smile disappeared, the veil dropped over his eyes—"I'll ponder what you said. Good-by, ma'am, and give my regards to Judge Bates."

Pinkerton escorted her to the main lobby where Bates was waiting. She stood before him, silent, ill at ease, and he looked at her curiously.

"Well," he said at last, "what happened? What did you think of him?"

She thought he must surely see in her eyes how her self-confidence had suffered. "I don't know, Judge Bates," she answered almost helplessly. "We—we practically quarreled. I feel I managed things very badly this morning. It's even possible I made a fool of myself."

Her disappointment in herself had shaken her badly and she was on the verge of tears. Judge Bates, hastily patting her arm, said nothing and quickly escorted her to his carriage.

51

THE SHOCK OF HIS QUARREL WITH ANNE HAD DRIVEN
Harry Heyward like a homing pigeon straight to Charleston. After
a few days he had no longer been able to endure either the thought of
Anne or the reality of Washington.

But on his way to Charleston the clatter of wheels over the rough
track sang a song of home-coming and heart's ease. And when his
train stopped for water at a dusty crossing in the shadow of a turpentine plant forty miles from the city, Harry gratefully dropped from
the lamplit coach into the darkness and the fragrance of the night.

In a rush of rapture he drank in the evening air. The pine barrens
and swamps that stretched without an undulation to the invisible
horizons of night flung back to him every scent and sound that he
loved. On this mild winter night the breath of spring was in the air.
In a few weeks, from the earth, from the pines, from the swamps and
the drainage ditch beside the track, would rise the odors of the land
he loved—the sweet tang of turpentine, the acrid, musky smell of
swampland, the sweetness of dogwood, jasmine, azaleas, and the rich
heavy scent of countless wild flowers. From all this flat, lush, darkling
land, with every branch hanging motionless in the sweet hushed air,
would rise a mighty torrent of night sounds, already beginning to be
audible—a loud, pulsating cacophony of crickets, tree toads, bull-
frogs, chirpers, katydids, and all manner of noisy insects, nameless
and unseen, a song of night and the earth that no low-country Caro-
linian ever forgets.

He heard the clank of the waterspout, then the bell rang and with
a rattle of link pins and gear the little train began to move. Harry
pulled himself up on the platform and stood there a moment before

he entered the coach. His heart was solaced and his spirit eased. He felt that everything in this land—the harbor mists of Charleston, the noonday heat waves shimmering above Meeting Street, the soft-lighted verandas at night, the silhouette of palms and blossoms and scented shrub, the affluence of Legare Street—all belonged to him, had somehow been brought into being by the very fact of his being alive, and hence should and ought to exist to serve him at his own behest and desire.

His train clattered through the night, over the lonely far-reaching earth, and finally drew to a halt in a smoky depot and sighed there and puffed and panted as over a race well run. And Harry's heart soared. He was in Carolina. He was in Charleston. He was South. He was home.

Harry had not told his mother the exact time of his arrival. He walked homeward alone, as in a dream, drinking in the moon-silvered pillars of St. Philip's Church, soaking in the names he loved—Stoll Alley, St. Michael's Alley, the old Pringle home, Clason's store with its candy striped awning—as he strolled down Meeting Street. At the East Battery wall he lingered, watching a few quiet lights on the silent water, turning to glance at the wide verandas of pleasant homes resting behind mellow brick walls and delicate wrought-iron gates. He thought to himself, This is where I belong. All at once the driving harshness and boorishness of Yankees, their smugness, their God almighty scramble for dirty dollars, their filthy little dingy frame houses, their crowded, ugly little towns, intolerable in summer, worse in winter, became anathema to him. He hated all of it with a fierce hatred, the proud and glacial North, the banging, clanging, brutal, coarse, smoky, filthy, slum-jammed, mannerless, bustling, money-grubbing North. And he had begun to fear it a little.

But now Harry felt whole and serene. He heard music from a nearby home, a distant piano, a young girl singing, and far down the street, through the open doors of a snow-white church, came the eloquent, urgent voice of a man of God haranguing his flock.

He walked briskly up Legare Street and turned in at the lofty wrought-iron gates, always open on the Sabbath, and walked up the wide azalea-flanked path that led to his home.

Inside there were flowers everywhere, and lamps alight, and the soft sheen of his father's rich rugs underfoot. Then his mother came from the library and poised on its threshold like some startled wild bird.

"Harry! Harry! You rogue!" She flung herself in his arms and kissed him again and again.

When he had composed himself she led him into the parlor and

53

stood looking at him happily. Alice Heyward was a striking woman, tall and willowy, with Harry's ash-blond hair and dark violet eyes under even darker, level brows.

"Dear Harry, don't say a word," she said, smiling a little too sweetly, placing a graceful protesting finger on his lips. "Charles heard all about it in a letter from Thomas. He'll be home tomorrow."

She saw the pain in his eyes and retreated hastily.

"We won't talk about it, not for a long time. I'm so terribly, terribly happy to have you here."

Her eyes devoured him while she stroked his hand gently.

"Dinner's almost ready—and don't dress. Come along to your room, dear. It's just as you left it—every last thing in it, darling. Don't ever leave us again for a long, long time."

They walked arm in arm toward the graceful spiral staircase. Halfway down the hall the door of his father's study opened and a girl in a black net evening dress splashed boldly with crimson poinsettias stepped toward them and halted in a posture of complete surprise whose genuineness a keener eye than Harry's might have suspected. But Harry's astonishment was real enough. He caught the flash of dark, brilliant eyes in the natural pallor of a beautifully oval face. She carried a graceful figure superbly, and her pale oval face was transformed by a smile so intimately amusing and frank in its welcome that Harry caught his breath. His mother, watching him, said easily, "Jackie, do come here. Don't scold me, Harry. I had no time to tell you we have a very charming visitor from Savannah whose parents I've just had the pleasure of visiting. Harry—Miss Jacqueline Desfosses, our guest for a fortnight—my son, Miss Desfosses—Mr. Harry Heyward."

For a fleeting instant Harry's heart tightened. Some dim instinct warned him that this was too pat. He tried to catch his mother's eyes, but they were now laughing a little triumphantly at Jacqueline.

He bowed gravely, studying the girl's lovely face for any trifling sign to support his sudden suspicion.

"I'm delighted to meet you, Miss Desfosses. Have you been here long?"

She glanced with charming guilt at his mother.

"I hope you'll forgive me, Mr. Heyward, but I've been fascinated by your mother and Charleston for over a week. Indeed, your mother has made me a most willing captive. My brother arrives from New York tomorrow and your mother insisted I meet him here and make your acquaintance—a double pleasure I couldn't resist."

So she had been here for over a week. She had been here before he and Anne had—— His fears fell away. He said gaily, "You make it

54

a perfect home-coming, Miss Desfosses. And I'm certainly going to dress. I'll only be a moment."

On the landing some impulse made him turn and glance below. The girl was looking up at him, her lips parted. His mother was smiling.

Six weeks later, after a courtship that seemed to him like a distant dream, Harry and Jacqueline Desfosses were married in St. Michael's Church and went to New Orleans on their honeymoon.

Harry was sure, following his sudden return to Charleston after his quarrel with Anne, that he had fought hard to keep his balance. But Jacqueline had flowed into his life like some lovely liqueur. He had fought against her very briefly.

For Jacqueline was so much that Anne was not—so quietly, subtly voluptuous, with a calm, placid, unhurried mind that he soon sensed was nothing but an outward and useful veneer over the deeper passions that possessed her. Although he had had no intention of doing anything of the kind, he had proposed to her only a fortnight after their meeting. When Harry had quite finished Jacqueline had leaned quickly toward him, sought out his lips, and pressed herself against him.

In the rosy unreal days that followed, the memory of Anne faded into some cold and distant wraith that mattered no more to Harry or the causes he sought to serve.

But, remembering his months of waiting for Anne, he was surprised at the rapidity of his brief courtship and marriage to a charming girl he had never heard of a few weeks ago. Yet all of his being, as if outraged and baffled for so long, had demanded such a course. He was tremendously happy.

Then, as from a lovely dream, Harry began to wake. It was late in March. A jarring sense of reality broke through the soft sensuous curtains in which his mind had been swathed for weeks. All Charleston was in an uproar, and men he knew, men with whom he worked, were openly calculating the day of decision that all of them knew was at hand.

On the night of April 12 Harry went to bed very early and tried vainly to sleep. A strange excitement gripped him, for he had made his decision. He would go to Washington, taking Jacqueline with him, and expose Anne. He would secure direct evidences of her betrayals, fling them in the laps of the Richmond leaders he knew, and then banish forever from his mind the memory of this woman who had deceived him and all the others.

Later he slept and dreamed. And it seemed to him that he was

55

standing on a high cold mountaintop when suddenly he slipped and fell. In an agony of suffering he felt as if he would never cease falling and that his life and everything it contained and all that he had never grasped and never understood were falling into oblivion with him. A blinding sheet of light split the void about him. The crash and roll of thunder filled his ears. . . .

Harry found himself standing alone in the middle of his room, stark-naked, covered with cold sweat, shouting unintelligibly. He stopped shouting and stood there shaking, listening. Dull booming concussions rolled in from the harbor and reverberated among the buildings of Charleston. He grabbed a dressing gown, flung it over his shoulders, and rushed to the window just as his mother ran into his room. Another flash of light—and he had just time to see a slight and lovely arc of red penciled in the sky over the distant water before his mother threw her arms about him even as another great concussion jarred the house and rattled the window frames. Her eyes were brilliant in the darkness, her voice triumphant.

"We're free, Harry! We're free! The war has begun! We have our own nation at last. They're firing on Fort Sumter, Harry. It must have frightened you, for I heard you cry out in your sleep. Hurry! Hurry and get dressed, darling!"

So that was it, that was it, he told himself. But he found no relief or reassurance in this explanation of the horror that clung to him from his dream.

"What time is it, Mother?" His voice sounded very far away.

"It's four-thirty, dear. Please hurry."

A few minutes later both of them were running madly toward the Battery and joined there a huge sea of awe-struck faces gazing out over the harbor. The Battery, brick walls, iron gates, rooftops, and broad verandas were covered with faces solemn and smiling. People half dressed, people in night clothes cheered, danced, hugged one another, and shouted wildly. Other people, somber and silent, stared into the dark sky as at a miracle, while the first screaming shells of the irrepressible conflict roared out of the guns of Moultrie and other harbor forts and burst in crimson flame and deafening concussions before the casemates of Sumter.

War had begun.

7

ONE MORNING IN THAT INCREDIBLE APRIL, FULL OF
Fort Sumter and Baltimore's assault on the Massachusetts regiments,
Judge Bates called Anne to his office. He handed her a paper and said
cryptically, "I think he's come around."

"What do you mean?"

"I had a long talk with Mr. Lincoln last night," replied the Attorney
General. "We discussed Maryland. He and Seward have had Hicks
over from Annapolis several times. At last the President is aroused—
he is ready to authorize the arrest of the Maryland legislature the
moment they convene. Here is the rough draft of your brief supporting such action, with a few proposed changes. Will you write out the
finished draft for me as quickly as possible?"

Her eyes shone with pleasure. This was what she had fought for
and dreamed of.

"That's most generous of you, Judge. I'll go to work at once."

Anne went to her rooms. She had needed more work to take her
mind off her anomalous and uncomfortable role in the capital. To
quarrel with Harry, to watch her Southern friends leave en masse, to
endure the tensions in her own riven family were one thing. But for
weeks to have had nothing important to which she could devote herself wholeheartedly, with which to compensate for these pressures, had
made her miserable. Even Mr. Evans, an uncertain quantity at best,
had performed his vanishing act with more than usual abruptness. She
had had a curt note one morning. He would be gone "for some weeks."
He hoped to have "the pleasure of renewing our acquaintance upon
my return."

She had awakened this morning depressed at the emptiness of her

57

personal life and utterly discouraged with the results of her work in the capital. Now, standing in the sunlight before her parlor windows, she felt a surge of purposefulness. She *was* needed. The President had confirmed her views on Maryland and she was to prepare the brief that would help transform an idea into action. She turned to her desk gratefully and, drawing paper before her, she set to work.

For almost three fantastic months following the attack on Fort Sumter, the country and the capital were in an increasing uproar. The torn administration, representing a divided, corruption-ridden, apathetic, unwieldy North, did nothing but discuss measures to cope with a situation wholly out of control. On July Fourth the new Congress convened in special session. And then the storm broke. Frightened senators and representatives and home folk who had hoped and prayed for any kind of peace that could be bought, decreed, or compromised without bloodshed awoke to the appalling fact that they were really at war. Virginia, North Carolina, and Tennessee had now also seceded.

The Army and Navy had all but dissolved in a flood of resignations as the ablest officers in both services rushed South to fight for their respective states.

The one Southern pillar of respectability left in town was Anne's intimate friend, John Breckinridge, nephew of a loyal and devout Kentuckian she loved. Breckinridge was now a Kentucky senator standing alone among the vacant black-draped seats of his Southern colleagues. To this pillar Anne still clung. Friendship and affection she had to have, and Breckinridge and his attractive young wife gave her both. Moreover, she wanted to show Wade and Secretary Chase and others of Mr. Lincoln's Yankee coterie that here, at least, was another well-born Southerner like herself who could retain his convictions and yet remain loyal to the Union.

Her faith in Breckinridge was blind and ardent. Both Judge Bates and Ben Wade told her that Breckinridge was under heavy suspicion, that he was shunned or treated with freezing discourtesy by his colleagues. But she clung all the closer to the handsome Kentuckian, convinced that of all her intimate friends of Southern sympathies Breckinridge was still to be admired, for only he had had the courage to come back to his seat in the Senate. And yet a vague fear shook her as she read his words in the *Congressional Globe* and saw that he was waging a lone battle against the whole pack of Unionists, a pack telling him in words and gestures that he was the one yellow dog left among them.

"I stand alone," he said in one of his first fiery speeches. "But I will speak. Under the Constitution I have the right to speak. The day is

58

not yet, but it draws nigh, when a terrible accounting will be rendered by those who are plunging their country into the vortex of ruin under the pretext of maintaining the Constitution. Nothing but ruin, utter ruin, to the North, to the South, to the East, to the West, will follow the prosecution of this contest. You have two confederacies now!" he cried. "Fight but twelve months longer, and you will have three; twelve months longer, and you will have four!"

There was logic in that. But logic and reason had fled. Facts were in the saddle. It made no difference, Anne reflected, what a man said or professed or actually believed any more. It was what he did, and only that, that counted now.

Then, on July 16, began an uproarious, frightening week that was to end on the twenty-third with the debacle of Bull Run and a panic-stricken city filled with dusty, exhausted, bloodied men and officers wandering the disordered streets.

The week began abruptly enough. It was a hot glaring summer day. Anne was walking past Joe Shillington's bookstore, when she almost bumped into Senator Wade, flushed and rude, hurrying out of the shop.

"Your friend Breckinridge is to speak in half an hour," he had said roughly, hardly stopping. "You'd better get up there and hear him. I understand the fur's going to fly."

He rushed off without another word. She had intended to go back to her rooms and work in the shaded comparative coolness of her parlor. Instead, as she watched Wade disappear around the corner, she opened her handbag. She had her gallery card tucked into a moiré pocket. She took it out.

Even before her Kentucky friend began to speak Anne had an uneasy premonition of what was coming. She sat taut as he started his address before a tense, hostile chamber.

This day, this man, this speech took on the curious strained unreality that often denotes the final stage of complete disillusionment. To Anne, in a most personal and painful way, his speech was always the Great Betrayal. For she was fond of Breckinridge. He had been as dear to her, as loyal and frank, as a brother. And the blindness of her devotion to him now made her bitterly aware of the accurate judgment of radical Yankees whose opinions of Breckinridge she had fought so hard to alter.

As she listened to Breckinridge's incredible assault on the President, as she listened to the venomous charges of this man who had protested his loyalty to her over and over and had been her gallant and entertaining escort at innumerable social affairs, he roused her to a fury of which she had not considered herself capable. For Breckinridge had

59

not only deserted the cause. He shouted defiance at the President and the nation in terms that enraged Anne.

"The President," he said, and the words were like bullets, "in violation of the Constitution, has made war on the Southern states for subjugation and conquest, has increased the Army and Navy, called forth the militia, blockaded the Southern ports, suspended the writ of habeas corpus, and without warrant arrested private persons, searched private houses, seized private papers and effects. And now, in his Baltimore speech, the President asserts that the state of Maryland is abolished. This, in every age of the world, has been the very definition of despotism."

It was so unexpected that Anne could not take her eyes from him even for a moment, and as though under a hateful spell she sat hearing him pour forth a stream of bitter, outrageous, and more personal attacks on the President.

Several days later, as though there might remain any misunderstanding of his real views, Breckinridge repeated his fiery denunciation in Anne's own city of Baltimore. Among other things, he destroyed beyond repair whatever bridges she still had to the South.

Stunned by the treachery of Breckinridge, Anne remained in her rooms for two days, poring over her files, dreading the attack she felt she must make on this man, and pondering the means and the method. Mail piled up on her desk, unanswered. She fought to strip away the last veils of illusion in which she had swathed a number of unpleasant realities that marked her own recent activities. All her own errors of judgment in the past year rose to haunt her. The emergence of the hated Republican party, a third party; the shock of Lincoln's election; the treasonable defection of friend after friend; her separation from Harry; all the warnings she had received and ignored; and now, most bitter pill of all, the betrayal of her close friend, John Breckinridge —these impacts now shook her and roused her to a cold fury.

On the evening of the third day she made a momentous decision and returned to her files. In them were all the confidential letters between the Southern governors of a decade ago. These letters had been tracked down, sought, and finally dearly bought with the blood of a young New Orleans journalist, Laroche Talbot, who believed in the Union. Three weeks after he had sent these letters Talbot had been found dead in a New Orleans alley, his face blasted away by a shotgun.

For several days she wrote and rewrote, cut and strengthened a paper into which she poured all her sense of outrage and all the startling facts she possessed about Breckinridge and his fellow con-

60

spirators. When her rough draft was completed she seized a blank sheet of paper and wrote:

REPLY TO THE SPEECH OF HONORABLE J. C. BRECKINRIDGE, delivered in the United States Senate, July 16, 1861. By Anna Ella Carroll of Maryland.

Her paper began:

"I have read with pain the speech of the Honorable John C. Breckinridge, delivered recently in the United States Senate, and with still deeper pain I now see him descending from his high position as a senator and come to Maryland to use the fallacies of that speech for the purpose of stimulating and strengthening the Confederate rebellion."

She went on: "I have in the spirit of friendship repeatedly repelled by my pen the charge of disunion heretofore made against him. I cannot but feel sorrow that one who has enjoyed under this government every degree of elevation but the presidency should at last prove himself recreant to the Union's cause."

She reviewed his charges against Lincoln and added: "These are grave charges, and if true the President should be made to suffer the extreme penalty of the law. But the major premise of the Senator, namely, that the President made war upon the South, is *untrue,* and I proceed to show that *no one in America knows this better than that gentleman."*

She reread the collection of treasonable letters from the Southern governors in her possession, the incredible document of the Confederacy, dated 1849, that Davis had given her in person, and she began a new paragraph:

"Secret but powerful efforts to dissolve this Union have been made in the cotton states since 1831; but, on the seventh of May, 1849, under the instigation of Calhoun, then the chief conspirator, a meeting was held in Jackson, Mississippi, when the secession party formally organized to form a *Southern Confederacy* upon the first act of the general government on which they could base a pretext. They there laid down their program, which the conspirators of 1860 and 1861 have faithfully acted out."

At this point she inserted every letter that Talbot had given her— letters from Quitman to Colonel Preston; from Governor Means of South Carolina to Quitman; from Quitman to Means; from Seabrook to Colonel Maxy Gregg; from McRae to Quitman—all of them, without a cut or omission of any kind.

She outlined, step by step, in devastating and documented detail, every development of this close-knit conspiracy. She wrote on, her pen driving across the white sheet.

61

"After the death of Calhoun in 1850, Senator Davis and his confederates in both branches of Congress agreed upon a provisional government and sketched a constitution for a Southern Confederacy! [Davis] managed by intrigue to have himself named its President! This document, and the proceedings of the conspirators, found its way into the hands of Mr. Clay through the offices of the author of this paper."

She hesitated a moment, then firmly crossed out "through the offices of the author of this paper" and substituted instead, "but under such circumstances as forbade any public use of it." She continued:

"In the running debate in the United States Senate, Mr. Clay made frequent pointed and personal allusions to Mr. Davis, in order to draw forth some remark which would justify the Southern Constitution's public use; but Davis, undoubtedly suspecting the motive, studiously avoided giving him the opportunity. That Constitution was similar to the one the traitors have now adopted, except that it specially provided for the acquisition of Cuba, Mexico, and all tropical America."

After discussing the traitorous letters she wrote: "Here we have every idea on which the conspirators are now acting; the withdrawal of South Carolina *to force the issue;* the assembling of the cotton states at Montgomery, Alabama; the organization of a Southern Confederacy; the forcing of the border slave states to choose between a Northern and Southern Confederacy; the proposition even of the Crittenden Compromise; the arming of the Southern states; the firing on Fort Sumter; with the hope *of drawing blood to cement the Southern States.* The doctrine . . . is the doctrine of the conspirators today, *that the government cannot use force against a state,* and if so, it is an act of war."

She went into a devastating analysis of the Pierce and Buchanan administrations and then wrote:

"I have it upon the authority of a senator who was present that Mr. Breckinridge united with the conspirators in their consultations and gave to them the influence and sanction of his high position. It is a phenomenon in the history of governments without parallel, and will be an everlasting disgrace upon our civilization, that Cabinet ministers, the Vice-President, senators, and members of Congress should for weeks and months, by the apparent sanction of the President of the United States, have wielded the powers of an organized rebellion for the overthrow of the Constitution and government they had sworn to support! Our fathers never foresaw that a few atrociously corrupt men would rise, without regard to the will of the majorities in their several states, and perpetrate the crime of double treachery against their state and federal governments! Mr. Breckinridge grossly insults the intelligence of the country by charging that the President made war against the South! The facts adduced establish beyond controversy that the President *did not* make war, as charged, *but that the traitors made the war* which now threatens the subversion of the government and endangers our national existence.

"Upon this fearful exigency, I proceed to inquire, what are the duties imposed upon the President by the Constitution?"

Anne thereupon went into a thorough discussion of reviving the war powers of the government which, she pointed out, had all but been destroyed by Buchanan.

It was morning of the fourth day when she finished her paper. She had scarcely eaten since she started it and had gone to bed each night exhausted by the intensity of her emotions and her efforts. Bright blades of noonday sun pierced the drawn shutters and crossed her desk as she rose and called Milly. She sent her for coffee and a light lunch and sat down to read over the last page. She picked up her pen again to add one fiery last paragraph.

"Better that Washington had perished like Hampden; that Jefferson had never drafted the Declaration of Independence; that Lee, Hancock, Adams, Franklin, Sherman, Charles Carroll, Livingston, etc., had died like Sydney and Russell upon the block, than that this Union, created to be the *daylight* to break the night of ages, should finally collapse, and *traitors* be permitted to write the epitaph: '*It lived and died.*' "

She reread the entire paper and her last act was to cross out her name of authorship.

"Let it stand alone," she said aloud, and after bathing and eating the food Mrs. Prescott had sent up, she drove at once to the printing shop of Henry Polkinhorn. There she ordered one thousand copies to be printed at her own expense. Then she turned around and drove home and went to bed and slept for fourteen hours.

The pages were printed. There in sharp black on white were the words as she had written them and intended them, fresh from Polkinhorn's presses, still fragrant with ink. Here was her "Reply to Breckinridge."

The same day the copies were finished she hired a messenger service to deliver them to a list of government offices, including the White House, publishers, newspaper editors, and the Associated Press. This done, she sat back and waited—but she had not long to wait.

The very next morning Judge Bates, his eyes snapping, appeared at her door with a copy of her pamphlet in his hand. He came in with a terse greeting and remained standing.

"I have just one question, ma'am," he said sternly. "Did you write this document?"

For one awful moment her heart stopped. Had it had some horrible effect she could not anticipate? She said faintly, "I did. I thought to—— What is the trouble, Judge Bates?"

"Trouble?" The Attorney General tossed the pamphlet on the table and put his arms around her. "My lord, Miss Carroll, it's tremendous. You've pulverized Mr. Breckinridge, absolutely destroyed him. Why in God's name didn't you put your name on it?"

She was so relieved and overwhelmed by this reception that for a moment she could not speak.

"I—I had my name on—I took it off."

"That was foolish, ma'am. Every government chief is demanding to know who wrote it."

She was dizzy with excitement and relief.

"Has—has Mr. Lincoln read it?"

"He has indeed, ma'am. He found it on his desk this morning. He canceled every appointment and studied it for an hour. He insisted on knowing who wrote it. I told Cameron I suspected it was you, and Mr. Lincoln sent me here to fetch you—and I see beyond a doubt you're the guilty party. He wishes to see you at once."

"Now?" Her voice sounded faint and far away. Bates smiled reassuringly.

"Now," he said gently. He sat down on the nearest rosewood chair and blew out his breath in a great "pouf."

"Lord, ma'am, you don't know what's happened. Maybe you did right to publish that anonymously. It's a bombshell. The press is already hammering Breckinridge—but this will finish him. My God, ma'am, where did you get those letters, those facts, those details even I have never heard of? Are they in those files Wade told us about?"

She nodded and rushed into her bedroom, calling out, "You'll have to wait five minutes, Judge. My hair looks impossible. Milly!" she cried. "Milly, come here."

She was back in a few minutes, her eyes shining, a handsome blue silk cape over her shoulders, a pert blue-and-white bonnet perched on her blond head. Judge Bates, usually a solemn, kindly, reserved being, bubbled and effervesced in excited confusion while they drove up the Avenue.

"You couldn't have timed it better," he kept exclaiming. "They're scrambling for more copies. Ben Wade and Thaddeus Stevens are passing the few copies they've got around the Hill like valuable contraband. I had no idea you wrote it until I recognized certain phrases. And that hammering of the word 'traitors' "—he laughed grimly—

64

"that was the final clue. That's all I ever heard you call your Southern friends."

They rolled up the graveled driveway to the White House and found Hay standing in the vestibule. Bates whispered to him, and Hay's grave eyes widened as they surveyed Anne a moment.

"All right, Judge," he said. "Let's go upstairs. He's in the study now."

Mr. Lincoln was seated in an ancient swivel chair behind a long dark desk. He rose inquiringly as Bates entered. His eyes strayed to Anne. Bates enjoyed his moment.

"Mr. President, the search you authorized has ended. Miss Carroll is the author of the 'Reply to Breckinridge.' She pleads guilty, sir, and I brought her here at once."

The President tried not to change expression. But his eyes began to sparkle with amusement and a surprise he could not hide. He pulled over a horsehair rocking chair.

"Please sit down, Miss Carroll," he said quietly.

An embarrassing silence followed. Mr. Lincoln looked from Bates to Anne and back as he absently fingered the pamphlet on his desk. Finally, as if to confirm Judge Bates's extraordinary announcement, he said, "You wrote this document, ma'am?"

"Yes, Mr. President. I've known Mr. Breckinridge a long time. I thought that——"

"Yes," interrupted Mr. Lincoln, "you must have known him a long time. You've shelled his woods, rolled him out flat, and tossed him to the bears. Where did you get your facts?"

She told him briefly of Talbot, the letters, her files, of Clay and Jefferson Davis, and her long, long study of the Southern conspiracy. He watched her silently and from time to time ran a rambling hand through his coarse sandy-black hair.

"Well, by jing," he said at last, using a favorite expression, "well, by jing!" He added suddenly in a different tone, "Where did you study constitutional law, Miss Carroll?"

She told him about her father, of her father's training, and of her studies in Baltimore. He began to finger the pamphlet again. He turned suddenly to Bates.

"Judge," he said sternly, "I have a bone to pick with you. One of your clerks made a slip the other day. Who is preparing the brief on the planned arrest of the Maryland legislature?"

"Miss Carroll, sir," said Judge Bates meekly. "She knows the ground so well that—I asked her——"

65

"I see," said Lincoln quietly. He studied Anne so closely that the color flooded her cheeks. "So you're writing the Attorney General's opinion on the legal grounds for the military arrest of a state legislature." Before she could answer he smiled. "I'm glad you are, Miss Carroll. I'm mighty glad you are. And I want to congratulate you on this paper."

"Then you're really pleased with it, Mr. President?" she inquired.

"Don't I make myself plain?" retorted Lincoln, smiling again. "You kind of took my breath away, that's all. I thought Wade or Bates here had a hand in it. I tell you frankly, ma'am, this pamphlet is powerful enough to insure the safety of the capital and keep Maryland in the Union. And John C. is through. You've cooked his goose. There's not a doubt of it. I can't say more than that. How many copies did you order? And, if you'll forgive me, who paid for it?"

She told him. His eyebrows went up and he stared hard at her. He stood up and placed his hand on her arm.

"Miss Carroll, I'll be as frank as I can. I almost owe you an apology. When I first met you at Willard's I couldn't quite make up my mind about you. I've met a few female politicians and had little use for them. You may remember our little tiff. Your advice on Maryland seemed extreme to me then. But it was I who did not at that time appreciate the critical situation in Maryland. Now I wish to say to you that this is a fine and statesmanlike document. It is devastating in its evidence. But what most interested me were your observations on the war powers of the President, included in this paper. I want to compliment you especially on that section. And I tell you now I intend to use your services further in this field. I want you to understand this place is open to you—that you are most welcome here any time. I mean that, and, Bates—you're my witness."

She smiled at him, her whole face alight.

"You don't know how happy and relieved I am, Mr. President. Judge Bates frightened me out of my wits this morning. I thought he had come to scold me."

But Mr. Lincoln had turned to the desk and was ruffling the leaves of her paper.

"Well," he said abruptly, "we're going to do something about this. Right now. Would you both mind going with me to the War Department?"

Wonderingly they went with him, out the west portal, across the frayed lawn, through the wooden turnstile gate that separated the White House from the big dingy oblong War Department building, with its striped awnings and pillared entrance. They went in the side entrance, facing the White House, and walked up two flights of stairs to Mr. Cameron's office.

"Mr. Secretary," said Lincoln with no preliminaries, addressing the shrewd, thin-faced man behind a roll-top desk, "we've found the guilty party. Miss Carroll wrote that Breckinridge broadside."

Cameron jerked himself to his feet and stammered astonished praise at Anne, his gray eyes gauging her closely. The President cut him short.

"Mr. Secretary, this paper's got to get around. Do you think you can put your War Department imprint on this document and get out fifty thousand copies at government expense?"

Cameron blinked.

"I guess we can if you say so, Mr. President. The printing office is jammed with contract forms and it will take time but——"

"Well, do it, Mr. Secretary," said Lincoln genially. "And I want five thousand copies for the White House when they're ready." He turned away, then hesitated and looked at Anne. He picked up the stub of a pencil on Cameron's desk and turned smilingly to her. "How do you sign your works, Miss Carroll?"

"You think my name should be on it?" she asked.

"I certainly do," said Mr. Lincoln. "Nobody else but you can back up those facts and charges. And besides, I'm going to see that a woman gets her due. How shall I put it?"

He picked up her pamphlet. His tall awkward figure leaned far over Cameron's desk.

"By Anna Ella Carroll of Maryland," she said firmly, and looked over at Judge Bates, who smiled back at her.

The President wrote her name slowly in a large scrawling hand across the title page and read it aloud.

"By Anna Ella Carroll of Maryland," he said solemnly. He slapped the pamphlet on Cameron's desk and straightened up. He looked at Anne, smiled a little grimly, and added, "And there, by the grace of Miss Carroll of Maryland, goes John C. Breckinridge of Kentucky."

8

THE LONG TIME OF FEELING LOST AND USELESS WAS over for Anne. Paradoxically, during the endless hot weeks of August 1861, her confidence rose like a welcome and returning tide even as fear and panic increased in the city. For the disaster that had overtaken the Union forces at Bull Run, a jarring reality in a world of delusion, had thrown the capital into chaos.

Men and women she knew were still fleeing in droves to Maryland. Several Cabinet members had packed their silver and crated their belongings. Night after night angry mobs and drunken men in every variety of smoke-stained, torn, and bloody uniforms poured into the noisy brothels that now filled the town, accosted respectable women before their own homes, and screamed derision, along with the rest of the public, at the lost generals who had led them to disaster.

Side streets were crowded with sutlers' wagons full of rotting food. Gangrene and tetanus raged through the new white-painted pavilions readied just in time for the wounded. A stocky major general named George McClellan had been summoned from western Virginia to replace the man disgraced at Bull Run, General Irvin McDowell.

In all this upheaval Anne was being pulled into a powerful stream that bore her along on the flood crest of new resolutions she had only half formed. Strong forces were being marshaled behind the scenes. She was becoming a vital part of these forces. She had never felt so alive, so much a part of her world and her times. Cameron, the Secretary of War, had brought to Washington an old friend of Anne's as his assistant—Tom Scott of the Pennsylvania Railroad—made him a colonel in the War Department, and placed him in charge of all telegraph and transportation facilities.

Scott, a strikingly handsome young Irishman in his early thirties, with pink cheeks, curling brown hair, and perfectly cut cameolike features, was an organizing genius who had risen rapidly in a few years from a clerkship in a small station to the first vice-presidency of the Pennsylvania Railroad. In his first weeks in Washington he had won fame for himself overnight by his brilliant measures of defense for the city following the rout at Bull Run. With him, from his Pittsburgh division, Scott brought a corps of young rail experts and telegraphers who made everyone's eyes pop. Among them was a flaxen-haired young powerhouse, a stocky Scot named Andrew Carnegie, who had strung wires from Annapolis to Washington and was one of Scott's right-hand men.

Anne was delighted to see Scott again, for she had met him often at her Baltimore home. And she was at last enjoying the sweet taste of triumph. Thousands of reprints of her "Reply to Breckinridge" had been run off on the presses of a dozen states. The President's official War Department edition was soon to be distributed. A personal friend of hers, James Tilghman of Baltimore, had passed out a thousand copies before his home in a few hours.

Under this galling fire Breckinridge had fled to Kentucky. Wade told her he had gone for good.

Never had her already considerable reputation for being able to influence public opinion shone so brightly as it did now. Wade was jubilant at her widespread recognition. "She's an extraordinary woman," he kept repeating to Evans, Stanton, and his colleagues in the Senate. "That little woman has a remarkable talent for putting over the causes she believes in—just remember Hicks, for instance—and now look at what's happened to Breckinridge! There's not an abler propagandist in this country."

Several senators, including Wade, set a plan on foot to send her to London as an unofficial ambassador for the Union cause. Wade was more disappointed even than Anne when the proposal failed to go through.

Early in September Anne received momentous news from Baltimore. The Maryland legislature, enraged by Hicks's stubborn stand and encouraged by what had happened at Bull Run, had secretly decided to convene on its own authority and vote immediate secession on September 17th. She had passed this information on to Bates at once, and the Attorney General hurried over to see her the following morning.

"We're ready to move," Bates announced. "I submitted the Maryland brief to the President and Cabinet yesterday. It met with unani-

69

mous approval. Here is a first draft of General McClellan's orders to General Banks, based on your information and dated ahead to the twelfth. Banks is ordered to arrest all the disloyal members of the legislature as soon as they convene."

She read McClellan's brief orders with rising excitement.

"That will do it, Judge, that will do it!" she exclaimed. "You don't know what I owe you for your support. There's no other way of dealing with this pack of traitors."

"Much of the debt is owed to you," retorted the Attorney General with a smile. "Meanwhile, I wish to give you a friendly warning. Colonel Scott has something up his sleeve. He's determined to see you next week."

He went on to tell her the difficulties the President was facing in prosecuting the war.

"You've no idea, Anne, of the pressure brought upon him day after day, from the highest sources in business and finance, to bring this conflict to an immediate close on any terms. The Treasury is empty and——"

"Do you mean to tell me," she exclaimed, "that Northern houses can't subscribe overnight to any war loans the government requests?"

"They can but they won't," replied Bates emphatically. "No, ma'am, the first stages of this war are being financed by subscriptions from the humblest people in the land—workers, farmers, and God-fearing folk in small towns. In a word, by patriots. Later on, when the bankers are sure which way the wind blows, they'll come in."

She was astonished when Bates laughed.

"What's humorous about such a situation?" she demanded.

"I beg your pardon," said Bates, "but I was laughing over a quick retort of the President the other day. McCulloch introduced a group of bankers to Mr. Lincoln and said in a low tone, 'They've come to see the Secretary of the Treasury about the new loan. I can vouch for their patriotism. As the Good Book says, "Where the treasure is, there will the heart be also." ' " Mr. Lincoln looked grimly at the financial brethren and replied immediately, 'There is another text, Mr. McCulloch, I remember, that might equally apply: "Where the carcass is, there will the eagles be gathered together." ' "

Anne joined in his laughter. Then she said, "Mr. Lincoln baffles me, Judge. He's so *slow*. He infuriates Mr. Stanton, who told me last week he'd written Buchanan that Mr. Lincoln was an imbecile and would ruin the nation in another sixty days. Mr. Stanton fully expects Davis to take Washington any time he wants to. And yet," she said slowly, "Mr. Lincoln has a quality I cannot define. He——"

Bates, smiling a little ironically, interrupted her.

"Let me define it for you. Mr. Lincoln is *not* a good executive. But he is a great mover of men and a remarkable interpreter of them. At our Cabinet meetings he reminds me of a long-legged old Roman charioteer riding herd on an incredible assortment of balky steeds. It will take time for the nation to get his measure. But he is a country man who knows how to think things through."

September ninth was an unforgettable day in her life. That morning when she picked up the Washinton *Star,* Anne had the grim satisfaction of reading the latest news about John Breckinridge. The day before, speaking to a gathering of Kentuckians in Bowling Green, he had announced that he was leaving the Senate to enter the Confederate Army.

"I exchange with proud satisfaction," he had cried defiantly, "a term of six years in the Senate of the United States for the musket of a soldier."

On that very morning, too, the War Department sent copies of Anne's "Reply to Breckinridge" to all government desks in the capital and to all embassies and consulates abroad. The distribution was by personal order of the President and correctly construed as his official reply to the departed senator.

That afternoon Anne was officially presented to members of the Cabinet by Mr. Lincoln. She had dressed carefully in a new and most becoming bright blue silk that accentuated the color of her eyes. She knew she looked her best, and she felt composed and at ease until the flood of flattery made her blush. The sight of Judge Bates, seated in his big leather chair, grinning at her, restored her, and she savored the moment to its full.

September was altogether a triumphant month for her, for Bates's increasing confidence in her was evident. The Attorney General, a mild man and still greatly worried over the forthcoming arrests of the Maryland legislators, without warrants or the right to habeas corpus proceedings, asked Anne to prepare a supplementary opinion in support of this radical action. She wrote a brief, concise paper during a week end with her family entitled *The Constitutional Power of the President to Make Arrests and to Suspend the Writ of Habeas Corpus—Examined by Anna Ella Carroll of Maryland. September 1861.*

This paper, too, was distributed in the thousands to the press and public officials by the President and Attorney General.

Ben and Caroline Wade, delighted by her success, honored Anne with a gay supper party to which they invited Judge Bates, Colonel

Scott, the new Assistant Secretary of War, and several of her intimate friends. She missed Lem Evans, who was still in St. Louis and would be for another week.

"Judge," she asked curiously, determined to clear up the mystery now that she had the opportunity, "what on earth *is* Mr. Evans up to, and just whom is he working for?"

Bates said with a candid smile, "On my honor, Anne, I don't know. He's thick with both Seward and Chase, but he's also running an errand or two for the War Department, while our friend Stanton is cooling his heels as a minor legal adviser in that department. That's all I know. And by the way," he added, changing the subject firmly, "you are looking very charming this evening."

She sat at his right at dinner with Colonel Scott on her left. Through the soup and the fish courses she tried vainly to talk seriously, but Tom Scott was in no mood for it. He ate like a hungry boy and regaled them with yarns of his early experiences in railroading. He concluded a long entertaining reminiscence by counting up the Irish in high places, including Anne, and suggesting an Irish League, with himself at the head to bring the war to a quick and triumphant close.

They were roaring over his banter before the meal was half through. But as they waited for dessert to be brought in he turned to Anne and faced her seriously. "Look here, Miss Carroll," he said, "why don't you stop all this writing and go to work for me?"

"May I ask your plans?"

Wade grinned and spoke for her.

"Hands off, Colonel. Miss Carroll is only waiting for the Maryland legislature to be tucked behind the bars, according to her prescription, and then she's going to rest."

"Rest?" exclaimed Scott in mock horror. "Whoever heard of the Irish resting? Why, this war is a railroad man's dream! What you need is a change, ma'am, from all that poring over legal fine print. How would you like to tabulate and organize transportation facilities for the twenty divisions of the new Army?"

Anne looked at him, surprise and pleasure bringing added color to her smooth cheeks.

"I mean it," Scott insisted. "Will you come to see me next week?"

She laughed. "Yes, I will, Tom. But only a social call."

Scott made a wry face. "I warn you, ma'am, if you enter my office you'll never begin your vacation. And now, Caroline, a big piece of that mince pie, please."

But later in Wade's pleasant parlor the easy atmosphere of the table vanished, and the talk was deadly earnest. Those who knew

72

what was really happening were badly frightened by the military crisis.

As Wade sketched what was being done Bates fell silent and Scott's fine eyes were a somber blue. At last he interrupted.

"The fact is, isn't it, Ben, that the rebels have the whip hand and everyone abroad knows it. They've got the whole damn country sewed up from Washington to St. Louis and west to the Rio Grande—an area greater than most of Europe. Thank God the railroads are ready. Worst of all, and this I tell you in strict confidence, of course, nobody in the entire War Department has come up with the ghost of a plan or proposed any projects of real value.

"Wait a minute, Colonel," the judge protested. "We've got a Mississippi expedition under way with Eads guaranteeing a dozen armored gunboats in three months. We've got Frémont in St. Louis, and McClellan in Washington planning to take Richmond by Christmas."

"Well?" said Scott challengingly.

Bates seemed astonished. "You don't think much of those activities?" he asked.

Scott glanced at the anxious faces about him. "I don't think Frémont can hold Missouri," he said at last. "As for McClellan and Richmond—what's he got when he gets it? Outside of the Tredegar Iron Works and the Bellona Foundry, I consider the town worthless from a military point of view. I know I'm against the mass of opinion. But this war's got to be won in the West—and the New Orleans expedition is the only plan that promises much. But where's the army for it?"

Anne, watching Judge Bates, saw a curious expression cross his amiable face.

Wade said gently, "Did you know, Colonel Scott, that the river expedition is largely Judge Bates's conception?"

Scott looked amazed. "Upon my soul, no! I saw Cameron's memoranda about it with Mr. Lincoln's approval attached. That's all. The forces called for looked pretty flimsy."

"They are," agreed Judge Bates grudgingly. "But if we get enough boats for Flag Officer Foote and enough forces in St. Louis, and if we can hold Missouri and Kentucky another six months—it can be done."

"Whew!" offered Wade. "That's a big collection of ifs, Judge."

They were all silent. After a moment Scott said, "There's another aspect to this. The Navy wants to take New Orleans from the Gulf. They claim that with enough heavy mortars they can smash the river forts. But the ships aren't even outfitted and orders have only just been placed in Pittsburgh for two hundred mortars and about fifty

73

thousand heavy shells, all yet to be cast. In short, we're hamstrung for time. The financial people are terrified. The war's costing two million a day, an unheard-of sum in any modern struggle, and we have nothing to show for it."

Anne broke into the conversation: "Colonel, I haven't any right to ask this. But—is Mr. Evans in St. Louis in connection with what you've been telling us?"

Scott hesitated. "Well, I guess there's no harm answering that," he said. "Yes, he is. What a war!" he continued. "The Attorney General—and no offense intended, Bates—conceives a plan to open the Mississippi to New Orleans. Chase, the Secretary of the Treasury, jumps in because Evans is reporting to him about the gunboats, and at the same time he also has to submit his reports to Seward in the State Department. Meanwhile, the President has the Blairs, and God knows who else, watching Frémont; others unnamed are watching the Blairs, and the poor damn War Department doesn't even know what to think of the rebellion. Cameron's too busy buying blankets, though he's going to St. Louis tomorrow to see what *he* thinks!"

Their earlier gaiety was never restored and the evening ended on a minor note.

Scott drove Anne home through the cool September air. Standing in the gaslighted hall of the Washington House, he managed to grin and regain a trace of humor in his voice.

"You enjoy ten hours' sleep tonight and you won't need a vacation, Miss Carroll, and please come to see me as soon as you can."

Anne watched him walk to the door, then, tired and depressed, she went slowly upstairs and stopped, startled to find her door ajar. Milly, in Cambridge for a few days, would not return until tomorrow. She clearly remembered closing and locking the door. Now she pushed it open, walked into the parlor, and stood motionless. In the dim light from the window, reflecting the glow of lights across the rear yard, she saw confusion and disorder. It took her five minutes to find a match in Milly's tiny room. When she finally lighted a lamp in the parlor she gasped at the havoc. Her entire suite had been ransacked. File cases lay empty on their sides. Her desk and been swept clear, a paper cutter thrust purposelessly into the polished surface. Desk drawers had been hurled into corners. The war maps on her walls had been slashed, even the window draperies torn from their rods. She went quickly through the wreckage about her desk. Very little was missing—but that little was important. Every copy of her 1850 letters had disappeared and she thanked God she had duplicates in Cambridge. Confidential letters from Chase and Bates, the latter in regard to the Maryland affair, were also missing. Then she saw that the paper cutter thrust into the desk had pierced a sheet of torn newspaper on which had been hurriedly scrawled in heavy rude lettering, "Death to a traitor!"

She sat down and stared around the room. Who could have done this—and why? she wondered. She was upset but not really frightened.

Her eyes wandered to the slender table with the gilt legs and marble top on which the lighted lamp shone down on a few personal belongings. Something about the table startled her. Then she realized that not a thing on it had been disturbed. Beside the lamp lay her mother's locket, a miniature depicting Julianna's father, Dr. Stevenson, alighting at Parnassus Hill; the double miniatures in leather frames of Thomas and Julianna, a small framed painting of Old Trinity Chapel, her Bible, and a little oblong basket containing a partially finished bit of embroidery.

There was only one person in the world who might have left that table untouched. She knew that Harry Heyward had returned.

9

WHEN SHE WOKE THE NEXT MORNING AND TOOK IN THE appalling ruin of her rooms she realized that the temper of the times had changed profoundly. The absurdly melodramatic had become commonplace.

If, on the pleasant lawns of Castle Haven a year earlier, anyone had prophesied that Harry would carry out such an invasion of her rooms and leave behind him a silly threat worthy of a popular novelist at his worst, she would have laughed at such a preposterous flight of imagination. But she did not feel like laughing this morning.

Immediately after breakfast she drove to Scott's office and told him what had happened. The Attorney General was also there.

Scott's blue eyes kindled. "We'll pick him up on sight. Do you know where he's staying?"

"I haven't any idea. I haven't see him since January," she said.

"Well, ma'am, Colonel Prentiss at the provost marshal's office and several others know him well enough. We'll find him. Meanwhile, I'm placing an armed guard in your corridor night and day."

"Nonsense, Colonel——"she began, but he cut her short.

"There's nothing ridiculous about this, Anne. We are cleaning up the city, and the traitors are snapping back. Rose Greenhow's in prison for forwarding a full account of McDowell's Bull Run advance to Beauregard. We have thirty other women behind bars—and McClellan is driving every drunk and deserter off the streets. Your part in this Maryland affair is well known. Besides, there's something else."

He was looking at her with an expression of deep calculation.

"What is it, Colonel?"

"Anne, I have some proposals to make. Judge Bates, here, has already discussed them with Mr. Lincoln. Beginning with an extensive paper on the war powers of the President, how would you feel about preparing a series of political pamphlets dealing with the major legal conflicts for the War Department to issue from time to time as questions arise?"

"I'd love it," said Anne emphatically. "On what basis do you want to handle this, Colonel?"

Scott appeared puzzled. Judge Bates was smiling a little.

"Well," said Scott hesitantly, "I've never commissioned a woman to do any kind of work. But I'm willing to draw up an agreement we can both sign and we can secure proper fees for such work from the general contingency fund to be passed in December. What do you think is——"

She interrupted him. "I think there's an easier way, Colonel. You and I have known each other for years. Suppose we make this a verbal agreement. I'll prepare the paper on war powers. You submit it for approval to anyone you wish. If it isn't satisfactory, we can forget the whole thing. If it's what you want, then we can discuss the proper fee."

Scott was obviously relieved by this suggestion, and they discussed further details for some time. Judge Bates, who had been silent till now, finally spoke up.

"Can you tackle this paper pretty quick, ma'am? All I want now is your idea of a general approach to the subject. If it's what we're after, why, you go ahead and do it your own way."

Gone were any plans of a vacation in Maryland. Anne had even forgotten what brought her here this morning. She leaned back and for some time marshaled her thoughts. At last she said:

"Judge Bates, it seems to me there is a direct approach to this whole matter. It is contained in a fallacy that American law is peculiarly heir to, and it stems directly from Blackstone, whose conclusions do not always apply to the American scene."

"How is that, ma'am?" asked the Attorney General.

Through the open window she heard a rumble of distant thunder and the curtains swayed in a puff of air. She chose her words carefully.

"In European nations," she said, "sovereignty resides in the government, not in the people. Their governments possess and exercise absolute power. But according to the American theory, sovereignty resides in the people. The American Government possesses only limited and delegated powers, not absolute. Many of Mr. Blackstone's most famous opinions have rested on this European conception of sovereignty, and it has taken half a century for the growth of American law to refute many of these applications to our own country. The

77

point is that in America it is the President who is the direct representative of the people—and not the government."

The Attorney General nodded. "That is correct—but what are you driving at, ma'am?"

"Simply this," replied Anne. "We all know the powers conferred on the President by the Constitution. They are seldom invoked during times of peace. But in time of war we are all unduly surprised by the extent of these powers, though they need only the stating of them to be made obvious. For instance, the Constitution defines the presidential powers and then requires him to 'preserve, protect, and defend' them *in any emergency*. And what does this mean? It means that when, in case of rebellion or invasion, the judicial and civil powers are weakened or made impotent the President is then made *sole* judge of the manner in which his powers may be executed for the public safety. He does not become a dictator by this. In fact, as a civilian in power he prevents the military from assuming a natural dictatorship in such a crisis. He is a *civilian* commander in chief, required to stay at the capital, in the presidential mansion, and to hold in his hands *civil authority* as supreme over *armies*."

The Attorney General's eyes were alight with interest. "That's sound enough, ma'am. Go on."

Anne's mind was working intently, surely, and she spoke without fumbling for a word. "Well, I've always felt the authors of the Constitution had a better understanding of the kind of crisis we face today than any of our contemporaries have. Take the writ of habeas corpus for example, Judge Bates—it is a great and fundamental privilege. But still, it remains only a privilege, and the public safety may at certain times require the suspension of *this* privilege as well as many others, or all. These fools in Congress insist on their right to advise, direct, and even command the armies they raise. They say they have the right. That is a lie. It is only for Congress to raise and support armies sufficient to smash rebellion. But it is the *President's* duty to command and direct these armies. And this military force, *directed by the President,* may employ every means known to civilized warfare. It may subject *all* persons, civilian and military, to military law. It may seize and use *all* property in its efforts to crush a rebellion, without regard to the ownership of the property, whether friend or foe. And all this, I repeat, under the personal direction of the President. You may say this is a fearful power, Judge, and it certainly is. But no popular government such as ours can live without it."

She paused, looked at Scott's intent face, then back to Bates.

"That," she said confidently, "is the preliminary ground on which I should approach the problem of the President's war powers."

Judge Bates got up. "All right. I'll take that," he said with obvious satisfaction. "That is the correct approach as I see it. We'll tell Seward and Cameron you've gone to work. They'll be required to give you any assistance you need."

Anne reached her rooms just as the heavens opened and a dark deluge poured down on the city while luckless pedestrians scampered for shelter in the yellowish gloom. In the upper hall she heard hotel porters restoring order in her ravaged quarters. They had the door open and a pile of papers and a shattered file drawer were heaped in the hall.

She walked in, smiling, and halted at once, shocked as she seldom had been. With an air of colossal presumption of which she had not thought him capable, Harry Heyward sat by the streaming window. Two porters on a short ladder were rehanging her draperies.

Harry rose instantly. He was white and the muscles in his hollow cheeks made her think of springs wound too tightly. He said quietly enough, "Don't create a scene, Anne. I've got to talk to you."

She was angry and incredulous. "Harry—get out! Are you insane—after what you've done here?"

"I won't take long," said Harry coolly. "So you knew it was I," he added. "I suppose it *was* obvious. Listen to me, Anne. I'll be brief. And I'm damn fool enough to warn you. I also have a confession to make. Until this week I had been unable to make anyone in Richmond take your activities seriously. The material I got here last night will change that. It's now on its way to Richmond. I've got proof at last of everything I ever charged you with, and I'm not alone in this any more. If you make another move on behalf of this ape in the White House or any of his dirty lackeys, you are marked for the payment a traitor deserves."

He looked at her steadily for a moment, and she was surprised at the strength and purpose in his eyes. He seemed to read her mind.

"I owe you something," he said firmly. "I think I see things pretty clearly that I've ignored all my life. I've married since I last saw you"—he was gratified to see her start and the color leave her face—"and I've found my own purpose finally. You should know what it is. You are watched every moment, Anne. There'll be no more warnings."

Before she could think of a word to say he turned and left. The two porters stared after him in amazement. She turned on them. "How did he get in here?"

"He done say he was a fren' of yohs—you was expectin' him," said the more vocal of the two. They guiltily gathered up their brooms and ladder and left.

She was dumfounded by Harry's rash visit. She was also annoyed at herself for being so stupid as not to raise an alarm as soon as she came in and found him here. For one thing, the morning's talk with Bates and Scott had left her with an exalted self-confidence which she realized she must guard against. For another, the habit of years had not been wholly erased. One part of her mind still thought of Harry as she had always known him. She had to force herself even now to face the fact that her former fiancé had become her bitter and perhaps dangerous enemy.

Half an hour later Milly arrived from Cambridge, and just before six Scott's sentry knocked at her door and took up his station in the hallway. For an instant she wished he had been sent before Harry arrived. But in her secret heart she knew she didn't mean it. Milly, frightened by what had happened during her absence, huddled by the parlor lamp, cringing a little at the crashes of renewed thunder rolling over the city.

Anne, her own nerves on edge, spoke rather sharply to her. "Milly, I'm going to lie down an hour. I'm dead. I'll talk to you later. Don't you dare disturb me."

She took off her clothes, put on a thin white silk robe, and lay on the bed in the oppressive heat. The thunder sounded like ten thousand batteries of war. It had been a chaotic, disjointed, frightening twenty-four hours. And Harry's mad melodramatics had put the finishing touch to it. She wanted to sleep and she could not. Time passed and above the uproar outside she half heard voices in the hallway, heard Milly at the parlor door, heard nothing for a moment, then saw a widening crack of light as Milly softly opened the door, saying timidly, "Are you awake, Miss Anne?"

"Milly, I told you to leave me alone——" she began irritably.

But to her astonishment Milly boldly entered her room and flung the door wide. "Guess you may change your tune, Miss Anne," said Milly triumphantly. "Mr. Mason, the clerk, come up. He say Mr. Evans is downstairs and wants to see you in a real hurry, right away."

10

FOR ONE STARTLED MOMENT SHE LAY MOTIONLESS, trying to absorb Milly's announcement. Then she bounced off the bed in a pleasant confusion of pink flesh and flying robe. Her fatigue vanished.

"You're sure, Milly, you're sure?" she cried, and saw immediate confirmation in Milly's bright eyes. "Bring him up here at once."

Milly's big eyes widened. With a suggestion of roguishness she allowed them to flutter over Anne's pink-and-white figure.

"All right, if you says so," she said, grinning wickedly. "But if I was you I'd have him wait five minutes, ma'am. You gotta put *somethin'* on."

Anne colored primly but could not help laughing. "That will do, Milly. Bring him to the parlor. It won't take me long to dress. And while you're downstairs, Milly, order supper for us both and serve it here. He'll be hungry. Roast beef, coffee, anything Mrs. Prescott has."

She took longer over dressing than she expected, hesitating between a soft rose silk dress Lem had never seen and an apple-green mull he had once complimented her on. Each, she knew, became her blondness. In the mirror, as she brushed her hair, she saw that the excitement of the day and her brief rest had heightened her color and that her eyes were bright and clear.

She had time to close the blinds on the sea of mud that filled the Avenue which resembled some watery inferno under the flickering oil flares that sputtered in the rain and marked the shallow excavations for the city's first streetcar line. A lampman, with his slender, flame-tipped stick, was lighting the gas standards.

She turned up the parlor lamp that poured warmth and intimacy over the marble-topped table laden with the personal belongings Harry had left untouched. She remained standing by the table, wearing the soft rose-colored dress and matching jacket, wondering why she considered Evans's appearance such a God-sent conclusion to an impossible day, and where he was after being in such a hurry to see her. Then she heard his long easy stride thudding along the hall carpet and his startled exclamation, "What's that?" when the sentry challenged him.

She herself had forgotten all about the sentry. She rushed to the door, threw it open, and cried out, "It's quite all right. Come in, Mr. Evans. They've got me under guard." She began to laugh, but there was a catch in her voice. "I've never been so glad to see anyone in all my life. You're—you're like a soldier home from the war!"

"What soldier—and what war, ma'am—and in God's name, what's all this infantry doing up here?" came his easy, humorous drawl.

And there he was, looming in the doorway like some sea monster risen dripping from the depths, clad in a long black rubber poncho and hood he had appropriated from the War Department.

He pulled off the hood and stood grinning amiably at her with the expression of some truant schoolboy who has foregone an important errand and wandered home long after he was expected. With his lean height and broad shoulders encased in the straight, military poncho, he seemed to fill the doorway. On his high cheekbones and along the strong lines of his jaw drops of rain sparkled in the lamplight. His gaze roamed from her cheeks to the rose-colored gown and came back to her blue eyes.

"May I come in?" he asked, and bowed low, half in earnest.

Then he laughed and strode into her parlor, spreading his poncho over the wood box to dry. He sniffed the flowers, touched her embroidery on the table, and sighed deeply.

"Home, did you say, Miss Carroll? I'll accept that."

She was startled not only by this sally but by a marked change in his manner and expression. He seemed warmer, more relaxed, a far different being, in fact, from the rather formal, distant, and contradictory creature she remembered. But his habits hadn't changed. He sat down on the sofa, placed his feet on a small rosewood chair, stretched his arms over his head, and exclaimed, "I can't believe I'm here, Miss Carroll. I've been to bedlam and back."

"You think you've escaped bedlam by coming back to Washington?"

"I've escaped it here," he retorted, glancing leisurely about her room. He looked up at the new maps tacked in orderly rows on the wide wall opposite the fireplace, at the lines of neat blue and red pins marking military positions, and at her formidable desk piled high again with papers. Finally he picked up her embroidery and traced a flower with one wondering finger and then put down the hoop and examined the little painting of Old Trinity Chapel. He seemed completely pleased with himself and with her and nodded approvingly at her rose silk dress and jacket.

"I reckon that's the only lovely thing I've seen in forty days," he said enthusiastically, his eyes traveling from the jacket to her vivid face and blond hair.

"Sallie made it for my birthday," Anne said, glad that she had chosen to wear this dress rather than the green.

He grinned and said with simulated surprise, "Oh—the jacket?" and laughed at her blush. He leaned forward, his eyes dancing. "And your hair, ma'am. I surely like it that way."

It was swept back rather loosely in graceful waves, fastened with a pearl brooch in a generous knot at the nape of her neck.

"You're always a pleasant relief, ma'am," he went on banteringly. "Why do most women haul their hair back smooth as glass and banish every curl as rigidly as they do their impulses?"

What had got into the man? The stern face was full of an easy, almost impudent good humor. She was a little startled, too, by the lazy intimate note in his voice and was not quite certain how to meet it. However, she said boldly, "I've never banished either my curls or my impulses, Mr. Evans. Do you think I should?"

"God forbid!" he said fervently, laughing and showing his even white teeth. But his eyes grew thoughtful. "What on earth's going on, Miss Carroll? You haven't told me—what's this sentry doing here?"

Not until she began to tell him what had happened did she realize how much she had been longing for someone in whom to confide. At first he listened quietly enough, glancing sharply about the restored room when she described its ruin. But when she told him of Harry's visit that very afternoon his face darkened and he got up and paced about the room.

"You made a bad mistake, ma'am. You should have turned him in at once. The sooner Scott collars him, the better."

She was astonished how rapidly his Texan drawl disappeared when he became angry. There was a twang in his voice that might have come from Maine.

"I'm just beginning to take him seriously, Mr. Evans," she said apologetically. "I——"

"Maybe I am too," interrupted Evans grimly. "What did he get?"

"A great many letters and a lot of material dealing with the Maryland legislature."

Evans jumped. "So that's it! My God, I almost forgot why I came

83

here running. He must have acted immediately on this Maryland affair. Haven't you heard what happened?"

"No." Her eyes widened and she stared at him in dismay. "Has there been some trouble?"

Evans shook his head. "No trouble—but a lot of excitement. Someone, through Harry evidently, must have warned the Maryland legislators last night. But fortunately the War Department was tipped off too. Late this afternoon General Banks, without waiting for them to convene, arrested enough of the damn traitors in their own homes to stop the whole affair. They've been rushed to Fort Lafayette in New York and Fort Warren in Boston. I've just come from Scott's office. Maryland's in an uproar, with rebel mobs in Frederick, where the legislature was to meet, and in Baltimore."

"But they *arrested* them?" She almost whispered the words. "You're sure?"

"I don't want to call Banks a liar." He grinned and pulled a paper from his pocket. "Here it is—'To the Secretary of State from General N. P. Banks, Headquarters in Maryland, September 20. Sir: I have the honor to announce the arrest of the following Maryland legislators: R. F. Salmon of Frederick County; R. C. McCubbin of Annapolis; William R. Miller, Cecil County; Thomas Cloggett, Frederick; Josiah H. Gordon, Allegany County; Clark J. Durant, St. Mary's; I. Lawrence Jones, Talbot; Andrew Kessler, Jr., Frederick; and Berman Mills of Carroll County.' There it is!" added Evans triumphantly.

"They've got the right ones!" exclaimed Anne jubilantly. "I know every one of them." She leaned back in her chair, relaxing with relief, and looked into his eyes. They were intent, alight with the excitement of his news.

"There's an awful uproar over this, ma'am. But, by heavens, secession in Maryland is a dead duck. We can pour Union troops and supplies through the state without a hitch. They're doing a war dance in Scott's office."

Anne got up impulsively and walked across the room toward him, her silk skirt making a soft rustle over her starched petticoat.

"Lordy, Mr. Evans, I've lived nine lives today. But this restores them all. I think," she said, "we owe ourselves a little celebration."

He was smiling, but there was a warning in his eyes that checked her. "Not yet. I've heard your story, but you haven't heard mine. Colonel Scott is coming here shortly."

"Scott! In heaven's name, why?"

"I'm in the dark myself," said Evans. "I think——"

He paused as Milly came in to say that their supper would be served in a few minutes.

"Supper here?" exclaimed Evans, delighted. "You'll never get rid of me, ma'am. Now then, let me tell you this briefly before we eat. To begin with, I rushed back from St. Louis because I became downright frightened."

"But what were you——" Anne began, then restrained her curiosity. "Forgive me. Please go on, Mr. Evans."

"I can't tell you exactly what I've been doing just yet. I'd like to, but it's impossible. I will say I was sent West to inquire into conditions in Texas and to take a look at Frémont on the way back." He frowned and paused before he continued, speaking each word with emphasis. "If you think conditions are disastrous here, I assure you they're ten times worse in St. Louis. Revolution is the word out there, successful revolution. Yet we've got to hold St. Louis. It's the key to the whole Northwest—and far more important than Richmond. And I don't know whether Frémont can hold it."

"I talked to a lot of people out there," Evans went on, "and not a single Army or Navy officer from Pittsburgh to Missouri believes Bates's scheme to force the Mississippi is feasible.

"As God is my witness, Miss Carroll, we've no plan of campaign whatever beyond the Navy's scheme to take New Orleans. The generals are waiting for the War Department to *plan* something. The War Department is praying to God the generals will *do* something. I've never seen such a state of affairs."

"Have you told Colonel Scott all this?" she asked.

"I reckon I did," retorted Evans. "And I'll bet it crimped his fuse a bit."

"Colonel Scott told me Cameron and Seward have been snarling at each other for weeks," she said, looking very serious. "Mr. Cameron charges Mr. Seward with trying to run the Army for him, and Mr. Seward claims Cameron is taking over the State Department. Scott suggested they change places and cancel their quarrel."

Evans smiled grimly. "There's no exaggeration in that. The confusion behind the scenes is incredible. I have had to report to four Cabinet officers, each of whom presumes to give me contradictory orders and advice. One of these days," he added, "I'll have to drop my disguise."

Milly interrupted them, ushering in two waiters laden with trays and linen. A gate-leg table was cleared and set up before the fire. Evans took his feet off the chair, propped some pillows behind him, and sat back comfortably. She thought he looked paler and more preoccupied than she had ever seen him.

"I wonder why Colonel Scott wants to see me again tonight," she said. "It seems to me I've seen everyone in Washington today."

"I haven't an idea," said Evans candidly. "He was mighty upset over my reports. But what he's fishing for, I don't know."

When the food was served Evans ate ravenously. She watched the color come back to his cheeks and deepen his tan. Fortified by a little port, he began to tease her about her maps.

"You came just in time to cheer me up," she said while Milly cleared away the dishes. "It's been a horrible week. I needed someone to rescue me, and you have."

"Then it's a double rescue." He laughed. "I had to think of myself too." He made a wry face. "I had to get away from the generals."

He got up from the table, walked to the window, and peered into the street.

"Well, we've caught a colonel anyhow," he announced. "Here's Scott himself in a tearing hurry."

A few moments later Milly ushered the Assistant Secretary of War into the parlor. Anne and Evans, standing near the window, caught at once his air of suppressed excitement. Without any preliminaries Scott asked Evans to wait for them in the lobby.

Anne, annoyed by his abruptness, protested. "Colonel! After all, Mr. Evans is my friend and guest. I——" She stopped, her expression demanding an apology. Scott offered none.

"My dear young people," he said sarcastically, "explanations later. You friend Mr. Evans and his reports have topped a disastrous day for me. Now then, sir, just leave us alone a few moments and we'll all be on our way."

Evans picked up his poncho and left. Scott sat down at the desk, took a notebook from his pocket, and looked sharply at Anne.

"Mr. Evans has tossed the fat in the fire with his reports," he began. "We can't go on like this. Anne, you've often mentioned relatives in St. Louis." He consulted his notebook. "Here they are, Mr. and Mrs. Charles C. Carroll, 19 Locust Street."

"That's correct, Colonel."

Scott snapped shut his notebook. "Can you arrange to visit them—at once?"

Anne's anger and astonishment vanished as she heard the urgent note in Scott's voice. He was not a man who ever overstressed trifles. His handsome face was tense. He was very much in earnest.

"I—I believe my sister-in-law Peggy, their daughter, can arrange it. But you know, Colonel, the St. Louis Carrolls are rabid Southern sympathizers," she reminded him, "though they respect my stand."

"Exactly," said Scott in a surprisingly satisfied tone. "Now then, we must work fast. I've talked to both Bates and the President this afternoon. Listen closely. Can you prepare that legal paper of yours in St. Louis—in six or eight weeks?"

86

He was so alarmed by Anne's look of dismay that he allowed her no time to answer.

"Miss Carroll, you must trust me. I need your assistance at once. All I can say at present," he added very deliberately, "is that the President prefers it done this way. . . . You know the Mercantile Library in St. Louis?"

She nodded. "It's an excellent one."

"Would you say it had sufficient legal facilities for the preparation of your paper?"

"Yes. It has the best law library west of Washington. But——"

"That's all I want." Scott jumped to his feet. "Do you know the librarian there now?"

"I don't believe I do. Why?"

Scott's eyes narrowed. "His name is Edward William Johnston," he said with assumed casualness. "He's an able, quick-tempered old boy —a fine scholar, a distinguished librarian. He also happens to be the brother of Joe Johnston, the Confederate general—and a kinsman and close friend of Albert Sidney Johnston, Confederate commander in the West. Do you understand?"

Anne's full lips were unsmiling, her blue eyes cold.

"Very well, Colonel, let's stop these subtle approaches. What exactly do you want me to do?"

"Please, ma'am, don't look at me is if I'm asking you to put on a disguise and play spy," protested Scott. "What I want——"

He talked without stopping for twenty minutes. He had conceived the plan of having Anne stay in St. Louis for a month, where she was to combine work on her paper for the President with on-the-spot reports about the situations Evans had warned them were brewing.

"What I want out there is a good reporter with the kind of advantages you have," said Scott forcefully, and went on to point out that as a woman of prestige, visiting a family of Southern sympathizers, her own kinsmen, her position would be impregnable. He walked up and down her parlor with quick nervous strides. "We're not asking you to spy on anyone, Anne. But we must have a quick and final estimate of this New Orleans expedition. I told Mr. Lincoln and Bates that your knowledge of land and water transport might be most valuable out there. I also want some better inventories of railroad rolling stock— and you can get 'em for me."

"And what about Mr. Johnston?" asked Anne shortly.

"Pump him. That's all. Just pump him," Scott answered. "We know he's in constant communication with both Joe and Albert Sidney Johnston in the West. And he loves to talk. He has an eye for the

87

ladies." Scott grinned for the first time. "He used to run the Roanoke Female Seminary in his younger days."

Obviously she was to be given no time to think, no time to consider so many, many things. In a tight little voice she scarcely recognized Anne whispered, "All right, Colonel. I'll go."

Scott grabbed her hand and shook it elatedly.

"Thank God! If you'll get your wraps, ma'am, we'll be on our way. We can talk further in the carriage."

They found Evans in the library chatting with the clerk. He took stock of Scott's mood at once.

"What have you cooked up, Colonel? You look as if you'd found all the cream."

"Never mind, sir." Scott grinned and helped them into his carriage. He gave no directions to his coachman, and they splashed westward along the Avenue for several blocks before anyone spoke.

"Colonel," Evans said finally, "I understand Miss Carroll has already told you about a young rebel named Heyward who paid her a visit. Can you nab him?"

"He left for Baltimore an hour ago," said Scott calmly.

Anne looked at him quickly. "How do you know that?"

"Captain Prentiss, from the provost marshal's, spotted him at Willard's bar this afternoon—and why on earth, ma'am, after seeing me and then running into young Heyward, didn't you turn him in when you had the chance? I can't understand that. At any rate, Prentiss followed young Heyward to the Baltimore and Ohio depot an hour ago and saw him buy a ticket to Baltimore. But Prentiss lost sight of him when a Vermont regiment got off the cars and jammed the waiting room. We'll check the cars at Baltimore. Prentiss didn't stop him before because he was hoping Heyward would lead us to some of his friends. But we'll pick him up tonight."

"You haven't got him yet," Evans remarked. He glanced at Anne and said acidly, "Mr. Heyward seems to have enjoyed a charmed life today."

Anne said nothing. For the first time she was convinced of danger. Scott and Evans took Harry seriously, and this on top of his violent threats to her, his going to Baltimore—once her own home, her center of operations—made her realize that she might be greatly underestimating Harry as a foe. Why had he gone there?

"Where are we headed, Colonel?" Evans asked. "I thought we were going to your house."

"Not for a while," said Scott blandly. "I have a little surprise for you both."

11

SCOTT'S HORSES SLOWED TO A WALK GOING UP THE slight incline past the sandbagged Treasury. Then they turned left on Pennsylvania Avenue, and through dripping trees Anne caught a glimpse of the flaring portico lamps of the White House. She looked at Evans and saw that his obvious surprise matched her own. Their carriage turned in at the main gate and halted by the sentry box. Scott produced his pass and spoke in a low voice with the captain of the guard. A sergeant saluted, and their carriage rolled up the circular drive.

"Colonel," she said accusingly, "are we seeing Mr. Lincoln at this time of night?"

Scott nodded guiltily. "Seward, too, I believe," he added.

She gave a little cry and heard Evans swear under his breath.

"Why couldn't you have warned us?" she said. "After a day like this! Tom, you're unforgivable. Besides, I'm a sight in this old cloak of Sallie's."

"This is not my doing," Scott said patiently and emphatically. "I've been under instructions all evening. Do you suppose I enjoy all this? I've been up since four this morning. And if you want company in your confusion—count me with you."

Plainly, they were expected. A doorman ushered them at once into a dimly lighted waiting room where they left their wraps. Young Hay came in by another door, greeted them noncommittally, and then led them upstairs and down the long hallway to the left to the door of the President's study. The great house, usually thronged with civilian and military callers, seemed huge, empty, ominous. Hay knocked lightly on the door, and the President's high uneven voice called out, "Come right in."

89

She saw Seward first. Clad in an untidy gray suit, the Secretary of State was standing by a tall window overlooking the south grounds and the river. She had never seen him without a cigar, and he was chewing an unlighted one now, slowly rolling it from one corner of his mouth to the other. Ash was scattered the length of his satin-faced waistcoat. His eyes seemed to rove about in two narrow slits, and his hair, which badly needed a brush, was limp and gray in the poor light. He was rocking slowly back and forth on his heels like the pendulum of some run-down clock. When they looked expectantly at him he removed the cigar from his mouth and flicked the dead ash carelessly on the carpet. His shrewd Welsh-Irish face wore a sardonic expression.

"Well, sir, here they all are," he exclaimed, addressing someone across the room. "Good evening, Miss Carroll. How are you, Colonel? I see you brought your convoy safe in port. Mr. Evans, I'm glad to see you." His husky voice betrayed an excessive use of cigars and snuff. His sharp eyes moved from one to the other.

Then Mr. Lincoln, in a far corner, folded a paper he had been reading and rose to greet them. His eyes rested on Anne, and she saw a hint of mischief and amusement in them.

"Well, Miss C., here you are again. And I presume you're about to remark, 'This is indeed a surprise.' "

"You're quite right, Mr. President. I was. And good evening, sir."

"I'm delighted to see you, ma'am," said Mr. Lincoln. "Hello, Scott. You look beat up. And good evening, Mr. Evans. We've just been discussing your report, sir.

"Sit down, sit down," Mr. Lincoln continued amiably, and watched in some amusement as Evans ignored a small narrow chair and leaned his tall figure against the corner of a desk. "I declare, Evans, you're still growing. Were you trying to get up above that St. Louis smoke? I don't believe we've ever stood up to one another, have we?"

Evans shook his head and laughed. "No, sir, we haven't. But you'd have me by half a head."

"Well, now, I can't take that. Here, sir—stand off the rug and let Seward be judge."

Anne saw that Seward wanted to get down to business and was irritated with this byplay. But Scott grinned and Evans got up and stood back to back with Lincoln. She was astonished to see that Lincoln topped him by a good three inches, although Evans had always seemed to tower above every crowd she had seen him in.

"You've got him beat, Mr. President," Seward said stiffly, "by several inches."

"That can't be, Mr. Secretary," protested Lincoln. "It must be that hair of mine." And he placed one hand on his head, pressing down the coarse black hair. As the two men laughed and separated Seward shook his head and said dryly, "Some of it's hair, Mr. President, but you'd still top Mr. Evans if you took off your shoes."

"Is that a fact?" asked Lincoln in such a mournful voice that they all laughed. Then he sighed and sat down and looked them over with his somber eyes as he idly tapped the paper he had been reading. They waited. In repose, Anne thought, he seemed very worried. He put on his spectacles again, opened the paper, and eyed Evans as if from behind a heavy veil.

"Well, son, there's not much to cheer about in this report——"

Evans waited a moment, then said simply, "There's not much to cheer about in St. Louis, Mr. President."

In the silence that followed Lincoln continued to study the paper in his hands while Seward showered more ashes on his vest and looked glumly at Evans.

"A long letter from Francis Blair confirms much of your report," observed Mr. Lincoln. He took off his glasses and polished them slowly.

"The adjutant general, Lorenzo Thomas, confirms all this," he said. "After his tour of inspection out there last week he told me the nation's forces aren't even sufficient to hold Missouri and Kentucky to the Union."

"The nub of the matter is, Mr. President," Evans said quickly, *"that there are no plans.* Nothing but this nebulous outline of a scheme to force twelve hundred miles of a great river with a dozen slow craft and a few thousand men. Sherman threw up his hands when I discussed it with him. He wouldn't even talk about it."

"Sherman's a sore point," Mr. Lincoln commented grimly. "He told Cameron in Louisville a few days ago that he needs two hundred thousand men to clear Kentucky. Cameron said to him, 'My God, where are they to come from?' He thinks Sherman is insane, as do others. He's got but fifteen thousand men now, and rifles for less than a third. Do you think Sherman is mad, Mr. Evans? He is very bitter, very upset, and there are queer reports about him."

"I'm sorry, but I don't, Mr. President," said Evans hotly. "I repeat —the trouble is, *we have no plan.* That we must recognize. In my opinion, the rebels will be recognized as a nation by foreign powers in a matter of weeks."

"That may be so," Mr. Lincoln said reluctantly. "Seward's been walking on eggshells. Both France and England are preparing to war on us, and if something ain't done quick, they will. The whole Cabinet is aware that a general European war with the United States is imminent."

91

They were shocked by these words.

"Mr. Seward," Anne said abruptly, "we've been under the impression that the threats from abroad were nothing but press campaigns carried on by commercial interests."

Seward drew another cigar from his pocket and chewed it reflectively.

"Young lady, we're all gambling. We don't know. Take this report from Adams in London on the eighth instant." He drew a sheet of buff-colored paper, obviously scribbled on with his own notes, from an inner pocket.

"Since July eleven thousand troops, some of the Empire's oldest and finest regiments, have landed in Montreal. British ships of war in the St. Lawrence include the *Black Prince, Chanticleer, Persia,* and *Australasia.* Adams reported five thousand more troops have sailed for Nova Scotia. Look at these sailings from Plymouth for Canada last month—the *Emerald,* the *Hero,* eighty guns; the *Sutlej,* fifty guns; the Fifth Dragoon Guards, the Grenadier Guards. And last week, the *Persia,* the *Parana,* the *Adriatic,* the *Niagara.*"

Seward looked at their strained faces.

"Do I disturb you? Enormous stores, including winter garments, sledges, and campaign materials for northern climates, are now massed in Toronto, Montreal, and Quebec. You may ask what all this has to do with St. Louis. Well, the Northwest has to be held, not only to ward off the English, but to prevent any junction between English forces and French forces striking north out of Mexico." He brought out another paper.

"Here is an important dispatch from Ambassador Clay in St. Petersburg. He writes, 'Prince Gortchakoff expresses his fears, should any reverse happen to us, that England would at once make common cause with the South. . . . I would prepare for war with England as an essential means to prevent the independence of the South before the first of April.' Dayton in Paris writes even more forcefully."

Seward coughed nervously and took time to light his cigar and immerse himself in a cloud of blue smoke before he spoke again.

"Thurlow Weed, who is going to Europe shortly, asked me last night if I thought we would be embroiled in a general European war within six weeks. I told him, 'It would seem so, but I don't know. We are still feeling our way.'"

Anne, who had come to know Seward well and had long admired him, was more deeply concerned by his observations than by anything said earlier. The Secretary of State was a reticent man and she had never before heard him speak so frankly or at such length.

"You see, Miss Carroll," he continued, "I have been assailed for proposing and even threatening war with England, or a general European war, in which to dissolve this civil conflict of ours. Now and then Mr. Lincoln has filed my teeth down a bit. But it don't seem to occur to my enemies that I have threatened a European war in order to forestall this very threat from others. I have, I think, temporarily frightened Palmerston and Napoleon." Seward raised his voice and shook his cigar at them. "But—and it's a very large 'but'—*we do not know where to strike.*"

Another pall of silence fell on them. Mr. Lincoln got up, clasped his hands behind him under his coattails, and walked over to Seward as if to address him, only to turn suddenly and face Anne.

"Well, young lady," he began, "we might as well tackle this head on. I take it from your presence that you have consented to go to St. Louis for us in line with Colonel Scott's plan. Now with this Mississippi project—this scheme for forcing the river and seizing New Orleans—we come to something far more urgent, something we must bring to a final decision at once."

He ran a worried hand through his coarse black hair.

"Seward put it kind of strong. But I guess he's right. We *don't* know where to strike. A long time ago I flatboated down to New Orleans. It's a tremendous river, no two miles of it alike in depth and current. I know something of that river, and a kinsman of mine, Stephen Hanks, is one of the best pilots on the Mississippi.

"Now then, when somebody tries to sell me a horse and twenty hired judges of mine look him over, stare at his teeth, check his fetlocks, roll his eyes, pound his chest, and run back to me and say kind of doleful-like, 'Well, Mr. Lincoln, that horse *might* run a race, and then again he *might* fall dead on the track,' by Jiminy, I'm suspicious of that critter. Just about everybody in the government, Miss Carroll, has been to St. Louis to take a look at that horse. Evans, here. Also Cameron, Scott, Bates, Foote, and a parcel of staff officers. Scott, here, and Bates are still for this Mississippi junket. But Cameron is getting a bit shaky, and I'm *mighty* shaky."

He stopped, noting Anne's bewilderment.

"Have you a mission for me instead of Colonel Scott's?" she asked.

"It's in addition—and multiplication," replied Mr. Lincoln. "We've got a stack of errands chalked up, if you'll run 'em. I told Scott to put his oar in first."

"I want to be sure I understand," said Anne slowly. "First, I'm asked to go to St. Louis to prepare a legal pamphlet on the presidential war powers? Then on the way I am to prepare various transportation estimates for Colonel Scott? And besides I am also to form some

93

judgment about the practicality of the Mississippi expedition? And all this in six or eight weeks?"

Her voice sank at the prospect. She loved the stimulation of hard work, enjoyed working under pressure, but such a schedule was more than she had ever attempted.

"Mr. President, it's impossible," she said, shaking her head.

"I know it is," he replied kindly. "But it's a last straw and has to be grasped at. It had not occurred to us, nor did it seem advisable in any way, to employ a woman on this mission—until Colonel Scott pressed the matter. He has great faith in your judgment." Mr. Lincoln smiled. "Miss Carroll, I've sent a heap of men to St. Louis and back. I'd like to see what one woman with a background like yours thinks about the situation out there. Maybe a woman might turn up something we men have missed. At any rate, I like to think so."

In spite of these flattering words the fact that responsible officials could improvise such measures at a moment's notice made her blindingly aware of the crisis confronting them all. For once she found herself wanting to refuse responsibilities, and yet she heard herself saying calmly, if reluctantly, "I've already told Colonel Scott I'll go, Mr. President. But under the circumstances I don't think too much should be hoped for."

Lincoln made no comment for a moment. But unexpectedly he came over to her and placed his hand on her shoulder. She had an uncanny feeling that he had been reading her mind.

"It may strike you as a mighty queer way of doing things, ma'am. But the fact is, and you must see it, we're all up a tree."

He hesitated a moment, then turned to Lem Evans and said almost brusquely, "I'm sorry to send you galloping back to St. Louis, Mr. Evans, before you're got your wind—but you know the ropes there and Miss Carroll will need an escort. I would suggest that you both visit the Ohio camps and, in particular, drop in on Sherman. Cameron don't like the man and I'm not satisfied with the Secretary's impressions."

Anne's quick acceptance of Mr. Lincoln's request seemed to have invigorated them all. Scott rose eagerly to his feet while Seward went over to the sofa and picked up his coat and hat. He turned to Anne, a grimly amused expression on his sharp features. But his eyes were warm and friendly.

"My congratulations, Miss Carroll. There are many times I could wish you were a member of this Cabinet. Good luck to you—and good night, Mr. President."

Scott, who had been studying with interest Anne's somewhat enigmatical expression on learning that Evans was to be her escort, paused long enough to tell Evans to take his carriage home and then he, too, left hurriedly. Mr. Lincoln walked over to the sofa and sat down, flapping a newspaper at the blue haze left by Seward.

"One of these days," he observed, "Mr. Seward will go up in smoke with his last cigar. He just about asphyxiated me tonight."

His face grew somber as he sat for a moment without speaking. "Evans," he began at last, "I want to ask you something. I understand you saw Eads in St. Louis. What did you say the speed of his gunboats will be?"

"Eads says five knots. He hopes for six," returned Evans.

Lincoln shook his head. "I've seen the river run through Fort Adams Reach faster than that. And its twelve hundred and eighteen miles from St. Louis to New Orleans—if the river ain't chewed it shorter these past few years." He added emphatically, "No, sir, I don't like the plan one bit."

Anne tried to visualize the great river she had never seen, bearing Eads's gunboats south to battle. Suddenly she spoke:

"There's a still greater disadvantage than the distance, Mr. Lincoln."

"What's that, ma'am?" he asked with interest.

"Disable any of Captain Eads's gunboats, or the transports for that matter, and they'll *drift south,* downstream, straight into rebel territory."

The President stared at the floor a moment and then glanced quizzically at Anne.

"I'll tell you what, ma'am," he said wryly, "I guess we need a river that flows the other way."

Mr. Lincoln got up and silently accompanied them to the waiting room where they had left their wraps and then walked with them through the darkened rooms to the main hall and the front portico. He stood in the doorway, gratefully sniffing the fresh air. When he took her hand and said good night Anne saw that he was regarding her with unusual sympathy, as if he were forcing himself to refrain from saying something to her which he wished to say very much.

Mr. Lincoln remained standing in the dimly lighted doorway as they prepared to drive off. Flaring gas lamps flung patches of shifting shadows over the gleaming wet lawns stretching to the fence and the wooden stile that separated the War Department from the White House grounds. A lone cavalryman and his horse splashed across Lafayette Square. The horseman absently saluted the guard at the sentry box and a little later turned north on Seventeenth Street.

The President raised his right hand shoulder high and waved at them briefly in a careless intimate gesture that warmed them both.

12

ON A MELLOW LATE SEPTEMBER AFTERNOON A MAUVE-colored mist softened the ancient Kentucky folds of Muldraugh's Hill rising above the wooded limestone bluffs about Knob Creek, some distance south of Louisville. The slanting sun, shining mildly through this rosy haze, gilded currant and blueberry bushes and wild grape, touched with magic the gnarled crab-apple trees along the winding, dusty Louisville and Nashville pike, and caressed redbud, wild rose, and reddening leaves stained with the first faint blood of autumn's wounds. Golden shafts of light hung quivering above dark and silent pools resting like green jewels among the shadowed hollows along the creek.

In a pleasant little hollow not far from the main road straggled several rows of tents and half a dozen brash new cabins, bedded down like a handful of interlopers among these quiet old hills and mountains.

A sergeant, in civilian trousers and a faded blue military blouse held at the waist by a single precarious button, plodded up the regimental street, a puff of fine dust floating away on the still air in tiny lazy spirals at each footstep. Before a large tent, on a slight rise facing southwest and marked by a rude board marked "Headqutrs," he drew himself up and saluted.

"They're at the sutler's store, sir. Major Armstrong will bring them along in about five minutes."

"Very well, young man. That's all I wanted to know."

The sergeant, like some toy automaton, wheeled about and plodded off while the little clouds of golden dust again marked his passage.

The bizarre-looking officer whom the sergeant had addressed seemed to be poured in a single sagging arc against the yielding canvas of a rickety camp chair. His feet were perched on a packing box. He

96

was a slender, loose-jointed man with rather small, intense, dark hazel eyes. His lean flat cheeks were burned raw-red from wind and sun. From the back of a close-cropped thatch of reddish-auburn hair a wisp of even redder hair near the neckline stuck straight out like a belligerent exclamation point. In any other region but this wilderness his clothing would have excited ridicule. He wore heavy dusty boots and rough trousers of new blue denim, but his officer's blouse, unbuttoned, was so faded and dusty as to defy detection of its basic hue. The crowning touch to this collection of nondescript apparel was a battered stovepipe hat, with a triangular hole clear through the crown, which rested cockily on the back of the sun-baked head. The face beneath it was lost in thought and puffing violently on the stub of a ragged cigar. From this figure escaped a low growl followed by a voice as rough as coarse sandpaper.

"Where'll we put 'em, Major?"

His aide, a dim figure in the recesses of the tent, seated on a folding cot and intently examining the intricacies of a new sword buckle, looked up in surprise and said reassuringly, "That's all fixed, sir. The gentleman will bunk with Major Armstrong. The lady will be settled at Calkins's farm down by the pike."

The man in the camp chair grunted angrily and blew out a huge cloud of swirling smoke. He shuffled several papers in his lap.

"What in the devil is Mr. Evans escorting a woman to St. Louis for when he passed through here on his way to Washington ten days ago? Is the War Department providing chaperons for females these days? Who is she, Bart? Ever hear of her?"

Major Denning got up and buttoned his tunic. His sharp eye had noticed the small group that had just left the sutler's store at the other end of the camp street.

"Yes, sir. Her name is Miss Carroll." He slyly eyed his commanding officer as if to gauge the effect of his next words. "Handsomely blond, General. I'm told she's a Baltimore newspaperwoman."

If he had fired off a small mine under the officer's camp chair the effect might have been the same. The feet on the packing box came down on the floor with a crash. The cigar butt was flung a good ten feet into the dusty company street hewn up the hillside.

"By God, you don't mean it! I won't have any jackal of the press in or about this camp. If I'd known that I'd have locked them both up in Galt House this morning and left 'em in Louisville to rot. Are you serious?"

Major Denning decided his little joke had gone far enough.

"Don't worry, General. She ain't practicin'. You saw the War Department telegram. Evans seems to be taking a rebel sympathizer

97

to her St. Louis relatives under official escort. But it looks queer. Evans told me last week he wouldn't be back this way at all."

"Well," said the other, "I'm damned if I see why we have to extend our hospitality to either of 'em. I intend to talk to Evans about this."

He lighted a fresh cigar deliberately and leaned forward, scowling at the cloud of yellow dust advancing on his tent and containing three plodding figures. When the figures finally halted before him, Major Armstrong, a stocky individual with a heavy black beard powdered with dust, stepped forward.

"Colonel, may I present our visitors? Miss Carroll of Washington City, sir—General Sherman. Mr. Evans, of course, you know."

"How do you do, General," said Anne.

The forbidding face stared at her, grudgingly grunted, "How do you do, ma'am," and at once turned to Evans. "What's going on, sir? We have no facilities in camp for visitors." Again he stared at Anne without removing his battered hat. "Miss Carroll will be greatly inconvenienced," he added in an unpleasant tone that suggested the entire Army would be far more inconvenienced than Miss Carroll.

Evans grinned amiably, stepped forward, and handed Sherman a small dispatch case.

"Not our doing, General, I assure you. Please glance at that."

General Sherman jerked out two sheets of yellow paper, ran through them quickly, looked up at Anne in astonishment, saying, "Why, I thought that——" and then clamped his teeth on his cigar again as he returned the dispatch case to Evans. The scowl never left him, but there was a subtle change in his gruff manner as he turned back to Anne.

"We'll be glad to have you join the officers' mess, ma'am, at once. I hope you have a strong stomach," he added encouragingly.

"Don't worry about me, General," she said coolly. "I've breakfasted and dined in five Ohio camps in as many days."

He caught a glint in her eyes and colored slightly.

"You would have been a lot more comfortable in the Galt House, ma'am," he said abruptly. "But I guess you can stand the food if we can. Take 'em along, Major. I'll be over in a moment."

A hundred yards away from Sherman's tent they sat down near the head of a long table made of rough planks set up in the open under a huge tent fly. A dozen officers, already eating, eyed them curiously.

"I don't like him," Anne whispered to Evans when Major Armstrong rose to summon an orderly. "And that absurd hat!"

"I don't think he likes you, either," retorted Evans pleasantly. "You'll both have to come around a bit."

98

A few moments later Sherman took his seat at the head of the table and began eating without a word. They plowed silently through watery beef stew, hard soda biscuits, vile coffee, and petrified pie with traces of apple between the stony crust. But Anne ate with gusto and, to Sherman's obvious surprise, downed three helpings of stew. He watched her curiously.

"How long have you been eating camp fare, Miss Carroll?"

"For about five days, General."

"Then you've got a mighty sound constitution, ma'am."

"I have an excellent constitution, General. In this air and these surroundings I could live on bark and swamp root if I had to, and I'm sure," she went on evenly, "it would be quite as nutritious as this stew."

There were several guffaws down the table which died away as Sherman, his face fiery, glared at the offenders. The meal was finished without another word, and in half an hour they found themselves seated in Sherman's tent with the General and Major Denning looking out at a riot of sunset color in the west. To Anne's relief Sherman had discarded the tile hat which now reclined rakishly on his cot. He had taken it off for comfort and not for manners, Anne decided. The atmosphere was still tense and both she and Evans waited impatiently for Sherman to ease the strain. As if forced to face an unpleasant duty the General at last pulled out three cigars, chose one carefully, placed the others in easy reach on the packing box, and, ignoring Anne, said abruptly:

"Well, sir, let's get this over with. I don't wish to appear too ungracious, but we're in a great deal of trouble out here. I understand from your papers that on this occasion you are traveling under Mr. Lincoln's personal orders. What is it you wish to know, sir—this time?" The last two words were impatiently emphasized.

Evans's keen eyes studied him.

"General," he said at last, "I know we're a damned nuisance. But I think you should know that both of us—both of us, sir—have been assigned a specific mission by the President and the Assistant Secretary of War, Colonel Scott. And I think the whole matter should be discussed with you alone."

"What——" Sherman started angrily, then nodded to Denning and said in a different tone, "All right, Denning, maybe you and Major Armstrong better play some chess for a while."

"Yes, sir. Very glad to," said Major Denning quietly, and both men stepped out of the tent.

More truculent than ever, Sherman turned so that Anne's view was more of his back than his face.

99

"I trust everything is now satisfactory, Mr. Evans."

There was more than a trace of sarcasm in his voice, but Evans ignored it.

"I know what you're up against, sir," he said patiently. "I'll put the cards on the table at once. The fact is, General, everyone in Washington is terribly worried."

"I hope so, but I don't believe it," retorted Sherman shooting gray puffs of smoke like a miniature battery into the cool evening air.

Evans went on as if he had not spoken. "Miss Carroll and I have been assigned to make a detailed report on the New Orleans expedition—in the very greatest confidence, and as soon as possible. We have been ordered to obtain an official opinion on this expedition from every important officer between Cincinnati and St. Louis." He reviewed the Mississippi plan briefly and finished with a quiet question, "Have you any reflections on the matter, General?"

For a few moments Sherman sat, his cigar flaring and subsiding like an angry torch. Then he exploded.

"By God, Mr. Evans, but you try my patience, sir. I have no reflections, no thoughts on the matter at all. Why should I? I don't know who in God's name thought up this wild-goose chase of yours. But it's downright nonsense, sir. I am sitting out in this wilderness, Mr. Evans, with fifteen thousand raw recruits, delegated to guard over three hundred miles of hostile frontier, while two rebel armies stand poised at either end of the state. I have a handful of Sharp's rifles, a few rotten European muskets, many of them useless, bought by corrupt contractors of ours abroad. That's all I have. But McClellan sits in Washington with a hundred thousand men for a frontage of less than a hundred miles. Frémont sits in St. Louis with sixty thousand trained troops for the same distance. And every man *I* want is siphoned off to one or the other."

His words came in sharp bursts like volleys of musketry.

"The situation is impossible, Mr. Evans. I have repeatedly refused a major command until the administration understands the real character of this war. That they do not—not in the slightest degree. We cannot even equip and clothe the handful of farm boys I've got. And yet these fools in Washington want my opinion"—he paused and sarcasm edged his voice—"on the simple little matter of opening up twelve hundred miles of the greatest waterway in the world through the heart of a huge area full of rebels armed to the teeth. They are just plain damned fools, sir, and you can quote me directly on that. I have begged and implored for proper measures out here until I dare not say more."

He swung abruptly around to Anne.

"You, ma'am, you seem to enjoy the confidence of Mr. Lincoln. Perhaps you are an expert. Perhaps *you* have an opinion on this river expedition."

His tone was courteous enough, but the veiled irony in it was unmistakable, and she kept her temper with difficulty.

"I'm not an expert, General Sherman, and I have few opinions yet on military matters. But as now planned, the New Orleans project seems to me to have very little force, even on paper."

"And what would you suggest in its place, ma'am?" he asked shortly in a distinctly bored voice.

He was leading her on to make a fool of her, and Anne determined that he should not. She looked sharply into his hazel eyes and said, her voice clear, controlled, and crisp:

"General Sherman, if you can equip and train one hundred thousand men in a few months, I would urge you to plunge straight south and break the Memphis and Charleston Railroad. It seems to me that that road is far more important than the Mississippi. It is the main artery for Confederate supplies and the only through road from the Atlantic to the Mississippi."

The tip of Sherman's cigar dipped in astonishment. Putting it aside, he leaned forward in his chair and now completely ignored Evans.

"Who gave you that idea, ma'am?" he demanded.

"General, I happen to have made railroads my business for ten or twelve years."

"Indeed," said Sherman, his eyes narrowing. "And what do you know of the Memphis and Charleston road?"

"A good deal," she retorted tartly. "It is the spinal column of the South. At the moment it is the most important railroad in this country. It is an almost direct route of seven hundred and fifty-six miles between Memphis and Charleston, including from west to east the Memphis and Charleston to Stephenson, Alabama, two hundred and seventy-two miles," Anne went on to enumerate without a pause, "the southern part of the Nashville and Chattanooga to Chattanooga, thirty-eight miles; the Western and Atlantic from Chattanooga to Atlanta, one hundred and thirty-eight miles; the Georgia Railroad to Augusta on the Savannah River, one hundred and seventy-one miles; and the South Carolina Railroad into Charleston Harbor with blockade runners at the city wharves, a final lap of one hundred thirty-seven miles. The rolling stock, as of June thirtieth last year, included eighty-three locomotives, one hundred and ten passenger cars, seventy-eight baggage cars, seven hundred and fifty-seven freight cars, one hundred and thirty-three coal cars, and some seventy-eight pieces of miscellaneous equipment. The roadbed is in fair condition, except for about

101

thirty-nine badly ballasted miles with poor rail between Corinth and Memphis. The road had ten thousand tons of new iron rail on order last year. About half of it has been delivered."

She paused for breath, then added emphatically, "That railroad should be taken at all costs, General. Its capture would disrupt the entire interior supply lines of the rebels from New Orleans to Richmond."

Sherman picked up his cigar and stared at her. There was a profound silence, suddenly broken as Evans tried vainly to smother his laughter. Then Sherman got up abruptly, flung his half-smoked cigar away, walked to the opening of the tent, and called to an orderly across the street to bring lanterns. He came back and looked down at Anne. Through the dimness of dusk she saw just the suggestion of a tired smile on his ruddy face.

"Well, ma'am," he said in a strangely gentle voice, "please accept my apologies for all that's been said and left unsaid tonight. I haven't talked to anyone with common sense for so long I can't recognize sound judgment when I encounter it. I'm not accustomed to meeting women with any opinions worth considering in these matters. I think we ought to begin all over again."

His sharp speech and rough approach were gone completely. He went to his desk and pulled out papers and maps, called back Major Denning, and for an hour chatted with them in the utmost frankness. To Evans's amusement, his whole attention was now centered on Anne. Once he remarked smilingly:

"You're right about the Memphis and Charleston, ma'am. But how do we get there? If they'd give me an army I could swing it. And Buell wants to use the Cumberland and Tennessee to get into east Tennessee to relieve the patriots there. But nobody will listen to us. Mr. Lincoln told me not six months ago he did not think he needed military men. He and the politicians really believe that a brief military demonstration will bring back the seceded states. They have a terrible lesson to learn. And if this area, now open to the rebels, falls to them the whole cause is lost."

"And you believe that may happen?" asked Anne.

"I think the Union cause hangs by a thread, ma'am. The only straw I grasp at now is Davis's stupidity. For Davis, too, is making terrible mistakes. He has gone on the defensive to save blood, believing King Cotton so necessary that foreign powers will at once recognize the South and foreign war will shortly shatter the Union. If he's right—we're finished. But I don't think he is."

"Mr. Lincoln is aware of all this," insisted Anne.

"He may be. But he don't show it and he made some idiotic remarks

102

to me last spring," retorted Sherman. "Your presence here is proof enough of his indecision. And it would be a lot better for them to have someone of a more sanguine mind than mine out here. You can judge by the press what they think of me."

Since the Eastern and Midwestern papers were in the midst of a vitriolic campaign charging Sherman with hysteria, cowardice, and downright insanity, Anne felt it would be most tactless to pursue the subject.

As he continued she began to warm to Sherman, to his fine cool intellect, his quiet realism, his long calm perspective on every problem he touched. He spoke fondly of Bardstown, his favorite stopping-off place, and the old Talbott Tavern where he had often stayed in his travels as a boy, and of pleasant Kentucky homes he had visited. When he touched on the war again she saw that his earlier rudeness and nervous tension had been a mask to hide his sensitive comprehension of an appalling picture that others saw only in small and unrelated sections.

A diversion occurred when Major Denning gravely rose, picked up Sherman's disreputable tile hat, and solemnly hung it on a coat hook. Sherman caught Anne's unguarded look of amazement.

"Guess I'll have to get rid of that plug tile of mine," he said with appealing candor. "I picked it up in Louisville two years ago—it's light and just fits. But it gets me into trouble. We found a young chap in civilian clothes the other night. He hadn't had time, he said, to get into uniform. I scolded the boy. He muttered something under his breath when he walked away. I thought he was swearing and sent Major Denning after him. You tell 'em, Major."

Major Denning laughed. "Well, the youngster stammered around and finally said, 'My God, sir, any general who wears a hat like that has a hell of a right to talk to me about a uniform.'"

Sherman joined in the laughter and added, "Still, a uniform is pretty important. I reckon I'd better send that hat back home to Ellen."

All during the following day Evans was in conference with groups of officers. Anne strolled around the camp in the morning, talking with young recruits, and spent part of the afternoon with Mrs. Calkins and her two towheaded youngsters. Enjoying herself, Anne found it hard to realize that this pleasant remote little farm was perched on the rim of war.

In the evening she and Evans dined with Sherman again, this time a pleasant, congenial meal.

"You know, ma'am," Sherman said frankly, "I detest the press. Out here they're nothing but scavengers who rush into print with every bit of secret information and conjecture they can lay their hands on for rebels to read the next day. But I want to tell you you're an ornament to your profession. And you and your young man have brains. I hope you both continue to use them. I wish you luck on that river project. Good night, ma'am. And my best wishes for the remainder of your trip."

While she lay awake on a rustling corn-shuck mattress in the Calkins farmhouse a phrase of Sherman's lingered in her mind. "Your young man." She resented it and she liked it. Away from Washington, Lem Evans treated her like any companion whose ability he respected, in a way, too, like a bright child whose precociousness amused and delighted him. Not since the night Lincoln had asked them to go on this trip had she caught a glimpse of the look she had seen then, that told her she was a woman—an attractive woman. She fell asleep vaguely depressed in spite of her diplomatic success with Sherman.

13

THE TRAIN THAT BORE THEM WESTWARD RATTLED
through the jammed yards of East St. Louis and came to a stop by a
long wooden platform close to the ferryhouse. All day long they had
watched troop trains and freight trains shuttling east and west across
prairie and pleasant Illinois farmland shimmering under a brassy sun.
An hour before they reached their terminus a violent thunderstorm had
raged and dribbled ragged streams through the badly fitted windows.

Now their goal lay before them. Beyond great stacks of lumber,
piling, military supplies, and the frame ferryhouse rolled the tawny
Mississippi in a wide shallow bend. Faintly visible in the murky haze
and gathering dusk was the city of St. Louis.

The sky was black with threat of a new storm when they left the
train and boarded the ferry. But as Anne followed Evans to the bow
and stood in the fresh breeze from the West and gazed at the chocolate
flood pouring past the ferry slip she was filled with excitement. Evans,
leaning against the rail, looked gloomily over the river.

Nothing in her experience had prepared her for the spectacle of
savage color and majestic vista that unrolled before them. The country itself was rather flat and uninteresting. It was the phenomenon of
conflicting weather forces that created the sweeping grandeur of a
scene from some dark myth of the gods. Two storms had collided over
the river an hour earlier, dumped forth a deluge, and then hung in
blackness over the city, while thunder growled and gashes of lightning
ripped across the sky.

On the western horizon the clouds had lifted slightly and then
seemed to settle in place, as if to afford a tantalizing peep through
their blackness at a brilliant and illimitable world of blue sky and

105

sunlight beyond. Through this long narrow azure slit the sunset sun flung a great cone of saffron light across the rest of the heavens. Over the river floated an eerie glow of brown suffused with a crimson that made men and women on the boat, workers on river craft, and all those in the open pause and stare at the unaccustomed wonder in the sky. A fresh breeze fluttered yellow whitecaps on the river.

Against the dark and distant city there seemed piled a low bank of snow pouring forth columns of smoke that rose above the river in an ominous black pall. Anne, peering intently, saw that this seeming bank of snow consisted of tier upon tier of river steamers—side-wheelers, stern-wheelers, tugs, propeller craft—tethered in one, two, three, and four tiers at right angles to the ranging levee. Half a dozen steamers were in motion, their huge wheels churning the brown water to a ghostly whitish-brown foam touched with red. A last bar of sunlight struck one of the boats, bright with banners, along its full length and it steamed northward like some strange craft made of delicate white icing on a sea of chocolate.

At last a bell clanged in the depths of the ferryboat. The paddles moved and the craft slid out of the slip and fought against the straining current. Anne leaned against the rail, fascinated by the strange welter of colors and vistas.

After some minutes she turned to Evans, her face rosy and her hair turned to copper in the curious light.

"I've never seen anything like it, Lem. Never." She drew a deep breath. "This is the West, the West I've longed for all my life."

The ferry was already approaching the levee, and the wilderness of river craft tethered there now took on shape and form and life. They saw row upon row of tall slender stacks, guy wires, gilded eagles, ornamental balls, coats of arms on pilothouses decorated with gingerbread woodwork; garish river scenes painted on paddle boxes; acres and acres of deck; miles of white latticed railing; ships with staterooms alight; others dark and silent but their lower decks swarming with life; furnace doors suddenly opened with flares of crimson flame that vanished again. Cordwood and coal were piled on boiler decks, with Negroes running about with hand trucks, though it was after five and loading had stopped. Here and there solemn, silent figures, as if carved against the rails they leaned on, watched without expression as the ferry entered its slip.

She caught a glimpse of the great levee and the riveted, rip-rapped riverbanks, fourteen miles of them, stretching away from the Rivière des Pères on the south to the northern limits of the city, the levee a four-mile tilted slope of granite blocks rising at an easy angle from the water. The summit of the levee was littered with gangways and piled with cordwood, with sacks of wheat under shelter and bales of tarpaulin-covered cotton wet with rain. In even rows were parked hundreds of wagons and drays, their horses bedded down for the night. Carriage lamps gleamed before the ferryhouse, and on the far side of the levee a solid wall of warehouses, saloons, ship chandlers, and restaurants provided a backdrop for two opposing streams of milling people pushing, shoving, and pouring in and out of yawning doors. Against this muffled din sounded the shrill and tinny tones of two pianos far away.

This, then, was St. Louis. Already it was early October and they had spent a precious fortnight visiting a dozen camps. But the knowledge of half an empty and waiting continent beyond, the fresh western breeze from sweet-smelling prairies, and the consciousness of all the harnessed forces of this vast water front linked to the great river bearing her into the city swept from Anne's mind all the fears and repressions of the capital city she had left behind. She had never felt so buoyant, so sure of her powers. And she wanted to share these feelings with the silent man beside her.

"Lem," she said quickly, "I want you to forget every doubt I've had about this trip. Something is going to come of all this. I feel it in my bones. I'm sure of it."

"If you feel that way," he replied, smiling but still grave, "then I'm sure of it too. But go slow. Wait until you catch the mood of this city. And don't forget—it's under martial law."

In the crowded waiting room they found her family—Uncle Charles, gray-haired, erect, pleasantly austere, a prominent lawyer in the town; and Aunt Anne, born in Snow Hill on the Eastern Shore, a plump, demure, and determined little woman in a severe brown dress, her brown eyes full of warmth and affection.

"Anne!" she cried, and they came together in a flutter of embraces, greetings, inquiries about the family and Peggy, and quick, shrewd glances at the tall figure of Evans. Aunt Anne, informed that Evans was on his way to New Orleans, beamed on him as a fellow Southerner and whispered to Anne, "At least, my dear, you're traveling in correct company, and very handsome company, I must say. Do tell us all about this sudden trip of yours."

As Anne turned to the eager, affectionate face of her aunt a wave of guilt brought sudden color to her cheeks. It was all very well to tell herself she was in St. Louis only to observe events and send her observations to Colonel Scott. But until this instant she had given little thought to the precarious situation of these members of her family, the parents of her brother's wife, of whom she was genuinely

107

fond. After all, she was enjoying *their* hospitality, staying in *their* home, and her escort was a confidential agent of the Union whose activities, if made known, would cause the Carrolls to reject him right now. And what if she told them the truth about her coming to St. Louis? For a few interminable moments Anne hated herself.

While they waited for their baggage her mind was filled with conflict. At all events, she argued silently, her cause was a just and crucial one. The ordeal would be brief. It was not easy to meet Aunt Anne's warm gaze and speak vaguely of legal work that could be done only in the Mercantile Library.

Fortunately Uncle Charles soon interrupted her.

"Now, now, ladies, I'm sure we're all famished. Come along to the Planters' and let's order our dinners first. We've a table there. I'd be delighted to have you join us, sir," he added, accepting the rangy Texan with a sharp look of appraisal.

Anne sensed the mood of the city at once. It was grim, bitter, brittle, a city surrounded by a cordon of blue regiments, filled with repressed and unassayable forces, charged with tension and, in the brilliantly lighted Planters House, roaring with a savage gaiety. The Planters, located on a slight hill at Chestnut and Fourth, opposite the almost finished courthouse with its impressive dome, remained the great Southern stronghold in a Southern city ruled by the Union through bayonets and martial law.

During dinner she chatted gaily enough with Uncle Charles, but the picturesque men about her held her attention. Tables were crowded so closely together that waiters could scarcely move. Wealthy planters, lawyers, city merchants, booted visitors and Westerners, mine agents and fur dealers from the Rockies, steamship operators from Vicksburg and Memphis crowded the bar, strolled about the dining room, and brought their drinks to packed tables, where they stood swapping news with their friends. And all of these men were loud, defiant, cheerfully arrogant, and about them all clung an air of secret knowledge and secret triumph. Watching a bearded Westerner in a plaid shirt, with huge diamond cuff links shining resplendently and incongruously from the rough material, she heard Aunt Anne say loudly above the din:

"My dear, we have a real surprise for you. Harry Heyward is coming to dinner tomorrow night. He was quite shy about it, but Uncle Charles insisted. He's a very old friend of yours, isn't he?"

She thought her blood would freeze. Evans, sitting directly across from her, did not change expression. But he looked down and began to toy with his spoon.

108

She managed to stammer, "But, Aunt Anne—is—is he in St. Louis?"

Luckily Aunt Anne was absorbed with a lobster salad.

"Goodness, yes. I thought you'd written him. He even told us you would be here today, though we knew that from your telegram. Harry said he was looking forward to seeing you."

Anne felt trapped in this garish, roaring room. Traveling, seeing new faces and places, had made her forget Harry. Now she remembered Harry's face the last time she had seen him—that cold hostility doubly frightening on the face of a friend turned foe. Aunt Anne, surprised by her silence, regarded her closely.

"What is it, child? You're pale. Are you ill? Here—drink some of this coffee."

Anne poured scalding coffee down her throat until she was blinded by tears. But she had time to recover herself.

"I guess I'm more tired than I thought," she said at last. She forced a smile. "I had no idea Harry was out here. I'll be delighted to see him."

But her buoyancy was gone and the rest of the evening was a torment. After dinner they drove to the Carroll home on Locust Street, a handsome frame house full of Eastern Shore furniture, Southern gimcracks, innumerable chandeliers, and gilt-framed pier glasses. And the Carrolls plunged happily into a long evening of exploring the endless labyrinth of family connections, gossip, and chitchat. Even Peggy's frequent lengthy letters from Cambridge could not satisfy her parents' insatiable appetite for family news and they questioned Anne delightedly.

She tried vainly to get a moment alone with Evans. Even when he left quite early the Carrolls crowded around them both and she had only the reassuring warmth of his handclasp and a certain glint in his eye to comfort her.

Later on Aunt Anne's affectionate chattering tongue pursued her to her bedroom.

"We'll have so many lovely long talks, dear. And where *did* you find that *striking* escort of yours? I'm sure *he* can alter your views. Oh dear, we won't talk about *that,* will we? I'm so sorry the children are all away. Nellie is married to a *lovely* gentleman in a dull little river town called Keokuk. Elizabeth and Anne are visiting Edward, who lives in Vicksburg, you know. Thank heavens, Vicksburg will never feel this war. . . . Would you like breakfast in bed, dear?"

On and on went Aunt Anne, careening merrily down one conversational chute after another. But at last she turned out the gas, kissed Anne on both cheeks, and tiptoed to the door. She could not resist one parting shot.

"I'm glad you're to meet Mr. Johnston at the Mercantile, Anne. A brilliant man and one, I'm sure, who will make you change your mind. We all have a right to our opinions, dear, but I do regret seeing even one Carroll on the wrong side. Good night, dear."

Anne felt suffocated in the darkness of her comfortable but strange room. How did Harry know? How did he *know?* He had even *anticipated* her arrival in St. Louis. She had been so sure of everything a few brief hours ago. Now her exhilaration had fled. She was uneasy to the point of fear.

Anne's whole orderly existence, her religious training, her lifelong association with men and women of breeding and polish, the comparative ease with which she had made her way had left her entirely unprepared to measure Harry's new role accurately. Still, she was obliged to consider the stubborn facts. He had not hesitated to ransack her rooms and seize her private papers. He had threatened her with death. He had gone to Baltimore for a purpose—and there he must have picked up her trail to the West. And he had not been apprehended. He was here in St. Louis, not only at large but brazenly planning to confront her in her kinsman's home. She must, on the surface at least, match his own bravado. Since she could not escape meeting Harry, she would do her best to take advantage of the occasion. She would weigh, if she could, why he was here—and how much he knew. Arranging for his arrest posed an insoluble problem for the moment, for even though St. Louis was occupied by Union troops, they were sitting on a barrel explosive with Southern sympathizers and Southern secret agents. If Harry had any knowledge at all of her reasons for visiting St. Louis his immediate arrest could very easily spell disaster for her. She had to wait until he first exposed his hand. And what, she thought in sudden panic, might Harry do to ruin Evans's mission when he found out that Lem was with her?

It was a long time before Anne passed into broken sleep.

14

MR. EDWARD WILLIAM JOHNSTON, THE WITTY, HAND-some librarian of the Mercantile Library, watched with interest the first arrival of the day. Looking disarmingly young and clear-eyed in spite of her restless night, Anne came straight to his desk.

"Mr. Johnston, may I introduce myself?" she began, handing him an unsealed envelope. "I'm Miss Carroll, niece of Mr. Charles Cecelius Carroll, whose note this is. I'm most anxious to make use of your legal library for a few weeks."

"I'm delighted to meet you, ma'am," said Mr. Johnston, his bright black eyes resting appreciatively on her for a moment. Anne had chosen the simple blue wool dress and rose pelerine carefully. He unfolded the note and read it quickly. "By all means. We're delighted to have you with us—you'll find several of your own works on our shelves. I'd like to compliment you on *Star of the West*. We have several well-read copies here. We're honored, ma'am, to have you work at the Mercantile."

"That's very kind of you," she replied smilingly. "I intend to combine a pleasant visit in St. Louis with work on a treatise on constitutional law I've had in mind for some time."

As they talked for a few moments Anne realized that he had no idea of her present political convictions and took for granted that her sympathies were the same as the St. Louis Carrolls. It was like a game, and for an instant until she remembered that this was part of war Anne felt a little as though she were cheating this pleasant scholarly man. When she was certain that he did not suspect her she began her campaign with a flattering smile.

"And how does it feel to have two such distinguished members of your family in command of Confederate armies, Mr. Johnston?"

111

He laughed and leaned over his desk, warmly confidential.

"I'm very proud of them both, ma'am. My brother, General Joe, has a huge command in the Shenandoah Valley, I understand. As for Albert, I haven't seen him in three months. But I hear from him often. And just between us"—his eyes sparkled mischievously and his head came close to hers—"he's building the finest army in Tennessee. Forty thousand fully equipped troops—and in three months he'll sweep every Yankee north of the Ohio right into the Great Lakes, where they belong. A gifted and brilliant man, Miss Carroll; I believe he's in Nashville now."

"You *should* be proud of them," she said encouragingly. "But I just came through Ohio and all the talk there is that Albert Sidney Johnston has over a hundred thousand men ready for action."

He flashed her a quick, good-natured smile, as one in exclusive possession of the true facts.

"I think we understand one another, ma'am. That's just pepper for Yankee eyes. Just the same, Albert's sitting on the Memphis and Charleston Railroad forging an army that will soon sweep the West."

"You think the Yankee prospects poor in these border states, Mr. Johnston?"

"Poor!" He looked at her in genuine amazement and pulled one end of his well-trimmed mustache. "Why, that's the first hint of doubt I ever heard from one of your family. I assure you, ma'am, the issue is already decided. Sterling Price's army will soon roll over Missouri. Albert Sidney will sweep the whole area from Cairo to Cincinnati. These Yankees can barely hold the lid on St. Louis. You can see that easily enough. And Southern independence and recognition by all Europe is a matter of weeks. I happen to know this, ma'am. I have the facts. Please set your mind at rest."

Matters had gone quite far enough. Anne was feeling decidedly reluctant in her new role. She preferred the direct approach to any problem. But she ventured one more question.

"You confirm every sentiment I've heard throughout the West," she agreed. "But what do you think of the rumors of a Union attempt to force the Mississippi?"

Mr. Johnston's expression said plainly that this was all nonsense.

"You mean those eggshells Eads is building?" He even laughed generously. "Madam, the Father of Waters is absolutely invincible. How can anyone imagine that a dozen small river craft with a few thousand farm boys will even get a hundred miles South, let alone twelve hundred? It's bosh and nonsense. Everyone out here knows it. No, ma'am. It's all over. And France and England will convince you of that at any moment."

She said meekly, "You may be quite right." Mr. Johnston beamed confidently and came from behind his desk. Leading her to the law library, he introduced his clerk, and, with a friendly nod, left her.

The Mercantile Library at Fifth and Locust was an advanced institution in a thriving, roaring city of one hundred and sixty thousand. Not only did Anne find all the old legal classics—Blackstone and Joseph Chettys; Chancellor Kent's early volumes; Coke, Fearne, and Fonblanque; Plowden and Powell; Bacon's abridgments in ten huge, dull volumes; Comyn's digest; Hargrave's state trials; Buller's *nisi prius* with complex cases compressed into five lines, a half score of important cases to the page; and good old Jacob's *Law Dictionary,* and all the other familiar volumes of her father's library that she had ransacked as a child—but there was an entire section devoted to a half century of new classics developed in American law. Here was the finest law library west of Washington.

She fell to work with pleasure and labored steadily until noon. Then a sharp diversion occurred. Hearing voices, she looked up and saw Aunt Anne and Mr. Johnston bearing down upon her. Aunt Anne had come to take her to lunch. An expression of bewildered surprise was registered on Mr. Johnston's handsome face. Disregarding signs of "Silence!" posted everywhere, Aunt Anne called out loudly at a distance of several yards:

"Time to rest a bit, my dear—and Mr. Johnston has a bone to pick with you."

Well aware of the nature of the bone, she gave that gentleman a dazzling smile. But Mr. Johnston was grimly bent upon confirmation of Aunt Anne's incredible information.

"I am anxious to clarify something at once, Miss Carroll," he said politely, his eyes fixed on hers. "Is it possible you are a Union sympathizer?"

"But of course, Mr. Johnston. I always have been—all my life."

Mr. Johnston could not have looked more shocked if she had just announced that she was about to enter a house of prostitution.

"Good lord, ma'am, why didn't you tell me this?"

"You never asked me, Mr. Johnston. I supposed the nature of my inquiries would acquaint you with that fact."

"Well, I never." He colored slightly but managed a wry smile. "I never expected to find a Carroll and one of the first ladies of Maryland lined up with these misguided Yankees."

"You'll find a number of them," she informed him politely. "My father, for one. Young Dr. Thomas Carroll, who's married to Aunt Anne's own Peggy, for another."

113

"I'm afraid I've made an ass of myself," said Mr. Johnston distantly. Without another word he turned and left them.

Luncheon with Aunt Anne was a brief and strained affair.

At four o'clock Evans called for her. He looked harried and anxious and said little until they had driven to the Planters House and settled themselves in a private parlor. Only a fortnight ago they had left Washington. But their visits to the Ohio camps, the informal, catch-as-catch-can conditions of living had quickly broken down the last barriers of formality and self-consciousness between them. It was impossible for her to reconstruct or even recall her earliest acquaintanceship with Evans. She felt as if she had been traveling and conferring with this man for years. In this enforced intimacy they had long since dropped their usual formal salutations. She didn't like "Lem" or "Lemuel." It didn't fit him. But there it was, and it was the name he used.

He was summing up the chaotic military situation.

"As the diplomats put it," he said with bitter humor, "the situation is deteriorating. I saw Frémont this morning, and by this time he's convinced I'm an informer and is sure I tattled to Mr. Lincoln. So does Jessie Frémont, just back from Washington. She's tossed all judgment overboard. She's confusing her beloved general with Mr. Lincoln every day of the week."

Anne said, as though such a meeting would not be touching off dynamite, "Lem, take me down there tomorrow. I've always wanted to meet Senator Benton's daughter."

"Don't try it," warned Evans. "I'll take you down there—but don't cross swords with Jessie Frémont." He grinned at her. "I don't want to be caught between you two Amazons."

Anne laughed. "You aren't very flattering, Lem. I promise I'll watch my manners. But I'd like to judge Jessie Frémont for myself."

"We'll see. Meantime today we're to meet Eads. We're expected at his office in an hour. It'll be a pleasure to talk to one sensible man after the morning I've had."

He paused, remembering something. The relief on his face was replaced by worry.

"Anne, I don't like this dinner idea with Harry. It's all wrong. The man should be arrested immediately."

She carefully considered her own reply.

"From many points of view—yes. But from the most important of all—no. It would be simple if we could be sure Harry does *not* know why we're here. But if he *does,* we can be sure he's not working alone. In that case his arrest, *while we are in St. Louis,* could be a

114

signal for an exposé of our purposes here. The moment we leave town I'm for having him arrested at once. But I beg of you, don't risk upsetting our whole applecart now."

Evans looked very gloomy but finally shrugged.

"All right. But it seems to me we're always finding reasons for *not* arresting Harry. The moment our mission's completed I want him behind bars. We must be on our way to Eads. But later tonight I think we ought to give the subject of Harry Heyward some very careful consideration. The whole situation is likely to get out of hand."

They found Eads in a cluttered cubbyhole on the second floor of the Army Administration Building. Eads, a sternly handsome man with a wide firm mouth like the jaws of a steel trap, was a native of Indiana and had been a brilliant designer of ship salvage machinery. He had promised the government eight or more iron-plated steam-propelled gunboats, armed with heavy cannon, in one hundred working days. He was about to make good his promise. There were seven gunboats at Carondelet, five at Mound City, and others at Cincinnati.

Eads examined their papers thoroughly and then studied them both while Evans questioned him for half an hour. Evans finally asked, "Then you won't hazard an opinion on their ability to force the Mississippi?"

"No, sir," replied Eads firmly. "That's not my business. That's the Army's. You'll have to ask General Frémont or the War Department about that."

"We already have, sir," retorted Evans, and gave him a quick résumé of their information.

Eads looked worried. "Well," he said succinctly, "they better unify their command in the West right away or they're finished. All I get out of Frémont is that if my boats are sent down the river he'll run twenty-five to fifty thousand troops along the banks and we'll all be in New Orleans by Christmas—he hopes."

"Have you seen at any time any detailed plans or approved documents in Frémont's possession regarding this New Orleans expedition?" asked Evans.

"None whatever," said Eads emphatically. "I've often thought the rebels might do well to permit such a loose-knit expedition to proceed without hindrance while they were sending strong forces past our flanks to sweep the whole Northwest clean. Jeff Davis must be mad not to try. The rebels could strike now and strike hard. Nobody's ready for 'em."

They sat in uneasy silence for a while, digesting these disagreeable reflections. Anne spoke first.

115

"Captain Eads, I've been wondering for some time—if your craft were disabled in midstream how could they be prevented from drifting down the river into enemy hands?"

"You ask embarrassing questions, ma'am," retorted Eads. "I designed these craft for patrol work and to support attacking land forces. They are invulnerable to ordinary fire power, as we now know it. They can blow most river fortifications out of the water and stand up to these forts at a range of a hundred yards and suffer little damage. But they must have plenty of water and plenty of land support, in my opinion, for any operations on the Mississippi. They are designed to patrol strong river points such as St. Louis, Cairo, Paducah. But if disabled on the Mississippi—they'd be lost without a doubt. For us," he added wryly, "the Mississippi flows the wrong way."

The words had a familiar ring. What was it Lincoln had said? Her memory brought it back almost instantly. "We need a river that flows the other way," the President had told her. She turned these words over and over in her mind, like a refrain whose hidden meaning eluded her.

After chatting a little longer Eads arranged to place a tug at their disposal in a few days. They left his office, feeling that they had accomplished little, and went to the Army telegraph office to file their daily reports to Scott. She was surprised by the rapidity with which Evans dashed off several messages in cipher and she remarked on it.

Evans grinned. "There's nothing to it. Here—read this and see what you make of it." He handed her the form and she read the following message: "T. A. Scott, Washington: The Mon Inn Dee Red per Pay gal Lee Can Inn Ale Tell pose Prow Ewe watt Lee Flat heem Tell eye chewed Moore Tom Mount free Meat two End N. V. Corn Inn Be Wood Itt.—Evans."

Anne laughed heartily. It was a relief after this trying day.

"It's nothing but nonsense, Lem. What is it?"

"It's a homemade cipher. Given the key, any ten-year-old boy could write that stuff as rapidly as I did. Strange to say, the rebels have never broken it and the War Department uses it on military wires it knows the rebels have tapped. But look, read it *backwards*. Read it just as it sounds, *phonetically*. You can read it easily. Try it, Anne."

At first amused, she began to read slowly, "It would be in corn
——"

" 'Inn Corn N. V. End'—that, if you please, is phonetics for 'inconvenient,' " said Evans. "Go ahead."

Anne began again. "It would be inconvenient to meet Free Mount —no, Frémont—Tom Moore—is that 'tomorrow'?" Evans nodded. Anne went on. "Should I tell him flatly—what you prow—no, pro-

116

pose. Tell Ale Inn Can—why, that's 'A. Lincoln'—tell A. Lincoln legal paper ready in month. Signed, Evans."

"You're doing fine," said Evans approvingly. "Now you know the War Department's cipher code—one of them, at least."

"And you mean the rebels can't break that silly method?"

"They've had experts working on it for months. The operators rattle it off very fast and also add embellishments and tricks of their own to confuse anyone tapping a wire. It hasn't been broken yet."

They filed their telegrams and Evans returned to his hotel while she went back to the Carrolls' to dress for dinner.

Long before she had finished hooking her green moiré gown several of the dinner guests had arrived. And as she fastened her mother's locket about her neck she was startled to hear Harry's familiar voice bantering Aunt Anne downstairs. His presence here seemed absolutely unreal; the evening ahead of her loomed like a nightmare. She felt as if the locket were a noose tightening about her neck.

Amazingly enough, however, the early stages of the evening were quite serene. As she descended the stairs, her skirt whispering across the polished wood, she saw Harry in the living-room doorway, handsome in ruffled linen and a long dark blue coat, surrounded by a group of Aunt Anne's friends. He was pale, his face rather drawn, but he eyed her candidly enough, bowed gravely, and greeted her as if he had left her only yesterday at some Washington levee. In fact, his very composure disturbed her more than any signs of open hostility might have done. Just then Evans entered, hat in hand, and paid his respects to Aunt Anne. The latter undertook to introduce him to Harry.

"Mr. Heyward—may I present Mr. Evans of Texas? He has been kind enough to escort Miss Carroll to this city and is soon to depart for the South," she said beamingly. "I think you two should know each other."

"I'm sure of it," replied Harry quickly without any sign of recognition. "How do you do, sir." He did not extend his hand, nor did he glance at Anne.

"I've heard a good deal of you, Mr. Heyward," said Evans evenly, his eyes never leaving the other's face. "This is quite a surprise. I understood you were in Washington."

"The surprise is not mutual, sir." Harry smiled coldly. "You are going *South,* sir? How far?"

"To New Orleans, Mr. Heyward, as soon as possible."

Harry suddenly flushed. "Indeed. I didn't know you had made such a fervent stand with the South."

117

Evans laughed. "Why, sir, I stand where I've always stood. You should know that."

Anne caught her aunt's baffled expression. The situation was dangerous and she put an end to it at once.

"Harry," she said, "you're such a surprising person. I heard you were in Baltimore a short time ago. How did you happen to come West so soon?"

They were surrounded by people now. He smiled and drew her away from the little group and strolled with her into the front parlor. She caught a flicker of what seemed to be regret in his eyes. Then it vanished. He said in a voice as sharp and startling as the sound of breaking china:

"I didn't tell you all my plans, did I? Quite careless of me. I thought you might have heard from Sallie. I started for Baltimore but got off at Relay House and rode over to Pikesville and Trenthan to see Tom Cradock about some of our Western property." He looked at her closely. "In fact, I stayed there for several days. Tom advised me to consult with Coke and Davis in St. Louis—and then Peggy wrote Sallie you were on your way to St. Louis for a visit. I thought this all most interesting and quite a coincidence. So on I came."

Sallie, Sallie, she thought, so careless about what she repeated. But her spirits came back with a bound. Then he didn't *know*. He might be curious, even suspicious, but he didn't know for certain. She spoke stiffly with him a few moments, then moved away to join another group until dinner was announced.

Harry sat at her left and Evans, she noted thankfully, was at a far corner of the table between two pretty girls from Paducah. Uncle Charles had gathered together a wide assortment of people representing many points of view, she discovered as dinner proceeded. Evidently he had taken care thereby to provide a protective screen through which individual hostilities found it hard to penetrate. Even with this precaution the dinner was scarcely a real success. The strain and tension seeping in from the city were almost palpable in the comfortable, candlelighted room.

Anne listened with relief to the engagingly mischievous asides of a young boy of sixteen who sat on her right. He was an alert, brown-eyed youngster named Dale Duncan, a distant kinsman of Nellie Carroll's husband in Keokuk, and in a humorously adult manner he repulsed all Anne's good-natured attempts to find out what he was doing in St. Louis. But when they rose from the table and sauntered into the parlor he whispered to her:

"I'm not trying to be rude, ma'am, so I'll tell you a secret. You seem to be the only Yankee present. I'm in the Union Army, the

118

Fifth Iowa, and I go to Cairo in a transport steamer tomorrow. I was sworn in this morning. But don't you tell the Carrolls. They'd scalp me here and now."

She was astonished and dismayed. He was such an innocent, fun-loving boy, with an infectious habit of grinning and solemnly winking one bright eye at the slightest joke or allusion they shared between them. He reminded her a little of a younger, less concerned Lem Evans.

"But, Dale," she protested, "why can't you wait awhile? Why did you have to join?"

"I didn't have to. I wanted to," said Dale stoutly. "Everybody in Keokuk joined. My cousin Pat is only fifteen, and he's out training at Rolla already. His mother, my aunt Hat, had a fit." Suddenly he became defensive. "Don't you worry about me, ma'am. I've been a crack shot since I was twelve. I can take care of myself."

"I'm sure you can. But—what does your mother say to all this?"

"Mom? Oh, she carried on something awful. Cried all one day. But Pop made her clam up. He said I'd be home before Christmas and the whole business would be finished before then."

"And you think so too?"

He grinned again. "I wouldn't mind a little longer, six months even. There's a lot of Keokuk and Davenport boys I know in our regiment and we're having fun. I got a Sharp's rifle today—they're hard to get —and all I want is a shot at some Johnny Reb and then we'll bring back Jeff Davis in a coffin, and I suppose I'll be helping Pop get in the crops next summer. Though I don't aim for farm life. I want to live in St. Looey when I'm older."

He was so excited over his coming trip to Cairo—he had never been more than twenty miles from home in his life—that when he came to leave to take one of the young girls home before the military curfew sounded Anne did an impulsive thing. Drawing him to a corner of the big square hall, she unfastened her mother's locket and pressed it almost surreptitiously into his hand. As his fingers closed over it she wondered at herself. It was unlike her to do such a thing as this spontaneously.

"Now you're one of the family, Dale," she whispered to him like some fellow conspirator. "Take it as a good-luck piece. It's very precious to me and it will bring you home safe and sound before you know it."

He was so surprised and pleased he could hardly stammer his thanks. While he examined Julianna's locket she told him something of its history.

119

"Ma'am, I'll wear it all the time. You're sure you want to give it to me?"

"I am indeed. And, Dale, when the war is over and you're a big businessman in St. Louis, perhaps you can send it back to me. But don't you let the Carrolls see it."

"Not a chance," he said with another of his absurd winks, and he bade her good night with a charming little bow.

She did not even see Harry leave later in the evening. Her first intimation that he had gone came when Aunt Anne led her aside in the living room, her bright eyes clouded with anxiety, her expression puzzled and a little unfriendly.

"Anne dear, have I been a fool?" she demanded. "I heard of Harry's marriage, but I still thought you and Harry the best of friends. Had you quarreled? I feel something is terribly wrong, and Peggy has scarcely mentioned Harry for ages. Is it just these terrible differences that afflict us all?" She suddenly looked helpless and worn and finished weakly, "I took it for granted——"

Anne's heart went out to her in quick compassion. At the same time she was stung with a renewed sense of shame over deceiving and taking advantage of her own family. For her own self-respect she must tell her aunt at least part of the truth, and she did so, emphasizing her political differences with Harry that had led them to cancel their engagement. That was as far as she felt it wise to go. But Aunt Anne was greatly upset.

"Why on earth didn't you tell me, dear? You didn't have to endure an evening like this for a moment. Good heavens," she wailed, "it's almost impossible to carry on social life any more."

Anne silently agreed with her. As she kissed her aunt affectionately she glanced around the room. Everyone had left but Evans, who was talking with Uncle Charles but trying to catch her eye.

"Don't worry about it, Aunt Anne." She patted the other woman's plump hand fondly. "These are most difficult times for all of us. And now, if you'll excuse me, dear, Mr. Evans is to take me for a short drive. He's leaving soon and we have some matters to talk over. I'll be back within an hour."

"At this time of night?" exclaimed Aunt Anne, aghast. "The city isn't safe! It's jammed with rowdies and military police. And it's nearly curfew time."

"We'll be all right," Anne assured her. "I need a breath of fresh air. We won't be gone long."

She did not enjoy the expressions on the faces of Aunt Anne and Uncle Charles as they watched her drive off with Evans in a closed carriage. Over the years they had come reluctantly to accept the fact that she was a responsible, grown woman who worked as hard at her profession as any man and who had for some time earned a considerable income, but they could not swallow such a flaunting of the proprieties.

"Whew!" said Evans, mopping his forehead as they drove down Fifth Street. "This won't do at all. Harry has marked me down for fair, and your family will have the whole story if we don't look out. And yet I've come around to your point of view—I don't think we dare have Harry picked up just now."

"We've been much too brash and naïve," exclaimed Anne, "not to anticipate possible complications. And Aunt Anne and Uncle Charles —I feel quite ashamed of myself at times. I'd never forgive myself if the poor dears became involved in something unpleasant. I'm half inclined to move——"

"Not yet," warned Evans. "You'd only have more complications. But I'm jumping into the Denton House on the water front tomorrow and laying low. You stick to the library for a few days."

Twice they were halted by patrols on the deserted streets before they reached his hotel. But Frémont's passes, secured by Evans on their arrival, were honored at once.

"How can we talk at the Planters?" asked Anne abruptly. He was silent a moment.

"I'm sorry to have to suggest it, but there's only one place, I'm afraid. You'll have to come up to my room for a few minutes. I've two letters from Scott and an urgent telegram to show you. They came after I left you this afternoon. I'm not sure we're not watched," he added with a look of concern. "But this can't be helped. We have very little time."

"Very well," Anne said reluctantly. "I suppose you're right. I'm afraid my welcome in town is already wearing thin."

"Go into the ladies' parlor for five minutes," said Evans in a low voice as they alighted. "There's a stairway there. I'll go at once to my room—264. At the end of the corridor. Up one flight. The door will be open."

Thankful that the ladies' parlor was crowded, she spent five minutes arranging her bonnet, then leisurely climbed the stairs and entered Evans's room unnoticed. It was a small room with nothing in it but a narrow iron bed, a huge walnut wardrobe, a deal table piled with newspapers, two straight chairs, and a strip of worn carpet.

"All I could get alone," said Evans, pulling a chair out for her. "They're packed four and five to a room here."

He drew a sheaf of letters from an inside pocket.

121

"I don't like this, don't like it at all," he said as if to himself, and handed her two brief notes.

"There's Scott's latest. They don't amount to much. He wants Eads's report and your estimates on rolling stock. The real meat is in this telegram."

She sat at the table and bent over the form, the precise script of the telegraph operator penciled over by Evans's cipher translation.

"Can you read it?" he asked anxiously.

"Yes." She read in a low voice, " 'Disregard Frémont. Halleck to replace him in November. This most confidential. Must have detailed summary on river expedition within two weeks. Decisions rest on this. Navy operations on New Orleans from Gulf via South Pass almost complete. Bates and L. now firm for joint river project. Give us all you can to support this. (signed) T. A. S.'

"Then they're committed to the New Orleans plan." She looked up at him with quick concern. Evans sat slumped on the edge of the brass bed.

"It looks like it," he agreed. He stood up suddenly and came toward the table, his whole attitude one of defiant determination. He repeated Scott's last phrase—"Give us all you can to support this"—and laughed shortly.

"What have we got?" he demanded. "Interviews with seven commanding generals and twenty-nine staff officers from Cincinnati to St. Louis, and not one of 'em with an ounce of faith in this New Orleans jaunt. All of Missouri and most of this town convinced the Union is finished. And who has supreme command out here? No one."

Carefully he began to go over the military situation as he saw it. He concluded:

"Anne, in my opinion two essentials are required of any effective blow to be struck. It must aim at the heart of the rebellion, not its perimeter. And Negro slaves should be brought in contact with Union soldiers. That event alone will blow the South wide open. But I'm becoming convinced *the North does not want to strike this kind of blow*. The attitude of the generals proves it. To them the South is a Pandora's box that nobody wants to open. But if the national government is to maintain itself it must smash rebel supply lines, seize railroads, and get at once to where Negroes can be reached and *armed*. Those blacks are important. Give them arms and enlist them."

Evans struck his fist on the desk and said abruptly, "I think we ought to tell them that in Washington. Tell them flatly there will have to be a new plan at once, a completely *different* plan." He stopped and looked at her in fierce perplexity. "But, my God, *what is it going to be?*"

Anne sighed. Her eyes felt hot and heavy, the skin on her face taut with fatigue.

Evans was regarding her closely now. After a moment he said gently, "It's late, we'll have to sleep on it. Come along, Anne—I'll drive you home."

The change in his voice dissolved her impersonal concentration. For the first time she realized that it was long after midnight and she was alone with Evans in his room at the Planters House. As she looked about the small, bare, smoke-filled room, she was aware with a little shock that she did not wish to go home at all. She was at home here with this man. She felt as if she belonged with him wherever he might be. The depth and certainty of this feeling revived her. In sudden comprehension she saw what the past hectic weeks had done. By swift, subtle changes she and Lem had been transformed from acquaintances to friends to this—a man and woman who looked now into one another's naked eyes.

Evans stood for a moment before her, and in his steady gaze she read the identity of his discovery with hers.

"Anne dear——" he began, and stopped.

The strain of their situation showed in his worried speculative eyes and in his air of trying to formalize the easy intimacy that grew so naturally between them. He picked up her cloak from the other chair and held it for her.

She managed to smile a little as she rose and let him place the cloak on her shoulders, whitely bare above her green décolletage.

"Take me home, Lem. I can't think any more."

They walked boldly downstairs and across the lobby to the stares of the night clerk and a Negro porter mopping the floor. When they stopped by the Carroll mansion, the lower rooms blazing with light, Evans stared at the bright windows a moment while his lips tightened.

"Do you want me to present your explanations?"

"No, thank you, Lem. I'll handle this myself." They got down from the carriage and stood apart. "Perhaps I'd better go the rest of the way alone," she said in a low voice. "Good night, Lem. At the library at three tomorrow."

On entering the hallway she found both Aunt Anne and Uncle Charles sitting bolt upright on the sofa in the living room. Aunt Anne rose and came to her, rigidly erect.

"My dear Anne," she said firmly, "we welcomed you here in spite of these times and your sentiments because you are one of us. You are a Carroll. But these hours and this conduct cannot be accepted. You are welcome to complete your visit, dear, but we cannot risk scandal and worse. We are Southerners, living in this city on sufferance and under martial law. You will have to observe the amenities, Anne, and I do not feel that Mr. Evans should be brought to this house again. And now—good night, my dear."

They stood in the doorway silently watching her climb the stairs.

15

TWO FEVERISH WEEKS PASSED. THERE WAS NO TRACE of Harry. Uncle Charles intimated he had departed for Chicago on business. Evans spent a great deal of time in the shipyards and Army centers, twice traveling west to the railhead at Rolla. Anne had taken a suite at the Everett House to serve as an office when she could not work at the Mercantile Library and to have a place to talk to Evans privately. But she was still staying with the Carrolls. She blessed the library, for her work there went well.

To her surprise she got along famously with Mr. Johnston, in spite of that gentleman's shock over her Union sympathies. In fact, the lively librarian seemed to consider it imperative to uproot her heretical fantasies and return her to the true faith of the South. Anne thoroughly enjoyed her morning tilts with him, the warmth of their remarks bringing many interested and amused readers about his desk. For Johnston was a man of cultivation and intellect, greatly interested in English history and literature, a witty raconteur, a vigorous and fluent writer himself, who immediately recognized Anne's talents and abilities.

Mr. Johnston regaled her one morning with a hilarious account of his famous but bloodless duel with John M. Daniel, the Southern editor, over the merits of Hiram Powers's celebrated statue of the Greek slave.

"I've no idea what we were trying to prove," laughed Mr. Johnston. "But we were very bloodthirsty—and we both missed. It was about as futile a contribution to the slavery controversy as could be imagined."

But little by little Anne persuaded him to discuss war plans in the

125

West. Under the pretense of gradually being convinced by his picturesque logic and then prodding his quick temper with pointed thrusts at the proper moment, Anne learned a great deal from him. He could not resist boasting of his two famous relatives.

And every two or three days she sent voluminous accounts of his gossip and claims directly to Bates and Tom Scott.

She was actually able to piece together the location of important units in Albert Sidney Johnston's growing army, especially as Mr. Johnston became more and more incensed with Jefferson Davis and the latter's reluctance to heed the General's demands and warnings in the West. In fact, she learned that the President of the Confederacy, convinced of active foreign intervention at any moment, was rapidly drawing off men and materials from Tennessee to reinforce Richmond and, ironically enough, was turning many of the troops over to General Joseph Johnston, the librarian's brother, in Virginia. This turn of events further loosened Mr. Johnston's ready tongue, and before long she knew that rebel forces in the West were not at all what they were claimed to be. The whole situation in Tennessee began to occupy her mind.

But every afternoon she dropped work on her paper for Lincoln and her drawing out of Johnston and plunged into a different world. She and Evans relentlessly explored the city and wound up on the water front each evening, gloomily watching the muddy flood of brown water that poured past the city, that seemed to carry with it every conjecture and faint hope they possessed straight into the heart of the Confederacy.

Her personal life came to seem bizarre, unreal, as if she were forcing her way through some strange and violent dream and would wake in her sunny room back home on the quiet banks of Church Creek. The realization that she had traveled to St. Louis in company with a man she had scarcely known before, that together, day after day, they were searching the city and the water front for some as yet concealed solution to a rapidly mounting crisis, and that in this constant companionship and shared purpose they were being drawn ever closer brought her both happiness and fear. Neither of them referred even indirectly to that revealing night at the Planters House. But since then a warm current of awareness had encompassed them and was bearing them toward what, Anne could not tell. In a few short weeks the intimacy they had not chosen would end with their work. Would they choose to continue it? *Could* they?

It was always at this point that the memory and the threat of Harry chilled her. Ironically, it was now Anne who regretted that Harry had not been disposed of, once and for all, by military arrest.

126

And it was Evans, preoccupied with the problems of Frémont, who began to pooh-pooh her fears and advise her to forget about him. No one in the Army, he informed her—and the intelligence system was excellent—had seen a trace of Harry.

But her anxiety only increased. She was more concerned for Lem's safety than her own.

During this first hectic fortnight the two of them had made themselves thoroughly familiar with St. Louis in long, almost daily expeditions inside the city and out. They had visited the Union regiments that reached from Carondelet to North St. Louis. They had driven to Compton Heights to watch new German regiments filling rows of tents that looked like slices of fresh white cake on the green beside the city's reservoir. They had looked down from the heights and seen the whole city on the pleasant plateau selected by Pierre Laclède more than a century before, and had been able to identify the dome of the courthouse, the spire of St. John's, the long thin line of the Pacific Railroad penciled across the meadows, leading westward to Rolla. And always to the east, they had caught the glint of sunlight on the river, the great river that flowed so inexorably from north to south.

They had ridden the Fifth Street cars that jangled haltingly five miles north to Bremen, a German settlement where droves of mules and rows of sales stables stank in the warm sun. There the streets were full of cracking whips and sweaty teamsters swearing in every variety of German at thousands of mules being driven through clouds of swirling dust to transports and barges that would take them to die on battlefields yet undreamed of.

They had gone to hospitals and homes crowded with wounded from the fierce summer battles at Wilson's Creek and the minor but bloody struggles at Monday's Hollow, Big River Bridge, and Underwood's Farm. And on Verandah Hill they had watched the drilling of new recruits to take the places of those who had fallen.

The whole city came to seem to them like some great structure overstrained, teeming with frantic activity. Brittle traffickings of the day were held under bayonets; everywhere there were Home Guards, seizures, incipient riots, and the smell of fear . . . death . . . murder. The Union barely held St. Louis, and that shaky hold was being threatened as rebel forces gathered in southern Missouri under Price.

But in this tense, highly explosive atmosphere Evans flourished. Every hidden faculty in him came alive. And his sense of humor, sardonic and often mordant as it was, was an invaluable tonic for Anne. In contrast to him, she suffered prolonged moods of depression, and

127

her sense of humor, unremarkable under ordinary circumstances, shriveled to inconsequence.

Fortunately for them both, Evans's humor, his teasing and chaffing made palatable the grim facts they were having to digest.

In her parlor at the Everett House they spent hours in amicable wrangles over the legal aspects of the war, but as the days passed she began to realize that Evans had a deeper and more abiding interest in strategy and that he had long been a student of military affairs.

"I caught the fever in the Mexican War," he told her one evening after they had filed their reports and were relaxing in the high-ceilinged room she called her office. "I managed to make a captaincy in three months," he added. "I learned a lot from a Regular Army man named Simon Buckner." He made a wry face. "He's with the rebels now and is a mighty able man.

"I want to show you something about the strategy of Price's position, for instance," he said, getting up suddenly and crossing to her desk where he unrolled a map of southern Missouri and bent over it.

But it was neither law nor strategy of which she thought as she studied his powerful head in the light from the lamp beside him. And the mental companionship they shared so ardently, she confessed to herself, was only an attractive screen for something deeper.

Lem Evans was a man to love and be proud of. In the turmoil of St. Louis he looked like a warrior and acted like one. She could hardly believe now that she had been surprised at first by the respect which St. Louis officers, from Frémont down, accorded his judgment and opinions. He had an intuitive talent for spotting fallacies and going to the heart of any problem he had under consideration. His mind had roamed far afield, but his instincts and modes of reasoning remained those of a shrewd frontiersman. And his highly detailed knowledge of the Tennessee and Mississippi valleys astonished her.

Their growing intimacy excited her. Men had admired her as a woman or as a lawyer, but no other man had ever given her, in addition to an awareness of warm personal approval, the absolute sense of partnership and equality which Lem Evans had given her in the past two weeks.

He was often direct, blunt, and sarcastic, but she had come to treasure his easy informal manners, the way in which he lighted a cigar, stretched out his legs or even put them on a low worktable she had and, with hands clasped behind his head, discussed their plans. Frequently he finished with, "Well, am I wrong? What do you think?"

Sometimes he was wrong and he never concealed his mistakes.

"I hadn't thought of that," he would say, or, "I reckon you're right. That makes a different picture."

128

As she stood beside him now, watching him trace with a strong sensitive finger a campaign he visualized for Price, and listened to his deep voice carefully explaining each move, she had a sudden desire to interrupt him, to ask, "But, Lem, what about us?"

He stopped and looked up at her. "Why, Anne"—he grinned—"you little rogue, I don't think you've been paying a bit of attention." He stood up and put his hands on her shoulders. "Tell you what, though, Anne, just the same we make a damn good team. Let's set up our own office of military affairs when we get back to Washington."

That night when he took her to the Carrolls' door he leaned down and kissed her lightly.

Afterward, in the wide walnut bed upstairs, she lay awake a long time, wondering.

As the days passed the real purpose of their being in St. Louis seemed as far from achievement as ever. Anne's paper on the war powers of the President proceeded smoothly; the information she extracted from Mr. Johnston was useful when pieced together, and Evans had met and made friends with all the men he had been sent to see. Still they were as far from solving the problem of a river assault on the Confederacy as they had ever been.

It had a curiously different effect on them.

One morning when Evans returned to meet Anne at the Everett House after his daily visit to General Frémont at the elaborate mansion in which the Frémonts had established their headquarters, his exasperation and impatience were plain to see.

"He's a madman or a genius," he exclaimed, throwing his wide-brimmed hat on the low table, pulling out a cigar, and biting off the end as he walked across the room. Lighting it, he smoked in quick angry puffs and tramped back and forth as he talked. "The man has tremendous ability, but it's so damnably undisciplined. General Schofield told me that right after the battle of Wilson's Creek last August, when General Lyon was killed, Frémont showed him and Frank Blair his personal map with a broad red line running straight through southwestern Missouri and northwestern Arkansas all the way to New Orleans. 'This is my route, gentlemen,' Frémont told them in that lofty manner of his.

"After Blair and Schofield left Frémont's office, Blair asked, 'Well, what do you think of him?' and Schofield spoke right out. 'It's a goddamned nonsensical plan by a harebrained amateur!' he told me he said. Blair, a real admirer of Frémont, remember, even went so far as to admit to Schofield, 'Well, John, I've been suspecting that for some time.'

129

"How can we get anywhere with a man like that?" Evans finished in disgust.

Anne sat up very straight.

"I thought for a while it might be a good idea to meet Jessie Frémont, but I've given it up, Lem."

"I'm glad to hear it," observed Evans. "General Jessie may still command St. Louis—but she's ruined Frémont. The Blairs are after him—and the Blairs are from Kentucky. You know the old saying, 'When the Blairs go in for a fight they go in for a funeral.' There's no point in seeing her."

"I'm afraid you're right. Judge Bates wrote me about her incredible interview with Mr. Lincoln a few weeks ago. He said Jessie left the White House in a rage, flaunting her handkerchief in the President's face and crying, "Sir, the general will try titles with you! He is a man and I am his wife.' "

"It sounds like her," said Lem. "She showed me a note her man wrote her a week ago. Something like this: 'My darling, My plan is New Orleans *straight*. Foote with his gunboats to join us on the river below. I think it can be done gloriously, especially if secrecy be kept.' "

Evans groaned.

"Secrecy! Why, Jessie's shown that note to everyone in town! The only comic relief in this depressing situation is Frémont's gang of foreign officers and their fancy wardrobes. Nice chaps, but completely mad. I'll except his German aides—some of them are first class. I suppose you know Colonel Joseph Weydemeyer, a former Prussian officer and socialist editor, helped plan the fortifications here. But that Hungarian Asboth is something different."

Evans flung himself on the sofa, put his feet on the table, and looked at her grimly.

"I saw that map of Frémont's and I said to Asboth a week ago, 'My God, General, you haven't got arms, tents, or supplies for Frémont's forty thousand men, let alone protection for the gunboats.' 'Is no need of tents!' grinned Asboth. 'In Hungary we make winter campaign. We sleep without tents, our feet to fire, though sometimes our ears freeze.' He wouldn't say a word about the gunboats. Is no gunboats in Hungary, I guess," added Evans venomously.

Anne pulled a clipping from an envelope on her desk and handed it to Evans.

"They're beginning to understand all this in the East," she said. "Look at this speech of Senator Sumner's. He blasted the whole administration and said that no adequate measures have been taken anywhere or are even in sight, and that not a department of the government has any idea of how or where to strike the rebellion. He

130

ended by saying, 'We cannot conquer the rebels as the war is now conducted.' "

"I'm sick of this treadmill," Evans said angrily after he had glanced over the paper. "Let's get to some conclusions right now." He drew a small envelope from an inside pocket and handed her some cipher telegrams from Colonel Scott. "In the first place, Frémont is through. Finished. There it is. The general suspects this. He's given orders that no dismissal notices will be accepted by him. But Scott knows his man. He's sending copies of the President's dismissal notice by three secret agents in disguise, one of them as a Southern planter. Frémont will be fired by the first week in November. Hunter will command until Halleck arrives. And Sherman, as he hinted to us, has resigned in disgust and gets here tomorrow. I'm for getting back to Washington at once. The whole mess is blowing up in our faces."

He lowered his feet to the floor with a thump.

"The whole thing's futile, Anne. If you still need convincing let me read you a remarkable paper Scott sent me in strictest confidence. How he got it I'd like to know. Listen to this."

He glanced at her white face, then read slowly and with great emphasis:

" 'This is a private paper and summarizes my conversation with the President on October 12. Political situation: Frémont ready to rebel—Chase despairing—Cameron utterly ignorant and regardless of the course of things and the probable result. Selfish and openly discourteous to the President. Obnoxious to the country. Incapable either of organizing details or executing general plans.' "

Anne's eyes were incredulous. "Who wrote that?" she demanded.

"John Nicolay—the President's own private secretary," retorted Evans. "And there's more. 'Financial situation: Credit gone at St. Louis, Cincinnati, Springfield—immense claims left for Congress to audit—overdraft today, October 12, 1861, twelve millions. Military situation: Kentucky successfully invaded—Missouri virtually seized. October here, and instead of having a force ready to descend the Mississippi, the probability is that the Army of the West will be compelled to defend St. Louis. This is the testimony of Chase, Bates, the Blairs, Meigs, Gower, Gurley, Browning, and Thomas, that everything in the West, military and financial, is in hopeless confusion.' That's it," added Evans, "and I think that finishes us."

Anne got up, went over to the window, and stood gazing into the street. After a moment Evans rose and sat on the corner of her desk where he could see her profile. Minutes went by. He rubbed his chin thoughtfully, glancing at her from time to time. Just at the moment when he thought she had reluctantly digested these devastating facts

131

and was about to agree with his conclusions, she whirled about, her fists clenched. She strode across the room and faced him with blazing eyes.

"I will not go back! Do you understand me? I will not leave this town until I find some solution that satisfies at least *me!* Do you hear? I'll rot here—but I won't go back to that paralyzed city and tell them I agree with them. Never, Lem! I won't! The more despair I encounter, the more pessimism, the more cowardice, the more apathy, the more indefensible acceptance I find that this Union is gone, is collapsing, is finished, and *that nothing can be done to save it,* all the more emphatically do I say that this Union *will* endure, that it *will be maintained,* that there *is* a solution to this tragedy which we have not yet found—*because we do not know where to look for it!* Go back if you wish, Lem. But I'll stay here. There is something here I have missed. I know it. I feel it. I intend to stay here until I find it."

She was magnificent, he thought. Small in stature as she was, she was nevertheless superbly—and futilely—magnificent. She still confronted him as if he were some opponent she would sweep from her path.

"There are situations so tremendous," he said somberly, "as to be beyond any individual control. I think this is one of them."

"It is *not!*" she said hotly. But her expression suddenly changed. "Lem dear," she added in a quiet voice, "you may do as you please. But I will not leave St. Louis until I find the solution to this catastrophe that I *know* exists."

16

AS IF IN MUTE ENDORSEMENT OF ANNE'S DECISION, A bulky packet of papers arrived from Eads the very next morning. These included passes to visit the shipyards at Carondelet and Mound City. But the most important enclosure was an invitation for Evans and Anne to board Eads's converted river steamer, *Western Star*, a survey ship, for a week's observation trip with a party of engineers bound for Cairo, where more gunboats had gathered, and up the Ohio to Paducah and Smithland. Several wives of Army engineers were traveling to Paducah, and Anne was invited to share a cabin with Mrs. Metcalfe, wife of a colonel.

When Evans joined Anne later in the day he found her in buoyant spirits. He read the invitations and was astonished at her enthusiasm.

"If we're going to stay on out here," he asked sharply, "why in God's name should we waste a week on the river?"

"For heaven's sake, Lem, let's go. My pamphlet is almost finished. I want to get out of this town for a few days and *think*. Above all, I'd like to see something of these rivers myself. We may get an idea. By all means, let's tell Eads we accept."

Since the *Western Star* was to sail in three days, on Friday morning, they decided to visit the nearby Carondelet yards at once. Late the following afternoon they shoved off on a government tug into the dusk and a fog-shrouded river, clearing with the picket boat and heading rapidly downstream. At Carondelet, forty minutes later, they inched through the fog and found their berth with difficulty. The night air was raw, full of mists and shadows and hints of rain to come.

Major Barton, in charge of the yard, met them, full of news.

"We've orders to deliver these craft by December fifth," he told them. "Supplies and guns are already pouring in, and we've no place to put them. Something's up. Come along and I'll show you the yards."

The night shift had just gone to work under great rows of oil torches that threw a lurid glare on the ways, derricks, and stocks. But the ways were empty. The last two of seven armored gunboats had been launched that morning. Big, black, ungainly monsters, they lay tethered together like quiescent leviathans drowsing on the dark brown flood that murmured against their flanks. They were swarming with men. Hand forges flared along the docks as blacksmiths and riveters worked at last-minute jobs. Every port and gangway was opened wide, while hustlers and longshoremen with hand trucks rushed stores and supplies aboard.

Major Barton first took them aboard the *Carondelet,* already designated as Captain Foote's flagship. They had to make their way carefully on the slippery crowded deck. Eight heavy guns were lashed together along with huge stores of salt pork, ammunition, tools, shovels, canned goods, and supplies of every kind piled in disorder in the very midst of riveters and carpenters. Great plates of armor and railroad iron lay here and there, still waiting to be bolted to the midship section.

The ships had not seemed so formidable from the docks. But as Lem and Anne wandered down their great grim gun decks, with the armored ports open to the night air, and noted the heavy oaken beams and bulkheads, twelve inches of solid oak overlaid with two and a half inches of armor and rails; and studied the huge black guns, yet to be mounted, and the interminable piles of shells, they were more and more impressed. These were no eggshells. They were among the most formidable craft ever designed. They were new and devastating weapons of war, already revolutionizing naval architecture. They were heavy, strong, built to endure battering. And they were armed with huge Columbiads, the heaviest guns ever mounted on ships.

"Lordy, they look tough and big," she murmured to Evans as Major Barton led them to his office. For another hour they went over specifications of the gunboats and listened to a frank discussion by the major of their advantages and limitations. They were as massive and formidable as they looked, Anne learned, but horribly, frighteningly *slow*.

When they were ready to leave a brief delay arose. Major Barton decided to ask the tug captain to give passage to St. Louis to fifteen armed guards bound for Benton Barracks. The skipper grumbled a bit about crowding his small craft, but the guards were soon embarked, placed in the after cabin, and the tug started back for St. Louis.

The fog had lifted, with patches of mist clinging here and there to the dark swirling water. A few dim stars shone remotely above them.

134

Pushing against the strong current, they were barely two miles above Carondelet, crowded in the pilothouse, when Evans spotted what seemed to be a swift picket boat cutting across their bows.

"He's pretty far out, Captain, if that's a picket boat," he exclaimed. "And he has no running lights."

The other craft swung parallel to their starboard side, about thirty yards distant. They were suddenly hailed.

"This is Picket Boat Six. What craft is that?" came a loud voice over the water.

"United States Government tug *Eagle*," the captain replied, pushing his head out the window. He added with quick suspicion, "What is the password, sir?"

There was no answer from the other boat. Evans stood up, his eyes straining through the darkness. The black shadow to starboard swerved toward them. The voice of the captain, now tense, rang out again:

"Keep off there—and give us the password."

Not a sound beyond the puff of her engines came from the approaching craft, a small swift tug with most of her superstructure removed. Evans swore in a low voice.

"God damn it, there's something wrong here. Anne! come along with me!" He almost dragged her from the pilothouse to the engine-room gangway. "Go down that ladder to the first platform level and stay there." She obeyed without a word and Evans ran to the after cabin where most of the guards were playing cards at a small table.

"Sergeant, you'd better get your men at the ready. I may be wrong, but I think we're being raided."

The sergeant goggled but issued orders at once and followed Evans, who pulled at the revolver under his coat and ran forward to the pilothouse.

The strange tug was not fifty feet away, and both ships were running against the current at about five knots. A loud voice came again through the darkness.

"Heave to, Captain, or you'll be in trouble. We want your two passengers. Stop your engines at once, or we'll fire through your pilothouse."

The captain swore. But the engine-room bell rang, the engines ceased turning, and the tug slowly drifted broadside to the current. Trying to detect any force on the other boat, the captain called out:

"You approach at your own peril. Who are you?"

Voices were abruptly raised on the dark craft now close on their beam. And Evans jumped, for he heard the voice of Heyward on the other ship and Heyward was saying, "Be quick about it, you fool.

135

They have only three armed men. Get that woman and the agent off at once."

"Very well, sir," came the reply, and the tug began to close in. In their own pilothouse Evans heard the quartermaster say in a scared voice, "Good God, sir, here they come!"

Evans whirled about to find the sergeant had mustered all fifteen guards on the portside, concealed from the onrushing craft.

"Sergeant, you're in command here. But for God's sake, fire on that boat. It's rebel—and they don't know you're aboard. They're after Miss Carroll and me."

"You're sure, sir?" said the sergeant, a big bluff farm boy in the Fifth Iowa.

"God damn it, yes. I recognize 'em. Fire on them."

The other tug's bow was in point-blank range. The reluctant sergeant speedily sprang to life. He said in a loud whisper:

"All right, boys—right along the pilothouse and the portside—ready—aim——" He straightened up suddenly and bellowed, "FIRE!"

The crash of fifteen old-fashioned muskets roared over the water and lighted up briefly in a lurid yellow glare a small tug, her deck piled high with coal, and a group of men armed with revolvers standing on her starboard gunwale. Evans caught a glimpse of Heyward flattened against the pilothouse. Even as the glare died away Evans heard shouts and screams, saw two figures tumble toward the water. Then blackness again. But where he had seen Harry he leveled his revolver, waited a split second as the tug rolled slightly, and then fired. For brief seconds revolver shots, yells, shouts, and curses filled the air. Behind him Evans heard a man grunt and slide to the deck. But another crash of muskets tore the night and a voice screamed out, "For Christ's sake, stop it! We've had enough." The other tug sheered off.

Evans ran to the pilothouse.

"Get going, Captain. Don't let them get away."

Engine-room bells jangled and with a quick lunge the tug forged ahead.

"Heave to, there," shouted Evans. "We have a cannon and we'll blow you out of the water. Heave to!"

"All right, don't fire," came the hasty reply, and the craft began to lose way at once. It was all over. They drew alongside the battered little tug a moment later and the sergeant and six men went aboard to take over the prize. Evans glanced in the engine-room doorway and saw a frightened fireman and Anne's white face staring up at him.

"Stay there a few minutes more," he called. "We got 'em. I'll be right back."

136

He jumped aboard the other tug and made his way forward, stumbling over two figures on the deck. Beside the pilothouse he found what he was seeking just as the sergeant, carrying a lantern, came up behind him. Harry Heyward was sprawled, half sitting, against the pilothouse, a hole through his shoulder. Blood seeped through the light gray coat he was wearing. He was unconscious.

"How many others?" Evans asked the sergeant.

"Two went overboard. Two dead on deck. Four wounded—and three ain't scratched. Couple of the crew in the engine room," replied the sergeant, putting his hand inside Heyward's shirt. "Still kickin'," he said cheerfully. "What in hell were they tryin' to do?"

"I told you. They were after that lady and me. Take 'em all inside, Sergeant, put the crew under guard, and stop the engines. We'll tow 'em to Government Wharf."

Five minutes later a picket boat, aroused by the gunfire, came charging downstream and alongside in a swirl of muddy foam. Evans went to Anne and brought her on deck. She was pale but quite composed.

"Was it—Harry?" she asked.

He nodded. "It was. And Harry is shot." He felt her start. "Right through the shoulder and nothing serious. But he'll be in bed a long time."

"Should I—should I see him, Lem?"

"My God—no!" replied Evans roughly. "We're getting out of here on the picket boat right now. This was too damn close."

On the picket boat they drank coffee and watched Eads's tug, now far astern and towing Heyward's craft against the surging current. Evans swallowed the last of his coffee and exclaimed in disgust, "We're fools. What's the matter with us?" he demanded. "Time and again we've refused to take Harry seriously. But even I didn't think he was up to this sort of thing."

She looked at him, her eyes wide with shock, and shook her head slowly.

As soon as they landed they drove to the arsenal and made a full report of the incident. Anne appeared to have regained her composure, but on the way to Locust Street she faced him abruptly.

"I can't do it, Lem. I can't go home yet. Drive me down to your hotel. I need an hour to pull myself together before I face Aunt Anne."

At the Denton House, facing the water front half a mile above the ferryhouse, they found the tiny parlor deserted. A spick-and-span little place, the hotel was frequented for the most part by pilots and quartermasters, and all of them had long since gone to bed. Evans

137

poked up the fire in a pompous round-bellied bit of a stove. In low voices they talked over what had happened.

"Where will they take him?" she asked.

"The House of Refuge, probably. Under arrest, of course. He'll be laid up at least a month. They've really got him this time."

"What do you mean?" she asked in a strained voice, but he was sure she knew.

He said gently, "For that business tonight. You know they'll execute him. They'll have to."

"No. No." Her words were a whisper. She wanted to ask other questions and could not.

He took her hand. "Please promise me one thing. Don't go to see him. I'll talk with him tomorrow."

She nodded. But the pent-up questions would not down.

"Lem," she said hesitantly, "did—did you do it?"

"Did I shoot Harry?" he asked bluntly. "Yes. I had to. We had a mighty close call. If we hadn't had those extra guards aboard——" He made an eloquent gesture.

"Did you," she hesitated, "did you shoot to—to kill him, Lem?"

He turned and for a few minutes looked at her with grave astonishment.

"Girl, I know you well enough to know your head rules your heart. It's a lucky thing right now. The Harry you and I recall may still have a warm place in your heart. But good lord, Anne, *this* man—this man on the river tonight—spelled disaster to both of us. Certainly I shot to kill. What else could I do?"

There was concern and something deeper in Evans's eyes as he looked at her and he realized, as she remained silent, that she could not answer his last question.

Anne was shocked. And her shock astonished her. It came not from Lem's words but from the overwhelming knowledge that she felt no slightest bit of affection for Harry. I've been waging my own Civil War, she told herself. Harry, the Harry she had thought she loved, had vanished as though he had never lived. Lem was right. The man on the river was not that Harry. Even if he had been, she would not have cared. . . . Lem Evans was the only one who mattered. The only one. She relaxed beside him on the comfortable worn sofa.

As they watched the half dozen little squares of glowing isinglass in the stove door staring at them like ruddy eyes, their nerves rejected all that had happened tonight. They thrust away these feverish events as if they were nothing but disturbing dreams.

The low mournful wail of a river steamer far away came to them faintly. A wall clock ticked drowsily in the hallway. They talked now and then, but briefly, almost in monosyllables, and for the most part they sat together silently, their shoulders touching in comforting, intimate companionship.

It was late. It was time for her to leave. But she did not stir, and Evans gave no intimation that he thought she should. He finally looked at her and then with a sudden gesture reached for her hand and held it close before he spoke.

"It's a queer time—and a queer place, Anne," he began, and his eyes were so intense that the color poured into her cheeks. "It's a queer time but the right time—and it has to be said. Listen to me." He took a deep breath. "I've got to tell you that I love you with all my heart, that I can't exist any longer without you, that I can never again afford to lose you for a moment. We belong together. On that boat tonight, the thought of what might happen to you nearly drove me out of my mind. For I love you—and if you'll have me I want to marry you, Anne, to have you with me always, to love you and cherish you . . . ."

He paused, as if dissatisfied with what he had said or how he had said it, and she was impressed by a strange blend of savagery and gentleness in his expression. She did not know it, but the savagery was Evans's reaction to time wasted, to the cautious thinking and careful planning he had indulged in all his life.

There was something of the same regret in Anne's reflections. And something else. She had known all along that she wanted something from men that was not only physical, not only mental, but that partook of some vague moral and emotional quality whose very nature had eluded her. She had only half guessed, now she was sure what it was. The additional element she demanded was a status of equality in a *life fully shared*—the acceptance of her *just as she was*—with no reservations. And Lem Evans was the first man in her life who had ever offered her such a partnership.

He must have sensed her thoughts, for he answered them immediately.

"As for anything you wish to do, Anne," he said passionately, "do it! I've never met a mind like yours. I want you as a wife, but I also want you as a cherished partner—in every respect, every degree. I want you to go on using every talent you possess as you, and you only, see fit. But I want you with me. For God's sake, Anne, can you love me as I so deeply love you?"

Her heart leaped in sudden and exhilarating freedom. She turned and placed her hand lightly on his arm. He read in her radiant face everything he wished to know.

"Why has it taken us both so long to understand this?" she asked.

139

"We've been such fools, Lem, waiting and wasting so much time. I must have thought it was impossible to bring two worlds of thought and feeling together. And I was so wrong! All those years in Baltimore—I wasn't really living. How did I ever get along? What did I feel or fail to see? I don't know. Perhaps the answer is I hadn't met you, Lem. Of course I love you and want you with all my heart."

He leaned forward a little hesitantly, as if she might vanish, as if she were some prize about to be snatched away. But she did not vanish, and her brilliant eyes, her half-parted lips, her pink cheeks and sweet fragrance filled him with sudden fire. He took her in his arms and his lips sought and found hers, and they remained in one another's arms for a long time, lost in the little parlor, lost to the feverish city about them so full of the clamor of war, lost to the tawny, tantalizing yellow flood that rolled past the levee in the darkness only a few yards away.

Later, much later, Evans looked up at the clock on the mantel and saw that it was a quarter of two.

"I'm taking you home, dearest," he said, smiling. "Someday, very soon, I hope, I won't have to——"

She interrupted him with a kiss.

"We'll have to wait a little longer," she whispered. "But not long, dearest. When we finish this assignment——" There was a warm unguarded look in her eyes and she put her arms about his neck and held him close. "Lem, you've given me new life. We'll find a way out of all this mess. We will." She kissed him twice and said breathlessly, "Now take me home, darling."

They drove the longest way they could devise to Locust Street without being challenged by too many patrols, and she was startled and made shy by the amazing change in Evans. His dark eyes snapped and sparkled and the high color in his cheeks made him look astonishingly young.

"Love and war—it's a heady mixture," he said softly, and then suddenly he remembered their narrow escape that evening.

"We don't have to worry about Harry any more, but I'm afraid he wasn't working alone. That trip on the *Western Star* is a capital idea. I'm all for it now. I'll be able to take you out of this city for several days. Furthermore, we'll be——"

She was not listening, for she broke in with the question women in love so often ask: "When did you first know you——"

"That first week end we spent with your family last winter. But you frightened me."

"Sh-s-sh, never mind," she warned him. "I was nothing but a stupid, wretched little egotist then. It took time and you to teach me. . . . Good night, sweetheart."

140

They kissed lingeringly at the curb, walked to the door, and kissed again. The war fell away and she felt a little oddly as if it were years ago; as if both of them, knowing only the security and sureness and ardor of youth, were standing in a quiet street before a quiet house under the ancient trees of some lovely village on the Eastern Shore.

She ran lightly into the house and upstairs to her room. Even the widening crack of light under Aunt Anne's door and Aunt Anne's accusing face and eyes advancing to meet her failed to disturb her.

"Aunt Anne," she said with a cheerfulness that silenced the angry reproaches of that estimable woman and struck her speechless, "I know you'll be greatly relieved. I'm a thoroughly impossible person and I've decided to move to the Everett House tomorrow. Will you help me pack, dear?"

17

THE *WESTERN STAR* CUT THROUGH THE BLUE HAZE OF
an Indian summer day, slipping past dim capes and shadowy islands,
pushing through the stubborn brown current of the Ohio a few miles
above Cairo. The uneven beat of the paddles—*flug*—chug—chug—
flug—chug-chug—as the long pistons began and closed each stroke
vibrated strongly through the ship, for she was being pushed to maintain a crowded schedule.

As Eads's guests, Anne and Evans sat in the pilothouse on the high
leather-cushioned bench once reserved for visiting pilots. Until the
Engineers got her the *Western Star* had been a fancy craft. Her ornate
pilothouse was like a spacious glass temple with a great wooden can-
opy edged in gilt gingerbread and topped by a fierce golden eagle on
a golden ball directly over the wheel. There were showy red-and-gold
window curtains; new green oilcloth on the decking; a round fat stove,
freshly polished; bell knobs of bright brass; and a wheel six feet in
diameter with gleaming brass-studded walnut spokes turning easily
this way and that under the sensitive hands of a Cairo pilot, Ben Sykes.
In the late afternoon sun the pilothouse glowed in a comfortable glory
all its own.

Even against the current the *Western Star* was making fifteen miles
an hour, weaving patterns of lacy foam as she gracefully rounded the
great bends or cut swiftly from one bank to the other to take advantage of quiet water as Sykes made some familiar but unseen crossing.

"I never thought I'd wonder why I wasn't born to be a river pilot,"
exclaimed Anne as Sykes spun the wheel abruptly, stood on one
spoke, and watched the ship, aimed directly at a steep bare bank piled
with cordwood, veer sharply to starboard, slip into calm water, and

142

rush along parallel to dense woods not twenty feet away. Heavy swells, caused by her passing, crashed through thickets and raised a great turmoil along the soft, overhanging shores.

Evans, leaning back, idly watching the ever-changing designs made by the sunlight reflected on the whitewashed ceiling, sat up and laughed.

"Isn't it enough for you to be a lawyer, a businesswoman, a propagandist, and heaven knows what else," he teased, "without taking in the Western rivers? As for this serene endless country—you'd think the war was on another planet."

Anne's smile died. "Oh, Lem, why did you have to mention the war? You remind me there's something I have to tell you. I sent a letter off at Cairo to Judge Bates, telling him about Harry. And—you won't like this—I begged him to arrange for Harry's exchange and parole. I had to do it."

He didn't like it at all.

"In God's name, why? I thought we'd decided where Harry belonged."

"Under arrest, yes," she said quickly. "But—you don't understand. I can't be responsible for Harry's death. I simply can't."

"So you're willing to have him go South again and keep on plotting against us?" he asked harshly.

She put her hand on his arm. "Lem, don't you understand? Besides," she went on in a low voice, "no matter how he has acted recently, I still think he's essentially an incapable——"

"There was nothing incapable about the man who plotted that affair the other night," snapped Evans. "By sheer chance we had those extra guards aboard. Otherwise——"

"Please, Lem, I know all that. I know I'm wrong. But I—— Maybe I'm softhearted," she said almost desperately. "I know you don't understand. But Harry will observe his parole, and—I'm sorry, Lem, but Judge Bates had to do this for me."

He was thoroughly angry. But the letter was already gone.

Fortunately a bell rang mellowly on the deck below and the mate put his head inside the pilothouse.

"Supper's ready, ma'am. We'll be tying up at Farrell's Landing tonight to take on wood. 'Sides, there ain't no room for us at Paducah."

After supper they explored the *Western Star,* wandering for a while through her long empty gilded main salon, like some magnificent frosted tunnel on the main deck, gloomy in the gathering darkness, with rows of prism-fringed chandeliers vibrating above them, and small gaudy oil paintings decorating every stateroom door. Then they climbed down crew ladders to the boiler deck, a blend of coolness and

143

flame, where a whole battalion of men, black men with rippling shoulder muscles shining with sweat, tended the fires, plunging cordwood through sixteen fiercely glowing fire doors under furnaces and boilers rising in shadowy majesty above them.

Later they got their wraps and dragged canvas chairs to the lee side of the wheelhouse and sat there, full of the rhythmic beat of the ship, full of wonder at the sky and a full moon flooding with silvery magnificence the black water, the black banks, and the endless ranks of bare trees.

Evans began to talk with unaccustomed fullness. First, of all the vast country he had seen—of the Tennessee Valley and his cross-country journey as a youth through the low country of Mississippi and Louisiana to the rich plantations of Harrison County in east Texas. He spoke, too, of his military life. Of Texas plains, of Fort Belknap, Fort Chadbourne, of Horse Heads Crossing on the Pecos, and the cruel dry emptiness of a land without limits. He spoke of his own affairs and the affairs of men with whom he mingled. And in this roving young lawyer and frontiersman Anne caught glimpses of a hard, driving mind that delighted in demolishing legends, myths, and sacred shibboleths with genial impartiality and sometimes with a ruthless force that frightened her.

"For heaven's sake, Lem, what political party do you belong to?" she finally demanded.

"I'm damned if I know," he responded with cheerful candor. "I've been a Democrat, a Know-Nothing, and now I've no label I respect. I've always despised the plantation owners, but up until two years ago I tried to defend slavery. Then Thad Stevens got hold of me and put me through his wringer. I had to square my beliefs. I had to face the fact that Negroes are people—that they're entitled to all the rights I am. That was a painful step for me. But Stevens made me take it. I *had* to take it. For above all things in this life I detest the exploitation of man by man—this robbing, pilfering, pushing, squeezing of blood, money, and labor from the poor, the ignorant, the helpless, or the plain unlucky."

Evans stood up, struck the ship's rail with the flat of his hand, and said with a violence that astonished her:

"It's a murderous society we live in, Anne. We pay best those who exploit us—the businessmen; those who cheat us—the politicians; those who destroy us—the generals; those who entertain us—the artists; and least of all—those who teach us, instruct us, and sacrifice their lives and labors for others. As for the legal profession—I despise it." The moonlight did not soften the fierceness of his face.

"And you an able judge and lawyer yourself? I don't believe it!

144

Did you ever dare express these sentiments in public?" Anne looked up at him.

His eyes began to twinkle and he laughed. "I reckon I did! I was one of the main speakers at the Annexation Convention years ago—and feeling my oats! I got up and turned loose on the ranchers, the Eastern bankers, and the wealthy planters who'd rigged up a court system in that empty state that was complicated enough to handle the calendars of New York and Pennsylvania."

"What did you say to them?" asked Anne curiously.

"I told 'em the whole contrivance of courts of juridicature is a medieval fraud upon the community; a system of leeches designed to rob the poor and humble and preserve the rich."

"Good lord! What happened then?"

"There was a large-sized riot," said Evans, chuckling. "When it was over, I went right on and told them—and this I deeply believe—that there's no question of right or wrong which a sensible savage is not as competent to decide as the ablest judge in the land; that I'd take any honest blacksmith's opinion today in preference to that of Taney or Reverdy Johnson. I told the whole convention—whenever the Speaker could get 'em quiet—that I absolutely contended that courts and lawyers should be suppressed in favor of popular tribunals, courts of the people, for the arbitration of all human differences in conformity to the benign principles of the Golden Rule." Evans paused and added ironically, "On that lofty note I closed."

"And how did they receive that recommendation?"

"For five minutes they screamed that I was an anarchist, a communist, a Jacobin, and worse. Then the boys gave me a vote of thanks for the best speech of the convention, voted in their court system, appointed me district judge, and put me on a list of Supreme Court possibilities for the following term. Finally we all went out and got drunk."

Evans sat down again and talked on, amusing her with stories of his political campaigns and the famous race in which he went down to defeat running for a second term in Congress against Judge John Reagan of East Texas.

"There never was a campaign like that, I reckon. Both Reagan and I were in fine fettle. Between the sixth of June and the first Monday in August one summer, we canvassed thirty-six counties in east Texas, joined in forty-eight debates, wore out an army of horses covering isolated communities from the Mexican Gulf to the Red River, from the Sabine River on the east to the Trinity on the west—often traveled all night to reach our next debate. Every one of our debates lasted five hours or more. We put on a show that roused the state—and Reagan won."

Evans looked grim for a moment. He said shortly, "Reagan was a smart man. We almost finished our careers in a joint debate at Jefferson. Reagan caught me on some questions I had trouble answering. I lost my temper, pulled my gun on him. He was just as quick and shoved his own gun against my chest. The crowd held its breath and watched us. I was really going to fire when Reagan grinned and said mighty quiet-like, 'Come on, Evans. Let's put up our guns. I don't want to kill you. I just want to go to Congress.' " Evans laughed easily. "Well, I put up my gun and a week later Reagan won. But that was a close shave."

Evans pulled his chair closer. "And what about you?" he said. "You're a pretty remarkable young woman, dear, if I may say so. You're completely feminine, blond, and disarming. Yet you're smart as a whip, and more successful than most men. I've often wondered why you left the kind of life your mother enjoyed and got tangled up in business and politics. Did your father keep you with your nose in a lawbook from the time you were born?"

"Not at all, Lem," she retorted. "I had just the same kind of childhood as anyone else on the Eastern Shore. I ran around with all the youngsters in the neighborhood—the Handys, Dennises, Hickses, Wilsons—oh, all of them. I swam, I fished, I learned to sail a boat, I fell off our dock. I was always getting into trouble for doing something I wasn't supposed to. Mother said I'd never be a lady." She smiled.

"Well, I guess I'm not the kind of lady Mother was, after all. She was horrified when I wanted to go to Baltimore and earn my own living. Poor Mother, she didn't realize it, but it was partly because of her. Mother had a happy life, but it wasn't the kind I wanted! I swore I'd never accept the life of a Southern woman—the fawning gallantry, the false chivalry, the little prison-house pedestals men built for them. Father adored Mother, but much of the time she was by herself out in Kingston Hall, working incessantly every day, supervising a huge estate, looking after all of us children—she had seven in twelve years— keeping track of two or three hundred slaves and *their* children! Mother died quite young." Anne sighed. "I'm not saying that her kind of life isn't a good one, if a woman has the temperament for it and a husband like Father. Most of the Southern women I know aren't so lucky as Mother."

"Wasn't it very hard to get started in Baltimore?" Evans asked. "I don't see how a woman can get any kind of work besides teaching."

"I was lucky," she said simply. "Father and Mother knew everybody and had lots of friends. Two of them, Dr. Bob Breckinridge, who

146

was pastor of the Second Presbyterian Church, and George Brown, once treasurer of the Baltimore and Ohio, took me under their wing. At first George Brown's important business friends, probably as a favor to him, let me prepare simple reports for them. But I loved the work and before long I was getting what I thought were huge sums, a hundred and even two hundred dollars, for shipping reports and what not." She looked at him and smiled. "I must have been an obnoxious little goose. I'm sure many people were shocked and I had to take a lot of patronizing and unmerciful joking from the others about my unheard-of ambition to enter business. But that's how I began."

"I never knew anyone like you." Evans shook his head in amazement. "What is it in life you like best?"

"Reality," said Anne with an unexpected force that surprised them both. "Reality—pleasant or unpleasant, dull or bright, cruel or fine. I like facts that *exist*, in spite of our preferences or passions. I love reality, Lem, but everyone I know seems to wish to escape it, as if reality were some wild beast about to spring."

"I reckon it is, often enough," retorted Evans.

"Not if you recognize reality for what it is," insisted Anne. "What fascinated me in Baltimore was the manner in which so many able men grasped at reality or fought to find it, and then tamed it and used it. They weren't afraid of change. They made change. They took science, invention, chemistry, machinery, good ideas and bad, explored them, experimented with them. Professor Morse, Ross Winans, Arunah Abell, the Latrobes, Alex and George Brown, Tom Swann—they were wonderful men. Baltimore is magnificent—I've always loved it! And yet in politics and government we fight change and experiment, fight it to the death. I'm guilty of that myself."

"Whew!" exclaimed Evans, looking a bit astonished. "You *are* sailing a lonely sea. An eternal search for a land of make-believe—that's the groping of most harried mortals."

Anne looked over the dark, gleaming water, scowling a little under the pressure of her thoughts.

"But one can't live that way. I detest what most people call ordinary times. I liked Mr. Emerson's words in Boston the other day, that if there's any desirable period to live in, it is the age of revolution. He said something to the effect that this kind of period is a very good one, *if we but know what to do with it*."

"The trouble is," said Evans dryly, "we admire Grandpa's revolution but never the one going on under our noses."

Gradually their talk subsided as the throbbing ship swept around a dark headland, and in the distance a single point of light in all that moon-swept wilderness flashed three times. Three mournful blasts

147

from the whistle above them echoed and reverberated along the river-banks. They heard voices in the wheelhouse. Bells jangled below and the ship lost way a little.

"Must be Farrell's Landing," murmured Evans regretfully. "We tie up there."

They shared a rising dislike of this little point of light shining so bravely in the velvet blackness about them—for they feared houses, people, clamor, and a river town that would shatter the mood that bound them. But there was nothing of the sort.

As the *Western Star* glided, with a great splashing of paddles, into the shadows of huge trees that hung over the water and poked her sharp nose against a soft bank piled with cordwood, they saw that the pin point of light came from a lantern hung on a small raft tethered to the shore. A single small cabin, dark and silent, was merely a blacker shadow against the bare black trees. A torch glowed from the forecastle, a plank was thrown out, a man skipped ashore, and a Negro's rich, languid voice on the bank called out, "Wood's a-ready fo' you, Cap'n Clempson."

For half an hour the furnace force and crew loaded cordwood. Then they vanished below. The clang of iron doors sounded as a night watch banked the fires. The light went out in the wheelhouse and Sykes and the mate stepped down together and regarded Anne and Evans with surprise.

"Ain't you folks ever turnin' in?" asked Sykes genially.

"Pretty soon," replied Evans lazily. "It's a mild night, Pilot. We're enjoying it."

The two pilots grunted good nights and disappeared. A cloak of impenetrable and lovely silence closed over the ship. A single riding light hung high at her stern. A lone bird chirped drowsily far away and the moon, now high, burnished the whole surface of the cove and flung great shadows from trees and low bluffs and deceptive banks across the shining river that swept out of sight into a cloud of silver mist.

For another half-hour they said nothing. Evans's arm rested lightly across her shoulders. Finally he moved slightly, wondering if she slept. But her face was turned to his, her eyes, opened wide, were startlingly clear and luminous, and her cheeks, shadowed with moonlight, were pink and silver under a halo of blond hair. Both his arms went about her.

"Anne!" It was a mere whisper, but it shook her. "Anne!"

148

18

AN ICY NORTHEAST GALE DROVE DOWN ON THE CITY OF
St. Louis, washing clean the gray levee stones, silvering the surface of
the river, and churning the water-front streets into streams of mud.

At five in the morning, a few days after her return from their river
expedition, Anne woke from a sound sleep and lay listening to the
steady drip of water from the eaves and the gurgle of rain water in a
corner drain. The very rains from heaven symbolized her thoughts.
For the riddle of the Western rivers oppressed her. Her mind was full
of the glimpses she had had of their vast tortuous courses and the
vital part they were already playing in the war.

She was also more disturbed about Harry than she cared to admit.
A military tribunal, in secret session, had determined that Harry had
been operating with or for certain unnamed parties on Beauregard's
staff; that the attack on their government tug had been planned as
part of a larger coup to seize control of the city a week later, a plan
now exposed and frustrated. There was to be a closed inquiry which
Evans would attend. Anne's presence during the incident had been
carefully concealed. And to her great relief she had a telegram from
Bates reluctantly promising to secure Harry's exchange under an ironclad parole.

Two days ago she had completed and sent to the White House one
hundred and twenty pages of carefully edited and finely written script,
the final draft of her treatise, *The War Powers of the General Government*. She had sent to Colonel Scott the inventories of railroad rolling
stock and river craft he had asked for, and a great deal of additional
valuable information gleaned from the lively brain of her librarian
friend, Mr. Johnston. All of her official tasks had been completed—
all save one.

149

And now, in the darkness, her head ached under the strain of concentration. Any stubborn opposition had always sent her flying into battle.

In the past month she had run into a solid wall of opposition to any decisive use of the Western rivers at this time. The considered opinion of every military man was against it. So was the prevalent feeling of pessimism, disbelief, and even downright ridicule. The more she ran against this wall, the more furiously determined she became.

Damn the Army! Damn these arrogant, smug, rude, pleasant, hesitant, polite, and gallant officers and men who repaid her inquiries only too often with frank wonder and ill-concealed hostility. But if the military experts and the entire Army had no faith, who in all the world might have? Who could offer better judgment or more soundly found information?

Who was there armed with knowledge that she had not sought out?

A sudden vision of the wheelhouse of the *Western Star,* of a long expanse of gleaming water, of brass-studded spokes turning under the hands of Pilot Sykes flashed through her mind. An idea struck her so forcibly that she almost cried out. She leaped from her bed.

"I'm a fool!" she said sharply as she searched with shaking hands for a match. "A plain damn fool!" Even in her excitement she thought oddly, Lordy, Lem's even teaching me to swear.

She lighted the lamp and sat on the bed a moment, her pulses pounding. It was a simple idea that had occurred to her, extremely simple and obvious, but it was filled with possibilities that she sensed rather than saw clearly. Seven days on these great rivers of the West and her examination of the river fleets and concentrations at Cairo and Paducah had enormously stimulated her imagination. And she had just recalled a bit of advice her father had given her years ago.

"My dear girl, don't ever forget that the solution to a problem, however difficult, may often be found in the first humble person you meet."

Well—she had forgotten. She was now appalled by the fact that not once during her six weeks in St. Louis had she or Evans ever approached the trained pilots of the Mississippi. It was true they had scoured the water front and talked with innumerable dock workers and shipwrights, even asking an aimless question or two of quartermasters strolling along the levee. But not once had they interviewed a master pilot in regard to the problem they were attacking. St. Louis, before the war, had swarmed with able river pilots. A few were still here, although most of them had fled southward. The Mississippi Pilots Benevolent Association, with scores of famous pilots, was at the

150

height of its power and prestige. And the association's rooms were not two blocks away from the Denton House where Evans lived.

If ever she had wanted to curse like some stevedore and relieve her outraged sense of good judgment, now was the moment. She glared at her desk, piled high with a vast disarray of topographical maps of the Mississippi from Cairo to New Orleans and South Pass: county maps, Army maps, state maps, surveyors' maps, War Department maps, a detailed sectional map of the Memphis area. Over them all she had spent hours. And not once had she discussed these matters with the river pilots to whom these maps were nothing but children's blocks.

She pulled on a dressing gown and hurried downstairs to the desk. The night clerk, an early morning paper propped on a table, was stirring a cup of coffee. It was six-thirty.

"Mr. Page," she asked abruptly, "have you any river pilots staying at the Everett House now?"

Mr. Page, although surprised by such an inquiry at such an hour, answered politely.

"Why, surely, Miss Carroll. Captain Scott lives here, but he's down the river. Mrs. Scott is here. Charley's been on the river all his life." He glanced at the dusty wall clock. "She don't get up till about eight. Then there's Elisha Fine and Harry Benham, but I ain't seen 'em around for a few days."

She thought a moment. In this instance another woman, especially the wife of a pilot, might be an ideal intermediary.

"As soon as you think Mrs. Scott is up and around, will you ask her if I may see her immediately? It's most urgent, Mr. Page. I'll be in my room."

"Glad to, ma'am. She's a right pleasant lady. Want a paper, ma'am? I'm through with it. There was a real ruckus down at Belmont yesterday."

She took the paper absent-mindedly and walked back to her room. There, to divert her impatient mind, she began to read the first fragmentary accounts of the battle of Belmont the day before. Grant, the commanding general at Cairo, she read, had taken three thousand men down the river twenty miles on steamers, acting under Frémont's orders to "make a demonstration" against rebel troops at Belmont.

The Belmont adventure had almost been Grant's undoing. His troops, landing on the Missouri side at Fort Columbus a few miles above Belmont, had won a quick cheap victory by blindly firing quantities of ammunition at fleeing rebels they had hardly glimpsed. But the rebels had returned in strength and swept Grant's disorganized men, full of captured corn whisky, back on board their steamers,

151

fortunately protected by the timely arrival of two gunboats. Grant himself, disgustedly watching the rout, had slid his horse down the crumbling banks and across the flimsy gangplank under fire—the last man aboard his steamer.

The account ended, "The dead and wounded will be landed at the levee late this morning. General Grant is expected to report on the proceedings at Frémont's old headquarters, probably to General Hunter."

Obviously the whole affair had almost turned into disaster.

At a quarter to nine Mr. Merritt, who with his wife ran the Everett House, knocked on her door.

"Mrs. Scott will be glad to see you at once, ma'am. May I show you to her rooms?"

She found Mrs. Scott a pleasant, almost pretty little woman with pink cheeks, graying hair, and bright black eyes. She appeared to be under great strain and Anne soon learned why. Captain Scott had piloted one of the steamers at Belmont, and the Pilots Association had not yet heard from him. In spite of her anxiety, Mrs. Scott welcomed her and Anne began. Representing herself as a writer from Washington engaged by the government to prepare a descriptive book on the Western rivers, she sat and chatted with the pilot's wife until she felt that the other woman had become friendly and would arrange an introduction.

Mrs. Scott finally rose. "Miss Carroll, I'm worried sick about Charley. I know he didn't expect any fighting when he left here last week. But I'll send him right over to see you the minute he gets here. I promise you that."

For the moment there was nothing to do but wait. Lem had also been out of town for three days. She wondered if he, too, had been at Belmont. She sat in her room, increasingly worried and nervous, until eleven o'clock when Mr. Merritt knocked. He had news that dense smoke had been seen over Duncan's Island, south of town. The Union fleet from Belmont would be at the levee within an hour. Anne hurried to get her dark blue bonnet and cape.

When she emerged from the Everett House a few minutes later a great crowd was pouring out on the wide esplanade above the levee and surging toward the foot of Olive Street where the boats were expected to land.

The rain had ceased, but low ranks of gray cloud scudded across the choppy water. The approach of the steamers, signaled by the pall of smoke over Duncan's Island and the distant gleam of ships' metal, brought a faint cheer from the crowd. Conflicting reports from the battle had filtered through town all morning. Union sympathizers regarded it as a victory in spite of the disgraceful re-embarkation of the demoralized troops.

But when six dingy steamers, one with a perforated funnel leaning to port at a drunken angle, finally tied up to the levee, sudden silence gripped the crowd.

The first three ships were jammed with the wounded and the dead, who lay on the boiler decks in rows of motionless, shrouded figures. Dusty, disheveled men of the Fifth Iowa stood against the crowded guard rails. Anne turned for an instant from the shocking sight and saw that a long train of ambulances and Army wagons had lined up at the rear of the levee.

Looking again toward the river, she saw furious activity. Gangplanks had been lowered and groups of officers rushed ashore, shouting to friends and relatives. But the men were held aboard. And now the dead and wounded were taken off. She shivered. This, indeed, was a portion of that reality she prided herself on facing so courageously. Yet she moved closer to the nearest gangway and studied the faces, so many faces, on litter after litter bearing haggard dirty men, some bandaged, some in blood-clotted clothing, some white and still, all waiting to be carried to the waiting wagons.

Some waved gaily or feebly at the white massed faces watching them; some grinned and cracked old jokes. Others did not move at all. The troops began to pour ashore. She was about to leave when a voice she recognized froze her heart.

"Miss Carroll, ma'am—Miss Carroll!"

She whirled about and found herself looking into the cheerful face of Dale Duncan being borne across the levee on a canvas litter carried by four grinning troopers. He looked feverish but quite well and she ran to him.

"Dale! Dale! For heaven's sake, what happened?"

He shook his head a little, still smiling, "Tell you about it later, ma'am. Could you come along with me? I'm sure the family ain't here."

She followed the litter to the ambulance and spoke to a medical officer checking a casualty list. He shook his head. "Impossible, ma'am." She pulled out her papers, showed them to him, implored him, "Please, please. This boy is a relative of mine."

Her papers impressed him. Most of the ambulances had rumbled off. There were only two men in the canvas-covered wagon that waited for Dale.

"All right. But don't go in the barracks. They're too busy up there."

153

The surgeon quickly examined Dale. While the boy was being lifted into the ambulance the doctor came over to her and said almost brutally, "I'm letting you ride with him, ma'am, because he's finished —and we happen to have room. He's shot through the chest. Don't let him talk if you can help it."

Wordlessly, almost without thought, she climbed to the driver's seat, then pushed back to the straw-covered flooring and found herself next to Dale, seated between two litters. The other two men in the narrow ambulance were asleep or unconscious. Dale's brown eyes regarded her steadily as they started on the long ride to Benton Barracks.

She could not believe the medical officer's verdict. There was color in his cheeks. His eyes were bright. She began to stroke his forehead lightly as they rumbled over the rough stones.

"Don't talk, Dale," she whispered.

But they had not gone five blocks when he began to tremble slightly and her free hand found one of his and held it tightly. Another few blocks and she felt as though her heart would break. Blood had begun to trickle from his mouth. She wiped away the blood with her handkerchief. He was breathing heavily and quite suddenly all the bright confidence in his eyes had been plucked from them.

"I got to talk, ma'am," he said thickly. "I can't make it. I know I can't.

"Please don't talk, Dale." Panic struck her. "You mustn't talk. You'll be all right as soon as you get to the hospital."

He shook his head. "I ain't all right. I'm done for, ma'am."

A little later he began to fumble at the blanket.

"Lift me up, ma'am."

With unexpected strength he pulled his hand away and tore at his breast.

Oh dear God, don't let me faint, she prayed, and shifted herself so that his head was on her lap. His groping hand seemed to be reaching for something. Without thinking she pulled the blanket down a bit to aid him and almost screamed. His torn dusty shirt was soaked with blood running through a thick rough bandage about his chest. He was pulling feebly at her mother's locket around his neck. Hardly able to see through her tears, she found the clasp and unfastened it. He opened his eyes and smiled.

"Take it back, ma'am. It's yours." He pushed it weakly into her limp hand. To her consternation he began to cry.

"Don't, Dale. Don't," she implored him. He was trying to talk again, trying in painful gasps to say something that was important to him. She leaned her head close to his and heard him whisper:

154

"I can't help it, ma'am—I feel so terrible. Don't tell anyone—don't ever tell anyone—but I never got a chance to do anything. Never used my gun. Not once. I—I just walked off that damn boat into a cornfield and something hit me in the chest. Never even used my Sharp's rifle. Don't tell anyone that. I——"

The bitter tragedy of the useless soldier overwhelmed him and he closed his eyes again.

She sat dry-eyed, stunned, Dale's head in her lap, her stained hands shielding his head from the shocks of the muddy street. He was very quiet. Later—they had not even turned through the stone gates of Benton Barracks—he raised his head abruptly, said very clearly, "Miss Carroll!" and then choked and fell back, while bright blood poured from his mouth over the blue of her cloak.

When they finally stopped and the three litters were slid deftly from the ambulance, she sat where she was without moving. The young captain, peering into the ambulance, exclaimed, "My God, Sergeant, there's a woman in there. Are you hurt, ma'am?"

She did not answer, and they pulled her out, almost roughly, and stood her on the ground. She swayed slightly, her eyes dilated, and the captain called out, "Get some brandy, Mac. She's badly off. The youngster's dead."

The brandy burned her throat. She was conscious of the jammed yard, the rows of litters on the withered brown grass, the crowd about the dispensary, the drivers shouting and swearing, extricating wagons from a mass of tangled vehicles. She saw a wagonload of dead driving down to the little mortuary behind the barracks. Only the sergeant now stood beside her. The others had too much to do. He was a stocky, red-faced German with a dirty glass half full of brandy.

"So. Better—*nein?*"

"Dale!" she cried. "Where is he?" She was still unable to grasp what had happened.

"*Bitte*—please to go home, madam." He said with sudden impersonal anger, "Gottammit, they never should sent the poy here. It was crazy to moof him. He was your poy?"

She shook her head and the sergeant walked with her to a crowded horsecar waiting at the corner. He even found her a seat, and in the turmoil and excitement no one paid any attention to her bloodstained cloak.

So she returned to the city, numbly clutching Julianna's bloodstained locket in one white hand.

155

19

SHE REMAINED IN HER ROOM THE REST OF THE DAY.
The shock of Dale's death had been great and she was stunned and
shaken by her first intimate look at war. But all she had seen, she
knew, was but a glimpse of war, the faintest beginning of beginnings,
a mere hint of the carnage and slaughter to come. What could she do?
What could she *do?* Somehow the Union must seize the initiative and
hasten this dreadful thing to an early end.

Mrs. Scott had left the hotel in midafternoon. Evans had not appeared. Pilot Scott had not appeared. She was alone. At six, Mrs.
Merritt brought a hot supper to her room. She began to feel better
and cleared the table and sat down at her maps again, though Dale's
face kept coming between her and the brightly colored papers.

This time she concentrated all her attention on that vital area of
the Mississippi Basin extending from Cairo to Memphis and including
the Ohio, Cumberland, and Tennessee rivers, the latter entering the
Ohio at Paducah, which she had recently visited. Again she was
fascinated by the overwhelming role of the Memphis and Charleston
Railroad, striking directly east from Memphis, the great backbone and
supply line of the Confederacy.

She traced the railroad eastward through Corinth, Tuscumbia, and
Decatur, in Alabama. Something shook in her mind. The river was
the problem—not the railroad. But the railroad led straight east,
through the whole heart of the Confederacy. And Evans had hammered home time and again that any effective blow to be struck
must rip into that heart, must tear open the Deep South, destroy its
great arteries, the supply lines.

The great and damnable Father of Waters not only flowed the

156

wrong way, but also it was merely part of the perimeter of the South. If the entire Mississippi River were seized the immense rebel hinterland would still remain to be conquered.

If there were only *some* river, *any* river, that not only *flowed the other way* but might give access to that hinterland. "Hammer the heart! Hammer the heart!" Evans had said, and all she could see was a rebel-held railroad leading to that heart. Once again, and quite mechanically, her pencil traced the Memphis and Charleston Railroad from Memphis to a point a few miles east of Corinth. There her pencil suddenly stopped and dropped from her fingers. Mr. Lincoln's comment, "I guess we need a river that flows the other way," a sentence echoed by Sherman and Eads, now roared in her ears. For she was looking straight at a river that answered this first great requirement.

She looked—and the new and breath-taking interpretation of this familiar map struck her like a blow in the face. Not a hundred miles east of the Mississippi, and paralleling it for another hundred miles, was a river that ran in an exactly opposite direction to the Mississippi, a stream that actually did flow the other way, *from south to north*. And a great bend of this stream lay but a few miles from the Memphis and Charleston Railroad and was later crossed by this railroad—twice.

She was looking at the Tennessee River, and she had stared at its wandering course hundreds of times and never understood what she did now.

Her mind worked at top speed as she traced its course eastward, upstream, and it flashed upon her in a single moment of stunning insight that this remarkable river met the greatest requirement of all, that it performed a function far greater than the Mississippi, that it met all that destiny demanded—and more. For here was a river that not only flowed out of the whole vast vulnerable heart of the Confederacy, and flowed in the right direction—from south to north—but its very source springs were within striking distance of Atlanta in far-off Georgia. It flowed through Chattanooga, only one hundred and thirty-odd miles from Atlanta. It actually paralleled the Memphis and Charleston Railroad for miles and was twice crossed by this key railroad between Decatur and Memphis. And it flowed across the Deep South, westward across north Alabama, through a corner of Mississippi, and *north* through Tennessee—straight to the Union stronghold of Paducah on the Ohio River.

She went back and retraced the steps by which she had arrived at this astounding discovery as if to dispel some tantalizing fantasy. But the more she studied this map, as if it were some astonishing vision

157

from another world, the greater became her conception of the role this river might play. The Tennessee River at once became a key to every strategic center of the South. And there was not only one river that flowed from south to north. There were *two*. East and north of the Tennessee flowed the Cumberland, swinging out of Nashville and flowing northwest and north to Smithland on the Ohio, also in Union hands.

Then she was studying Mobile Bay and her eye raced northward along the courses of the Alabama and Tombigbee rivers. And how close the railroad and the Tennessee River were to the headwaters of the Tombigbee! and how close to Chattanooga, on the Tennessee, were the headwaters of the Alabama! And how close, too, was all of this vital area to Atlanta and the approaches to Charleston and the sea, and the broad valleys reaching northeastward to Richmond!

She dared not carry the germ of her great idea any farther. She knew nothing of these rivers, nothing of their currents, soundings, or navigation. Until she did, she dared not venture farther. She could not even afford to believe in the upheaval going on in her mind.

She knew the Cumberland and Tennessee had been suggested as avenues of relief for Union sympathizers in eastern Tennessee. But even this local operation had not been deemed practical, for the rebels had constructed two wilderness works named Forts Henry and Donelson on these streams near the Kentucky border. Surely the War Department, the Engineers at least, had examined these water-courses and rejected them, perhaps because they were navigable only two or three months of the year.

But, as this map held her hypnotized, she could not stop the great forward leaps of her imagination. Dimly but surely she began to see the outlines of something vaster—an over-all strategy of the war—opening up avenues of cleavage that could draw and quarter the Con-federacy as no other route even suggested. Gone were the perimeters of the Confederacy. The Atlantic and Gulf coasts, the whole length of the Mississippi, fell away into shadow.

With her new gift of vision Anne was staring straight into the exposed heart of the whole rebel area, and the magic function of the Tennessee River exalted her.

She walked excitedly about her room for an hour. How could they all have been so blind! The more she studied the Tennessee Valley, the more glaring became the blindness of all of them. For another great fact burst on her consciousness, as if suddenly released by her earlier discoveries. She had studied the political complexion of this area many times. And contrary to most civil and military opinion, the whole farming belt along the Tennessee, much of north Alabama,

158

and almost all of east Tennessee, while nominally rebel territory, had remained loyal to the Union. This she knew to be true. And this meant that even with only limited forces available the Union armies could successfully invade this land. They would, in sober fact, be invading territory for the most part loyal. And this loyal belt ran right up to Chattanooga and the gates of Georgia!

About nine that night Evans found her in her rooms standing by a window, staring out. She was tense and terribly excited, her blue eyes blazing in a paper-white face. About her were her maps, marked and noted, strewn on her bed, on the floor, and torn crumpled sheets of paper tossed everywhere. He had come in with muddied boots and grime on his face.

"Hello there, I've been down the river to Belmont and listen to this——" he began, and then stopped short, shocked at her appearance. "Great God, Anne, what's happened?"

She began to tell him coherently enough of the day's events. Then the long-overdue storm broke and she clung to him, sobbing, for the memory of Dale and the other tragedies of that day would not even begin to fade.

Later, while he ate a hastily assembled supper, she told him about her visit to Mrs. Scott and her idea of talking to a river pilot. He struck the edge of the table with his hand.

"You're right," he said vehemently. "We've been stupid. Incredibly stupid. I've heard of Charles Scott, by the way. He's a first-rate pilot —been on the rivers all his life. It's quite possible he could help us."

She was eager to share with him the first dim outlines of the ideas seething in her mind. But she could not bear to have them both disappointed if the whole plan were a mad dream. First she must ask the pilot one question. She forced herself to spend the evening helping him draft reports and dispatches of their river trip and the results of interviews at Cairo to be sent to the Attorney General and Tom Scott. When they had finished and he rose to go, he told her that Harry had been placed on the *Helena* that afternoon with a large group of exchanged officers and political prisoners and was now on the river bound south for Memphis.

"I didn't think it best to see him again," said Evans. "But I was told he was amazed he'd been exchanged and that he was convinced you and I had full details, possibly even new plans, in our possession for the Mississippi River expedition. I breathed easier."

"I don't wonder," she said in a low voice. He noticed her pallor and took in the disordered maps and paper-strewn floor once more.

"Still battling?" he asked sympathetically.

159

To his astonishment she came over and put her arms around him and kissed him hard, then pushed him, while he protested, to the door.

"Lem," she said with an odd and exciting smile, "this weary brain of mine is beginning to bloom again. Tomorrow is Sunday. Captain Scott *must* come to see us. He has to. And I want you over here early —and all day, mind. I have to get lots of sleep. And now, good night, sweetheart."

After he had gone she undressed, got into bed, and slept like a child.

Evans breakfasted with her at nine and at eleven o'clock he was sitting at her table, writing the last of his cipher telegrams. Anne, walking nervously up and down, through parlor and bedroom, had made him jumpy. A few minutes after eleven the hotel boy knocked on her door and she ran to open it.

"Pilot Scott's in the parlor, ma'am. He's waiting to see you."

"Lem!" Her voice was almost hysterical with relief. "Don't move out of this room! Wait until I come back."

The door slammed behind her with a crash that rattled the little room and left Evans openmouthed.

In the parlor of the Everett House she walked as if on eggshells to meet the man who had come to see her. At first, sitting stiffly upright on the narrow horsehair sofa, he appeared stolid and likely to be unresponsive. When he rose to greet her she was immensely reassured. He was a tall, wiry man who moved easily and quickly. He was wearing a rather nondescript pepper-and-salt suit, with a heavy gold chain securely anchoring a watch hidden in a pearl-gray vest. But what impressed her most about the pilot were the shrewd, intelligent, bright brown eyes that watched her so warily from under shaggy level brows. Below a mass of thick curly brown hair his high clear forehead gave him a surprisingly almost scholarly appearance. His face, the color of mahogany, was crisscrossed with fine lines.

There was something about his settled watchful wariness, together with a kind of well-knit timeless solidity, that made her think of some age-darkened carving from resistant driftwood. He was altogether a remarkable figure. There was a touch of Southern drawl in his voice. "Cap'n Scott's my name, ma'am. Charles M. Scott. I reckon you wanted to see me," he said.

"Yes, Captain Scott, yes." In tumbling haste she repeated the role she had played for Mrs. Scott, mentioning her book, her interest in the Western rivers, and a possible history of the war. Her shaking hands

160

showed him her credentials. He seemed completely unimpressed, and the suspicion in his eyes seemed to increase.

"I'm only a pilot, ma'am. I know the river channels. That's all. Don't see where I can help you much. I been up thirty-eight hours without sleep."

He was obviously puzzled by her nervousness and remained standing although she had seated herself before him. His eyes told her he wished to leave.

"Please sit down for just a moment, Captain Scott," she pleaded. At last, to her great relief, he did so, sitting on the edge of his chair as if ready to flee, and watching her intently.

"I understand you are a Union pilot, Captain Scott, working for the Army—and that you were at Belmont this week."

"Yes, ma'am. I am—and I was," he said briefly.

"For whom do you work?" she asked.

He hesitated and his eyes narrowed. "Wa—al—I'm General Grant's chief pilot, ma'am. I'm aboard his headquarters boat, *Belle of Memphis.*"

He noticed her startled expression and his alert brown eyes never left her face.

"Then you've been a long time on the river?" she asked eagerly.

"Rivers, ma'am. All of them. About forty years."

Forty years? It seemed incredible—he did not look a day over fifty. He must have read her thoughts, for he said stiffly, "I keelboated when I was thirteen, ma'am. Cooked for three years for crews on the Tombigbee."

"Captain Scott," she said unsteadily, "let me be frank. I am terribly upset this morning. A very dear friend of mine was wounded at Belmont and died yesterday. But—but Mr. Lincoln himself has asked me to find out what rivermen think of the Army's New Orleans expedition. That is the real purpose of my seeking you. I am writing a book about this war. You are an experienced pilot. These New Orleans plans—what do pilots think about them? Have *you* thought about them, Captain Scott?"

He evidently had. He scowled and pushed back his unruly hair. His cheeks puffed out as he vainly looked for a cuspidor. Then he relaxed and studied her for a few moments. Suddenly he barked, "So Mr. Lincoln asked you to find that out?"

She nodded, not daring to trust her voice, and he snorted contemptuously.

"Then why'n hell don't his generals talk to the Pilots Association?" he said with quick vehemence. "It's sure death for any man, ship, regiment, command, or expedition now figgered to go down the river

161

now, next month, the month after—or till hell freezes, beggin' yore pardon, ma'am. Every pilot in the association knows that. But nobody's ever asked 'em."

Surprisingly enough, he began to thaw out as she questioned him about the Mississippi, fearfully exploring his mind, wishing to lead him on to the terrible question that tightened her throat. It was the mention of the Mississippi that turned loose, with a rapidity which amazed her, the storehouse of river lore he possessed. Scott began to talk. He talked easily, rapidly, in pungent, picturesque phrases, of crossings, chutes, riffles, the bend above Island 66, the great bend at New Madrid, the square crossing at Higgins's woodyard, the clouds of bagasse smoke at night that blinded pilots and had lined the wooded banks with wrecks for miles, the crossing marks at Hole-in-the-Wall, the shape of Walnut Bend, the strength of the current in Fort Adams Reach, the exasperating intricacies of Hat Island, Twelve Mile Point, Nine Mile Point, and every sounding on the approaches to New Orleans. Above all, he emphasized the bluffs along the east bank in Tennessee. "It ain't possible to take, sneak by, pass, or crawl under Vicksburg by the river, ma'am. Anybody tries is a plain damn fool and food for the devil."

She said timidly, "Do you know the whole river from St. Louis to New Orleans like this, Captain Scott?"

He looked at her scornfully, pityingly.

"Ma'am," he said quietly, as if soothing a baby, "I know every snag, riffle, pass, bank, crossing, marker, dead tree, reach, sounding, bluff, chute, island, and the difference in water level by the month from two hundred miles up the Missouri to Cincinnati and back to N'Awleens. If you got six hours I'll recite 'em."

She took a deep breath and began to warm to this amazing creature.

"Mobile Bay," she said abruptly. "Have you worked there?"

"I tol' you, ma'am," he retorted with a trace of irritation, "I know *all* the rivers from the Gulf to Pittsburgh. If you want soundings on the Tombigbee or Alabama rivers, or three channels through the delta besides South Pass—you can have 'em."

"All right, Captain Scott," she said breathlessly, her cheeks flushed. "Then tell me this——" She paused and moistened her lips. *"How much water is there in the Tennessee and Cumberland rivers? Can the Eads gunboats get up either of those streams? Think, Captain Scott! Think hard, and give me your best estimate."*

"Ma'am, let me tell you something," retorted Scott explosively, his weather-beaten face a darker hue, "I don't think, guess, estimate, or calkerlate. I *know*. An' don't you fergit it. Now then, yes—those scows of Eads can get up the Cumberland, to Nashville in high water, mebbe, but only 'bout fifty miles up from the Ohio at low water. But up the Tennessee—yes, ma'am, *all the way,* most any time."

She jumped from her chair and stood over him like some supplicant.

"*All the way,* Captain? In heaven's name, how far is that?"

"As fur as any fool wants to go these days," retorted Scott, his sharp eyes twinkling. "Plenty of water in the Tennessee all year. Right to Pittsburg Landing, to Hamburg, to Florence, and clear to the foot of Muscle Shoals in north Alabama. You seem mighty excited, ma'am," he added dryly. "You thinkin' of goin' there?"

"Oh dear God!" she exclaimed fervently. "Stay here, Captain Scott. Just five minutes more, I implore you. I have a friend to bring down."

She vanished in a swirl of petticoats and dashed up the stairs. As soon as she reached the landing she called out: "Lem! Lem! Come here!" and rushed down the carpeted corridor toward her rooms.

Hearing her cries, Evans ran into the hall. The light from a window at the end of the hallway outlined the figure rushing toward him. She stopped short a few feet away, almost bursting with the pent-up force of her ideas.

"Lem, listen to me! Listen to me and tell me what you think! What would you say to——" She paused and fairly gulped for air. "What would you think of diverting the Western armies from the Mississippi, putting them on transports, taking the entire gunboat fleet, and hurling the whole force up the Tennessee River—not the Mississippi, the *Tennessee,* Lem—right into the heart of the traitors' nest, straight into Mississippi and Alabama, straight to Chattanooga, just one hundred and thirty-eight miles from Atlanta and the rear approaches to Richmond. *Look at this map!*"

She dragged him into her parlor, tore the map in her eagerness to unfold it, traced with flying fingers the major outlines of her plan. He was looking at the map as if it were going to bite him.

"Well?" she demanded with sudden belligerence, frightened by his silence. "Say something!"

But he could not. For the first time in his life Evans was looking at the map through her eyes.

"Lem," she pleaded. "Please, please."

He straightened up with an oddly blank expression on his face.

"It may be so," he said cautiously. "I had never thought of it. There's plenty of water?"

She told him of her conversation with Scott. "He's downstairs right now, Lem. Please."

But he bent over the table again, as if invisibly bound to her map.

When he finally turned around his eyes were black points that bored into hers.

"When did you think of this?" he demanded in a strange voice.

"Yesterday—oh, I don't really know! It's been coming on me. Quickly, Lem."

"Wait a minute, Anne." He was struggling to combat the magnitude of her discovery.

"By God!" he finally exploded. "I do believe that's it. That's the move! It's got to be!"

"Then I'm determined to have it done!" she cried excitedly. "And come downstairs quickly, Lem. He's a strange creature. I'm afraid he'll leave."

They ran downstairs and found Scott warier than ever, completely baffled by the hectic reception he had met. She introduced Evans and said with quick frankness:

"Captain Scott, please trust us both. I've been most upset, as I told you. Please believe in us. Mr. Evans is doing confidential work for the War Department. We cannot obtain information about these rivers from the Army. They seem to know nothing of the subject. If you will help us I'll make it very much worth your while."

A little more slowly this time, Captain Scott thawed out again. She found almost immediately that he had little but contempt for the Army, and again she played upon one of his prejudices. He damned again every half-baked plan ever projected for forcing the Mississippi.

"It can't be done in a month o' Sundays with every rebel lyin' dead in bed," he exclaimed, and began rambling on about the state of the Army which, he said, was full of nothing but spies, traitors, and malingerers. Anne drew him over the ground he had covered before and noticed Evans's rising excitement. Finally his eyes signaled her and he took over the questioning of Scott.

"Captain, just to digress a moment, what is your opinion of Frémont?"

Scott pulled the end of his mustache and his shaggy eyebrows almost came together.

"Well, sir," he said at last, almost slyly, "he's like fried wool— greatly mixed."

Evans burst out laughing. "Well, sir, that's the shortest and best definition of Frémont I ever heard."

They chatted about Frémont a bit and then Evans switched the subject abruptly to Mobile Bay.

"Tell me, Captain, could a deep-water fleet and armored craft get over Dog River Bar at high water?"

164

"Wa-al, that's a problem, sir. They might have to lighten the heavier ships a mite. But they could make it on the proper tides."

"How far up is the Tombigbee River navigable for gunboats, Captain?"

"Clear to Demopolis for the next five months," said Scott emphatically.

"And the Alabama River?"

At top speed, Scott began to rattle off soundings and data on markers and crossings, running up both rivers from Mobile Harbor. Evans watched him, practically openmouthed with admiration.

To their astonishment they found Scott was widely read; he discussed in considerable detail the character of all the great rivers of North America.

"The Mississippi needs a lot of taming," he observed at one point. "The engineers can spend years on it. My own idea is a series of flood-control dams, and power dams, maybe. Also a proper ship canal right across Illinois to control the water level in dry seasons. The Great Lakes can stand the necessary tapping."

Another hour, packed with Scott's comments, went by.

"You ever been up the Tennessee around Muscle Shoals, Captain?" Evans asked innocently. Scott's face turned the color of an overripe plum. He sat up very straight, arms akimbo, his sinewy fists on his thighs.

"I been asked a lot o' questions, mister. I don't know yore game. But I reckon I'll do a little talkin' now to set you folks straight on a few things. Fust off, about myself. I told this lady I keelboated on the Tombigbee as a boy. I cooked at thirteen. Used to float down on the cotton boats to Mobile, work our way to N'Awleens, steamboat up to Memphis, walk cross-country to Eastport, opposite Waterloo, on the Tennessee. Then up the Tennessee, cross to the Tombigbee, an' start all round the circle again. You, Mr. Evans, you wuz prob'ly in knee pants when I took the first steamboat up the Tennessee in '31. I laid the warps for her over the Muscle Shoals."

"Good lord, Captain, I remember that. I was born within a few miles of the Muscle Shoals. I was seven years old then." He turned eagerly to Anne. "It was a great event. Fifteen years before I left for Texas. By heavens, Captain, that was the old Knoxville, wasn't it?"

Scott grunted but looked pleased. "It was the Knoxville, all right."

"Later on, in '38," he continued, "I helped Gen'l Winfield Scott take out the Cherokees. A dirty deal on them redskins, it was, too. I was mate on the same boat that brought 'em out from Fort Cass, opposite Calhoun, on the Tennessee. Then I served ten months under

165

Sam Houston and fin'lly settled in N'Awleens. Elisha Fine taught me pilotin'. So did the LaBarges. Later on I worked with Uncle Davy and Captain Sellers, a North Carolina man an' the best god-damn pilot on the river, beggin' yore pardon, ma'am. Also worked the *Natchez* of Vicksburg with Captain Tom Leathers; the *Altona,* fast as a reindeer; the big three-decker *Mayflower* that burned seven months after her first trip; I reckon I piloted a heap o' good boats— mostly the *Ed Shippen, Belle of the West, Eclipse, Princess, Ben Franklin No. 6,* and last year the *General Quitman* till the war broke out."

"When did you get out of New Orleans?" asked Evans a little sharply.

Scott regarded him coldly.

"Mr. Evans, there was a hundred and fifty-three association pilots in St. Louis when Sumter was fired on. About a hundred and forty-seven headed South. They figgered whoever held the lower reaches ran the river. About six of us who were already in N'Awleens came back Nawth. I come up in June, with a quarter interest in my boat, the *White Queen.* I got as fur as Memphis when General Gideon J. Pillow grabbed us. He refused us passage to St. Louis and locked me up. I busted out and headed for Cairo, went to Ohio to get my wife, brought her to St. Louis, went back to Cairo, reported to General Prentiss, and along about September twentieth, I reckon, was put on Grant's headquarters boat, *Belle of Memphis.* There's my story. What's yours?" he concluded truculently.

Something in the timbre of Scott's voice, under the soft layers of years of living in New Orleans, had caught Anne's ear.

"Captain, are you by any chance from Ireland?" she asked.

For the first time on that momentous Sunday, Scott grinned broadly.

"How'd you guess that, ma'am? Yes'm. I was born on the Auld Sod, but my old man was a native of Ohio. Ma was on a visit to Londonderry. When I was three we came back and I was raised in Pittsburgh. Then I went to Ohio and married. Ella Anna Fish, her name was."

Evans laughed and looked teasingly at Anne. "Miss Carroll's name is Anna Ella, and she's Irish too," he said gravely.

Scott grinned. "Well, either way, forwards or backwards, it's a good name, ma'am."

But in spite of these pleasantries Scott dropped back into his old shell of suspicion. He said a little sharply after further conversation:

"Let's get down to tacks. What's all this pullin' and haulin' about these rivers? If I can trust you folks, I'll help. But in this rotten town I don't trust nobody, an' that's a fact."

Evans ran upstairs, came down with every official paper in their possession, and spread them before Scott. But Anne, greatly excited, went even farther. To Scott's obvious surprise she got up and closed the door, then sat next to him on the sofa and began to tell him the truth.

"Captain Scott," she said, "I'll be frank. Now that you've confirmed my hope that the Tennessee River is navigable, it is my idea to divert all the available Union forces from this absurd New Orleans project, push them instead up the Tennessee into Mississippi and north Alabama as far as Muscle Shoals, and put the Union Army astride the Memphis and Charleston Railroad. We're going to urge the government to do this and to seize Mobile and push our forces northward from there. From these new bases it should be possible to move quickly on Chattanooga and Atlanta, to push across Georgia to the sea, and drive up the coastal valleys to Richmond, if necessary, to split the Confederacy in two! That's why your information is so vital, Captain. Neither Mr. Evans nor I, nor anyone else, apparently, thought of the Tennessee for such a purpose. I now believe it to be the sole key to Union victory. Do you see what you've done for us?"

In growing astonishment Scott studied her for several seconds. His bright brown eyes became brighter. She heard him breathe deeply.

"Good lord, ma'am, you—you mean this ain't been discussed with the military?"

Evans quickly interposed:

"Just that, Pilot. The President, who knows something of these Western rivers, is the man to convince. That we have yet to do."

Scott whistled in greater astonishment. But his judgment was rushing to confirm their own conclusions.

"By God, it makes sense," he said slowly, "the only sense I've heard or seen out here. You folks have something, something mighty big. No doubt about it. Why——"

Scott had a maplike mind. As his mind's eye roved up the Tennessee Valley, startling vistas opened before him. His eyes snapped with excitement as they turned again from Evans to Anne.

"You folks know what you've got on the fire?" he barked. "Look here, ma'am——"

He got up, walked across the room, suddenly turned and faced them.

"It's right. It's right," he burst out. "You put a strong fleet up the Tennessee and you can turn the flank of every damn fort on the Mississippi clear to Vicksburg without firing a shot on that river.

No doubt about it! And every town and battery on the Cumberland, too. Good God A'mighty!" He was visualizing all the Tennessee River and its contiguous territory. "Columbus, Memphis, Vicksburg on the right. And on the left flank—Bowling Green, Nashville, and Chattanooga. Not a one could stand if this were carried out right. And Mobile, eh? And the Tombigbee? Why, Chattanooga ain't but a hundred and thirty-odd miles from Atlanta! You can bust the South wide open that way—and it's the only way!"

Scott mopped his forehead, abruptly sat down, breathing heavily. He was stunned by what his imagination now encompassed in this simple advance up the Tennessee.

"Why'n hell ain't the military thought of this?" he demanded.

"You pointed that out, Pilot," retorted Evans. "Has Grant or anyone else ever asked you about these rivers?"

"Never did," replied Scott. "They don't trust the pilots. Most of 'em ran South, don't forget." He ran a hand nervously through his hair.

"Let's get this straight," he said with a trace of his old suspicion. "You two mean to sit there and tell me you figgered this out yourselves—and my information on the Tennessee clinched it?"

"Yes," replied Anne, but Evans roughly interrupted her.

"No, Captain, I hadn't a damn thing to do with this. Get that clear. I'm as stunned as you are. The credit for the whole idea belongs to Miss Carroll. It was she who talked to your wife, who begged her to get you over here."

Scott looked at Anne unbelievingly, but there was a light in his brown eyes he could not hide. He was lost in wonder again.

"By the Lord, ma'am, you're right. The Tennessee *is* the true key, the only key, to the whole situation. Ain't a doubt about it." He grinned ruefully. "Wonder I didn't think of it myself. But great Jehovah, folks, how you aimin' to put this thing across?"

It was Evans who now got up and paced the room.

"Let's tackle this bit by bit, Pilot. What are you planning to do the next few days?"

Scott seemed surprised. "Wal, I don't rightly know. My old lady's got a lot of fixin' for me to do in the new house, and Grant's given me ten days to git back to Cairo. The *Memphis* blew a cylinder head at Belmont. I ain't got a boat for a few days. They've promised me the *Emerald*."

Evans stopped before the pilot. "Captain, suppose I secured your release from the general for two weeks. Would you undertake a survey trip with me to the mouths of the Tennessee and Cumberland rivers?"

168

"For whut purpose?" demanded Scott.

"Why—soundings, getting the draft of the gunboats and river craft. Determining just how feasible this whole idea is."

Scott looked at Evans pityingly, even scornfully.

"Mr. Evans," he said, as if he had been insulted, "there's no need of that. I can write out all the soundings you want on both rivers right on that wall there. Eads has all the information you need on the gunboats. I know all about the transports."

"In that case, would you work with us?" He caught a stubborn refusal in Scott's eyes and added quickly, "May I ask—what do you make a month?"

"Five hundred dollars a month and found," said Scott laconically, and then grunted, "But not in this man's Army."

Anne was astonished at such pay, not having known that it was the regular wage of first-class association pilots on the river. She looked quickly at Lem's face. If he was surprised, he did not show it.

"Well, sir, I'm prepared to get your release from Grant for two weeks and pay you five hundred dollars to work with us in mapping out this whole scheme and backing it up with your figures."

Scott opened his mouth, closed it, leaned back in his chair, and rubbed his nose thoughtfully. Finally he snapped, "I'll take it."

To his obvious amazement Evans pulled out a great wad of currency and counted off five hundred dollars. Scott stared at the money, then quietly picked it up and folded it into a worn brown wallet.

"Only with Grant's say-so," he said brusquely. "What time you want me to go to work with you folks?"

"Tomorrow morning at nine o'clock—right here, Captain. You'll have your proper papers. I want to add we both owe you a great debt, sir, a very great debt. If you'll play with us we'll repay it tenfold."

Scott got up, smiling broadly, and unexpectedly gracious.

"I'll play. I take it everybody's to be mighty mum about this."

"Good lord, yes," said Evans emphatically.

"Don't you worry none. I'll take my money this once—and that's all. It's my belief," went on Captain Scott solemnly, "that it's the duty of every man to do all the good he can for his country without regard to self. That is my ruling notion. That's why I got out of New Orleans and lost my shirt. But I don't meet too many of like kind. If you folks are square, I'll play with you as long as you want."

"You won't regret it, Captain," said Anne fervently. "Then you'll be here tomorrow?"

Don't you worry," retorted Scott, grinning. "And if your friend here can wangle a two weeks' pass from the Old Man at this kind o' time—that's good enough for me. Good day, folks."

They heard him pound off down the street before they dared break the hush that lay between them. Evans was gazing at the vacant chair Scott had just left.

"Where did you find him? Where did you find this fellow?" he insisted. "He's got the whole damn country in his head. Every bit of it."

He got up and took Anne's arm. She was saying, "You see, Lem, it can be done with the forces we have, for most of Tennessee and north Mississippi and Alabama is loyal. You understand what that means? And that blessed Tennessee, it runs the *right way*. It runs north——"

He didn't hear her at all. He was shaken with excitement. He led her upstairs, down the hallway, into her room, and began immediately to sharpen pencils, lay out maps and tracing paper, rulers, military protractors, and other paraphernalia. Silently, on the same side of her table, they both sat down. Together they went to work.

20

TOM SCOTT'S SERVANT CAME TO THE DOORWAY OF HIS study at nine o'clock on the evening of November 30.

"Miss Carroll, sir," he announced.

"All right, Jim. Tell her I'll be down in three minutes."

His face grave, the Assistant Secretary of War picked up a batch of papers and glanced through them, then quickly descended the stairs. His visitor was standing by his desk in the library, smiling, and he was struck by her handsome appearance. A sharp wind had whipped high color in her cheeks. Her hair was swept back in blond waves under an impudent turban of autumn brown that emphasized its golden lights. Scott was instantly aware of some new quality in her. There was an assurance in her bearing, a maturity of expression, and an eloquence in her level gaze that impressed him.

"A thousand welcomes, my dear lady," he exclaimed with all his old charm, studying her shrewdly. "When did you arrive in town?"

He pulled out a chair for her. She put her muff on the table and sat down much as if she were paying him a mere social call. But as he watched her Scott began to feel unaccountably on the defensive. Her whole being seemed charged with energy and determination. Her blue eyes were very bright and never left his face, and she must have guessed his thoughts.

"I've come to do battle, Tom," she announced at once. "You might as well be prepared for it. And I warn you—it's going to be a real Irish tug of war. I went up to spend a few days with Millard Fillmore in Buffalo. I had to talk to him. We prepared some papers for you."

She did not tell him that Evans had traveled with her and edited her whole presentation at Mr. Fillmore's home.

171

"So Millard's giving you legal advice?" queried Scott.

"Not exactly. But he's a very dear friend and knows how to construct a concise brief out of sound arguments, even in military matters," she said pointedly.

"Will you have some sherry?" Scott temporized. "That's a chill north wind—though I see it's brought roses with it." He glanced smilingly at her cheeks.

"Thank you, Tom, I will," she replied, and leaned back in the deep chair and relaxed a little. He was eying the papers she had removed from her muff as if trying to gauge their contents, and she noted the set of his jaw and the glint in his Irish blue eyes. So it's going to be a fight, she reflected, and decided to give him a little more time.

"And you, Tom, and Washington?" she asked after a swallow of sherry. "Are we still going to the dogs?"

He turned the glass slowly and appeared to examine the color of the wine before he spoke. "We've gone," he finally said. "I think Europe will be at war with us in sixty days. The British are enraged over this Mason and Slidell affair. Have you seen any London papers?"

She nodded. "Some."

"Look at this sample of the British press." He gave her a marked copy of the London *Morning Chronicle* of a fortnight earlier and she read the following paragraph:

Abraham Lincoln, whose accession to power was generally welcomed on this side of the Atlantic, has proved himself a feeble, confused, and little-minded mediocrity. Mr. Seward, the firebrand at his elbow, is exerting himself to provoke a quarrel with all Europe in that spirit of senseless egotism which induces the Americans, with their dwarf fleet, and shapeless mass of incoherent squads which they call an army, to fancy themselves the equal of France by land, and of Great Britain by sea. While these mischiefmakers stagger on at the head of affairs, their only chance of fame consists in the probability that the navies of England will blow out of the water their blockading squadrons and teach them how to respect the flag of a mightier supremacy beyond the Atlantic.

Without comment she handed back the clipping.

"Read this." He handed her a memorandum from the Navy Department. "The entire British and French navies are being readied for war," he said. "There are mass meetings all over England. Eight thousand more of their best troops sailed for Canada from Plymouth and Southampton last week."

As she studied it, her lips set in a firm line.

"I *have* been away," she said. "I had thought, in spite of Seward,

172

that this was chiefly a press battle. I had no idea how far things have gone."

"That's not the half of it," returned Scott. "A tremendous struggle on a world-wide scale may be shaping up. Cassius Clay cabled yesterday from St. Petersburg that the Russians are enraged by the British moves. They're the only power friendly to us on the Continent. Prince Gortchakoff promised Clay he'll place a Russian fleet in New York Harbor, and if the French insist on pushing their insane Mexican venture he'll place another Russian fleet in San Francisco Bay. And he will! He told Clay they're still smarting over the Crimean War and will positively not permit England or France to gain any supremacy over here. They're worried, too, about Alaska and their fur trade."

Scott was watching her keenly and lightly tapping the arm of his chair. She voiced a silent prayer, took a deep breath, and plunged into the heart of her problem.

"Then some immediate military success on the part of the Union is especially imperative now, is it not?" she asked in a deceptively mild voice. "I have some new material on my proposed Tennessee campaign, Tom. Frankly, because of this fresh information, I ignored your brief note that came just before I left St. Louis. Have you come to any new conclusions on the matter?"

It seemed to her as if Scott braced himself anew, and his head with the handsome features and brilliant blue eyes went up a little defiantly.

"There's no use mincing words, ma'am. Our final decision was in that letter. Bates and I discussed your suggestion thoroughly. But Bates is determined to clear the river to New Orleans and I confess I lean to his opinion. Welles is already talking of having Farragut head the huge expedition now being fitted to take New Orleans from the Gulf through South Pass. The two expeditions could join forces at New Orleans. This is what Bates wants. However, I did outline verbally to McClellan the suggestion of a gunboat advance up the Tennessee. I also mentioned it to Andrew Johnson."

"And what did they say?" she asked tensely.

"If you must know," said Scott mildly, "McClellan said, 'Not even a tyro would propose such an absurdity as an unsupported river expedition up a shallow stream directly into hostile fortified territory.' He said that furthermore it would need a hundred thousand troops marching by land just to protect the boats. Anyway, Senator Johnson, from Tennessee himself, stated flatly he didn't think there was nearly enough water in the Tennessee for any such purpose. I'm afraid that disposes of the matter."

Anne's face was crimson.

173

"The senator," she snapped, losing her temper, "either lies or is an idiot. As for McClellan—he's a fool. My respect for McClellan vanished long ago."

Scott sat up abruptly. His vigorous voice hardened.

"Just a moment, ma'am. The general happens to be the commander in chief of our armies with a degree more military experience than your own. And Johnson knows Tennessee as well as his own back yard. He laughed at the idea."

Scott was thoroughly angry. She bit her lips and began again, holding up the papers in her lap.

"Tom, let's not quarrel. Please. But the general and Senator Johnson are completely mistaken. This is too vital, too important. I ask only one favor. The suggestions I sent you on a Tennessee campaign were loose, tentative, unsupported by a mass of relevant facts now available. Please consider them merely a general introduction to the complete plan I have here. I beg of you to sit down now and let me read the over-all plan to you. You can then examine the other material at your leisure. I'm convinced I can change your mind. You know we all face ruin if some sound plan is not put into action soon."

Scott shook his head. "I can't do it, Anne. I'm swamped with a dozen projects. Leave it here if you wish. I'll look it over in the next few days."

But the force of her own faith overwhelmed her and made her recklessly insistent. She managed to control her temper, but she stood up quickly, walked over to Scott, and threw all the papers but one onto his lap. Even Scott was inclined to flinch before the determination blazing in her eyes.

"Colonel Scott," she cried, "I won't leave this house until you've gone through this material. It is a sound plan, and Mr. Evans and I believe it to be the *only* plan that can possibly save the present situation. We've sweated and fought to create this plan.

"Mr. Evans feels as strongly about this as I do. You have important problems, but none more important than this, for absolute disaster confronts us all. Unless you examine this material at once I will never raise another finger for you or the department or any other branch of this paralyzed administration. Now, please sit back and allow me to read this paper."

Fiery color poured into Scott's handsome face, and he was almost on the point of ordering her from the house. But there was something about her that made him pause, the same intangible magnetic quality that had struck him when he first greeted her. The thought flashed through his mind that a great change had come over this woman since

174

he had last seen her. She was regal, magnificent, taut with a fervor and faith and excitement that, for all his anger at her overbearing insistence, forced recognition from him.

She stood motionless while he looked at her, trying to make up his mind what to do. For the first time since she had known him she saw his gaze falter for an instant, and in that instant she knew she had won her first victory. He said unexpectedly, "Why didn't Judge Evans come with you?"

"I begged him to," she replied. "He refused." Scott was astonished to see her blush. "He—he said it was my plan and I should present it. He told me if I thought I needed to call out the reserves he would be glad to come over."

Scott smiled a little. Then he snapped, "All right. Read it. Read it—and I'll listen."

She walked back to her chair, her hands shaking a little. She smoothed two sheets of paper on her lap and began reading aloud, with great deliberation, her clear ringing voice the only sound in Scott's library.

" 'November 30, 1861. To the Honorable Thomas A. Scott, Assistant Secretary of War, Washington, D.C.,' " she began. " 'Sir: The civil and military authorities seem to me to be laboring under a great delusion in regard to the true key of the war in the Southwest.

" 'The true key is not the Mississippi River but the Tennessee.

" 'It is a fact that the eastern part or farming interests of Tennessee and Kentucky are generally loyal, while the middle and western parts, or what are called the planting districts, are in sympathy with the traitors, but, except in the extreme western parts, the Union sentiment still lives.'

"In other words, Colonel," she interpolated, "we will actually be invading a *loyal* belt of territory, not hostile lands, and this is most important, considering the forces we have available."

She continued: " 'Now all the military preparations made in the West indicate that the Mississippi River is the point to which the authorities are directing their attention. On that river many battles must be fought and heavy risks incurred before any impression can be made on the enemy, all of which could be avoided by using the Tennessee River. This river is navigable for middle-class boats to the foot of the Muscle Shoals, in Alabama, and is open to navigation all the year, while the distance is but two hundred and fifty miles, by the river, from Paducah, on the Ohio. The Tennessee offers many advantages over the Mississippi. (By using the Tennessee) We should avoid the almost impregnable batteries of the enemy, which cannot be taken without great danger and great risk of life to our forces, from the fact

175

that our boats, if crippled, would fall a prey to the enemy by being swept by the current *to him* and away from the relief of our friends; but even should we succeed, still we will only have begun the war, for we shall then fight for the country from whence the enemy derives his supplies.

"'An advance up the Tennessee River would avoid this danger, for *if our boats were crippled, they would drop back with the current and escape capture;* but a still greater advantage would be its tendency *to cut the enemy's lines in two by reaching the Memphis and Charleston Railroad,* threatening Memphis, which lies one hundred miles due west, and no defensible point between; also Nashville, only ninety miles northeast, and Florence and Tuscumbia, in north Alabama, forty miles east.

"'A movement in this direction would do more to relieve our friends in Kentucky and inspire the loyal hearts in east Tennessee than the possession of the whole of the Mississippi River. If well executed *it would cause the evacuation of all these formidable fortifications* upon which the rebels ground their hopes for success——'"

She glanced up at Scott. His arms were folded, his head lowered, his face expressionless, and his eyes were fastened on the paper in her lap.

"Tom," she said, *"every stronghold on the Mississippi can be turned by the flank*. You do not need to send a single craft down that river. And a *sine qua non* is that Memphis and Charleston Railroad. *You have to have it."* She went on reading, "'—and in the event of our fleet attacking Mobile, the presence of our troops in the northern part of Alabama *would be material aid to the fleet.*

"'Again, the aid our forces would receive from the loyal men in Tennessee would enable them soon to crush the last traitor in that region, and the division of the Confederacy would do more than one hundred battles for the Union cause.'"

Once more she interrupted herself. "When you examine those maps, Tom, look at that area from Chattanooga eastward, from the headwaters of the Tombigbee and Tennessee rivers, a large section of which, I repeat, is loyal to the Union. From that area you are looking straight eastward to Atlanta, down the Savannah River to Savannah, and up the valley approaches to Richmond. You can forget the back country. Seize the railroads, and with the forces at your disposal you can cut the Confederacy to pieces in a matter of months. Now I'll finish.

"'The Tennessee River,'" she continued, "'is crossed by the Memphis and Louisville Railroad and the Memphis and Nashville Railroad.

At Hamburg the river makes the big bend on the east, touching the northeast corner of Mississippi, entering the northwest corner of Alabama, forming an arc to the south, entering the state of Tennessee at the northeast corner of Alabama, and if it does not touch the northwest corner of Georgia comes very near it.

" 'It is but eight miles from Hamburg to the Memphis and Charleston Railroad, which goes through Tuscumbia, only two miles from the river, which it crosses at Decatur, thirty miles above, intersecting with the Nashville and Chattanooga road at Stevenson. The Tennessee River has never less than three feet to Hamburg on the shoalest bar, and during the fall, winter, and spring months there is always water for the largest boats that are used on the Mississippi River.

" 'It follows, from the above facts, that in making the Mississippi the key to the war in the West, or rather in *overlooking* the Tennessee River, *the subject is not understood by the superiors in command.' "*

She sat back and waited. Scott's face was a mask, betraying nothing. But he repeated her last words, a little grimly, a little wonderingly, as if to himself, ". . . *the subject is not understood by the superiors in command,"* and stared at her for an interminable time.

"Let me have that. I'll go through the whole thing right now," he said at last. "Can you find something to do?"

He seated himself at his desk and went to work on the imposing pack of papers she had flung in his lap. There were tables of troop transports, gunboats, estimates of rolling stock, a treatise on the Memphis and Charleston Railroad, a complete roster of all available forces from Cincinnati to Cairo, plus those in Missouri, including the regiments encamped at the railhead at Rolla. There were estimates and comments from Eads.

Then came the incredibly detailed reports of Pilot Scott, with data on soundings, crossings, markers, and problems the gunboats would encounter. Voluminous reports of not one river but seven—the Tennessee from Paducah to the Muscle Shoals; the Cumberland from Smithland on the Ohio to Nashville; the Mississippi from Cairo to Vicksburg, including a study of two important tributaries, the Red River and Yazoo River; the Tombigbee River, from its sources in northwest Mississippi to its junction with the Alabama River above Mobile; and the Alabama River, from northeast Alabama to the Gulf of Mobile.

For at least two hours Scott read and pondered, and the only sound was the rustling of Anne's papers as he turned them. To steady herself Anne had picked up Chancellor Kent's *Commentaries* and forced her-

177

self to read page after page. But as time went on her nerves reached a breaking point. Once Scott got up abruptly, went to the window, pulled back the blind, and stared into the street. And she could not keep silent.

"What is it, Tom? Can I clear up something?"

He swung around, his blue eyes dark and troubled. He said roughly, "Don't talk to me. Let me alone."

He turned to his table, spread out the map she and Evans had traced in her little parlor at the Everett House in St. Louis, and for another half-hour sat studying it, his head in his hands. At the very instant she thought she must say something to relieve the now intolerable tension, Scott rose slowly to his feet, came across the room, and planted himself in front of her. His expression made her heart leap.

"Well," she managed to say, "what do you think of it—now?"

Scott expelled his breath as if he had been holding it all evening.

"My dear lady," he said quietly, "I'm not sure. I don't dare tell you exactly what I think of this. Not yet. But I'll venture this much. I'm not a military man. But I believe you have solved this problem by one of the surest, most penetrating strategical studies I've ever seen. But my God," he said wonderingly, as if to himself, "what problems this raises! How is such a plan to be presented? *Who* is to present it? Under whose authorship is it to be executed? How is it to be carried through?"

Her heart pounded with excitement. She felt as tired and triumphant as though she had run the whole course of the Tennessee River.

"Tom," she said after a moment, as if prompting him to an obvious conclusion, "Mr. Lincoln is still commander in chief of the nation's armed forces."

Scott jumped as if she had stuck him with a hatpin. He took out his watch and studied it. She knew by his face that he had made an immediate decision.

"Are you willing to sit here another hour or so?" he demanded.

"Of course. All night if you wish. What are you going to do?"

Scott's actions answered her. He ran into the hallway and called out, "Jim! Get me a hack at once and bring me my hat and coat."

He hurried back to his table, gathered up her papers, and pushed them into a leather dispatch case. Then he came over and unexpectedly kissed her on the cheek.

"We're going to find out at once, ma'am, whether we're both mad or whether you've cracked the toughest nut we've faced since this war began. I think you have. It's now ten minutes of two and I'm going to rout Mr. Lincoln out of bed and make him read this. And if he don't shoot me at dawn I hope to be back here by four. Just hang on

178

here, ma'am—and pray. Jim will get you coffee or anything else you wish. Pray, madam, pray."

He fairly ran from the room.

Scott dashed up the few steps to the wide portico of the White House. The colored watchman and the two guards in the dimly lighted hallway looked at him curiously.

"Yes, sir, Colonel Scott?"

"Get Mr. Nicolay down here at once," he said, and paced back and forth until the slim young secretary appeared hastily clad in a dressing gown, his slender bearded face heavy with sleep.

"Hello, Colonel. What are you doing here?"

"John," said Scott as forcefully as he could, "you've got to get Mr. Lincoln up at once. Something's happened."

Young Nicolay looked dismayed. "What is it, Colonel?" Then his face lighted up. "Is McClellan on the move?"

"God, no. I'd wake the whole damn town if he were. Nothing like it. But I have an urgent report here that the President must read immediately. It's vital."

"Colonel, he's exhausted," Nicolay protested. "He went to bed only an hour ago after a bad session with Seward and Chase. He's terribly depressed. Can't you delay this until morning?"

"No, sir, I can't. I have to get his opinion at once. And if Mr. Lincoln needs a tonic, John, this may be it. Get him up—and I'll take the consequences."

Nicolay reluctantly pattered off in his slippers. For ten long minutes Scott walked up and down the dim hall. Finally Nicolay reappeared.

"Come along, Colonel. But go easy with him—he's in a vile humor."

Scott went briskly up the stairs and followed him down the long hallway to the President's study. Lincoln was standing in the cold unheated room, looking about as wretched as anyone could at that hour, a brown flannel dressing gown pulled over his long nightgown, and worn carpet slippers on his bare feet.

There was no friendliness in the cavernous eyes, and Scott almost faltered for a moment. His Irish temperament was always leading him to act on hair-trigger impulses, and he wondered himself what difference a few hours could make. But his whole nature had warned him not to lose an instant and his determination surged back.

"What is it, Scott?"

"Mr. President, I won't apologize, unless you ask me to do so, for routing you out of a warm bed—and I trust when you've heard me out you won't ask me to. I have here a plan to move the Western armies, a plan so filled with immediate possibilities and future pros-

179

pects that it should be read by you at once. For if you approve it, not a moment should be lost in its execution. I beg of you, sir, to sit down and read it. You can leave out the tables and figures to save time. We'll have those checked."

For an astonished instant Mr. Lincoln looked as if he would have liked to use his long arms to toss Scott out the nearest window. But he went wearily to an old leather chair near the fireplace and turned to Nicolay before he sat down.

"John, have one of the boys set a little fire in here. I'm freezing. All right, Colonel, let me have it. And whose report is it?"

Scott hesitated. He had carefully folded under the salutation of Anne's report containing her name.

"Mr. Lincoln," he said slowly, "I have a favor to ask. Don't glance at the heading, folded under. Read it, sir, if you will, as an official report of my department—and then I hope we can both discuss it on its merits."

Mr. Lincoln leaned over and picked up the little case on the desk containing his spectacles. His dark skin was sallow and worn, his coarse hair and beard like a tangled mane. He put on his glasses slowly and looked up at Scott with an almost sullen impatience.

"You tackled me at about the worst time you could, Scott. I'll have you boiled in oil if this could've waited."

Scott did not dare reply. He went over and sat on a corner of the desk and watched a yawning colored boy light the fire. Outside a northeast wind had risen and boomed about the corners of the building. Mr. Lincoln carefully arranged the papers in his lap. He slouched far down in the deep chair, his chin almost resting on his chest, his eyes ranging somewhat upward through his spectacles as he held each sheet before him and began to read. A few moments later he kicked off one slipper and extended his bare foot to the fender and the fire whose warmth was beginning to fill the room.

Half an hour later the President looked up. His face was as gaunt and uncommunicative as ever, but there was an odd note in his voice.

"Who wrote this, Colonel?"

"Have you finished it, sir?" asked Scott, smiling and relaxing.

Mr. Lincoln grunted, frowned, and went on reading.

For another half-hour there was not a sound beyond the faint cheerful crackle of the fire. Lincoln finished with the papers, carefully shuffled them in order, placed them in his lap, and leaned back, staring into the flames. Scott's heart fell and he was finally about to speak when Lincoln spoke.

"God Almighty, Colonel—*whose document is this?*"

Before Scott could answer Lincoln abruptly kicked off his other slipper, rose quickly to his full height, and in his bare feet advanced on Scott, his eyes shining, his whole face glowing and transfigured in an expression Scott never forgot. He came straight up to Scott and embraced him, then stood off a moment, his eyes sparkling, his whole face so changed from the somber man Scott had met that he looked like a condemned man granted a last-minute reprieve.

"God bless you, Colonel, for coming here as you did. God bless you! Never in all my born days have I experienced a happier moment than this. Never."

"You believe in that plan, sir?"

"Believe in it! Scott, I'll let you in on a secret that will tell you more than volumes could about my state of mind. I have been ransacking military textbooks in the Library of Congress for two months. I have talked myself blue in the face with staff officers and generals, trying to see light, trying to find a plan. In my desperation, Scott, I have been on the point of proposing to the Cabinet that I take the field myself. I mean it. As I have repeatedly told those in command, 'If something ain't done soon the bottom will fall out of the whole affair.' "

Lincoln swung his arms excitedly.

"I'm no Army man, Scott. But I know something of this river country. And this plan, in my opinion, is sound, Scott. Sound, new, and inspired! Above all, possible of being worked with the forces we've got, not what we'd like to have, *for much of that territory to be invaded is, as the author suggests, loyal territory*. And in my reckoning it ain't only an immediate prospect, but it may contain the master key to the whole damned rebellion! I can't express to you what I feel about it, Colonel. But by jing, I can breathe again and believe in something!"

He was walking around like a man drunk with exhilaration, his long arms swinging in his emotion, his bare feet scuffing the carpet. He suddenly jerked around and the deep gray eyes fastened on Scott.

"Well, let's have it, Colonel! Whose idea is this? I've a mind already to place the officer responsible for this at the head of the armies and send McClellan back to his railroad."

Scott drew a deep breath. This was a night long to remember.

"If you'll fold back that first sheet, Mr. President, you'll read the name of the person whose sole conception this project is. The person who devised that plan conceived it alone, developed it, gathered all the data, and presented it to me in this form not five hours ago. I never saw it before."

Mr. Lincoln scuffed over to the desk, picked up the top sheet, and slowly unfolded it. His jaw dropped. He stared unbelievingly at the single sheet of paper for a full minute before he turned and looked at Colonel Scott, his eyes wide.

"God A'mighty, Colonel!" he said in a voice not much above a whisper. "God A'mighty! What are we going to do now?" He stopped, lost in contemplation of his own amazement. "What in tarnation are are we going to do? Where is she?"

"Sitting up at my house—waiting," replied Scott.

Lincoln fingered the paper a moment and studied the penmanship. "She had it copied, I see. I would have known her writing. Colonel," he said suddenly, "bring her over here." But he glanced at the mantel clock, shook his head, and laughed. "I guess it won't do, not in this rig. And I don't know what I could tell her." He glanced sharply at Scott. "How did it hit *you?*"

Scott had to laugh. "Just as hard, Mr. President. Just as hard. She had to talk me into reading it. I almost sent her packing. All I can say now is—my brains have exploded."

Lincoln was looking wonderingly at Anne's report, and he spread out the big map she and Evans had prepared.

"How did she do it all?" he asked Scott. "How did she do it all in six weeks? She turned out her paper on the war powers of the government in four. It's at the printer's now. How did she do it?" he demanded again.

Scott shook his head. "I don't know," he replied. "She's beginning to frighten me. What kind of a job did she do on your paper?"

Mr. Lincoln grinned.

"To answer that, I reckon you should have seen Seward's face. You know we both planned her pamphlet as the first of a War Department series. But when Seward read it he rushed over here and insisted it be issued under the seal of the Department of State. We didn't change three sentences. And, Scott, it's loaded with ammunition—for *me*. It's going to help me over a heap of high fences when those folks on the Hill start getting tough with me next month. . . . Did Evans work on this Tennessee business?" he asked suddenly.

"I gather he helped her draft it. But Evans wouldn't come along with her tonight. He said the whole plan was hers."

"Who is this pilot namesake of yours—a Pennsylvania relative?" grinned Mr. Lincoln.

"No, sir," laughed Scott. "But he's an Irishman like myself, a wild Irishman she turned up on the river front. She told me he lived in New Orleans for a long time. He's been on the Western rivers forty years."

"Lord Almighty," said Mr. Lincoln. "It's incredible, Colonel, just damned incredible. It sounds like pure fiction and whole-cloth fantasy." He sat down abruptly on the worn sofa and held his head in his hands, frowning at the floor. His high-pitched voice rose in a humorous wail. "But what are we going to do with this thing, son?

What are we going to do with it? Here we have the answer to a nation's prayer. We're both convinced of it. And it's the creation of a civilian! And to damn it to all perdition and the Army, Scott, what's more, *the whole thing is the work of a woman!*" He laughed in dismay or perplexity, Scott was not sure which.

"Well, you've given me the baby, Colonel. I'll nurse it awhile and show it to Cameron and McClellan. You run along and get some sleep. And tell that young lady, if you can, just how I feel about this. I've shed twenty years with you tonight. And not a peep about this to anyone, Scott. Not a word!"

21

DESTINY, DOZING IN THE ANTEROOM OF TIME, BEGAN to stir, to move, to stride through the streets of the capital with footsteps of muffled thunder.

Destiny's next incalculable move occurred one morning in early December when Senator Wade, in one of his blackest moods, dropped in at Joe Shillington's bookstore to pass the time of day.

Wade had recently been unanimously elected chairman of the new Committee on the Conduct of the War, consisting of three senators and four representatives, endowed with wide powers and now engaged, in view of the mounting crisis, in frantically sifting all schemes and suggestions for a practical plan of action. The Radicals in Congress, appalled by the disasters of Bull Run and Ball's Bluff, were determined to ferret out causes of the North's military stagnation. The Committee on the Conduct of the War became a stinging prod, a club, and often an invaluable and infernal nuisance to the administration throughout the war.

On this occasion Wade was harried and exhausted by a futile all-night wrangle with his committee. Joe Shillington, an observant listener and tireless collector of political gossip, was soon chatting with him beside the little stove that warmed his popular gathering place, packed to the rafters with books, magazines, and newspapers.

Mr. Shillington, accustomed to tot up his clients' symptoms, early-morning complaints, and facial expressions in accordance with the political winds of the day, was alarmed by the old senator's poor color and general air of ill-tempered tension.

"Senator, what's the matter? You look like some messenger from beyond the Styx."

"By God, I am one," replied Wade. "Joe, I'm beat. I got to bed at

184

five this morning and couldn't sleep. We've had every general in the East up on the Hill this month and kicked their bottoms around the committee room. And I'm in absolute despair. They tell us what they want, what they need, what the contractors give 'em or fail to give 'em. But not a goddamn officer will tell us what they plan to *do*."

Joe Shillington shifted his weight and said casually, "Colonel Scott dropped in an hour ago. He was asking for you."

"What about?" asked Wade quickly.

"No idea," said Shillington candidly. "But something's burning him. He picked up a copy of General Casey's *New Infantry Tactics,* said he had a problem he couldn't solve, asked about you, stood around a bit, and said he was going back to his office to ruminate. Something's eating him, Senator. Why don't you drop in on him?"

"I will. Thanks, Joe. I have a bone to pick with him anyway."

Wade drove at once to the War Department and was ushered into Scott's office on the second floor without delay. His feet on the desk, Scott was scowling, staring out the window, his handsome face reflecting the identical bafflement mirrored in Wade's aggressive features.

"Howdy, Senator, what's on your mind?" asked Scott without much interest. He had an excellent idea of the state of Wade's mind.

Wade grunted, sat down, bit off the end of a fresh cigar, and lighted it, watching Scott closely.

"Tom," said Wade wearily, "I've spouted this for a month now. You and I understand each other. For God's sake, what are we going to do? The committee is wild. Chandler is after Mr. Lincoln's scalp. Over in the House, Thad Stevens threatens to raise his own brand of hell. We've looked at everything. Why? Why? *Why*—after eight months of war, with the nation bankrupt and seven hundred thousand men sitting on their collective tails—haven't we got a plan, or the merest suggestion of some practical project?"

Wade's heavy jaw thrust forward. He was angry at Scott's lack of expression.

"What are the nincompoops in *your* department doing, Colonel?"

Scott swung around in his chair, his pink clear cheeks flushing a little, a curious expression in his brilliant eyes.

"Hold your horses, Ben. I'll tell you something. I'll tell you why I've been knocking my own brains out for two weeks. There is a kind of a plan that not a damn soul in the city, outside two or three sworn to silence, knows anything about. None of the generals, save McClellan this week, ever heard of it. And Mac——"

Wade took the cigar out of his mouth and stood up, tense and hostile.

"Are you telling me there is a *military* plan of which the Committee

185

on the Conduct of the *War* has not been told? Is it anything you believe in?"

"God help me, Senator," said Scott, his voice strained, "I've been forced to believe in it. If we could put it through with great secrecy I'm convinced it could ruin the rebels in the West and open up the entire Mississippi Valley to Union arms."

"In the West?" cried Wade, greatly excited. "I thought you were referring to some final evidence that McClellan might actually move that fat seat of his out of Gadsby's restaurant. *What is this plan, sir?*"

"Ben, I'm sworn to silence on this. Before God, I can't tell you. You'll have to talk to the President. He's had it under advisement for two weeks."

"Two weeks!" thundered Wade. "What is he trying to do—hatch it himself? What the hell is all this about, Colonel?"

"Ben, the only man who can tell you is Mr. Lincoln."

Wade was profoundly shocked.

"You sit there and tell me there's a war plan in existence that you believe in, that has never been submitted to my committee, that has not been discussed by any of the commanding generals, and that Mr. Lincoln has had in his pocket *for two weeks?*"

"That's right," said the Assistant Secretary of War, looking thoroughly unhappy. "Don't judge him too hard, Ben. He felt he had to submit it to McClellan first, in all fairness, and Mac sent it back to him only yesterday. He turned it down."

"God damn McClellan," said Wade blazingly. "All I demand to know is this: *Does the President believe in this plan?*"

"Without reservation," said Scott forcefully. Wade threw his cigar on the floor, his face flaming. Rage broke through the last of his reserve.

"Well, great God Almighty, if I ever witnessed such unconscionable bedlam, chaos, and worse. Is every man in this town bereft of guts and the power to decide? Can't Lincoln *act?* Can't *Cameron* act? Can't *you* act, Scott? By God, we might as well cover the Long Bridge with roses and invite the damn rebels in to take over this cesspool of paralysis! Why, hell and damnation, I've a mind to——"

Scott had long since become accustomed to the old senator's profane outbursts.

"You're wasting your time, Wade," he said evenly. "Go and talk to the President. I can't help you." But some of Wade's anger was reflected in his eyes. "I'd go right over, if I were you."

Five minutes later Wade confronted Nicolay talking with a congressman in the corridor outside the East Room of the White House.

"John, is Mr. Lincoln in his office?"

"Yes, he is, sir, but——" began Nicolay, and then caught the full savagery of the senator's expression. "Come along, sir, we'll see what we can do," he added quickly, and they mounted the stairs.

There was no delay. The President would see Senator Wade immediately. Mr. Lincoln, his spectacles on, glanced up from a document he was reading.

"Hello, Wade, what are you doing in this part of town? I thought the Senate tax bill——" He stopped and watched Wade, who had stepped back and violently slammed shut the door Nicolay had left ajar.

"What's the matter, Ben?" he asked easily, and took off his glasses.

Wade gave him a quick pungent account of his night-long meeting and his talk with Scott. Mr. Lincoln looked worried and unhappy. He got up and went to the window. His eyes were harassed when he turned and faced Wade.

"There is a plan," he said slowly. "I think it's feasible. So does Scott. McClellan don't. That ain't all. There are three other great obstacles to it."

"What are they, sir?" demanded Wade belligerently.

"You haven't read it," stated Lincoln mildly.

Wade lost his temper again.

"Read it! How could I read it when it seems to have been in your pocket for two weeks, sir! As chairman of the Committee on the Conduct of the War, I deeply resent this kind of treatment."

"Oh, tarnation, Senator, let's both get off the driver's seat and look at this thing together," said the President, his sallow face coloring. "Here"—he fumbled in a desk drawer, pulled out a document, and handed it to Wade—"settle down in that chair and read it. I couldn't turn it over to your committee until McClellan had a look at it. I got it back just yesterday. The general turned it down completely. This is a copy and no author announced. When you've done with it I reckon we'll talk about it."

Wade skimmed through the document while Mr. Lincoln's pen scratched steadily. Finally the senator rose, breathing heavily, his eyes shining.

"Mr. President, do you know what you've got here?"

With a rasping squeak of his swivel chair Mr. Lincoln turned and took stock of Wade's excitement.

"Now look here, Ben, take it easy. Scott and I both went through the same tantrums. I do know what we've got. We've got a lion by the tail and we don't know how to tame it. I believe in that plan. I see you do also. But let me point out a few stubborn facts. McClellan has

187

damned it, rendered his sober judgment that it's suicidal to advance upon a navigable river without great military protection ashore. He said flatly that he would never assume the responsibility for such a move. Moreover, members of my Cabinet, the majority of them, insist that in purely military matters I defer to the views of McClellan and Halleck. There are two other great liabilities in that plan. One of them—*it's the work of a civilian,* and you know how jealous any military man is of outside interference."

"This is the work of a civilian, not of a staff officer or the War Department?" asked Wade, his eyes wide with astonishment.

"That ain't all by a long shot," replied the President. His thick brows lifted quizzically. He pulled his nose a moment and looked at Wade, as if gauging the effect of his next remark. He managed to smile a little.

"Ben, I've always heard you don't cotton much to the frail sex, with the exception of your devoted wife. That so?"

Wade was completely mystified by this conversational shift.

"Why, sir," he said a little defensively, "I'll admit I don't like to see them poking their noses into men's affairs. But what in God's name has all this to do with——"

"Wade," said Mr. Lincoln slowly, "that document in your hand, from stem to stern, is the work of one individual—a civilian, and, Lord help us, *a woman!*"

Wade seemed to freeze in his chair.

"You're joking, sir," he exclaimed. Lincoln shook his head a little sadly.

"I don't joke about all things, Wade."

"Then who is she?" Wade almost shouted.

"That's the handiwork of Miss Anne Carroll of Maryland, and no one else. I believe you know her," said the President mildly. He leaned far back in his chair to enjoy the effect of this information. "And now, Senator, suppose you sit down and tell me how *you'd* go about putting this plan into execution."

Wade was now profoundly shaken by the morning's events. He saw in this plan, as Scott and Lincoln had seen, something daring, fresh, and original that could be done at once, *with the forces available,* and that was an element no other plan they had examined remotely possessed. He saw, too, through Anne's eyes, a vista of possible developments beginning with this plan that dazzled and awed him.

For half an hour he expounded, argued, and pleaded with the President, attacking vigorously each fresh objection they encountered. One of these was Attorney General Bates's commitment to the New Orleans expedition. But it was the problem of making the Army and

188

the generals accept Anne's plan that stumped Lincoln. To Wade, however, this was not the crux of the matter. He was thinking of something else. Both men were now standing, occasionally walking up and down the study, often interrupting one another, often warily circling one another like two opponents. Wade came to a decision of his own.

"The whole thing boils down to this, Mr. President," he said finally. "This plan is bigger than any of us. *You know we are now in the last extremity, and you have to choose between adopting at once and executing a plan that you believe to be the right one, thereby saving the country, or you will defer to the military men in command and lose the country. Isn't that the case, sir? Isn't it?*"

Lincoln was silent a long while. He was staring broodingly out the window at the foundation of the Washington Monument.

"I guess that's it, Wade," he said finally without turning around.

Wade waited for him to continue. But the President was silent. Wade jumped into this silence armed with certain conclusions he had already reached.

"Then, sir, our problem becomes still further simplified. You are the Commander in Chief of our now idle forces. The War Department has authority to issue proper orders and suggestions to the generals in command. The problem, as I see it, now becomes this: *to appoint as Secretary of War a man of force and determination who believes in this plan and will see that it is carried out, come hell or high water.* As for Bates, leave him to me. He's a close friend of mine and a friend of Miss Carroll's. I guarantee to handle him."

The President was obviously startled at Wade's suggestions. He circled the room once, quite agitated. Suddenly he struck the palm of his hand on the desk.

"All right, Wade. We're all in a tight corner. All right, I *will* take the initiative on this." The very words seemed to fill him with sudden fire. "But—you are suggesting, I take it, that Cameron is not the man for this job? Is that correct?"

"What is your opinion, Mr. President?" asked Wade coldly.

Their eyes met. They studied one another for several moments, and there was mutual understanding on their faces. The President said:

"I reckon we both know Cameron ain't the man for it. We're at loggerheads now. He hasn't the qualities for it. That's certain. You any candidates?"

"I have one—I can think of others," replied Wade quickly. "The best man for the job, Mr. President, is Cassius M. Clay of Kentucky— your Ambassador at the court of St. Petersburg. He's a two-gun, two-fisted Kentuckian who can make the fur fly in putting this plan into action. Above all, sir, he can handle the generals."

189

"And Cameron?" said Lincoln quizzically. "What do you propose I do with him?"

There was a long silence, broken when Wade struck his hands together sharply.

"I have it, sir. Just exchange 'em. You can cable Clay and start him back. Cameron, if eased out properly, will take to the diplomatic field like a duck to water. His friends will testify to that. St. Petersburg is not only distant," he added with a malicious smile, "it's on the road to Siberia."

The President guffawed, then looked serious.

"That will take time, and suppose when Clay gets here he don't go for this plan?"

"He will, Mr. President, he will. Thad Stevens and I can make him."

Wade paused. The time element alarmed him. "Mr. President, give me twenty-four hours. Let me come back here tomorrow afternoon with a slate we can look at together. I have in mind one or two candidates on the ground."

Mr. Lincoln's swarthy face was now flushed with excitement and Wade could hardly contain himself. The President accompanied him to the door.

"By jing, Wade," he said softly, with an infectious smile, "I do believe we've hit something. Let's try to pick someone here at home. I've got to talk to Seward about this. But come around tomorrow at four. And in any event, Cameron for Clay might be a horse trade we can work at. I think Seward would accept it. I'll talk to him. And you, sir, can tackle the Attorney General."

Wade rushed down the stairs and almost bowled over Nicolay in the hall.

"What on earth's going on, Senator?" asked Nicolay anxiously, seeing the sweat on Wade's face.

Wade looked at him with an expression of dazed incredulity.

"I'm damned if I know yet, John." To the other's astonishment, he pumped Nicolay's hand enthusiastically. "But I've either been shot out of a cannon—or Uncle Abe and I are riding hell-bent for glory! Good-by, John. And God bless you!"

Wade calmed down a bit as he hastened out of the White House grounds. He was struck by another impulse, an impulse founded in the cautious care with which he attacked each new problem. He walked rapidly across the dried winter grass of the west lawn to the War Department and returned to the Assistant Secretary's office. Scott was still there.

"Well, Ben," rapped out Scott, watching the old senator closely and echoing Nicolay's question, "what happened?"

For a few moments Wade stood silently before Scott's desk, mopping his forehead. His mind was racing like a stallion released after a winter of grueling confinement. His dark eyes burned militantly into Scott's.

"Colonel," he said, "I came back here to ask you one important question. To your knowledge, Colonel, has anyone else in the War Department had access to or seen Miss Carroll's plan? I've got to know."

"You've read it? What did you think of it?" parried Scott quickly.

Wade almost pawed the air. "What can anyone who digests it think of it? The whole damn project is pure inspiration, and you know it. Can you answer my question, Colonel?"

"Certainly, Ben. I gave a duplicate I made to one civilian in the office who spotted it on my desk and demanded its nature. I thought he had long since earned the right to read it."

"And that man, Colonel?" asked Wade.

"Edwin M. Stanton," replied Scott.

Excitement of great intensity glowed in Wade's features. He was obviously delighted, and his delight was even now forging a new and formidable purpose in his mind.

"You don't mean it! You don't mean it, Scott! Where is he now?"

"Ought to be over at Winder's Building. He had a brief to show General Dix this morning. What are you up to, Senator?"

Wade went to the door, then turned and faced Scott, who had risen behind his desk and was looking at him anxiously.

"Scott, I'm going to blow the top off this goddamn town. And you'd better be around to help pick up the pieces." He added in a calmer voice, "You don't know what you've done for me today, Tom. You don't know what you've done. But God bless you for it. I'll be here tomorrow."

At Army Headquarters in Winder's Building on Seventeenth Street, directly opposite the War Department, Wade cooled his heels for a half-hour outside the door of General Dix's office. At last the door opened and a stocky, barrel-shaped figure, laden with briefs, attempted to scuttle past Wade.

"Not so fast, Edwin. I've been stalking you."

Stanton stopped short.

"Why, bless my soul, Ben!" He added slyly, "Looking for a job?"

"Maybe." Wade walked down the hall with him. "I came to take you to lunch, Edwin."

The heavy-set figure with the bushy beard and bright dark eyes behind heavy glasses shook his head.

"I'm sorry, Ben, but I have an appointment at Willard's with Meigs and Gower."

"No, you haven't," said Wade flatly. "But we'll eat there and you can pay your respects."

"It's quite impossible——" Stanton began brusquely.

Wade stopped him. He said in a low voice, "Edwin, I've just read the document Colonel Scott gave you a few days ago—the Tennessee campaign. You and I are going to talk it over. *Now!*"

Stanton dumped his briefs on a hall table and looked cautiously about the empty corridor. He peered intently at Wade.

"You've actually read it?" he asked. Wade nodded. They stared silently at one another.

"What did you think?" asked Stanton, and saw that Wade was shaking with instant excitement.

"Look at me. You have your answer. But *you,* Edwin—that I must know at once."

Stanton took off his glasses, rubbed them absently on the lapel of his coat, never taking his eyes from Wade.

"I thought," he said at last in his soft voice, like silk over cold steel, "that it came straight from God, that it contained every answer to every prayer I've uttered since the fourth of March last."

Wade took a deep breath and seized the other's arm.

"Then you and I are going to Willard's, sir," he said firmly. "I may not eat, Edwin. But, by God, I can talk at last."

22

DURING DECEMBER ANNE AND LEM EXPERIENCED
every degree of suspense. Not a word about the Tennessee plan came
to them from Tom Scott or anyone else. And then Evans ran into Ben
Wade one evening at Willard's bar. The old senator gave him an angry
warning.

"Evans, get busy and collect every bit of evidence you can on behalf
of Miss Carroll's suggestions for the Tennessee campaign. We are
going to have to fight for this plan. Don't overlook a thing."

Just before the holidays Anne's State Department pamphlet on the
war powers of the general government was released by Secretary
Seward to the press associations and copies were sent to members of
the House and Senate, as well as government officials at home and
abroad.

Even Evans, who had helped Anne correct her galley proofs, was
surprised by the paper's scope, its reception, and the clear impact of
its formidable authority backed by the State Department. The document was frequently referred to on the floor of Congress. Sitting in the
House gallery one afternoon with a copy of the pamphlet in his hands,
Evans watched Alexander S. Diven, a prominent representative from
New York, rise to answer an attack on the President made by Representative Samuel C. Fessenden of Maine.

Said Diven earnestly, "I think there is no one hardy enough to
contend that the power to meddle with the domestic institutions of any
state was delegated to Congress. But if anyone wants to see that argument answered he will find that a clever woman has done it completely. The same one, in her cleverness, has also answered my friend
from Ohio, Mr. Bingham."

At that point a member of the House called out, "What is her name?"

Diven replied, "She signs herself Anna Ella Carroll. I commend her answer on the doctrine of the war powers of Congress to those who have been following the phantom of states' rights and misleading the people, and I recommend it to another individual, a friend of mine, who has given a most learned disquisition on the writ of habeas corpus and against the power of the President to imprison men. He will find that, too, answered by Miss Carroll. I am not surprised at Miss Carroll's sound legal talent and convincing analysis. The French Revolution discovered great political minds among Frenchwomen, and I am happy to see a like development among ours."

Evans had smilingly reported this to Secretary Chase the following day. But Chase had not smiled. And he had spoken very earnestly:

"Mr. Evans, I wonder if you fully realize Miss Carroll's position in the capital. Attorney General Bates referred to her a few weeks ago as 'the great unrecognized member of Mr. Lincoln's Cabinet.' Many others regard her in the same light. That is more than a phrase. It is the simple truth."

Evans, remembering Wade's recent admonition, was worried again by the silence surrounding Anne's other paper. He went directly to her rooms. Among other arrangements he had made with her on their return from St. Louis was one to share their libraries and files on matters in which both were engaged. She was out and he sat down to examine her now-famous pamphlet again. Issued under the seal of the State Department and subtitled *United States Civil War Pamphlets—II,* it was a powerful paper, and one of Anne's opening paragraphs caught Evans's eye: "It must be apparent to all that this is no petty strife, but one of those great contests of arms which make eras in the war-cycle of history. There are now seen standing face to face more than a million of men, armed for murderous combat. *Yet to these is committed the question of civilization on this continent.*"

But Wade's warning about the Tennessee plan was uppermost in his mind and he turned to her files. They were filled with letters from men of political importance, North and South. Many of the more personal messages amused Evans. That gem of gallantry, Mayor Fernando Wood of New York, among a number of sprightly notes, had just written her: "I told the archbishop that if he does not wish to reveal the information you seek he should flee at once, now that you're en route to New York. For I know you well enough to be convinced that no man, however cool, cautious, and diplomatique, can escape you."

He laughed at a typically impulsive note of Anne's to Secretary

Chase in April 1861 that read, "Dear Guv, I'm rushing to Annapolis to head off the madness of the legislature. These miserable fools! Heaven help us from such." There were also letters from her publishers. Ten thousand copies of her *Great American Battle* sold in three months. Seven editions of *Star of the West*. He saw many communications from Susan B. Anthony, Lydia Child, Clara Barton, Elizabeth Cady Stanton, and fees, ranging from $1,000 to $2,000, for Anne's services at various political conventions.

But Evans frowned when he came to her list of private charities. They were entirely too formidable in relation to her income—case after case of large contributions to prevent the separation of Negro families, five hundred dollars to a Signora Maris who wished to found an Italian paper in New York devoted to Garibaldi's fight for freedom, check after check mailed to anti-slavery societies.

He was scowling at an item of $1,000 to "Mlle. Gabriele Falk of Weimar, Germany," when Anne came in.

"Lem," she said mischievously, "you're prowling through my personal files. And why such a fierce scowl?"

He laughed and pointed accusingly to the memorandum he was reading.

"Who were you trying to bribe with a thousand-dollar bill?"

"Oh, *that*." Her expression grew serious. "I couldn't resist it, Lem. Gabriele's father was a brilliant contemporary of Goethe and Schiller, a champion of free education in Germany. Three years ago the town of Weimar celebrated the centenary of his birth. When I saw poor Gabriele biting her nails in New York without a penny to pay her passage home—well, I shipped her off with her children for a six weeks' visit. You must meet her sometime. Did you know she was born and lived in Martin Luther's old home?"

Evans laughed again and gave up. They had other matters to discuss.

While waiting for some word from Wade they spent the holidays at Trenthan, Sallie's and Tom Cradock's comfortable new farm home out the Reistertown Road, on Cradock's Lane, a mile or two from Pikesville. Evans saw there that other side of Anne—a love of domesticity and family warmth and gossip that always surprised and greatly moved him. During the week end all the Carrolls came over from Cambridge and Baltimore, and on Sunday everyone attended services at nearby Garrison Forest Church, once a frontier house of worship, situated on a lovely woodland hill with innumerable Cradocks, long associated with the old church, now sleeping in the surrounding yard.

Neither the Carrolls nor the Cradocks could ignore the upheaval

195

caused by Anne's emergence in a new and startling role in the life of the capital. Sallie was taken aback by it, and Anne's sisters and neighbors, all Southern in sympathy, were confused and impressed by this latest surge of her prestige. Moreover, just enough news of Anne's adventures in St. Louis, including her journey on the river with Evans, had wafted eastward to upset the household somewhat. They were inclined to disapprove of Evans as a Texas Unionist, but they couldn't help liking him, being a bit intrigued by him, partly because this tall, striking man was obviously devoted to Anne, partly because he was involved in activities that were a complete mystery to them.

But that Anne and Evans were in love, that they were quietly planning to marry, none of them, save Sallie, ever suspected. Sallie did not suspect it. She knew it at once.

In November, a week after her return from St. Louis, Anne had come unexpectedly to Trenthan alone. Sallie had noticed a change in her then. Watching her like a cat as they chatted affectionately, she had studied Anne's face, her manner, her expression. At last she could not restrain her curiosity.

"You've fallen in love with Judge Evans, haven't you, pet? You——"

"Yes, I have," replied Anne promptly. "Lem has the finest mind I've ever met—and the truest heart. We haven't made any announcement yet, Sallie. But we plan to be married in the spring, just as soon as our current assignments are finished."

Sallie had promptly burst into tears.

"I can't understand you at all," she wailed. "You rush madly about the country—and we all love you so!" she exclaimed a little chaotically. "And what is to become of you? You've had the pick of the finest men in Baltimore and Washington for years—and ignored them all. Then we thought you'd chosen Harry Heyward, and now in the midst of this uproar we're living in you suddenly give your heart to a raw frontier judge. It doesn't make sense, dear. It isn't that we don't like Judge Evans. We all do. But he's such a strange creature. He just doesn't *belong,* here or anywhere. I think it a great mistake," she added with the almost smug authority of a happily married woman.

Anne had kissed her fondly.

"Don't be so upset, sweet. After all, I'm the one who loves Lem."

But Sallie had been deeply disturbed. She had gone to her room and wept a little, but when she emerged in an hour with an air of martyred dignity she did not refer to the matter again. Nor had she at any time during this Christmas visit of both of them.

Listening to them together, even Sallie, however reluctantly, had come to see that Anne and Lem belonged together. They shared

196

a gaiety and wholehearted companionship which in some ways Sallie envied.

In lighter moments they often chaffed one another about their plans for the future. Anne's ambition for years, she confessed, had been to own and edit a newspaper in some county center, and Evans amused himself by picking out preferred sites in Texas for such a venture and then speculating on Anne's activities in that new environment.

"We might take over Austin," he said once. "All you need is a small press, a couple of fonts of type, and a Maynard rifle over your desk. I'll wager you could stir up the state in a matter of weeks, dear—and if I'm on the bench I can always get you out of trouble."

"You may need a newspaper editor for the same purpose, darling," she retorted.

With rather sudden finality the holidays were over and they found themselves on the cars clattering back to Washington. As they rolled across the winter landscape Anne handed Evans a paper on which she had been working, a supplement to the Tennessee plan, prepared at the request of Colonel Scott, who wished to answer some objections of the Navy Department. Evans was impressed by her final paragraph to Scott which read: "If you will look at the map of the Western states you will see in what a position Buckner would be placed by a strong advance up the Tennessee River. He would be forced to back out of Kentucky, or, if he did not, our forces could take Nashville in his rear and compel him to lay down his arms."

Evans folded the paper with an impatient gesture.

"We've got to put this plan through, that's all. But the Navy is hard to sell. Some whiskered commodore told Wade he thought this scheme 'a risky diversion.' The Navy's outfitting a tremendous expedition to take New Orleans and naturally doesn't relish your plan a bit."

In the smoky Washington depot they found Caroline and Ben Wade waiting for them. The last remnants of their holiday mood vanished. With the curtest of greetings, Wade drove them to his home. They all sensed he was bursting with news, but he discussed no official activities until after they had had dinner. Then, with a flair for the dramatic which he never neglected, he seated them and faced them from behind a small table and impressively cleared his throat. Caroline, who had taken up her knitting, smiled admonishingly.

"Ben dear, I know you're forever excited. But please try to control that horrible profanity of yours."

Wade grinned and then tried to appear hurt.

"My dear, I thought I was among friends," he said reproachfully. Then he glanced very seriously from one to another of them. "I may

197

as well tell you at once that tomorrow afternoon the President will announce the name of his new Secretary of War and that that gentleman will be in office within ten days. When that happens——"

"You can't do this, Ben," interrupted Anne. "You've got to tell us who the man is or nothing will make sense. Who is he?"

Wade hesitated, looked hard at Anne, and then barked, "Edwin McMasters Stanton. His choice was inevitable."

If Wade had said Jefferson Davis, his audience could not have looked more horrified.

Anne spoke first.

"Are you mad, Ben? The President will never accept him. Neither will leading Republicans. Mr. Stanton is a Democrat. I admire him. But for more than a year he has been saying vile things privately and publicly about Mr. Lincoln. They detest each other. I think the idea is preposterous, if I may say so."

"Nevertheless, you are entirely wrong, ma'am," Wade answered evenly. "Yesterday afternoon I brought Mr. Lincoln and Stanton together for the first time. Mr. Lincoln already *has* accepted him—— Wait, now." He paused for their exclamations of incredulity to subside. "Mr. Lincoln told me last week that he would approve my suggestion of Stanton, provided Stanton promised to execute Miss Carroll's Tennessee plan. But he was concerned about Stanton's past, his relationship to Buchanan, and what leading senators might think. However, I was ready for that."

Wade then went over again his visits to Scott and the President, Stanton's discovery of Anne's plan, and the fact that Stanton considered it the only possible solution to the present crisis.

"Stanton himself," went on Wade, "brought up every objection to his appointment that could possibly be made. His dislike of Lincoln— he hadn't even seen the man since his inauguration until yesterday. Their old enmity, dating from the Manny-McCormick case in Cincinnati; the problem of what to do with Cameron; the distrust of many Republicans who hate him, and many other matters."

Wade paused again and made an expressive gesture with his hands.

"All these obstacles," he said emphatically, "have been swept aside. The Senate will confirm Stanton at once upon my blanket endorsement and that of Thad Stevens in the House. I have told various members only as much as I felt necessary—that we have a plan of campaign in which Mr. Lincoln, Stanton, Colonel Scott, and I believe, and which Stanton will see put through. That was all they needed. They are all in the bag, ma'am," said Wade, addressing Anne, who was rigid with astonishment. "And why?" he demanded, raising his voice almost to a shout. "Because they have exhausted every plan and project. Because they distrust Cameron. Because they are panic-stricken *and don't know what to do!*

"Besides, they have a secret admiration for Stanton and what he did to save the country in Buchanan's regime. They know he is a steam engine in pants. That he has the guts to kick the bottom of any general he don't like. Fessenden told me that if I could sell Stanton to Lincoln they'd take him in a minute. When I told Mr. Lincoln that, God bless him, that fine soul said never a word against Stanton, and I know Stanton has hurt him deeply. 'Then he's our man,' he told me. I think he, too, realized Stanton is the one ruthless, honest, driving force that can save that bastardized wreck called the War Department."

Wade lowered his voice and said more calmly, "But I want you to remember this. The one factor that clinched this remarkable deal was Miss Carroll's plan. That, and that alone, did it. Stanton can't talk about anything else. He knows Richmond is hogwash. He knows this war has to be won in the West. He's convinced, and told me in so many words, that Miss Carroll's plan, with all its implications, contains the key to the entire war."

Wade stopped to allow these words to sink in.

"I still find this hard to understand, Senator," Evans said slowly. "Stanton has been extremely bitter about Mr. Lincoln. Hasn't he made any conditions of his own?"

"One," said Wade. "He insists that he is to have an absolutely free hand in the War Department and complete command of all communications. He intends to yank out every private wire leading to McClellan's headquarters five minutes after he's in office. All communications will pass through Stanton. Not an officer in the Army can telegraph his wife or ask for buttons without having his billet-doux pass through Stanton's hands. Oh yes, he also wants power over the press and threatens to close up any newspaper he thinks is hostile to the war effort."

Evans whistled.

"Senator, Washington is going to explode when this goes through."

"You're damn right it is," retorted Wade cheerfully, "and I'm looking forward to it. But take a look at the rest of the picture. Cameron has cooked his own goose. The President wants him out—is furious at him—for the Secretary of War had the presumption to publish his annual report a fortnight ago without showing a great deal of it to Mr. Lincoln. In this report Cameron publicly urged that Negroes be freed and armed to fight the rebels. Well, I believe that too. Stanton wrote that passage, though Lincoln didn't know it. But Lincoln hit the ceiling anyway and tried to recall the whole report. The border states,

199

particularly the President's own state of Kentucky, understand that this war is being fought to maintain the Union. They don't give a damn about the Negroes. Nor does most of the Army.

"And now," Wade continued, "the debacle in the West has hit the President in the face. Halleck writes that the German regiments have mutinied over Frémont's removal. The Treasury is bankrupt. As to public opinion—look at the papers. They're yelling for everyone's scalp."

Wade looked at his watch, ran his hand through his white hair, and relaxed a little.

"Just one more word. The utmost secrecy must be observed in all this, not only now—but right along. The generals, Halleck, Buell, Hunter, McClellan, and others, are even now at each other's throats. They've got to have their heads knocked together. They've got to be picked up by the scruffs of their necks and have Miss Carroll's plan forced down their throats, with Lincoln holding 'em on his lap and Stanton pushing the spoon."

This homely picture made them laugh in spite of the tension Wade had created. Even Wade laughed. Then he said quietly, "I've had the fight of my career to get this thing started. I'll tell you something more in strict confidence. Colonel Scott has already left for the West with a letter of secret instructions. Unknown to the Western commanders, he is fully empowered to organize and prepare the greatest military machine in this nation and send it crashing up the Tennessee River when the President gives the word.

"These armies," said Wade violently, "*must* be moved. When Scott says he's ready, the President is going to *make* them move. That action will be taken in a very few days."

They sat in stunned silence and watched Wade raise his untouched glass.

"Colonel Scott has an enormous and crucial work to do. I propose we wish him Godspeed. I propose we drink to the resounding success of the Tennessee plan."

23

A FEW DAYS LATER MR. LINCOLN SENT FOR ANNE. IT was January 11, and Washington's unpredictable weather had produced the kind of sunny mild day caressed by a warm southern breeze that made one feel that the trees along the Avenue were about to burst into full bloom and crocuses and tulips were pushing their way up through the steaming soil. Men walked about with loosened collars, overcoats on their arms, hats in hand, sniffing the fragrant air, wondering where winter had fled, and caring not.

The President had invited her for a short drive. Evans accompanied her past the guardhouse near the sandbagged Treasury building and to the east door of the White House and left her with a solemn warning that his smile belied.

"If you two aren't back by five, Anne, I swear I'll turn the whole Army of the Potomac into a search party. . . . Good luck."

Five minutes later Mr. Lincoln's carriage rolled from the stables and the President strolled out with Nicolay and Mrs. Lincoln's seamstress, Elizabeth Keckley, a handsome free colored woman. Mr. Lincoln was wearing a well-fitting light pepper-and-salt suit, the first time Anne had seen him in anything but black, with a soft collar and loosely knotted black string tie. He looked fresh, animated, and younger than she had ever seen him. Spying her tiny French blue bonnet, he exclaimed, "Good afternoon, ma'am, I'm happy to see you have a hat that won't give in to a Washington breeze."

As they talked idly with Nicolay and he handed her into the open carriage, two armed cavalry guards went ahead of them to the street and waited. Mr. Lincoln placed a gray slouch hat on the box seat and sat bareheaded, looking eagerly up through bare branches at the warm blue sky.

"Where to, ma'am. Where would you like to drive? Silver Spring, Chevy Chase?"

"Anywhere for a bit of country," she replied. "And I leave the route to you, sir."

"Then it's Rock Creek and a glimpse of Georgetown," he replied, and gave directions to the driver. They drove across Lafayette Square and out Connecticut Avenue until they entered the winding Rock Creek road, with a glimpse of the red brick houses of Georgetown in the distance on their left, and the white pillars of the old Lee mansion barely visible in the warm haze across the Potomac. Then they plunged through the woods where Rock Creek flashed and rippled in the sun.

"I've wanted this for weeks," said Mr. Lincoln. "I guess I'm celebrating that paper of yours by putting on this spring suit today."

"You should wear gray more often, Mr. President," she said boldly. "It's most becoming and you look years younger."

"Do I?" he answered, obviously pleased. "Well, Mary don't think it's quite dignified. I've got a closetful of Springfield clothes I never get a chance to wear."

They chatted easily for some time, basking in the warmth of a perfect afternoon. At last, however, Mr. Lincoln began to question her closely about her St. Louis adventures, especially about the pilot, Captain Scott. She told him everything she could about him and he nodded vigorously.

"Some of those old boys like Scott can upset an army of experts, ma'am. I think you and Scott did just that."

Later he ventured to tease her mildly about Evans and was surprised to see her blush. He said reassuringly, "Evans is all right, ma'am. I'm glad you like him. Do you see him often?"

She answered frankly, "Mr. Lincoln, I'm very fond of him. We see a great deal of each other." She could not meet his bright speculative eyes.

"I understand, ma'am," he said gently. "And I wish you both good luck. A little affection means a lot these days."

She murmured some reply and watched his face as he glanced over the pleasant countryside. No photograph by Brady or anyone else, she thought, could do that face justice. It was a face that moved through a thousand delicate gradations of line and contour, light and shade, in a range of expression from grave to gay, from the rollicking jollity of laughter to a serious faraway look with prophetic intuitions. She thought of John Nicolay's remark to her: "There are many pictures of Mr. Lincoln, ma'am. But there is no portrait of him."

Today he was gay and assertive, teasing and gentle, and, she sensed, filled with the force of a number of decisions he had made. They rode a quarter of a mile in silence before he said abruptly, "What do you think of Stanton, ma'am?"

It was a difficult question and the directness of it made her cautious. She picked her way slowly through her reply.

"I think he has an ungovernable temper and has said many outrageous, even libelous, things about you, Mr. President. But if these factors can be forgotten, then I think . . ." And she embarked on a concise tribute to Stanton's talents. He listened thoughtfully until she had finished.

"Well, I reckon you're right. And those factors you mention have been forgotten—locked up, anyway," he added with a mischievous expression.

"You are actually going to choose him?" she asked.

"I have chosen him," he said, and enjoyed her surprise. "Just between us, ma'am, at this moment your friend Salmon Chase is carrying a note to Cameron appointing him to St. Petersburg and stating that Stanton will take his place."

"Lordy, then it's really done!" she said breathlessly.

"Yes, and I'm ducking behind the nearest stone wall," said Lincoln, grinning. "I'll let Wade handle the opposition."

The creases of humor settled into lines of seriousness.

"But what I wish to talk to you about, Miss Carroll, is this: You know and I know that this Tennessee business has to be kept an almighty secret. Wade and Stanton want me to jolt the armies of the West a bit with an order putting them on the alert. What do you think of it?"

"I don't like it," she said frankly. "Why single out the armies of the West? That would indicate clearly that action is planned out there. Why not an order to all the armies?" she asked significantly.

He considered this but did not comment. Then he turned and looked directly at her, smiling slightly.

"Miss Carroll, tell me—do you think I've had the 'slows' as charged? Do you think I ought to assert myself over the chiefs of the armies, as some suggest?"

"Yes, I do," she replied, a little frightened by her emphatic tone. She added hastily, "But I don't begin to know all your problems."

He smiled ruefully.

"I guess you make it almost unanimous. I still have faith in McClellan. Old Winfield Scott sold him to me without reservation; said he was the finest soldier and organizer in the country. But I wish now he'd said he was the best fighter. Your friend Bates has about given me up. He wants me to push these people. Well," he said quickly,

"I'm going to now. But how? I'm no military man, and no armies of this magnitude in these days have ever been commanded anywhere by anyone."

An idea flashed through her mind, an idea that glowed and grew.

"Might it not be possible, Mr. Lincoln, to use this action in the West as a lever to make McClellan move?"

"It would be mighty desirable, ma'am, but how? An idea McClellan don't believe in won't change the General's mind."

"It could be made to," she insisted. "If you, as Commander in Chief, issued a general order for an advance, as you've suggested; if you addressed it to all the armies and directed its execution on a specific day, say a week or two *after* the Western campaign is to begin, wouldn't this help conceal the direction of the move we know is to be made and at the same time eventually force McClellan to move? If he failed to act, *following your order,* would not a successful campaign in the West place him in a most embarrassing position from which he would have to move—or lose his command?"

Mr. Lincoln put his feet up on the box seat opposite them, placed his hands behind his head, and gazed over the barren faraway hills with a dreamy expression in his eyes.

"Great Jehoshaphat!" he said once, and after a while laughed as if to himself. They were driving homeward now and he finally put his feet down and sat up very straight.

"It's something to chew on," he said minutes after her remark. "It's certainly something to chew on. I'll talk to Stanton. I'll let you know what I think of it. And now let me give you a brief warning, ma'am."

"On a day like this?" she asked lightly, but his eyes were concerned and she waited.

"Maybe you don't need it," said the President. "But once this campaign of yours starts you'd better be ready for anything. I know little about war, ma'am. But in a situation as extraordinary as this, once this Tennessee affair is launched anything can happen. Most control will be out of our hands. It'll be up to Halleck and Buell, and neither of 'em has a ghost of an idea of what's coming off. They may pull together, and they may raise hob with the whole thing. You'd do well to remember that."

"Is Halleck to lead the expedition?" she asked cautiously.

"Let me ask *you* a question first," said Lincoln with a sudden note of sharpness in his voice. "Who in your opinion is the ablest officer in the West, ma'am?"

"William Tecumseh Sherman, without a doubt," she said promptly, and Lincoln looked astonished.

204

"That's a queer thing," he said slowly. "Others have said the same. I had a long letter from his wife, Ellen, a few days ago pleading with me to clear him of all the talk of breakdown and insanity and to give him a proper command. I wanted to, but I decided that was the Army's business, McClellan's business. Why do you think so highly of him?"

She told him about the long September evening she and Lem had spent with Sherman at Muldraugh's Hill.

"Muldraugh's Hill!" he said softly. "Who'd ever have thought an army would be there? I used to swim in Knob Creek as a youngster right in the shadow of that old ridge. . . . Well, you may be right about Sherman. I hope so. We kind of got off on the wrong foot last spring when his brother, Senator Sherman, introduced us. . . . Did you meet Grant?" he asked abruptly.

"Unfortunately, no. But Captain Scott, his pilot, has told me a good deal about him."

"Well, you and Pilot Scott are two reasons, among others, why Grant's the one who's being picked to go up the Tennessee," said Lincoln mildly. "Besides, he's in charge at Cairo. But don't repeat any of this yet. And don't feel too bad about Sherman. He'll probably go along. I like Grant. I like everything he's done. The way he handled Paducah when he took it over—his proclamation there was a little masterpiece."

The afternoon sun was low as they drove briskly back along Connecticut Avenue.

"I have one more request, Miss Carroll," said Lincoln teasingly. "My requests seem to come in bunches where you're concerned. In your spare time would you like to plant yourself in the House and Senate galleries now and then and keep track of the confiscation and emancipation talk that's going on? By the way, what do you really think of our Massachusetts ornament, Charles Sumner?"

"His manner is a little too pontifical for me," she commented. "But he has a brilliant mind and I count him a close and treasured friend."

"He's one of mine too," said Lincoln quickly. "You know, Charles Sumner is my idea of a bishop."

She laughed. "I've never seen a bishop wear such gorgeous clothes. He's the Beau Brummell of the Senate, without a doubt. But his interpretation of the legislative powers of Congress always irritates me. Senator Sumner seems to consider himself a high priest appointed to abolish slavery."

"Well, you keep an eye on him," admonished Lincoln genially. "I have an idea Sumner is going to start a big fire one of these days. He

205

will have to be answered again. But we've talked quite enough business for one afternoon."

Later he sighed regretfully as they rolled through the big gates of the White House.

"That's the finest afternoon in a long time, ma'am. And if you'd care to go upstairs, Mrs. Keckley will look after you. Tell our friends I'll join them in a few minutes."

"It's been perfect, Mr. Lincoln."

He had escorted her to the door and she saw Mrs. Keckley approaching. The President took a few steps, then quickly turned.

"Miss Carroll," he called, and she waited while he came back. "Yes?"

His face was again the one she remembered so well—dark, melancholy, inscrutable—and she felt a little shaken by this transformation. He stared at her intently.

"Ma'am, the day and the company have been so pleasant I quite overlooked a plain word with you. I don't want either you or Mr. Evans to leave this town for a while, certainly not without letting me or Stanton know where you are. We may need you soon."

She stood stock-still while he walked away down the corridor.

24

THE HUMAN VOLCANO WHO WAS EDWIN McMASTERS
Stanton erupted on the morning of Monday, January 20, 1862. Well
before eight o'clock the nation's new Secretary of War marched up
to an oblong three-and-a half-story building and grimly surveyed the
dingy structure that was to be his official home. Then, barrel-chested
and formidable-looking, the man who hated inaction, indecision,
and incapability stalked through the front entrance.

Within the day he had sorted over his panicky employees like so
many secondhand goods tossed on a counter. Immediate promotions,
transfers, arrests, and dismissals piled up like snow in a blizzard. An
army of carpenters invaded the premises. Desks and furnishings were
torn out of offices, moved elsewhere, tossed into the yard, and the
whole building by evening resembled a summer pavilion on the slopes
of Vesuvius borne along on a stream of resistless lava.

On this first day in office the new Secretary of War *ordered* that
"the War Department will be closed Tuesdays, Wednesdays, Thurs-
days, and Fridays against all business except that which relates to
active military operations in the field. Saturdays will be devoted to
the business of senators and representatives; Monday to the business
of the public; and the Secretary of War will transact no business and
see no person at his residence."

But the upheaval in the War Department building was as nothing
to the storm that raged through the corridors of the Capitol and the
columns of the Northern press over Stanton's abrupt and astonishing
appointment. Lincoln's official acceptance of Stanton five days earlier
was a puzzle no one could solve.

Late in the afternoon Anne drove to the Capitol with Caroline

Wade and spent an hour wandering through the jammed cloakrooms, enjoying herself. The stupefaction of leading Republicans and Northern representatives was a sight to behold. Wade, grinning ironically at his wife and Anne from his doorway, stood like a rock in the midst of a whirlpool of mystified men.

"Certainly I vouched for Stanton, sir. He's all right. Ask Thad Stevens. . . . The Senate committee investigated his qualifications thoroughly, Mr. Bascomb. . . . My dear sir, I have no idea. . . . He's all right, I tell you. Ask Old Thad. We guarantee him." This with a humorous shake of his leonine head. "Hello, Morrill—yes, Seward and Chase *might* have had something to do with it. I couldn't say. . . . Where did you hear that, Bingham? I don't know anything about it." And: "Just ask Thad Stevens. He feels as I do."

Ben Wade and Thaddeus Stevens allayed their fears. But the mystification over Stanton's appointment was never dissipated.

Two days later Colonel Scott secretly arrived in town. He was to leave again for Pittsburgh in six hours, and Stanton called an immediate conference in his torn-up office. Present were Mr. Lincoln, Stanton, Scott, Anne, Evans, and Senator Wade. A small green-shaded lamp was the only illumination. Mr. Stanton made a gesture toward the President.

"Will you take charge of this meeting, sir?"

"No, Mr. Secretary, I won't," said Lincoln, smiling. "This is your baby. I'm going to listen."

The new Secretary of War took off his glasses and polished them, his somber dark eyes absently blinking at the lamp. Then he spoke in his familiar silky voice.

"This is a situation unparalleled in my experience," he began. "All of us here are civilians—one of us a woman. Yet upon this little group has devolved the necessity of striking an immediate blow to destroy this rebellion. We have the extraordinary responsibility of making the Army act according to a plan in which we believe but in which the Army's highest commanding officer, General McClellan, does not. You may say this is risky and most unorthodox. That is true. But the generals cannot or will not move. The crisis demands that they do— and we will now see that they do. We must launch the Tennessee plan, and once it is under way we will try to explain it to the proper commanders as it progresses. At present we dare not disclose this plan to the Army. They would haggle over it, debate it in public. This cannot be allowed to happen. The whole value of it would be lost.

"The incredible situation we confront has arisen because the Union cannot last another sixty days unless some thunderous blow is struck.

And still every commander in the West assures me no move can be taken for weeks—late spring at the earliest. That is too late.

"Miss Carroll's plan," Stanton continued, measuring each word, "has become the keystone of an arch of attack on a tremendous scale that Mr. Lincoln, Colonel Scott, and I have envisaged. A giant nutcracker, if you wish to call it that, is to crush the South in five months —six, at the latest. In a very few days the President will order a general advance on all fronts.

"But the complete success of this plan *depends upon a simultaneous move in the East*. McClellan will be ordered to take Richmond at once and *not stop there*. He is to plunge straight South, astride the railroads, and lay waste the land. If necessary, a portion of the Army of the Potomac will be rushed west to Tennessee to back up the main drive there. Colonel Scott has devised much of this. Two great armies are to advance east and west simultaneously. They are planned to meet in north Georgia or east Tennessee in the area between Atlanta and Chattanooga. The Navy is to operate against Southern seaports, opening them up as we advance, and using them as bases of supplies for inland movements in co-operation with the armies. In that way, and only in that way," said Stanton explosively, "we believe this rebellion can be destroyed in five months. . . . Now a word as to my own share in these proceedings."

Stanton picked up two or three sheets of paper from the table.

"When I first saw Miss Carroll's plan early in December," he said slowly, "I thought it came straight from God. I had long considered a similar route to split the Confederacy. But all of my ideas depended on good roads and on huge armies, not yet available, which would have to fight their way inland and be supported by extended supply lines. And this is midwinter. I never thought of the Tennessee River, or any other river, nor to my knowledge did anyone else. Furthermore, I had never realized that large sections of north Mississippi and Alabama are loyal to this Union, as Miss Carroll has so cogently pointed out, and should be willing to permit the forces we have available to maintain themselves there.

"Moreover, behind this military paralysis of ours I smelled treason —and treason in high places. So that I will not be misunderstood let me read to you certain portions of the draft of a letter I sent to Erastus Corning of New York a few days ago."

Stanton adjusted his spectacles and glanced quickly at Anne and at Mr. Lincoln, leaning motionless against a bookcase.

"I wrote this to Corning," began Stanton. " 'My dear Sir: Washington City is the worst base for *any* operation against the Southern states which could possibly be selected along the whole frontier. The purpose of this concentrating of all power in Washington is *to prevent the possibility of active operations* and *not* to have a *combined or concerted* movement. *These delays have been deliberately planned.* In a little while it will be too late.

" 'The battle which puts down this rebellion is to be fought in the West.

" 'But no plan of concerted action, no effective communication, even exists between the three Western departments. I do not believe today that Generals Buell, Halleck, or Hunter have *the least idea* of what's to be done in this department or theirs, nor do I believe that any one of them can make *any* movement *except by dictation from Washington.*' "

Stanton threw down the letter and struck the table with his fist.

"By dictation from Washington! And I say thank God for the President, who has had the courage to take command in this crisis, and for Senator Wade here, who has fought so hard to get our armies in action. I think the senator could name, if he would, the traitors even now in the House and Senate who have insisted that our huge armies be paraded here in futile force about the capital.

"We shall also see," said Stanton somberly, "how far this treasonable paralysis extends when things get under way. For the success of our plan depends upon full co-operation from McClellan and a possible diversion of part of his Army to the West when the proper time arrives. And now I refer you to Colonel Scott, who has been working like a Trojan to set this great force for action. Go ahead, Colonel."

Mr. Lincoln sat down, reached for Stanton's letter, and studied it soberly. Colonel Scott, his pink-cheeked Irish face still fresh in spite of no sleep for the better part of two days, looked at them and attempted to smile.

"We are trying to get the Army to sense our plan, to arrive at its possibilities themselves, without letting them get a look at it," he said a little sardonically. "This much has been done." Scott ran his eye down a long memorandum. "General C. F. Smith's reconnaissance of Fort Henry and the Tennessee early this month was personally ordered by the President. Smith reported the river navigable and Fort Henry lightly held and easily taken. At that time I was in Cincinnati conferring with Buell and later with Grant. Grant went to St. Louis to force the issue on Halleck by requesting permission to advance up the Tennessee. But Halleck waved aside the request and sent Grant packing! So much for that. It only proved Mr. Stanton's assertion that any action at all *must be dictated* from Washington. Buell suspects what we are up to and is for our plan but feels it most dangerous and doesn't want the responsibility.

210

"Mr. Evans, here, has been of great assistance in all this. I can tell you now that a secret session of the Frémont investigation in December revealed that Mr. Evans has been operating under a special commission from Seward dated last August. He is the State Department's confidential agent for Texas and Mexico. The Frémont inquiry showed that his task was to block any attempts by French forces in Mexico to join with the British coming down from Canada in the West; that he took part in General Butler's scheme to land a Union force at Matagorda Bay and wrench Texas from the rebels. Since that plan was found impossible to execute, Mr. Seward has now kindly loaned Mr. Evans to the War Department for various secret missions.

"Now as to my own operations. I have carried with me to the Western governors a long list of secret instructions from Mr. Stanton. That letter calls for the greatest striking force ever gathered—well over three hundred and fifty thousand men—for the drive up the Tennessee. Notice the scope of these demands upon the Western states, in addition to what they have already provided."

Scott thrust a mass of reports across the table. The little group picked them up and studied them as Scott went on talking. The reports, all of them rushed to Washington over a ten-day period, revealed at once the magnitude of the planned operation.

Fifty-five Ohio regiments to be in the field by February 1—seventeen new regiments to be formed in seven days, five new regiments in thirty days—76,380 men in all. Twenty new battalions of artillery, one hundred and forty men each; thirty-six hundred 13-inch mortar shells delivered at Cairo; twenty-seven carloads of gunpowder from the Messrs. Du Pont in Delaware sent West via the Pennsylvania to Louisville; thirty thousand stand of .54-caliber Austrian rifles rushed West from New York, with six hundred sailors for Foote, by special train.

Five new regiments of Michigan infantry, including the Tenth at Niles, the Twelfth at Kalamazoo, the Fourteenth at Ypsilanti, the Fifteenth at Monroe, to leave for Cincinnati at once. From Indiana, forty-four regiments of infantry, nine battalions of artillery, three regiments of cavalry.

On and on mounted the lists. New regiments in the West to back up the Tennessee campaign: Illinois, forty-three; Indiana, eight; Iowa, fourteen; thirty-eight new mortar boats delivered at Cairo; seventy-nine locomotives from eight railroads mobilized at Pittsburgh. Eighty river steamers piled up at Louisville. One firm alone, Clarke and Company of Pittsburgh, to provide thirty to forty boats handling four thousand men per day, to be rushed West from the Army of the Potomac.

211

Scott summed up his efforts.

"The arms situation is very bad. We've ransacked Europe for every kind of firearm. Look at this—rifles and muskets in *eleven* different calibers—U.S. muskets; Prussian smooth bores, .72-caliber; Saxony rifle muskets; Enfields, .58-caliber; French, .53-, .57-, and .59-caliber; Minié rifles, .70-caliber. For the cavalry, Hall's carbines, Jocelyn's, Sharp's carbines. Europe is cleaned out."

Scott went into great detail on the government's bill to seize all railroads to facilitate the campaign in the West, allowing them to handle twenty regiments per day of eight hundred and fifty men each from Washington to Covington, Kentucky, via Pittsburgh and the Ohio River. He showed them detailed timetables and finally wound up:

"As I wrote Mr. Stanton this week, the whole thing is an immense, a vast undertaking. *But it can be done.* My orders were 'to organize all the regiments, all the stores, ammunition, arms, artillery, rolling stock, and steamers into a single force able to crush the South, push eastward via Chattanooga and Atlanta, and join McClellan's army in the east, following the fall of Richmond.' "

In the silence that followed Mr. Stanton turned to Lincoln.

"Haven't you some comment on all this, Mr. President?"

Lincoln shook his head.

"Not much, beyond praise for Scott's and your great work," he said. "I've sent a flock of telegrams to Halleck trying to get him together with Buell and fix his eyes on the Tennessee. It did little good. He telegraphed me New Year's Day that he hadn't had a word from Buell, wasn't ready to co-operate with him at all, though he might be in a few weeks. Then he told me too much haste would ruin everything in the West.

"Too much haste!" exclaimed the President angrily. "That telegram got me mad. I at once ordered General Smith up the Tennessee to reconnoiter Fort Henry, decided on Stanton, and saw to it that Scott here had a free hand in the West."

"Well, sir," said Wade vehemently, in his first words of the evening, "all we ask, when Stanton and Scott get this big gun aimed at the South, is that you, Mr. President, pull the trigger—and pull it hard."

Mr. Lincoln stood up and reached for his tall hat on the bookcase. The others, strained and silent, were watching him.

"Don't worry, Senator," replied the President in a strong voice, his eyes on Stanton. "This gun is going to go off *in the next ten days.* And as you put it, I aim to pull the trigger myself."

<h1 style="text-align:center">25</h1>

IN THOSE DRAMATIC LAST DAYS OF JANUARY THE WAR
Department was sealed off, in a silence of complete seclusion, to
officials, the public, the nation itself.

Then the silence was broken, shattered, in fact, by a whole series
of unprecedented orders that poured for almost a week out of Stanton's
office.

In the remotest hinterland of the North men knew that at last
action had been ordered, that crashing events were at hand.

For the first time in the war the President boldly declared himself
the Commander in Chief of the nation's armed forces.

Just twelve days after Stanton's confirmation Mr. Lincoln presented
to an astonished Cabinet his first great war order. He read this order to
his Cabinet personally, not for their sanction but for their information,
and the order was issued the following day by the War Department.
It read:

President's General War Order No. 1

Executive Mansion
Washington, Jan. 27, 1862

Ordered: That the 22nd day of Feb., 1862, be the day for a general movement of the land and naval forces of the United States against the insurgent
forces. That especially the army at and about Fortress Monroe, the Army
of the Potomac, the Army of Western Virginia, the army near Munford-
ville, Kentucky, the army and flotilla at Cairo, and a naval force in the
Gulf of Mexico be ready to move on that day.

That all other forces, both land and naval, with their respective commanders, obey existing orders for the time, and be ready to obey additional orders when duly given.

213

That the heads of departments, and especially the Secretary of War and of the Navy, with all their subordinates, and the general-in-chief, with all other commanders and subordinates of land and navel forces, will severally be held to their strict and full responsibilities for prompt execution of this order.

ABRAHAM LINCOLN

On this very Monday, a week after Stanton had taken over the War Department, Anne met him outside his office. He remarked cryptically, "Our advice on forcing the Eastern armies to move has been accepted, ma'am. I refer you to Mr. Lincoln's next order which we will issue on Thursday."

And then it came, in the following form:

President's Special War Order, No. 1

Executive Mansion
Washington, Jan. 31, 1862

Ordered: That all the disposable force of the Army of the Potomac, after providing safely for the defense of Washington, be formed into an expedition for the immediate object of seizing and occupying a point upon the railroad southwestward of what is known as Manassas Junction, all details to be in the discretion of the Commander-in-Chief, and the expedition to move before or on the 22nd day of February next.

ABRAHAM LINCOLN

The thunder of Lincoln and Stanton knocking on the gates of war never ceased during that tremendous week.

On Monday there was the President's great order; on Tuesday Stanton ordered the arrest of General Stone in connection with the disaster at Ball's Bluff the preceding fall; on Thursday came the President's virtual ultimatum to McClellan. Stanton, enraged by a mass of fraudulent deals for defective arms and supplies from Europe, had also issued on Wednesday a remarkable document destined to forge in America the greatest industrial machine ever seen.

This momentous order from Stanton directed that "all outstanding orders, agencies, authorities, or licenses for the purchase of arms, clothing, or anything else in foreign countries, or of foreign manufacture, for this Department, are revoked and annulled."

A storm broke in the Senate over this order. Wade reported that Seward had violently protested the order to Stanton, warning him that "it will greatly complicate the foreign situation." Stanton had shouted, "It will have to be issued, Mr. Secretary, or very soon there will be no situation to complicate."

Talking to Anne and Evans, Wade said, "The effect of this order will make America in a very short time the greatest industrial giant

214

among the powers of the world. In one stroke Stanton is creating this giant by forcing us to produce all our own war material and stopping the flow of our gold abroad.

"But the uproar in the Senate got so bad that I finally persuaded Senator Fessenden to announce this afternoon that military moves are about to be launched that will satisfy every Union man and astound the world. That took the wind out of their sails. . . . But come in here a moment if you want a bit of fun."

They followed the senator into his office, where he picked up several copies of the New York *Times*. He was grinning delightedly.

"I just wanted to show you how Raymond's paper is going crazy. Their man Galway in Cairo can't figure out what's going on. Here are sixteen guesses—all of 'em wrong."

Wade read a number of strongly contradictory dispatches.

"Listen to this from Galway yesterday: 'The whole movement in the West is incomprehensible. All prospects of a fight on the Western front have evaporated.' "

Wade laughed. "Here's another: 'Colonels and privates tell me they've no idea where they've been or where they're going. Something important may have been done under my very eyes, but, if so, I have not seen it.' " He snorted. "That's Galway's only accurate observation. He says here it's lovely weather in Paducah and despite the ban on liquor our noble Army, having nothing else to do, manages to get drunk. I hope it's damn strong liquor," he said, throwing the papers on the floor.

They looked at Wade and the old senator said mildly, "At 10 A.M. tomorrow the President, as Commander in Chief, will convey orders in cipher to General Halleck in St. Louis, ordering an immediate advance up the Tennessee River to begin *within three days*. And God rest Halleck's peace of mind when he reads those orders!" Wade finished with a grin.

The great disjointed python of Union military power, its separate segments stretched in idleness and impressive majesty in a hundred smoking camps westward from Pittsburgh to Cincinnati, over the bare hills, the brown fields, and the mud-filled winter roads of the border states to the citadel of St. Louis, suddenly stirred, moved restlessly, began to turn and twist under the stinging prods of burdened wires bearing orders from Stanton and the War Department.

The dormant segments of the python began to move toward one another, coiled together in longer and longer segments, joined together at a score of predetermined points, became almost overnight a unified two-tailed monster, one tail at Cincinnati, the other at St.

215

Louis, its head at Cairo, the whole placed under enormous pressure, coiled to spring, goaded and pushed by startled commanders and now, at last, ready to strike the first great deliberately planned blow of the war.

Over the Western rivers rose palls of smoke and showers of sparks from tall stacks that glowed like torches in the night as dozens of transports, tugs, supply ships, gunboats, and fast dispatch vessels raced under forced draft for Cairo and Paducah. The dust of endless baggage trains drifted on the winter winds from the jammed highways of five great states. Columns of confused, excited men struck their camps and moved in solid masses down dusty roads, muddy roads, over stubbled fields, through the bare woods, pouring in a swollen noisy tide toward the crowded docks and levees of a score of river towns.

In his second-floor room at the Planters House in St. Louis, General Henry William Halleck, the tall, scholarly commander of the Union armies of the West, sat comfortably reading a treatise on American military bridges by his own Chief of Staff, General George W. Cullum, who was at that moment enjoying a cup of coffee in the Planters dining room. Halleck was a handsome man, forty-six years old, with large black eyes, heavy brows, and a high massive forehead that gave him an expression of great wisdom and effectually concealed the empty mental processes of a third-rate clerk.

He had just turned a page when General Cullum rushed into the room, his face flushed.

"General," he shouted, "you had better come to the telegraph office at once. There is no New Orleans expedition, sir. Everything available at Cairo and Paducah under Grant and Foote is to be hurled up the Tennessee and Cumberland rivers immediately."

Halleck stood up, and General Cullum never forgot the expression of astonishment that altered his scholarly features. "Who signed those orders, Cullum?"

"The general order in cipher was signed by the President, sir. All other instructions bear Stanton's signature."

Ten hours later regiment after regiment, to the crash of bands and crowds singing "John Brown's Body," was pouring down Pine Street to board a score of transports hastily massed at the levee.

In the adjutant's office of the small frame hotel in Cairo used as Grant's headquarters a stocky, plain-faced man with a short ragged beard sat smoking a meerschaum pipe and shuffling two or three letters on his lap. A face appeared at the door.

216

"You want to see me, General?"

"Yes, Pilot. Come in here."

Captain Charles M. Scott entered hesitantly, his eyes on the letters in Grant's lap.

"How long have you been in communication with these Washington people?" asked Grant bluntly, his steel-blue eyes studying the pilot's face. He held up the letters.

"Less'n three months, General," said Scott hesitantly.

"Scott——" Grant paused a moment, as if puzzled by something. Then he began again: "Scott, have you had any idea we were heading up the Tennessee River?"

He did not miss the flicker of fright that passed across the old pilot's face. Scott dared not lie to his general.

"Wa-al, sir, you might say as how I kinda smelt things movin' in that direction, sir."

"I see." Grant's face was a little grim. "Take your letters, but return 'em. And I want you to bring me any others in your possession. At once. That's all, Pilot."

At midnight, off the Cairo levee, under a lowering sky and a raw northeast wind, Flag Officer A. H. Foote, commanding the Union naval forces on the Western waters, conferred with his officers in the wardroom of the gunboat *Conestoga*.

"The situation is this," he said. "The following gunboats under my command are already under way to Paducah. The *Essex*, Commander Porter; *Carondelet*, Commander Walker; *Cincinnati*, Commander Sternbel; *St. Louis*, Lieutenant Commanding Pauling; *Taylor*, Lieutenant Commanding Quinn; and *Lexington*, Lieutenant Commanding Shirb. This craft, the *Conestoga*, Lieutenant Commanding Phelps, will weigh anchor immediately and proceed to Paducah. If I so decide, we shall begin the ascent of the Tennessee on the morning of the fourth. Low water is reported at Paducah, but Captain Charles Scott, General Grant's pilot, tells me that scouts report floodwaters from heavy rains pouring down the river near Hamburg. That's all, gentlemen."

In the back room of Grogan's Saloon a few days later, in the pleasant river town of Paducah, Captain Scott was playing checkers with Mr. Hicks, another river pilot, a man with the white beard and deep blue eyes of a patriarch. A squat bottle of Kentucky bourbon sat on the table, was frequently hoisted, gurgled happily.

The room rocked with the celebrations of a mass of farm lads in Union blue guzzling beer, bourbon, and half a dozen varieties of fiery oil-fumed corn whiskies, the best of them not a week old. Broad Kentucky accents collided with harsher voices from Minnesota, Michigan, and Missouri. A straw-haired private leaned back and wiped his lips.

"Hell, I ain't done nuthin' but walk around this damn Kentucky mud for three months. Ain't had a woman since I left Saginaw, Jed, an' thet's a fact."

"Who has?" demanded the bearded corporal surrounded by a group of grinning youngsters. "You can't git within——"

He stopped suddenly. They were all motionless. Pounding footsteps thundered in the alley, the door burst open, and a red-faced sergeant poked his head in the room. The boy who wanted a girl exclaimed, "Christ, they're yankin' us all in." No one else uttered a sound.

"Git outa here, every damn one of you," shouted the sergeant, his eyes blazing with excitement. "Git. The whole Army's movin'. We're goin' on the river. We're goin' to fight. You damn cornhuskers, drop that beer and move."

In a bedlam of shouts, overturned chairs, hastily drunk beer spilled on tables, tunics, and over the floor, the crowd rushed out. Pilot Scott alone remained, his unconcerned eyes roving over the disorder, over his checkers strewn on the floor. Mr. Hicks had gone. Everyone had gone. Captain Scott raised the squat bottle and emptied it leisurely. Grogan approached him curiously.

"What's the matter, Charley? Ain't you goin'?"

Captain Scott winked. "Plenty o' time, Tim."

Grogan sensed that Scott rested comfortably upon some knowledge of his own.

"Where they goin'?" he asked with caution. "New Orleans?"

Scott looked at him, rose, wiped his lips, and started for the door.

"No, sir," he said, "not by a damn sight. It's up the Tennessee, Tim. Right across Tennessee and east. Right across the rebels to where a man in blue kin reach right out and grab Jeff Davis by the throat."

He said this with such positive authority that Grogan was staggered.

"You knew this, Charley?" His little pig eyes widened at Scott's confident, confirmatory nod. "Say," he whispered, "how long you known?"

"I reckon about two months," said Scott coolly. " 'By, Tim, and hold a bottle for me. I'm comin' back with a thirst."

26

EARLY SUNDAY MORNING, TWO WEEKS LATER, EVANS called for Anne at her rooms in Washington. Fort Henry, with a small garrison, had fallen to Foote's gunboats ten days ago, and Grant had marched in. Then the nation had been forced to wait and watch the slow piling up of a tremendous struggle before Fort Donelson, just north of the town of Dover on the Cumberland River and twelve miles overland and east from Fort Henry.

Anne was greatly upset by this development.

"My lord," she exclaimed to Evans, "they don't need Donelson. All they need do is plunge straight up the Tennessee and leave Donelson behind. It would fall of its own weight."

Evans shook his head. "Maybe—but it's my guess Halleck is scared to death of this whole move. He don't dare leave those rebs behind. Besides, the men in the field are now in command."

Twenty-seven thousand men under Grant were massed against seventeen thousand rebels in Donelson. Yesterday, an endless Saturday, had brought a succession of disasters. Foote's gunboats, overconfident after an easy success at Fort Henry, had ventured on close-in fighting on the Cumberland and been battered back, heavily damaged. Foote himself was wounded. Springlike weather had turned to snow and freezing gales. The river was flooding. Men and boys had frozen to death by the score after flinging their blankets away in unseasonable heat and two days later finding themselves assaulted by sleet, ice, snow, and a raging blizzard from the north. And yesterday afternoon everyone in the War Department had felt stricken as wires poured in telling of Pillow's triumph in driving back Union forces under McClernand and Lew Wallace and seizing the Charlotte road.

219

Donelson was already being celebrated as a rebel triumph in Nashville. Anne, fearful that the Tennessee campaign had collapsed before it had begun, had scarcely slept. Her confidence had been badly shaken and she felt apprehensive.

Evans went to a small cupboard and poured himself a stiff amount of brandy. When he tossed off a second glass she exclaimed, "Lem, are you ill?"

"Never done this in my life," he replied. "But I can't stand this waiting. I don't understand what's gone wrong."

"I can't either," she agreed. "I'm frightened to death. Let's go to the office."

They hurried wordlessly along the dreary Avenue and found a score of carriages, with side lamps still smoking, and weary coachmen stamping their feet in the War Department yard.

The telegraph office was in the large room on the first floor, west of the rear entrance and directly opposite the Navy Department building. Present were Mr. Lincoln, leaning wearily over a high desk, a heavy gray shawl dangling from his shoulders; Stanton, his tie awry, his eyes bloodshot; Chase, Secretary of the Treasury, handsome and pale; Bates, Colonel Scott, Major Eckert, superintendent of telegraphs; Carnegie, David Homer Bates, manager of the office; John Tucker, Colonel Scott's assistant in charge of all Army transport; Anson Stager, the cipher expert; clerks, armed guards, and many, many others. They were all silent, chilled with long waiting, depressed with unanswered expectations.

"What is it, Mr. Stanton?" Anne whispered.

His face was gray with fatigue.

"We're not sure," he managed to say. "Yesterday we thought Donelson lost. During the night news came of C. F. Smith's great charge bottling up the rebels. Then our wires were out. After they were fixed we heard nothing until a flash came from Paducah at five this morning. The telegram said that Floyd and fifteen hundred had escaped by steamer before dawn but that Buckner had asked Grant for terms of surrender. We can't understand it after Pillow's victory for the rebels yesterday. Grant's reply to Buckner arrived an hour ago and I sent for you. We've heard nothing since."

He handed her a yellow tissue. The message read:

Paducah, 8 A.M. Sunday, February 16. Following reply sent by General Grant to Buckner commanding Donelson at seven this morning: "Yours of this date proposing armistice and appointment of commissioners to settle terms of capitulation is just received. No terms except an unconditional and immediate surrender can be accepted. I propose to move immediately upon your works. U. S. Grant, General Commanding."

220

"That's all we've had," said Stanton.

"All!" breathed Evans. "I guess it is. That's the end of Donelson."

"We're not too sure, Mr. Evans," retorted Stanton. "The Charlotte road was open to the rebels clear to Nashville yesterday afternoon. If they were so badly off why didn't they take it and get clear away? Nobody could have stopped them. There's a rumor Nathan Bedford Forrest's cavalry got out this morning. We can't figure what's happened at all."

For half an hour they talked in low voices, listening to the clatter of telegraph keys, watching cipher clerks pass to and fro with decoded messages. And then suddenly an operator called out sharply, "Here's something. Quiet, please!" A cipher operator named Tinker took the sheets from the telegraph clerk as fast as they were filled. His pencil drove rapidly through the decoding until he flung it away and stood up, shouting:

"Grant's done it! He's done it! Donelson has surrendered unconditionally with over seventeen thousand men, the entire garrison, and all supplies. Pillow and Floyd have fled, leaving Buckner in command. Grant's at Buckner's quarters now." Tinker glanced at another tissue and cried excitedly, "Albert Sidney Johnston got into Nashville last night from Bowling Green. Hundreds of rebels froze to death en route. The city is in a panic and scouts report Johnston will retreat southward and burn it to the ground. He——"

But the rest of Tinker's account was lost in the uproar that exploded in the room. In an instant Anne's confidence flooded back and for one lightning moment she savored the sweet full sense of achievement. Evans swept her into his arms and Stanton's emotion poured out in phrases of pious triumph.

"The will of Providence—glory be to God—this is the Lord's doing."

"I thought Grant was out there too, Mr. Secretary," ventured Evans, grinning, but Stanton was already circling the room, pumping everyone's hand.

In the midst of this scene Anne was struck by the expression on Mr. Lincoln's face. He had joined in their first great moment of exuberance, his eyes sparkling, his face beaming. Now he stood a little apart, talking to Judge Bates, a sad smile on his face so lined with fatigue. He looked utterly lonely.

"What's the matter with Mr. Lincoln?" she asked Stanton, and was astonished when the Secretary's eyes filled with tears. He put his lips to her ear.

"It's Willie Lincoln," he said. "The boy is desperately ill." Stanton added almost savagely, "He's dying, ma'am. The President has been up with him all night. Mrs. Lincoln is prostrate."

221

She was so shocked she could not reply, and Stanton said abruptly, "You'll excuse me, ma'am. I must get an hour's sleep. Will you see me in my office at one?"

"Yes," she said wonderingly while he went away, and she turned to find Mr. Lincoln at her side. He held both her hands in his a moment without speaking. He was smiling, but the expression in his eyes tore her heart.

"Ma'am," he said slowly, "I reckon none of us will ever forget this moment. The months of waiting are over. I can't begin to tell you what is in my heart. But someday I'm going to try." He beckoned to Evans, who joined them. "Do you know, Evans," he went on, still holding Anne's hands in his, "it was just a little over four months ago that I asked you and Miss Carroll to go to St. Louis. Just four months. I have to go to Mrs. Lincoln now. But one of these days we'll all sit down together and decide what is to be done. God bless you both."

He turned away. Anne, mystified, whispered to Evans, "What did he mean by that phrase, 'we'll all sit down and decide what is to be done'?"

"He means," said Evans grimly, "that he is going to see that you get recognition for this work. And so are the rest of us."

At one o'clock that afternoon Anne stood looking out a window in Stanton's office. Evans had gone again to the telegraph room below. The full impact of the shattering triumphs in the West was now striking the capital and being conveyed over the humming wires of the nation. A huge crowd had gathered before the White House. The park was jammed and lesser crowds swirled about every government building in view. Anne felt as if she existed in some pleasant, icy calm, but she was quite conscious of the falseness of this feeling. Her heart was pounding violently. Stanton met her and made no attempt to conceal his glee. He whisked a chair in front of his desk, bade her sit down, ran over and locked the door, and peered out the windows as if some prying interloper might be clinging to the rainpipe. He gulped a glassful of water, tossed off his coat, although the room was not warm, and finally sat down as if forcing himself to the inaction of his chair.

"Well, madam," he began explosively, "there are no words for an occasion like this. None whatever. I certainly can't find them. As individuals we can never repay you. But the Union can, and will."

She was breathing rapidly and hardly knew what to say.

"I—Mr. Stanton, if this plan can be completed within the year I would be the happiest person alive."

"It is going to be. It is within our power," exclaimed Stanton. "My

222

God, madam, do you know what has now happened? All Kentucky and half of Tennessee are lost to the rebels, and only eight weeks ago we wondered if we could hold St. Louis! Nashville will be surrendered. It cannot stand. Johnston has lost the whole of central Tennessee without striking a blow. He's got to get out, for Buell is already on his way to Nashville. And Fort Columbus, ma'am! A great Gibraltar on the Mississippi—outflanked, gone, as you predicted. It can't stand with Grant in its rear at Donelson. Every rebel stronghold on the Mississippi from Cairo to Vicksburg is now outflanked and threatened by Grant's armies and this ingenious campaign. If our armies press on, as we shall order them to do, and seize the Memphis and Charleston Railroad, the way you showed us will be open to Chattanooga, perhaps to Atlanta and the sea, and this war can be ended in a matter of months."

The sweat of excitement stood on his high forehead.

"Army Headquarters have been struck dumb," Stanton continued. "Their brains have been split wide open. They see everything that lay concealed only forty-eight hours ago. Buell is begging Halleck to get going. It is most curious what an idea can do, ma'am."

She shook her head a little wonderingly. She had a curiously detached feeling, as though she were standing a far way off, watching another identity, another Anne. The past twenty-four hours were like a dream from which she must soon awaken.

"Well," exclaimed Stanton, "Seward is beside himself with joy. The news is being poured abroad, with a few harmless Seward embellishments, I might add. Britain and all other foreign pirates will think twice and twice again before they dare move on this victorious Union. . . . And now I have a few personal matters to discuss with you. First, as to you and Mr. Evans."

He had moved so quickly from the general to the particular and the intensely personal that she was completely taken aback. Her blue eyes widened and color rushed to her cheeks. It was Stanton's turn to be embarrassed. Without another word he got up and went to the window, where he remained for several minutes, his back to her. When he turned and walked slowly back his assurance seemed to have melted. He took off his glasses and wiped them, and his large dark eyes blinked at her in shy owlishness.

"Forgive me, Miss Carroll. I'm no diplomat. I never have been. And it is a most delicate matter my blundering self has to consider. I have to ask you something, for it is vital to what comes after. You see —I can't help but feel"—he stumbled badly—"let me put it in a blunt and stupid manner. Are you and Mr. Evans engaged, ma'am, as rumored, or have you such intentions?"

223

"Is it necessary that you ask such a question, Mr. Stanton?" Her eyes searched his unwaveringly, but she was annoyed.

"Yes—on my honor it is—and if you will answer me frankly I'll tell you why," he replied solemnly, sitting down again at his desk.

"In that case, Mr. Stanton, I have to tell you Mr. Evans and I are very much in love and intend to marry quite soon."

She was not expecting the dismay so apparent in his eyes. He put on his glasses and leaned back rather limply.

"Yes," he said, as if to himself. "I was afraid of that. I was afraid of that."

"What is it you fear, sir?" she asked sharply.

He disregarded her question.

"Miss Carroll, purely as a matter of personal sacrifice, would you put off or delay such a move for a time? Let me tell you why." He went on quickly, noting the storm signals in her eyes: "As two confidential agents, you and Mr. Evans are invaluable to this department and the Union. Both of you can operate together or independently. We have in mind a great deal of important work for both of you to do —and Mr. Lincoln, I know, is relying upon you for the preparation of certain legal papers. If you marry now, if you are known in Washington as man and wife, I believe, and I know, that it will seriously impair your mutual operations—not so much Mr. Evans's, perhaps, but certainly yours. A married woman in our day cannot undertake or execute assignments and move about socially in quite the same way you do now."

"I have been aware of that for some time," she said coldly. But his distress was so genuine that she felt conscience-stricken.

"Believe me, dear lady," he went on, "any private and domestic blessings anyone can secure in these dreadful days should be twice encouraged and appreciated. But you and Evans are not anyone. You know my opinion of you. And his judgment of military and legal matters is well-nigh flawless. But it is you women who have to stand the curse of our prejudices in this prejudiced age. I say only this—that as the wife of Judge Evans the singular prestige you now enjoy in your own right would be greatly diminished. I have not been a trial lawyer twenty years for nothing, ma'am. I'm sure I don't need to expand on the position of women in our society and before the law today. Both of us know it well."

She sat looking out the window for some time, and old fears and the echoes of half-forgotten warnings disturbed her. For it seemed to her that, whenever she had rushed to embrace love and affection and the companionship of men, at once many prejudices, the demands of her own will, or even profounder forces, rose up to bar her way. Had she raised her own obstacles? she wondered. She could not be sure.

And yet, most reluctantly, she found herself forced to agree with Stanton.

As if to hammer home these thoughts, a roar of cheers rose from the crowd in front of Winder's Building across the street, and an instant later the concussion of cannon firing at regular intervals across the river rattled the window frames and even within this room made the quiet air quiver.

These were the first great artillery salutes to the fall of Forts Henry and Donelson and the triumphs in the West. From the ring of forts about the capital they were destined to roll and reverberate over the Potomac and echo thunderingly from Arlington Heights until far into the evening.

She did not know that tears were pouring down her cheeks until Stanton leaped to his feet, came over to her, and laid an arm about her shoulders.

"If you feel so deeply, ma'am," he cried in a strained voice, "marry him, marry him at once, and I'll be delighted to stand for the gallant man. I suggested this only as a slight delay until we're out of the woods. I beg of you to forgive me."

She shook her head and tried to wipe away the tears.

"It's not just what you've said, Mr. Stanton. I was thinking of so many things——" But to her consternation she couldn't stop weeping. She had indeed been thinking of many things—of Lem's warm brown eyes and how dearly she loved him, of Julianna's locket, of Dale's bright blood on her dress, of Sallie and her father, of Grant's and Buckner's farm boys lying in the stained snows and frozen swamps of northern Tennessee, while a few blocks away from her men shouted and laughed and poured into the warm bars of Willard's and the Metropolitan, and swarmed into churches or brothels or into the streets to celebrate victory, each according to his wants and desires.

And not five hundred feet away, in a darkened bedroom of the White House, she had remembered, the President's son lay dying.

In some strange way Stanton seemed to sense her thoughts. He was an intensely emotional man, and as he saw the struggle in the woman before him he was filled with self-reproach and pity.

"Go to him, Miss Carroll. Go to him," he said finally. "And for God's sake do as your heart dictates. I blame myself a great deal for bringing this up. I think what has upset you most, however," he added shrewdly, "is not so much what I have said here as what has happened elsewhere in recent days. I think you were thinking, as I am, of the carnage that is now to follow with no power to stop it. On occasion, life calls on us to endure too much. Yet we must endure. And this is such an occasion. . . . Where is Mr. Evans?"

"Downstairs, waiting," she replied, and smoothed her gloves and composed her face.

"Then don't keep him waiting any longer," said Stanton brusquely.

When she rose he escorted her to the door, his own eyes moist. She said impulsively, "Bless you, Mr. Stanton, for your understanding. You are a very good person, and I don't think a little postponement by Mr. Evans and me will hurt us at all. You are a very good person."

He seemed greatly moved by these last words.

"I thank you for that, ma'am. Very few people in this town would agree with you."

"Let's walk," said Evans when they reached the sidewalk. "Let's walk down the Avenue and swallow all this excitement at a gulp."

She had told him nothing of her interview with Stanton, but she saw that his expression was strained.

"What's troubling you, Lem?"

"I just read some rebel casualty lists," he said. "Two companies from Harrison County were at Donelson—the Texas Invincibles under Captain Hill was one. I know a lot of those boys. Cole Clough commanded the regiment. Hill and Clough were good friends of mine. They were both killed on Saturday."

But he began to recover his spirits when they caught the full view of the Avenue and the Capitol in the distance. The Avenue was jammed from curb to curb with vehicles, stalled horsecars, Georgetown busses, and a screaming, laughing, yelling mass of people.

She told him briefly of her talk with Stanton. He looked at her intently and saw the distress darkening her eyes. He stopped and took her hand.

"I don't like it," he said roughly. "I don't like it at all. And I don't consider that the matter is settled for longer than just a little while. But you and Stanton may be right, although I hate to say it; perhaps we'd better work awhile—work and wait. But not too long."

The sense of achievement she had known that morning belonged in another lifetime. At what cost she had bought that triumph, she saw now. The same cause that had brought them together was now holding them apart. It was a cause greater than either of them, a cause which neither could abandon, nor even dream of abandoning.

As they strolled along a kind of numbness took hold of her. In the midst of the celebrating crowd even with Lem she was alone.

Willard's blazed with light, echoed with yells, and up Fourteenth Street a volley of shots was answered with the dull boom of a small brass cannon in someone's yard. Opposite the City Market, where

226

Louisiana Avenue crossed Pennsylvania at Sixth and Seventh, was the greatest show, with an audience of screaming guests leaning far out the windows of the National and of Brown's Hotel. A great crowd from the poorer districts had assembled here, and drunken soldiers had cleared the south side of the Avenue and set up an impromptu race track. Dashing wildly about were a score of buggies filled with laughing girls, the horses sagging under hilarious soldiers riding astride in twos and threes. In the center of this mad merry-go-round a tar barrel blazed fiercely, sending up a column of black smoke, casting a ruddy glare over the buildings and grinning faces.

The sight of hordes of unescorted, disheveled young girls rushing about startled Anne into awareness.

"Where did they come from? Who are they?" she said, turning to Evans as though she did not believe what she saw.

"The provost marshal calls them McClellan's Reserves," Evans answered solemnly.

"You mean"—she caught the gleam in his eye—"they're all prostitutes?"

"In polite language—yes," said Evans, grinning.

"My lord," she said, interested and shocked, "it's an invasion. There must be thousands of them."

"There are," agreed Evans. "Stanton wants to clear 'em all out."

"Well, I should hope so," she exclaimed, watching two young females, practically bare to the waist, prancing about in the cold air on a teamster's wagon driven by five howling soldiers.

"You can hope, my dear, but it can't be done," said Evans emphatically. "Raise an army and they'll have their women—and not alone the Army! Webb, the poor badgered police superintendent, raided the Club House, a very fancy place next the First Baptist Church on Thirteenth Street, last Friday night and found the entire membership of an important Senate committee snug in bed there. Poor Webb apologized and fled in horror."

Evans laughed.

"You must forgive me, Anne, but even the provost guards were joking over the names of the bordellos listed for raiding. There's Mrs. Wolf's 'Wolf Den' and Mrs. Hay's 'Haystack'—these are real names known through the Army—the 'Devil's Own,' the 'Ironclad,' 'Fort Sumter,' the 'Blue Goose,' and 'Madame Wilton's Private Residence for Ladies.' My choice of names," he added gravely, "goes to 'Headquarters, U.S.A.,' and Madame Russell's 'Bake Oven.' But a lot of them are rich, cushy bordellos, and the authorities just don't dare touch 'em."

"Lordy," exclaimed Anne, "that's quite enough. Come along, Lem."

227

They pushed their way back to Willard's, watching rockets soar into the sky to the south from the grounds about the unfinished Mall and the Smithsonian Institute.

Another hour of aimless, feverish greetings from friends and acquaintances jamming the rambling hotel and they went out into the cool air again and walked slowly home. Cannon, revolvers, and muskets were going off all over the city. But once they were in Anne's rooms the uproar sounded muffled, far away, like some mad distant ghostlike Army performing mystic rituals of victory on this long-awaited winter night.

Here they relaxed. Evans built a fire, and after Anne had settled herself with her embroidery he picked up the current *Harper's Illustrated Weekly*.

"Good old *Harper's*," said Evans gravely. "They say here it's still New Orleans straight——" But he happened to look up and caught a bright warning in her eyes. "All right, sweetheart," he laughed, "the devil take this war for a while and I'll read something of Mr. Dickens called *Great Expectations* which could not, for you and me, be a fitter or a finer title."

The fire crackled merrily and he began to read in a pleasantly flexible voice, with the faintest trace of a drawl, about Pip and Mr. Pumblechook and their fine feast from delicacies "had round from the Boar."

" ' "Here is wine," said Mr. Pumblechook. "Let us drink, Thanks to Fortune, and may she ever pick out her favourites with equal judgment!" ' "

Evans stopped reading and picked up his glass of brandy.

"There's a toast I——" he began, and then leaned forward the better to see Anne's face in the lamplight. Her eyes were closed, her fingers idle. "Why, you're asleep!" he exclaimed reproachfully.

"No, I'm not," she said in a drowsy voice. "Please go on, Lem."

He continued reading, but from time to time he glanced over the pages at Anne, enjoying her rosy face, the warmth of the room, and the cheerful crackle of the fire, while far away, muffled shots and concussions reverberated so distantly as to seem in another world. At last he neared the end of this installment of *Great Expectations* and read:

" 'We changed again, and yet again, and it was now too late and too far to go back, and I went on. And the mists had all solemnly risen now and the world lay spread before me.' "

Evans's voice died away. He folded the magazine, laid it down, and said very clearly, "Lovely, isn't it, Miss Carroll?" and smiled in the silence that followed. He watched the slight shadow under her long lashes, watched the delicate lace fichu below her throat rise and fall with her breath.

"You're cheating, Anne. This time you *are* asleep," he said, leaning forward, speaking in a whisper.

But he really didn't seem to care, for he stretched out his legs with a sigh of contentment, found a cigar in his waistcoat, got it alight, and then leaned back, smoking slowly, letting his eyes caress her face while a great happiness welled up in his heart.

27

A FLOOD OF VICTORY CELEBRATIONS SWEPT THE
nation. Gone, forgotten, hurled away were all the bitter disappoint-
ments, the delays, the inexplicable blunderings. All depressions vanished in a pouring out of emotion that brought surging crowds day
after day into the streets of the cities of the North.

The prestige of Grant shot skyward, and "Unconditional Surrender"
became the byword from Boston Light to the Golden Gate.

The war was all but over.

The press proclaimed the immediate doom of the rebellion. "The
Beginning of the End" screamed the heading on *Harper's* leading editorial. "Rebels Finished!" shouted *Leslie's*. "How Long Can the Rebellion Last? Not Much Longer," asserted the New York *Times,*
answering its own question. And *Harper's* again exulted, "The Gulf
to Cairo, a thousand miles, will be cleared by March 15."

Pilot Scott came to life in a stream of vivid, picturesque letters that
now poured in on Anne with intimate firsthand information on the
movement of troops in the West. For Scott, the only riverman thoroughly familiar with the Tennessee, had piloted the whole expedition
from Cairo to Fort Henry, mostly at night, on the steamer *Emerald*.
His letters were quaintly phrased, weirdly spelled, full of shrewd
observations. He had pushed himself into the front lines at Donelson
to see the fight. "Bridges' Rifles and Sharpshooters," he wrote, "did
all the Fighting Indian style today. Every man in the Regiment can
Kill his Man at 400 Yards. Every Shot so Accurritt not a Man dared
show his Head above the Breast Works." . . . "Dead, Mutilated,
Sick, Tortured, and Wounded Everywhere. I would Hang all those
who brought on this Miserable Awfull Business. There is no Doubt
but this is the hardest fought Battel with the greatest Destruction of

230

Life ever fought out on this Continent." And in a lighter vein he wrote in another letter, "I see by the Press our noble General S—— led another charge today. Stuffe and Nonsense! General S—— could not Charge across a Nurserry unless he was Stoked Full of Stimoolants."

In the Washington *Star,* Anne read of the demonstration of fifteen thousand people before Army Headquarters in St. Louis. General Halleck had graciously appeared in an open window and shouted:

"I promised you when I came here, with your aid, to drive the enemies of your flag from the state. This has been done, and they are now out of Kentucky and will soon be out of Tennessee."

She read on. Later that night more than fifty thousand celebrating citizens stormed the Mercantile Library, where she had worked so quietly, and set off rockets and cannon and read the Declaration of Independence and the Preamble to the Constitution and made long and windy speeches in the light of great bonfires.

A brief item caught her eye. It stated that Mr. Edward William Johnston, librarian of the Mercantile, having refused to take the oath of allegiance, had been summarily discharged and had retired to his residence at Glencoe. She sighed and wondered what Uncle Charles and Aunt Anne thought of all these proceedings.

And in the War Department, Mr. Stanton, a wry expression on his face, filed away the Army's angry charges of Grant's debauchery at Cairo, which had arrived on his desk at the very moment of Donelson's fall, and sent Grant's name to the President nominating him for the rank of major general.

Near panic was reported in Richmond, Chattanooga, and New Orleans.

The week was one of public triumphs and private sorrows. For on the night of the twentieth, the idolized blue-eyed son of the President died, and Caroline told Anne that Mrs. Lincoln had wept and moaned for hours, demanding that the wild celebrations of the city be silenced, and vowing never again to enter the room where Willie died or the Green Room where he was to be embalmed.

The magnitude of what had happened, and happened so suddenly, made Anne long to be with Lem. They snatched brief bits of intimacy and peace in long walks together, in short visits to Trenthan and her Maryland home. Both were convinced, as others were, that the war was all but over, and all their plans, based on this expectation, were plans for a home and new activities together in Texas.

Just how much Lem had come to mean to her Anne realized sharply one evening when he hesitantly informed her that he was leaving for Richmond early in March under Stanton's orders.

At first she did not grasp his meaning.

"Richmond! What on earth—— Are you going there under a flag of truce, Lem?" Her instant fear for his safety seemed to stop her heart.

"No," he said slowly, "no flag of truce. Stanton wants an immediate report on the effects of your campaign on the Davis crowd. I have several men to interview. You see"—he flinched a little at her pallor— "I'm to be there four days as a secret agent of the War Department. I'm sorry, my darling."

The shock of this announcement made her regard with little interest a summons to come to Wade's office about nine. She had never even considered the possibility of Evans operating directly in enemy territory, and the thought terrified her. Evans, too, was subdued and silent as he escorted her to Wade's office. But the senator was greatly excited. He addressed Anne at once.

"My dear lady, there's to be a full-dress debate in the House on Monday and a determined inquiry to ferret out the author of the Tennessee campaign. Thad Stevens and I tried to head it off. It's impossible. The House is wild with excitement. After damning everybody in the Army and the government for six months, they're now beating their breasts and screaming for a hero. To a man, they demand to know who devised this campaign."

Wade's dark eyes rested broodingly on Anne for a moment. He said slowly, "This put us in a bad corner. It raises a great many questions. The point is—what are we going to do? How are we going to do it? And what are we going to say?"

Evans got up, his face reddening, and before Anne could speak he said harshly, "Let's get this straight, Ben. Why shouldn't Anne be acknowledged as the author of the Tennessee plan at once? What's all this hedging of yours about, anyway?"

Wade looked most uncomfortable.

"Wait a minute, Evans. What do you think about this, ma'am?"

Anne hesitated a moment. "What difference does it make just now, Ben? Later the record can be——"

"That's wrong, dead wrong," interrupted Evans sharply.

"By God, I don't know," said Wade. "We're faced with a humdinger. I had hoped this wouldn't come up now. Let me show you something. I got these from Stanton."

He pulled a file of dispatches from an inside pocket and riffled through them.

"Old human nature's at work," he said grimly. "The hats tossed in the air a few days ago are now coming down. Look at this. Halleck and Buell, who were planning to steal the pie from each other a fortnight ago, are now hurling angry telegrams at each other like two

232

cross boys, furious at a third obscure youngster they'd overlooked. His name is Grant, and he stole all the pie on the Tennessee while they sat on their bottoms, dreaming. A third confused spectator is McClellan. He don't know what to do. All three generals are worked into a lather against Grant."

"But how can they be?" cried Anne angrily. "The crowds are screaming for McClellan. They think he planned the whole thing."

"But McClellan *knows* he didn't." Wade's voice rang like steel. "And Halleck knows *he* didn't. Buell knows *he* didn't. And Grant only obeyed orders. But the others aren't even sure of *that*. We may have pushed the generals off the dock, but they still haven't learned to swim. It's a hell of a mess. Look at these wires. Here's Halleck charging Grant with insubordination and McClellan advising Halleck to have Grant put under arrest."

"Why, that man is mad!" exclaimed Anne.

"Go ahead. Read the rest of them," ordered Wade. They did so, and saw that Halleck had placed C. F. Smith in command and ordered Grant to remain at Donelson, pending his probable arrest.

They were dumfounded. Wade was in a rage.

"Rawlins wired Stanton that Grant wept for an hour over that ultimatum. These fools are all convinced," Wade continued angrily, "that one of the four has double-crossed the other three. *But which one?* In the midst of this mess our exalted Congress is about to present to the nation a glorious, gleaming idol for public worship, an untarnished, unsung hero! Ye gods!"

But Evans was angrier than ever. His tall figure advanced on Wade.

"Ben, you shock me. I don't believe, in the long run, the nation or the Army will resent the civilian origin of this plan, or the fact that a woman conceived it. The people will glory in it. The knowledge that one of their own, and a woman at that, with the help of a first-rate river pilot, showed the Army where to strike—why, it may seem a bit incredible, but it will give the whole people a feeling of sharing in these victories."

Wade was weakening.

"I'm at war myself on this, Evans. But it's a risky gamble. Suppose it don't work that way. Look at those telegrams. Suppose the Army became a laughingstock, the generals disgusted with one another, because after eight months of bickering they didn't know what to do— and a woman told 'em. I think now the truth should be told. I'm willing to take that chance. But I tell you flatly, I don't know whether the President or Stanton will agree."

"Have you talked to Mr. Stanton about this?" asked Anne.

"I told him about the House inquiry. He went wild. He's busy battling with Halleck over the telegraph. Stanton won't stand for this persecution of Grant. Says he don't care if Grant sleeps with every wench south of the Ohio and is drunk in the bargain, the country won't stand this treatment of the man who carved out these victories. Of course he's right. But the result is, we're to meet with Mr. Lincoln and Stanton in the President's study at ten tomorrow, before he goes to church. We'll thrash it out then."

"Let's get one thing clear," said Evans, "Are you with me—or against me, Ben? There's a disaster in the making if this is handled wrong. I'm not just fighting for you, Anne, though that's primary. But I'll be damned if I'll stand by and see the credit for this whole idea fastened not only on the wrong people but on people completely undeserving of the honor. It's a matter of integrity, history, and principle. It's more than that. If the truth is not made known now the lie to be substituted for the truth will tarnish everyone touched by it. Anne must be brought into the open at the proper time. And the proper time, the only time, is *now*."

"Let's talk about something else, Lem," she said gently. "Leave it to Mr. Lincoln. At least something's been done, and something accomplished. Let's drop it."

But in spite of these words, being only human, she did not rest well that night. As Evans had intimated, the question of authorship of the Tennessee plan was at once military, political, and personal. She had worked hard; like any man, she would enjoy a little public credit. And yet she knew quite well that her getting it was a far from simple matter.

These reflections of hers were confirmed when she saw the worried expressions of Lincoln and Stanton the next morning. Wade was more cheerful. He said to her, "Evans is right. We're going to fight for you." But Evans himself, leaning against a corner of the President's desk, looked worried. When they were all seated Mr. Lincoln towered gravely before the marble mantel and fireplace, his face worn with grief and fatigue. He managed a wry smile, however.

"Let's hear the arguments first," he began, "then we'll canvass the jury. I understand Mr. Conkling and the House demand that the author of the Tennessee plan be made known and the people be given an opportunity to acclaim their savior. Well"—he looked them over solemnly—"I guess we got ourselves up a rabbit hole and don't know how to turn around. I've been talking to Stanton—but you've been close to this, Evans. Let's hear from you first."

Evans carefully went over again his arguments of the previous evening. They were now strengthened and often eloquently expressed.

234

Mr. Lincoln nodded and scratched the side of his face. He looked quizzically at Wade.

"What do you think of this, Senator? Have you discussed it with the Committee on the Conduct of the War?"

"Lord no, sir," replied Wade. "I never dared mention the truth to anyone. The committee is convinced McClellan and Stanton got up the whole business. All except Chandler. He said Mac would have retreated to the North Pole before he thought of this." A sudden look of surprise crossed Wade's features. He frowned, then said abruptly, "Mr. President, do you realize yesterday was the twenty-second, the day assigned in your General Order No. I for an advance *by all our forces?* And that your Special Order No. I commanded McClellan to move his Army on that date? I'd forgotten all about it in this excitement. What is McClellan doing?"

"Nothing," said the President laconically.

There were subdued exclamations. Wade made a quick angry gesture but kept his temper. He leaned back, like some heroic figure cast in granite, and looked up at Mr. Lincoln. His broad expressive mouth might have been drawn with an iron rule.

"Mr. President," he continued, "yesterday I was against making known the truth of this situation. I deemed it politically inexpedient. I thought I had a hundred sound reasons for believing that to present Miss Carroll to the nation at this time might disrupt the delicate relations of the Army command, create distrust of the military among the people, and provide a foundation for further intrigue without end. But Mr. Evans has cogently undermined many of these arguments. His trust in the generosity and faith of the people I share. I talked about this at some length with Caroline last night and——"

"Ah," said Mr. Lincoln, interrupting him and smiling broadly. "And what did Caroline have to say?"

They were amused by Wade's confusion, and the old senator suddenly laughed at himself like a clever boy acknowledging a pose.

"Well," he confessed at last with a touch of unaccustomed bashfulness, "Caroline put it all a lot better, a lot stronger, and a whole lot longer than I did. In fact, she wanted to march on the White House at four this morning before she'd let me sleep. And I had to get my own breakfast."

"What does she want us to do?" asked Mr. Lincoln curiously.

"Why, by heavens," exclaimed Wade, "I think myself it's a pretty good idea. She wants the Speaker of the House to lead Miss Carroll out on the House rostrum at the height of the debate and simply announce, 'Gentlemen, here she is. This is the sole author of the Tennessee campaign. I present Miss Anna Ella Carroll of Maryland.'

235

And then Mr. Conkling, or whomever you choose, can tell the whole story." Wade hesitated ever so slightly. "Mr. President," he said emphatically, "I would like to see that done myself."

"God in heaven, no!" roared Stanton, shaking his head.

Mr. Lincoln looked very sober and turned to Anne.

"I reckon we all realize this is pretty serious. How do you feel about this problem, ma'am?"

Anne, in complete control of her feelings now, smiled and shook her head.

"I won't be a party to this decision. No opinions, no reflections, no judgments, Mr. President. I think it's entirely for you to decide."

"And you, Stanton?" asked the President after studying Anne a moment.

Mr. Stanton looked most uncomfortable. The war minister was sitting upright on the very edge of his chair, his head motionless, but his eyes turning from one face to another. His short upper lip was pulled tight against his teeth. He was torn by an inner conflict, for his hatred of the generals and his admiration of Anne had collided with an even deeper vein of profound judgment.

"I have to differ with Senator Wade—and Mr. Evans," he said forcefully. "I yield to no one in my recognition of what Miss Carroll has done. Furthermore, I intend to guarantee that full justice will be done her extraordinary work. But the time for that is not now. Let me show you why."

The fingers of both Stanton's hands drummed on his knees.

"The real cause for caution," he went on, "lies much deeper than we have indicated. In my opinion, only half the enemies of this Union are to be found in the rebel armies. The other half are to be found in the very councils and leadership of the administration. Yes, I will say it, among the generals themselves. These enemies of the people are as eager to pounce upon this government at the first slip, the first major blunder, as any of Jeff Davis's hirelings."

The war minister pursed his lips a moment, then said forcefully, "I'll be brutally frank. Mr. Lincoln, as President, has as yet no great hold upon the affections of the people, though he is beginning to gain it. The Army has not yet found itself, though it has made a glorious beginning. In all respects we are dealing with a great and delicate war machine hastily thrown together, a thing of patchwork, corruption, and patriotism. But it is destined to be the greatest war machine ever created." Stanton almost shouted, "It is destined to be an avenging host under hardened leadership with which we can smash and destroy the rebels from Manassas to New Orleans."

His voice moderated, became silky again.

236

"I bring all this up because the intolerable jealousy among the generals bears directly upon Miss Carroll. Grant's victories have upset the whole military applecart. Excuse me if I am frank in this group. But Halleck is a cream puff; Buell a non-entity; McClellan, once my good friend——" He stared absently out the window. "I will say it," he exclaimed. "This man has no heart in his cause. He is fighting for a boundary if he fights at all. Our great difficulty is to make him fight anywhere.

"Mark my words, if we go before the nation and tell them that a young woman and a humble river pilot, who would probably be shown out of any drawing room in this city, had had to present the nation with a plan, and our Chief Executive then had to force this plan on the Army, against the violent objections of its commander, General McClellan—good God, sir"—Stanton gulped a mighty breath of air— "we would ruin what prestige the Army has. We would cause further havoc among the generals. We would create profound distrust of the Army in Congress. And the commanding generals, if they are told a woman planned their first victories, may and will quite rightly suspect she may be planning their subsequent campaigns, as indeed she may be. No military command would endure for a moment in such a situation. I would be the last to demand it of them.

"No, sir," concluded Stanton. "Miss Carroll must *not* be recognized at this moment. I take it upon myself to see that she will be at the proper time."

Mr. Lincoln sat down on a horsehair sofa, his long legs sticking out like stilts straight in front of him, his head sunk on his chest. Anne's eyes never left Mr. Lincoln's sallow, drawn face. At last the President sighed and put his hands behind his head and gazed absently at the ceiling.

"We-ell," he said reluctantly, "I guess Stanton wins. I was of two minds about this until I talked to Seward. He don't know the whole story, but he guesses plenty. The foreign situation was worse than anybody knows. These victories have changed it completely. Seward cabled Dayton in Paris that we've all but ended an attempted revolution, and Adams reported that pressure for foreign interference has vanished in London and elsewhere. The Secretary is overjoyed."

The President sat up a little and his eyes rested on Anne. He smiled rather sadly, she thought.

"But I just don't think we can tell those folks abroad right now that a woman pulled us out of the swamp. It wouldn't be believed in the first place. And, believed or not, it would damage what little prestige we've got a-plenty. The fact of the matter is, ma'am," he continued in a kindly tone, *"I dare not go before the people at this time and tell*

237

them that the Union armies of the West are moving under the direction of a civilian, and a woman at that."

To Mr. Lincoln's obvious surprise, Anne laughed.

"That's putting it much too generously," she said warmly. "And I think this occasion has become much too solemn." She smiled at them before she went on. "I'm not a modest person and I should like to have my contribution recorded at the proper time, but I quite agree with you and Mr. Stanton. Right now it would be a great mistake to inject my interests into the delicate situation that has arisen." She turned to Stanton. "What happens to Grant, by the way?" she asked curiously.

"Grant stays," said the Secretary, "and our friend Halleck is going to be ordered into the field at once. I intend to get him away from his books and find out if he can fight."

Mr. Lincoln spoke to Wade. "I guess the best way to handle this House inquiry is to get Mr. Conkling up here this afternoon and have him draw up a resolution protecting Miss Carroll's interests. All we need do is tell him that certain persons have been concerned in the War Department's planning operations whom we deem it advisable not to proclaim at the moment, and that the whole business will be announced at what we consider the proper time."

After discussing the proposed resolution at some length they rose to go. Anne saw that Wade and Evans were anything but happy. She was halfway down the corridor, talking with Wade, when she heard the President call her. She went back to the door of his study.

"Come in a moment, Miss Carroll," he said, and after she had entered he closed the door. He was much upset and did not speak for a few moments, running a restless hand through his hair and walking slowly about the room.

"I feel very bad about this, ma'am," he said finally, with a strange note of humility in his voice. "It don't ring right, yet I don't know what else to do. I've cautioned myself not to adopt this course on the sole grounds you're a woman. That wouldn't do at all. I reckon we'd have to do the same were *any* civilian involved like this. But I'm still uneasy. In fact, ma'am, I feel plain guilty about this. I asked you back here because I want to tell you that I will make myself personally responsible for the recognition of your great services." His eyes brightened at her warm smile. "I personally will draw up the necessary resolutions at the proper time. I want you to know how I feel and keep this in mind while you go on working."

Her eyes filled with tears.

"Please don't say another word, Mr. President. Don't mention this again," she implored him.

The grief, the faraway expression on his face cut her heart.

"Is Mrs. Lincoln any better?" she asked as she went to the door.

"No, ma'am," he said abruptly, and seemed strangely helpless as he stood there. "Even strong sedatives don't help Mary much. Willie was her love and life, and now Tad's ill, though it ain't much. But I've never seen a woman grieve so, ma'am. I don't know what to do."

Thinking of what Mr. Lincoln had to bear, she walked slowly to the main hall where Lem was waiting. He was struck by the sadness in her eyes.

"What's the matter, dearest? What happened?"

She shook her head quickly.

"Walk with me, Lem. And don't say a word. I want to cry—and I mustn't."

28

ON MONDAY A TREMENDOUS CROWD PACKED THE
House galleries. The corridors were jammed with men and women
besieging members and sergeants at arms for additional admissions.
Rumors that the unknown author of the Tennessee campaign would
be formally announced had swept the Sunday gatherings in the city.

In the cloakrooms, crowded with House members standing in
groups or darting about as they caught sight of close friends, an angry
buzzing confusion reigned. Stanton's arrogant silence had enraged
them. All week congressmen had pried, questioned, and buttonholed
Cabinet ministers and War and Navy officials.

Evans was moody, silent, watching the scene with grim detachment,
while Anne held tightly to his arm. In a few days he would be in Virginia.

Many senators had come over to the House floor to watch the proceedings. Evans, thus far self-absorbed, became for the first time aware
of Anne's increasing nervousness as they walked up to speak to Wade.
She looked extremely well, dressed in canary-yellow silk, inset with
small panels of dark blue, and wearing a yellow turban which matched
her dress and was bordered with blue forget-me-nots which brought
out the color of her eyes. But her hands were endlessly twisting a
delicate gold chain and handkerchief ring that hung from her waist.

Wade was more upset than they had ever seen him and deliberately
avoided any talk with Evans.

"You'd better go to the gallery, Anne," he directed her. "I plan to
remain at the rear of the House floor with Thad Stevens and see that
this goes off properly."

She had tried to tell herself she would be quite composed on this occasion. But as she climbed the wide steps to the gallery with her hand on Evans's arm, her nerves tingled and a queer tightening caught at the pit of her stomach. It was not going to be easy, especially since Evans had said hardly a word from the time he had come to her rooms to get her. They found their seats and she leaned toward him and whispered, "Lem, please—don't be like this."

He started a little, looked down at her, and finally smiled.

"I'm sorry, sweetheart. But this whole business mightily upsets me. I'll be glad when it's over."

He patted her hand briefly and took his own away. But she reached for it again like a child grasping for support.

"Hold my hand, Lem," she pleaded. "I'm shaking. I wish I hadn't come."

And so he held her hand in both of his and felt her soft shoulder pressing mutely against his own. In spite of their feelings they were soon absorbed in the scene.

On this Monday, February 24, 1862, in the second session of the Thirty-seventh Congress, every member able to be present sat in his place. At high noon the chatter in the galleries and on the floor ceased all at once and a hush fell across the chamber as the Reverend Thomas H. Stockton arose and began a benediction. The Reverend Stockton gave thanks for victory and prayed at interminable length for the safety and continued sagacity of the President, the Cabinet, the Senate, the House, and all the people of the nation. A little breathless, the minister had hardly seated himself when the clerk rose and in an utterly bored voice read the House *Journal* of the preceding Saturday.

Then the Speaker stood up and announced that the regular business was a call on the committees for reports. There were two or three brief remarks on Colorado Territory lands and a resolution by Mr. Trimble on the military railroad to be constructed from Danville, Kentucky, to Knoxville, Tennessee.

Mr. Trimble sat down and Mr. Roscoe Conkling arose quickly, was recognized, and announced in a loud, clear voice, "I beg leave to offer a resolution, not for action at present, but that it may lie on the table."

The Speaker said quietly, "The clerk will read the resolution."

The tense galleries leaned forward and amid a complete silence the clerk read slowly:

" 'Resolved by the Senate and the House of Representatives of the United States of America in Congress assembled that the thanks of Congress are due, and are hereby presented to, Generals Halleck and Grant for planning the recent movements *within their respective divisions,* and to both these generals, as well as to the officers and men

241

under their command, for achieving the glorious victories in which those movements have resulted.' "

"Is there any objection?" demanded the Speaker.

There was no objection. Anne felt moisture gather in her palms.

"Is that all? Is that all there is to it?" she whispered to Evans in surprise.

"Wait," said Evans tensely, "it's not all, or I miss my guess."

Mr. Cox, a portly member from Ohio, rose.

"I move that the resolution be referred to the Committee on Military Affairs."

But Roscoe Conkling had remained standing. The House had realized that something important lay concealed in the purpose of this apparently innocuous resolution. In the hush that followed Conkling said slowly and impressively:

"My purpose in offering the resolution and asking that it may lie over without action now is this: I believe the officers named in this resolution are entitled to certain credit, and I desire the resolution to await future action, perhaps amendment, and I care not what particular disposition of it is made at present."

Conkling paused a little, as if for further emphasis, and then said very deliberately:

"*I would like to call up the subject when the House and the country shall be put into full possession of all the facts in the case,* including the reports to be made by the different generals, and when we shall know whether these victories were organized or directed at a distance from the fields where they were won, *and if so by whom organized,* or whether they were the conception of those who executed them. I have, as I have said, very little care whether, to this end, the resolution takes a reference or goes to the Speaker's table."

An excited chatter rippled across the floor, and the Speaker half lifted his gavel. But the member from Ohio, Mr. Cox, obviously surprised, rose and faced Conkling and fenced with him a few moments, discussing possible credit due the Committee on the Conduct of the War, and, seeing no flicker of interest on Conkling's face, went on to say that the clauses of his resolution must be most carefully drawn "to the end that no one entitled to credits shall be excluded from them."

Then Mr. Cox sat down and looked expectantly at Mr. Conkling as if to demand, "And now, sir, let us have the real meat without any quibbling." But Conkling proceeded with a great deal of caution. Again he said with a marked deliberation that could not be overlooked:

"I will take occasion to say now that I venture to predict that the truthful histories of these victories will demonstrate that *not alone* to

242

the modes of doing things, nor to the sources of movements which until recently prevailed in military affairs; not alone to the agencies which were at work when Congress met; *not, by any means, to these alone* are to be attributed the brilliant successes in the West."

These words caused an immense stir in the galleries and on the floor, especially among the Illinois delegation, to whom McClellan, who had gone to the Army from a vice-presidency of the Illinois Central, was a sacred idol. Mr. Fenton of Illinois rose and hastily offered in place of the resolution a flowery tribute obviously composed on the spot. Conkling at once objected strongly, pointing out again that the purpose of his resolution was to hold open the whole matter of the credit for the Tennessee campaign until all credits were finally assigned.

Anne looked to the rear of the floor and caught sight of Wade arguing violently with Thaddeus Stevens.

Mr. Cox was on his feet again after a final word with Stevens. Addressing an Ohio member, he said loudly:

"The gentleman says he does not believe in organized victory at a distance. But it may turn out otherwise, when this matter comes to be examined." He paused and added slowly, *"It is significant of one directing head and design in these recent victories that both flanks of the enemy, West and East, have been stricken and paralyzed at the the same time."*

There was another great stir in the chamber and a violent debate ensued among the partisans of the various generals. Finally Mr. Olin, a trim, dapper member from New York, rose and tried to pour oil on the troubled waters. With considerable unction he announced:

"It is sufficient for the country at present that *somebody* has planned and executed these movements."

But it wasn't sufficient for the House or the galleries. Everyone in the chamber now knew that a major mystery had been presented and that it concealed a known candidate for the nation's honors under a cloak deliberately devised by someone in authority. The drama of the situation held Anne and Evans spellbound, for tension was rising all over the House. Behind her Anne heard a woman say, "But, Ned, don't they *know* who planned the campaigns? It seems ridiculous."

"They know, but they won't tell," snapped the man with her, "and the rest of the pack are pressing to make 'em tell."

"Well, I never," said the woman, subsiding into puzzled silence again.

Anne, watching Wade, pulled at his arm.

"Wait, Lem—I think the resolution's going through. They're ready to vote."

Mr. Kellogg of Illinois, having attacked the resolution and tossed

243

verbal bouquets at McClellan, sat down with the indignant attitude of a gentleman who has discharged his full if disagreeable duty. And now Mr. Washburne, also from Illinois, rose and they saw Conkling's forces moving in for the kill. Said Mr. Washburne, hastily moving for action:

"I disagree with the views of my colleague as to the resolution. I cannot agree with him that it reflects upon anybody. I suggest that it should go to the Committee on Military Affairs, and hence I call the previous question upon the motion of the gentleman from Ohio, Mr. Cox."

Mr. Burnham now rose to his feet.

"I renew the motion," he called out clearly.

There was an uproar in the galleries as the excited crowd suddenly realized that they had been cheated, that the brief storm was over, that the name of the author of the Western victories—and it was now glaringly obvious that there was such an author, deliberately concealed —was about to be indefinitely pigeonholed.

The Speaker restored order and a member asked that the resolution be read again. The clerk read it amid a profound silence. By an oral vote the motion to table the resolution was denied. The previous question was seconded and the main question ordered to be put to the House. And under this operation the main question was passed and the resolution was referred to the Committee on Military Affairs.

Anne and Lem leaned far forward to watch the scene. A violent argument had broken out in the press gallery. On the floor a mass of vociferous members crowded about Conkling, Wade, and Thaddeus Stevens. Spectators chattered angrily. Many of them were flocking toward the exits.

Above the din Mr. Morrill of Vermont could hardly be heard as he rose and addressed the Speaker.

"I move the rules be suspended and the House resolved into a committee of the whole to take up the Appropriation Bill and that——"

They waited until the galleries were almost clear. Evans leaned back and sighed.

"Well, Miss Carroll," he said with a touch of obvious irony, "how do you feel?"

She patted a strand of blond hair into place and smiled at him bravely.

"Do you love me, Lem?" she whispered. To her surprise his eyes became moist and he looked at her with an intent expression she could not fathom. Then he boldly leaned forward, pressed her to him, and brushed her hair with his lips.

"You are my heart and soul and everything I cherish," he said with a rush of feeling. "There's no one like you—no one in the whole wide world."

They left the gallery and made their way along the crowded corridor until they came to Wade's office. When he saw them he at once ushered out several protesting members and closed the door. He looked tired and still avoided Evans's eyes. But he said to Anne, and there was iron in his voice:

"I want to thank you and congratulate you, ma'am, for enduring that ordeal. Will you both join Caroline and me for luncheon at the Metropolitan? I have a number of things I want to talk about."

All at once she felt weary, and the thought of food repelled her, but over Wade's shoulder she caught the expression in Evans's eye.

"Yes, Ben, I'll be glad to," she said. "There are several points about this proceeding I want to be clear about. After all"—she flashed him an oddly wistful little smile—"I don't always admit it, nor am I always permitted to, but I'm human. It was more of an ordeal than I expected. Frankly, I did not enjoy myself. And now, if you'll excuse me, I'll retire to the ladies' parlor and primp a bit."

After she had gone Evans remained in his favorite position, half reclining, half seated on the corner of Wade's desk, staring moodily at the preoccupied senator. Wade, his feet apart, his hands clasped behind him, was standing in the middle of his big red rug, his head lowered like an angry bull's, a scowl on his face as he looked out the window across the Capitol grounds. In the corner a handsome colonial clock in a great mahogany case gently ticked off the seconds.

"Well," said Wade abruptly, without turning around, "how do you think she took it?"

"Put yourself in her place," retorted Evans, his voice like chipped steel. "How would you take it?" Then he exploded. "God damn it, Ben, it's wrong. A great and terrible injustice has been done. I know it. I feel it. And everything in me cries out against it."

Senator Wade angrily bit off the end of a fresh cigar but failed to light it. He turned slowly around and his black eyes burned like coals in the weary pallor of his rugged face. For the first time that morning he looked directly into Evans's eyes and what he saw there only deepened the disturbance within him and the growing expression of guilt on his features. When he spoke his voice was harsh and strained.

"I think so too, Evans. I've tried not to. But, by God, I think so too."

245

29

RIDING A TIRED BLACK HORSE OF UNCERTAIN LINEAGE,
Evans entered Richmond from the west by the Danville road in the
dismal dusk of a day in early March. A Navy tug had taken him to a
desolate landing on Aquia Creek. He had slept in cornfields two nights,
pushed his way overland on three shifts of horses provided at prear-
ranged points by Union spies. He had a new identity. He was John
Albright, cotton merchant of Galveston. The original possessor of the
voluminous papers he carried had been found dead on a field at Occo-
quan, shot down by a Union rifleman as he was returning to a local
tavern after conferences with rebel supply officers.

Street lamps were being lighted as Evans walked his horse along
Broad Street, across the bridge, and finally tethered it to the hitching
post before the Ritchie House, only a block from the grilled balconies
of the Spotswood Hotel. He went immediately to a dirty little room
under the eaves, reserved for him by a Richmond contractor, a paid
informer of Union sympathies. There he sat for an hour, until it was
quite dark, idly reading a newspaper, actually organizing in his mind
the program of his visit. He was far more nervous than he cared to
admit. For the first time he was operating as a secret agent in the political and military heart of the Confederacy. It was not likely that
Texas men he knew were in the Southern capital. If they were—he
threw the paper to the floor and sat a while longer in the feeble flare
of a single gas jet, thinking. He was to confer with only three men
in Richmond, two Georgia legislators named Deming and Cartwright,
authorities on the rebel supply system, and with Edward Pollard,
editor of the Richmond *Examiner* and possessor of one of the keenest
minds in the South.

Evans took a deep breath, got up, carefully brushed his travel-stained coat, and walked downstairs and out of doors.

He had passed through Richmond just a year ago. A year ago! A swirling, colorful mass of 140,000 soldiers and civilians had been poured into a quiet charming little city, now jammed with camps, arsenals, furnaces, and wagon trains; its pleasant hills covered with pretty white tents, one camp called "Chimborazo" in nostalgic memory of the Mexican War. The city a year ago had seemed like some gay and gorgeous masquerade conceived by Walter Scott and every worshiper of the pageant of chivalry.

Fascinated, he had lingered a week in town, in the warmth and haze of early spring, marveling at the endless round of balls, concerts, fetes, and levees, at the lovely ladies of the town who rushed out daily to bake bread for their favorites in the regimental kitchens.

He had watched the Hampton Legion arrive from South Carolina, with wagon trains piled high with trunks, and every handsome member attended by a body servant to accompany him to the front. He had dined royally at Zetelle's and in the evening watched the arrival of the Louisiana Zouaves, Wheat's command, small, tough men with gleaming dark eyes. He had seen the quaint and sinewy Arkansas riflemen, the soldierly Virginians and Georgians, the picturesque, drawling North Carolina "Tarheels," and, on the day he left, the dashing Texas Rangers who came piling into town in and atop five long troop trains. Many of them he knew, and they told him they were disappointed to have to stop over in Richmond. They hoped to be in Washington in a matter of days—although Sumter had not even been fired upon!

Those Texas Rangers were tall, sunburned, hard-drinking men who walked about with the swagger of good-natured arrogant owner-ship and command, sweeping the pretty girls off the streets and into their camps and rooms with a force and gallantry quite irresistible, a conquest that aroused the ire of rival regiments. They were men who had taken as a great compliment old Zach Taylor's remark in the Mexican War that "they were anything but gentlemen or cowards."

And how greatly all this had changed. In so little time, in just a year. Everything, everyone seemed gray, drawn, dazed. Gone were the brilliant uniforms and sparkling camps. Gray mist clung to the sullen James and the stagnant, torpid waters of the canal crowded with gray deserted barges, clinging together as if for protection. The few people about moved swiftly like silent wraiths or clung to lighted areas like pale moths.

He shook his head over the spectacle and wondered where all the gaudy uniforms were packed away and what the Hampton Legion's

247

trim body servants were doing now—probably digging latrines and ditches in northern Virginia. But he had a dangerous day ahead and he soon went back to the Ritchie House, ate a quick supper, climbed to his room, and slept.

Shortly before ten the next morning he entered the office of Edward Pollard, the distinguished editor of the Richmond *Examiner*. Pollard was a solid, forceful-looking man with a magnificent head, a clipped gray beard, and an extraordinary pair of piercing gray eyes. There was about him more of the speculative, analytical judge than the aggressive journalist whose pungent, deliberate comments and summaries, personal and political, made him always listened to and sometimes feared in the councils of the Confederacy.

He accepted the identity and papers of Evans without question and asked Evans what he wished to discuss.

"We folks in Texas," said Evans almost casually, "would like to know the effect of the Tennessee campaign on the minds of Mr. Davis and his Cabinet. We were assured in New Orleans a few weeks ago that the Yankee generals could not and would not fight before late spring, and that Britain and France were to open war on the North by late January. That was the pap we were fed eight weeks ago, sir."

"I understand you, sir. Here is an able editor and a good friend of mine, Mr. John Daniel, writing in this paper two months ago that the Union is dead, that 'the puerile miserable straggling squads of benighted Yankees idling before our defenses must shortly pack up and go home,' and more balderdash of the same." Pollard threw up his hands. "That was published the day before Grant unleashed his great campaign."

"And what has been the effect of that campaign upon the President?" asked Evans mildly.

Mr. Pollard scrutinized Evans but seemed reassured. He said frankly, "Everyone has been struck to the heart save Mr. Davis. We were all taken by surprise, having been informed by everyone in and out of the Army that no major action could possibly take place in the West before late spring. And mark my words, Mr. Albright, if the Yankees get the Memphis and Charleston Railroad and make proper use of it—we're finished. Look at the importance of that road."

Pollard launched into an analysis of the Tennessee campaign that fascinated Evans. Pollard, he reflected, sounded exactly like Anne preaching the same sermon from another angle.

"You think the Yankee generals appreciate all this?" Evans asked finally.

"Good God, they must," exclaimed Pollard. "How else explain what they have done? In a single stroke our whole country lies exposed, including Mississippi, Alabama, even Georgia. Our whole Western defense has collapsed. And in spite of Yankee lies and our own, Vicksburg has not even been fortified. It can be had for the taking. The back door to Charleston and Richmond is now open if the Yankees only knew it. Everyone sees this but Davis."

"But we've been told," said Evans in a tone of desperation, "that Albert Sidney Johnston has an enormous force at Corinth ready to roll back the Yankees. That is the information in New Orleans."

"Mr. Albright, for the sake of our Texas friends I would like to tell you the truth as I see it. But I cannot. However, I will say this. Never was a more brilliant soldier treated more shabbily by Davis than Albert Sidney Johnston. Why, as far back as January twenty-second, Johnston wrote a devastating letter to Adjutant General Cooper here in Richmond, predicting this whole Tennessee attack and pleading for men and more men. I doubt if the letter was ever answered."

Pollard struck the desk top with his fist. He was thoroughly angry.

"I don't know what to tell you to tell your friends, sir. In my opinion, if the Yankees in the West simply keep on walking and don't sit on their tails the way they're doing in the East, we're through and Mr. Davis might as well pack his bags."

Evans, in mentioning Davis and the Tennessee campaign, had tapped a wellspring of deep resentment in Pollard. For Pollard detested Davis.

"Mr. Albright, perhaps I'm being a little too frank with you. It's a habit of mine—and gets me into trouble. But Mr. Davis is a child in administrative matters. He knows nothing of the delegation of authority. He has under him a willing, docile, hypnotized people, eager to fight. He has brave soldiers, the finest officers on the continent commanding a huge territory most difficult to conquer. And yet he is as madly obsessed with Richmond and a hundred miles of Virginia countryside as this mud turtle McClellan. He sees nothing else.

"Moreover, Mr. Davis is at heart a Southern planter. He believes implicitly that all Europe will die for lack of cotton. He cannot understand why the great powers have not already fallen upon the North. As for his government, you should see how its orders are spurned by many of our governors. They've told Davis time and again to mind his own business when he tries to requisition troops and supplies from the sovereign states of Georgia and Mississippi. 'By Gad, sir,' they say, 'are we not fighting for states' rights?'

249

"The fact of the matter is," said Pollard with sudden force, "Mr. Davis is a charming, able, and subtle conspirator—and little else."

Evans said slowly, "I take it, sir, you intimate that the formation of our Southern nation was planned and executed by a small group of men led by Mr. Davis?"

Mr. Pollard's expression was extremely cautious, but he did not back down.

"Yes, sir, you understand me. The mass of people in our South have had little to say about their affairs, one way or another, for thirty years. They have been treated like dogs and they do not know it. The real power has been a close-knit group standing even above and beyond the slaveholders. This group has ruled the South and Washington for years. It was this group that planned a Southern empire. They saw in the Southern portion of this continent, and in Central and South America, new careers, untold wealth, vaster powers. War took such men neither by surprise nor force. They had plotted it. They desired it. They took it in their strides. And the rank and file, the plodders, the people of both North and South, will now die on a thousand battlefields to gratify their desires. This war, sir, was planned in the very committee rooms of the Capitol in Washington, often by no more than a dozen grasping, ruthless, ambitious men.

"I will only say in conclusion," remarked Pollard, "that the man best calculated and best able to wreck and betray our cause has been appointed to defend it. It is a strange fatality, for Davis has charm, conviction, and an exclusive faith of his own. But he is the fatal error of the South and I predict, if he remains in power, he will defeat the whole galaxy of Southern generals.

"And now, sir," said Pollard with a broad smile, "I've talked far too much and far too indiscreetly. I would use your own discretion in telling our Texas friends something of this. Inform them, rather, that blunders may be remedied, that we are doing our best, that we abide by our faith and our cause."

Evans got up and took a deep breath.

"I'm mighty grateful to you, Mr. Pollard. But I still believe, sir"—and his conviction impressed Pollard because he did believe it—"that the South has not yet tapped its great resources. This war is still a war of amateurs. When the amateurs become professionals—then we shall see what may happen."

"I hope so," said Pollard heartily. "But the amateurs in the South may never get another chance. Good day, Mr. Albright, and I should be pleased to hear from you when you've returned to Texas."

"You will, sir," said Evans heartily, "and my thanks for your great consideration. Good day, Mr. Pollard."

Evans went directly to his room, locked the door, and wrote down every remark and comment of Pollard's that he could recall. This done, he folded the tissue dispatch paper into a tiny roll and placed it in one of the cartridge cylinders of his revolver. Then he went out to lunch and decided to look up the two men from Georgia during the afternoon.

Three days later he wrote out a series of abbreviated notes on his further observations, spent an hour placing all the tissues he had between the outer and inner soles of his left boot, and prepared to leave Richmond early Sunday. A series of talks with the two Confederate congressmen and minor officials in the quartermaster general's division, to whom he had secured introductions, confirmed every comment he had heard from Pollard. The South was on the verge of collapse in the West.

Late Saturday night, somewhat against his better judgment, he dropped in for a drink at the Spotswood bar. That favorite resort had recovered a bit of its former spirit and was jammed with politicians and officers. After half an hour's talk with a sutler from Mobile, Evans moved quietly to the far end of the bar and decided to leave, for the sutler had asked him some pointed questions on conditions in Galveston that Evans had a hard time answering.

He had tossed off his final small glass of raw bourbon and was wiping his lips when a pleasant voice, strangely familiar, spoke close beside him. More alarming than a gunshot, the voice was saying very clearly, "Good evening, Mr. Evans. Enjoying your stay in Richmond?"

30

EVANS TURNED VERY SLOWLY TOWARD THE MAN
leaning on the bar at his right elbow. He looked into the gray eyes of
Harry Heyward. For a few seconds neither man moved. They might
have been two old friends casually studying one another's features.
But Evans's mind was racing. His first impulse was to shoot it out,
but passage to the dining room and the street was barred by scores
of men standing about and talking noisily. Harry interrupted his
thoughts quietly, "I reckon you had better come up to my room
where we can talk, sir. Just walk along to that door and keep your
hands free. And upstairs to the right. I have you covered."

There was nothing else to do. Evans turned, pushed through the
crush to the carpeted hall, and walked upstairs, Heyward a few feet
behind him. Harry said in a low voice:

"Just a few doors, sir, to 309, on your left. The door is open, the
light is on. Walk in and stand in the middle of the room."

Once inside the room, Heyward produced an ivory-mounted derringer, faced Evans, and closed the door, turning the key in the lock
behind him with his left hand.

"Don't move your hands, sir. Where do you keep your gun?"

"Under my left arm," said Evans shortly. He was a little astonished
by Harry's calm command of the situation. He had expected an uproar, an immediate denunciation, or a call for the patrol, or all three.
Harry's tactics had him off balance momentarily.

"Sit down, Mr. Evans," said Harry sharply, indicating a worn
rocker under the gas jet. "We have a lot to talk about—and little time.
I intend to turn you in within fifteen minutes. Now, sir—what are you
doing in Richmond? I don't mind telling you, you gave me quite a
surprise."

"I have nothing to say," said Evans abruptly. "You'd better do the talking."

"Then I will, sir," said Harry easily. "I reckon a little exchange of information is in order. Let me see the papers you're carrying. And don't move forward in that chair."

With painful reluctance Evans pulled his wallet and papers from an inside pocket, wondering if he dared risk a sudden assault when he handed them to Harry. But the latter forestalled him.

"Don't move. Toss them on that table," he ordered. Evans did so. Harry's left hand ran through the papers and his eyes widened.

"Our situations, since we last met, seem neatly reversed," he observed.

Evans said nothing but caught the intense gleam of satisfaction in Harry's eyes. Harry studied the tanned features of his enemy somberly.

"Mr. Evans," he said slowly, "while I was—was convalescing in St. Louis I learned a great deal. Among other matters, I found out that you and Miss Carroll were much interested in the Western rivers —that à deux you made a little excursion to Cairo and, I'm informed, examined the mouths of the Cumberland and Tennessee rivers. Tell me, Mr. Evans, did Miss Carroll, either alone or collaborating with you, have anything to do with the Yankee's sudden shift from the Mississippi to the Tennessee? Did she? Did she?"

He rapped out the question like rifleshots, his eyes boring into Evans's. But Evans's expression was bland and he answered casually, "That's a pretty fantastic notion, sir."

Harry tried desperately to read the face of the man before him and to discover the truth there. Ever since last fall when Harry had lain in the House of Refuge in St. Louis he had done a great deal of painful thinking. Anne and Anne's doings plagued him profoundly. In spite of their decisive quarrel, in spite of his marriage to Jacqueline, Harry felt strangely and strongly bound to Anne. And he had pondered Anne's purpose in the West in a steadily increasing conflict of jealousy and bafflement. Hearing of her trip on the rivers with Evans and noting the sudden shift of the Army's interest to the Tennessee, the shadow of an intuition, dim, vague, and unstated, had rocked his mind. Now, as he confronted Evans, Harry was as close to the truth as he ever got. For he had been deeply humiliated by the extent to which he had allowed himself to be deceived in Anne. As a result he was now ready to believe anything about her talents for treachery to the Southern cause, even to his present preposterous suspicion that she might be responsible in some measure for what was happening now in the West. But sensitive as he was, Harry was still not a man to trust his own apperceptions completely. They had failed him too often. On this March evening in an upstairs room at Spotswood's, as he studied Evans's inscrutable face, he sensed some of the truth but dared not face it completely.

Evans, guessing a little of what was passing through Harry's mind, was furious at himself for bringing this disaster upon himself and Anne. Why in the devil had he lingered at the Spotswood bar, the most prominent gathering place in the city? When he thought of what might happen to Anne he winced.

"I have one request," he said quickly. "I'd like to write a note to Miss Carroll, here and now, that you can forward. Otherwise, she may suffer needlessly. She and I were to be married."

"No!" said Harry, almost in a whisper. "You're lying."

Evans saw that he was off guard and sent home another bolt.

"You know, don't you, that it was she who interceded for you in St. Louis? I wanted you shot. She wouldn't hear of it."

Shock and conflict of purpose lay in Harry's eyes. Again they searched Evans's hostile face, and this time they found the correct answer. And yet, plainly, he could not accept what he found, in spite of what he knew of the close association of Anne and this crude Texan. That she loved him, he could not believe, but that Anne would intercede for him, Harry Heyward, was a fact that he had more than half suspected and refused to face. Now it enormously complicated the decisions he had to make. Harry's actions were as unexpected as the new knowledge he was trying to digest. Moving abruptly, he tossed his derringer on the bed, walked over to the window, and stood with his back to Evans. It was a series of unconscious actions which left Harry defenseless and Evans free to act.

But Evans did not act and later on he could not quite explain why. Perhaps it was because he and Harry had at last taken each other's measure. And this understanding drew them together until Evans had an uncanny feeling that he and Harry were old friends who had reached a painful impasse; that in a sense they were two parts of a single being bound to Anne and neither of them could break these bonds.

But Harry was still a man of surprises. He asked quietly, "Mr. Evans, are you carrying dispatches to the Yankees?"

"I am, sir," said Evans, deciding on no more evasions, and surprised by this naïve question.

"Well—of course." Harry stroked his chin a moment. "And what have you learned in Richmond?" he asked with sudden fire. "You have found the South demoralized by these disasters. You have found that Mr. Davis does not trust his generals, especially Albert Sidney Johnston, the finest of the lot. You have found that all the delusions I myself have cherished have reigned supreme here in Richmond, and

254

that the dictatorship of facts has now set our brave world spinning. But let me tell you something, Mr. Evans——"

Harry's deep gray eyes burned brightly in his fine face.

"It would not matter if you carried every fact and figure we have back to your Yankee idiots on the Potomac. They would not believe them either. It has taken me a long time, Mr. Evans, to discover we all live by our wishes and fears. If your Yankees acted according to facts they might now have the South for the asking. You may know this. I suspect Miss Carroll knows it. But your generals and politicians do not dare believe it. They will ponder, discuss, plan, and endlessly debate. They would set your figures against a friend's surmise and eventually discard both. And meanwhile"—and Harry's voice rang through the room—"the South will have risen from these dreadful blunders and delusions and will yet strike, and fight, and finally carve out a bright and glorious victory. If you had lived, sir, that is what you would have lived to see.

"As for Miss Carroll ——" His voice faltered, and he began again. "As for Anne, it may be that among the lot of us she will remain undefeated. There is a clarity in her that men cannot tolerate. And if her thinking is as right as it is clear, then there may be something wrong in our Southern cause of which we are not conscious or have not been apprised.

"I have always loved Anne and she has always been too much for me. Never, until now, could I admit it. But she has won at every turn. There is something in her I cannot fight. Perhaps it is something that should not be fought. And yet, sir, if I acknowledged that, my world might fall in pieces. I might have no authentic reason for being what I am. Do you follow me?"

In spite of his own crucial predicament, Evans was fascinated.

"I understand you very well, sir," he said evenly.

His words, and a certain intimation they conveyed, brought back to life Harry's hostility. He leaned lightly against the window sash and regarded his enemy.

"All right, sir, now to our own business. Having heard these things —what would you do in my place? Suppose I am sitting in your chair, sir. For the moment I am you. Would you turn me in, consign me to the firing squad, or turn me loose in a moment of sentiment, or exact a binding parole? Suppose I am to marry the woman you love. If you were I, what would be your decision, sir? Come now, Mr. Evans, give me an honest answer."

Seconds ticked away and Evans was forced to admire the other man, once again in command, his gaunt, well-molded head flung back and the waves of ash-blond hair catching the light that also brought

255

out the whole structure of his handsome face. Harry had pushed him into a bad corner. God damn him, he thought, God damn him.

Finally he cleared his throat, surprised at the dryness in his mouth. There was dull anger in his voice. "You know the answer, Mr. Heyward, as well as I. You talk too much. I'd turn you over to a firing squad at once."

The muscles in Harry's face tightened. He nodded grimly, but strangely enough did not move.

"That's right, sir," he said loudly, as if he were a professor standing in a classroom and some bright pupil had given him an unexpectedly correct answer. Evans was nonplused. The man was inexplicable, unpredictable. He was certainly suffering, but all traces of his inner conflict, all his indecision, had vanished. He was a man about to make the only decision he could make, reflected Evans, and his heart began to pound. He felt suffocated. By God, he did not want to die! All at once Harry jerked himself away from the window. His left hand shot into his coat pocket and came out holding Evans's long black revolver. Rage contorted his features.

"God damn you!" he cried out in a loud voice. "God damn your soul to hell!"

He hurled the revolver clear across the room. It crashed against the wall by the door and fell on the thin carpet with a heavy thud. Harry's lean body trembled. He advanced threateningly on Evans.

"Get out!" he shouted. "Get out of here before I kill you. God damn it, get away from me and don't ever let me meet you again."

Evans stepped quickly across the room, picked up his gun, unlocked the door, never even glanced at Harry, and darted into the hall, slamming the door behind him. He drew a deep breath, stumbled in his relief, then walked weakly along the hallway, down the stairs, and into the street.

In the room he had left, Harry waited until Evans's footsteps had died away. He stood by the window, torn again by indecision. He wanted to throw himself on the bed in the old, old infant gesture and rail at his lot and sob out his frustration, his weakness, his final humiliation. But strangely enough he could not. He glanced a little guiltily in the mirror and his eyes were very steady and very bright. He could not quite understand what he had done. For he had a sudden sense of well-being and did not dare ask himself why. He took off his coat and threw it on the bed, turned down the gas, and pulled the little rocking chair over by the window, which he opened. For a long time he sat there breathing in the mild night air and looking out over the rooftops of Richmond and a bit of the James River curving to the left. His own behavior mystified him, but he did not care to probe his

256

motive for it. Instead, enjoying his solitude, he savored the first measure of happiness he had experienced for so long that he was afraid it would flee if he stirred. But when he finally went to bed it had not flown. It did not, in fact, quite ever leave him, then or later.

31

ANNE'S DELIGHT OVER LEM'S SAFE RETURN FROM RICH-
mond was so great that he dared not tell her of his encounter with
Harry until several days later. At first she was shocked, then her
eyes brightened and she pointed out eagerly, "I knew I was right in
fighting for Harry's exchange. He's sent you back to me, Lem."

He was about to observe derisively that if the Army had had its
way with Harry the incident in Richmond need never have occurred
at all. But seeing her expression, he thought better of it.

Having filed his reports with the War Department, Evans was enjoying a few days of complete freedom. But he watched the papers
closely. A tremendous battle was brewing in the West. A huge attack
by the combined Union armies on Corinth, Mississippi, Johnston's
stronghold, was rumored imminent.

One morning, trying to ignore the general tension, he lounged before a fire in Anne's rooms, running idly through an issue of *Leslie's
Weekly* while Anne sat on her sofa drinking hot chocolate. Maps
and papers were scattered all over the room. Evans, amused by a
florid account of the elaborate, much-disputed reception Mrs. Lincoln
had given in February, slapped the paper on the table and came over
and kissed her.

"And how is my 'delicate aerial blonde' this morning?" he asked
gaily.

"Please don't tease me," exclaimed Anne. "What are you talking
about?"

He picked up *Leslie's* again, struck a pose, and announced, "They've
done you proud, Anne. Sandwiched right in between Miss Livingston
and Mrs. Donn Piatt. Listen to this while I crawl at your feet."

With affectionate amusement he read *Leslie's* salute to Anne:

" 'Miss Carroll, a charming blonde of the purest type, wore a dress of white illusion, with a succession of puffs reaching almost to the waist. The effect was very fine and harmonized admirably with her delicate aerial style of beauty.' "

Anne laughed with him.

"It was *all* illusion, Lem. I'm five pounds overweight and Kate Chase was impudent enough to remark that I was becoming 'pleasingly plump.' I hate her! And I found my first gray hair a week ago—honestly. Don't you dare tell a soul. But dear *Leslie's* and its lovely lies—I'll renew my subscription this instant."

A shaft of sunlight played across her hair and he thought she had never looked lovelier. But her eyes were dark with anxiety.

"Don't ever mention Richmond again, Lem. I can't bear it. It was slow death with you away. How did I exist before——"

"Before what?" prompted Evans, smiling at her solemn expression.

"Before I met you," she said simply. "I can't understand it. Living, working, existing alone in that neat little house in Baltimore, staring at a pile of newspapers every morning."

"You haven't changed that habit," laughed Evans, glancing at the papers strewn about her room.

Her eyes laughed back at him. "You're not just a change, dear, you're a whole revolution."

They talked of less personal things and finished their chocolate.

"How's Old Mars?" asked Evans suddenly.

"I don't know," she said. "I wish you'd go down with me this morning and see him in action. He's established a 'morning hour' for the general public, which means everyone with an ax to grind, and it's something phenomenal. But he's already raised an army of enemies, Lem, and frankly I—I just don't know how to deal with him."

"I never heard you say that about anyone. What do you mean?"

"You'll see," she said enigmatically.

After a brisk walk they made their way through the crowded corridors of the War Department to Stanton's dingy, plainly furnished office. Stanton's "morning hour," held five days a week, was a spectacle unparalleled in the memory of Washington.

In the midst of a scattered group of cowed clerks and secretaries Stanton stood on a small dais supporting a high desk at one end of the fairly large reception room. A messenger stood at his elbow.

Once the doors were flung open, a solid mass of supplicants poured in and crowded about the stocky, spectacled figure, a belligerent Sir Oracle staring coldly at the throng. In half a minute Stanton had mentally separated the sheep from the goats. Once the room was

259

filled and the doors closed, the Secretary pulled out a fat silver watch, glanced about the room, rapidly estimating the pace he would have to maintain to clear the place in an hour. Then he fixed his eyes on the first caller he had chosen and called out forbiddingly, "Well, sir, what do *you* want?"

Anne and Evans had crowded into the last available space.

The breakneck speed Stanton maintained in disposing of these petitioners paralyzed the most poised. Men who had traveled hundreds of miles and carefully rehearsed flowery pleas for some favor, important only to them or their families, would be enraged to be interrupted, after one or two pompous sentences, by Stanton, who grew livid and yelled, "Pure tripe and nonsense, sir. Get the hell out of this room."

The whole scene rapidly became an organized turmoil. Once Stanton looked straight at Anne and Evans, seemed surprised, and frowned fiercely at them. Evans waved his hand in a gesture signifying they were present only as spectators, and Stanton, looking relieved, rushed on to his next case. But in all this bedlam of shouting confusion Anne saw that Stanton probed like a surgeon and missed nothing important.

Over the heads of a fascinated crowd Stanton's voice rolled and reverberated.

"Take this pass to the hospital, madam. You will be admitted at once." . . . "Damn it, sir, how dare you make such a request in this place?" . . . "See General Meigs about that, sir. It will take but a moment." . . . "That form is now correct, Mr. Adams. Present your contract to General Dix in the morning." . . . "Who the hell sent you here? Mr. *Seward?* Well, you go back and tell Mr. Seward it's none of his damn business. Tell him I said so." . . . "Hello, John. What? Well, why didn't you say so last week. Take this pass and get out—and good luck." . . . "Not another word, sir. I know your filthy face. You've hounded me for a week. If I catch you in this office again I'll have you under arrest." . . . "No, madam, I have no jurisdiction there. See Commander Fenton in the Navy Building——"

In exactly one hour the room was cleared and Stanton noisily washed up in a small adjoining lavatory, sprinkled cologne generously on his beard, and briskly signaled Anne and Evans to enter his office. His shifts of mood were phenomenal and he appeared now not to have a care in the world. He clapped Evans on the back, congratulated him on his Richmond trip, and fussed over Anne like an anxious father.

"I detest these morning sessions," he declared. "But I believe in them. They provide direct contact with the people and I learn about

260

matters that would never come to my attention through official channels. I'm bold enough to feel that I catch a few glaring injustices now and then and throw a little needed fear into the corrupt. And many of these Army lads have no place to turn to."

Chatting briefly on Army matters, Stanton gave them a few tidbits of information.

"After a perfect snowstorm of telegrams," he said, "Grant is back in the saddle. The campaign against Corinth, in north Mississippi, has begun."

Abruptly Stanton went to the window, sniffed anxiously, and opened it wide.

"This damn cologne drives me crazy," he announced with a wry smile. "But after choking on the breaths of yokels who seek to embrace me before they've digested their foul breakfasts, I have to use it."

Then, changing the subject suddenly, he turned and said to Anne, "Don't bother me for a few days, ma'am. Call on me Saturday. In confidence, I have to tell you my friendship and trust in McClellan are ended. He has flatly disobeyed the President's special order to move his forces; he is interfering in the West and is now engaged in a battle of dilatory words and letters with both Mr. Lincoln and myself. He may ruin everything we have planned. And don't show up here for a week, Evans. We'll have plenty for you then. And now, my friends, good morning to you both."

Anne's anxiety about Stanton had been dissipated by this brief if brusque interview. But a storm between them was brewing. For ten days, following the Saturday he had appointed and an occasion on which he had failed to appear, he had refused to see her. He scribbled a peremptory "No!" and "Not yet!" on two notes she sent him. And she had to see him.

She waited patiently enough at first, for she knew Stanton was overwhelmed. He was trying to do too much, and everything at one time.

Stanton's measures were harsh. He raised up enemies on every hand. He was pushing and prodding the motionless McClellan in the East, urging on the almost equally reluctant Halleck in the West, and at the same time ferreting out corruptions on a colossal scale. He was planning his own expedition to capture the Norfolk Navy Yard. He was organizing an amazing river navy of his own on the Ohio, acting under his personal orders, much to the rage of the Navy Department chief, Secretary Welles. Other schemes were boiling in his restless brain. No war minister in the nation's history had ever possessed such enormous powers, such an ungovernable temper, and such relentless, hounding energies. The people hailed him, the press trailing after them; the Army sullenly opposed him; the Navy actively fought him.

But for more than two weeks Anne was unable to get near him, and the delays in the West had her frantic. One evening at dusk, when she was by herself, she saw him in a corridor of the War Department. He was talking angrily to young Captain Piatt, an official of the Judge Advocate's office and an old Ohio friend of Stanton's. Anne made a mistake. Advancing impulsively, she boldly interrupted Stanton.

"Mr. Secretary," she said sharply, "it is absolutely necessary that I see you without further delay—and by tomorrow afternoon at the latest." The instant she heard herself she regretted that she had not chosen less peremptory words. Nevertheless, she was not prepared for their effect.

Stanton did not answer her at once. But when her words had sunk in he whirled on her, his eyes full of animosity, his lips snarling, and his whole expression so savage and fanatical that she was appalled. When he did speak he screeched rather than shouted:

"God damn you, madam, I'll send for you when I want you. Get out of this building. I'll have no petticoats around here now or later. You are not to enter the telegraph office again. Do you understand?"

Captain Piatt, horrified, placed a hand on Stanton's arm. Stanton shook it off and said, "Damn it, keep out of this, Donn!" and attacked Anne again. "You think with your simpering manners and eternal meddling you can give orders to *me,* make demands on *my* time, and *tell me* when I shall see *you?* I'll allow no females to interfere with me, ma'am. Get home where you belong. I don't wish to see you again, ma'am, now or ever. For God's sake, let me alone and take yourself away from me. Go! Go! *Go!*"

She was so stunned that she leaned against the wall, her eyes filling with angry tears. She was quite unable to speak, and Piatt came to her side and said in a low voice, "He's not himself, ma'am. Come along. I'll be honored to escort you home."

She was shaking so by the time Piatt found a hack that he feared hysterics before he could get her home. She cried once, "What is it, Captain Piatt? I know I shouldn't have sounded so arbitrary. But he knows me well enough to realize——" She broke off. "What did I *do?*"

Piatt's good-looking, sensitive face was gloomy and troubled.

"Madam, I don't know," he said in a puzzled voice. "He's not well. But the cause of these outbursts is a mystery to me. I have endured several of them. So, I understand, have Mr. Lincoln and Seward and many of Mr. Stanton's closest friends. I beg of you to try to forgive him."

"I can't," she cried on the verge of tears. "He's unforgivable. I never want to see him again."

Captain Piatt tried to comfort her. "Ma'am, I don't know what to say. I've known Mr. Stanton for years. In Steubenville he was liked and admired by everyone. Ten years ago he was a witty, gay, friendly young man. He would do anything for his neighbors, and people loved him. But when I met him in Washington last year, after a long absence, I hardly knew him. He was distant, hostile, gloomy—and I had counted him my closest friend. He has since insulted me. He has insulted Mr. Lincoln to his face. And Mr. Stanton's doctor has warned him twice he is subject to rushes of blood to the brain and should avoid all excitement."

She listened closely.

"I didn't know that," she said, surprised by Piatt's information.

"Did you know he has had two attacks of vertigo since he has taken office and was carried home from his office unconscious only two weeks ago?"

"No," she whispered. "That's horrible. Do you think he's gone out of his mind?"

"I do not," said Piatt emphatically. "But he is torn to pieces by some inner turmoil. And he is in a terrible state about this war. My lord, madam, you have no idea of his insolence. Only the other day Owen Lovejoy brought instructions from Mr. Lincoln to Stanton. And Stanton told Lovejoy, 'If he gave you that order, the President is a damned fool.' Lovejoy rushed back to the President and reported Stanton's insult. He told me Mr. Lincoln just grinned and told him, 'If Stanton said I was a damned fool, then I must be one, for the Secretary is almost always right and generally says what he means. I think I'll step over and see him.'"

But Anne could not get over Stanton's outburst.

"What can I do, Captain Piatt?"

"Don't do anything, ma'am," warned Piatt. "I predict Mr. Stanton will offer his abject apologies in a few days and forget about the matter."

"Well, I can't and won't forget such insults!" she exclaimed, indignation replacing her wounded feelings. "I can't and won't work with such a creature. And yet I *have* to——"

The captain escorted her to the door of the Washington House.

"Ma'am, just sit tight. Please wait, and try to rest and forget this shocking incident."

She could neither rest nor forget. For several days, however, she shunned the War Department. Then late one afternoon, having had

263

to deliver some papers to John Tucker, Colonel Scott's assistant, she hurried along the corridor outside Stanton's reception room, intent on leaving the building at once. As she passed a closed door she heard a woman's voice call out almost in a shriek, "But you must. You *must!*"

Stanton's rolling voice came to Anne clearly. "I cannot, madam. I cannot."

She wanted to leave. But the urgency in the voice of the unseen woman halted her where she was. After a brief struggle curiosity led her around to the side door used by Stanton's clerks. She slipped quietly into the far end of the room and stood transfixed at the scene before her.

In the center of the room stood a thin, distraught woman in a faded green jacket and frayed shawl, a market basket on one arm, and three dirty, wide-eyed children, two little boys and an older girl of about six, clustered about her skirts. The woman had been crying, and only her anger, as she glared at Stanton on his dais behind the high desk, staring past her out of the window, prevented her tears from flowing again. One of Stanton's clerks, behind a low table, had stopped working and, pen in hand, was watching the scene. An old janitor, waiting to sweep out the litter of torn paper and cigar ashes, leaned on his broom, looking at the woman and her brood with mild but sympathetic attention. There was no one else in the room.

In that wide forbidding space before the dais only the woman seemed alive. Her eyes were desperate, bloodshot, frightened, and one hand kept nervously plucking at the thin shoulder of the older boy. Her voice was thin, piercing, like a frayed wire about to break. She was obviously trying to say what she had already said in some new and cunning manner that would move the motionless figure poised above her.

"But he ain't bad," she insisted. "He's a good man. We been married this month nigh to seven year, and I ought to know. He only come back a day and night. He was on his way back with a lunch I packed him when they took him. Mr. Sec'cary, before God, we need him. He's the father of these here youngsters. If he ain't killed fightin', we want him back. I got no money, sir, nothin' but a pittance from his allowance."

"That is no concern of mine, ma'am," said Stanton harshly. He picked up several official papers clipped together. "Your husband, ma'am," he said in a clipped metallic voice, "is from the Thirty-third Ohio. He deserted last spring at Cincinnati and spent four days in your home. He was court-martialed and received a suspended sentence on recommendation of his superior officer because you were ill and your home was only fifteen miles from his camp. He has been arrested twice on minor charges and served sentence. When Colonel Moore's regiment was ordered into line in January he deserted again and was picked up by the provost marshal a mile from your home with three days' rations in a bag. He has been sentenced to be shot and I have approved that sentence. There is nothing that can be done."

"There is, there is." Her voice raised to a scream. "You can't kill him. You shan't. God will strike you dead for this! Is it a crime he loves his wife, that he loves Jamie and Mary, here, and Jed—and a baby boy I buried a year ago? Tom is a good man. He ain't never raised a hand against anyone. He farmed and he raised these chil'ren in the fear of God. And he's all I ever had. *All I ever had,* do you hear? You are a terrible, wicked person if you allow such an awful crime—and my children and I will curse you and haunt you into hell and damnation."

Her voice broke, shifted into a minor, wailing key.

"You cain't do it, Mr. Sec'cary. You know you cain't——"

"Get out," roared Stanton. "Get out of this room."

Anne was appalled by Stanton's behavior. He stood rigidly hostile, his beard flung up at an arrogant angle, his black eyes devoid of expression, still staring straight through the steel-rimmed glasses at some distant point past the window. He never once so much as glanced at the woman. The room quivered with a clash of wills as the woman faced him defiantly, her small brown eyes burning with hate and hopelessness. But Stanton's bellow had frightened the children and all three of them began to cry, the youngest breaking away and running toward the door, where he abruptly wet his trousers and clung screaming to the doorknob, unable to turn it.

At the sound of the children's crying, the woman wilted. She gave a little moan and flung herself on her knees before Stanton's high desk and clutched its heavy legs as if they were Stanton's own. All defiance fled out of her. She moaned and swayed and cried over and over, "Oh Lord, save him. Oh Lord, have mercy on him and save him."

At last Stanton moved. He whirled on his clerk, glaring at the openmouthed wretch as if he would tear him apart.

"God damn it," he shouted, "get her out! Take them all out of here!"

Without a glance at anyone, without noticing Anne almost in his path, Stanton strode the width of the room, flung open the door to his private office, and disappeared, slamming the door shut behind him with a crash that dislodged little clouds of dust from the dingy ceiling.

265

Anne held her breath as the clerk rose stupidly, halfheartedly, dreading his mission. But there was nothing to dread. The woman's will had broken and she lay crouched on the floor, whimpering. The clerk raised her up. Anne, her throat sore with the lump in it, marshaled the children together. The clerk turned them over to attendants in the outer corridor.

Then he came back and faced Anne. Neither of them could say a word. The clerk was rather undersized, with a sandy, sparse mustache over a weak mouth. But some spark within him flared now. He hitched back his thin shoulders and stared at the door of Stanton's study. He looked at Anne and his eyes narrowed, and finally he spoke.

"By God, ma'am," he said softly, "that's more than I can take. He can fire me, but I am going to tell him what for. I been here six months, but I never seen worse than that."

Without thinking, she followed this transformed little man. He did not even knock on Stanton's door. He opened it firmly and took a firm step inside. But one step was all he took. He stood just inside the room, his hand on the knob, and Anne peered over his shoulder.

"What is it?" she whispered.

The clerk pointed, and he whispered back, "He's sick."

For a moment she thought he was right. In the dim light from half-drawn blinds she saw Stanton lying on his back on the old haircloth sofa in the corner. His heavy strong figure rolled and twisted and both hands covered his face. He was moaning a little and the sound of his breathing in the confines of the room was labored, asthmatic, and tortured.

"Go get a doctor right away," she said to the clerk in a low voice. "I'll stay here with him."

The clerk darted away and she walked slowly over to Stanton's side and pulled a straight-backed chair from the wall and sat down. At first she thought he was in some paroxysm and was unaware of her presence. But he had evidently heard her, for he pulled his hands away from his face and quickly seized one of her hands in both of his and held it in a crushing grasp. Tears poured down his cheeks and all at once, between his sobs, he began to say over and over:

"God help me to do my duty! God strengthen me. God help me!"

Her hand went to her throat.

"Mr. Stanton! Don't!"

But the tormented man could not be stopped.

"How can I go on with this?" he whispered. "I couldn't look at her. I couldn't stand her eyes. I know the boy, ma'am. His father used to farm near Cadiz. But I can't pardon these lads. *I can't do it!* Somebody has got to make this Army stand together and fight. And

I haven't the strength to do this, day after day. God help me to do my duty. I cannot do it alone."

She was powerless to say a word and sat there stroking his broad moist forehead until the now frightened clerk came back with a doctor. The doctor gave Stanton a sedative and a prescription, warned him to rest a day or two, and after a low-voiced consultation with Anne left to order the Secretary's carriage brought round to the door.

But in spite of Anne's pleas Stanton made no move to go. He sat dejectedly on the edge of the sofa, his eyes lifeless, like a doomed soul awaiting punishment.

"What *is* it, Mr. Stanton? What *is* it?" she asked repeatedly, and fought back her own tears, for the man's plight went straight to her heart. He was shaking as if with the ague, and from time to time he passed a huge soiled handkerchief aimlessly over his face. Then one of his hands seized hers again and fastened to it and his flesh was like ice. The gesture seemed to release something in him, for now he could speak.

"Miss Carroll," he said in a dull voice, "please sit here with me a few moments longer. I must talk to someone."

32

COMING FROM STANTON AFTER HIS ARROGANT BE-
havior, these words astonished her. But there was no doubting his
terrible distress.

"What has happened?" she managed to ask.

He shook his head. "I have been beside myself all week. I have
to beg you, ma'am, to forgive these outbursts if you can, for I cannot
control them. What I said and did to you the other day has been
killing me. I have hurt outrageously some very dear friends in recent
weeks. And I do not know how to undo the damage. That I could
assail you so after all you have done—I owe my very office to you—
is something I cannot endure. Will you please forgive me?"

Stanton spoke in exactly the tone of a frightened child who fears
a dreadful punishment unless he is absolved.

"There is nothing to forgive, Mr. Stanton. If there is in your own
heart, believe me, it is forgiven. I know the terrible strain you are
under. I know what you have to contend with every day. But this is
something very different, my dear friend. If you possibly can, talk
about it, tell me about it. Try to unburden yourself."

With a real attempt to regain his composure Stanton sat up and
said quietly enough, "Madam, I do not know what seizes me at these
times. This woman today—she was the last straw. But these attacks—
all I am conscious of is that I must die; that some force or power
dooms me to die and to destroy and wreck and insult everything I
hold dear in the process. And my heart fights against this and my head
splits with pain—and then I'm undone. I cannot go on. And I cannot
die. There is too much that has to be done."

She thought fleetingly of what Captain Piatt had told her and realized that she was dealing with a soul-sick man, a man who obviously was not mad in any real acceptance of the term. She chafed his cold wrist a moment, then said firmly:

"You really must talk about this, Mr. Stanton. You said as much a few minutes ago. Now you are trying to escape from doing so. What is it that disturbs you so at these times? I know it is far more than—than these recent happenings or that ordeal of yours this afternoon. I do want to help you, but I don't know how unless you tell me what is the matter."

There was a quality in her voice that seemed to give Stanton courage. But his eyes were puzzled. He sat a little more erect, looking straight before him. He began to talk haltingly, as if to himself.

"I don't know, Miss Carroll. I don't know what these moods are. But I will tell you something not even my wife knows. I have a perfect horror of death. A terror of it. All my life long Death has sat at my board, slept in my bed, stalked me by day and by night. In some moment of darkness, before I am ready for it, it will have its way with me."

"But why—why should you feel this way?" she cried, shocked by the undoubted force and belief in his words. "You have everything to live for. Why?"

"Let me tell you something of myself, ma'am. Perhaps you can understand this terror, for I cannot." His hands plucked restlessly at a frayed edge of the horsehair sofa.

"I must speak of it," he said abruptly. "I have struggled for years with this sense of death and dissolution. I first encountered death when I was not quite thirteen. I was coming home from school one cold December day. The door of our house opened and my father came out, smiling, and waved a greeting to me. All at once he fell—or I thought he did. But he shook and twisted about horribly. I ran to him and when I reached him I found he was dead. They told me it was apoplexy. I—I cannot bear to think of it now."

"Then don't," she urged. "That was all long ago."

"There is no time or distance to such hurts," said Stanton. But he cleared his throat harshly and drove on:

"When I was nineteen a terrible cholera epidemic swept Ohio. That was in '33, I believe. One afternoon a bright girl I liked very much—the daughter of a doctor with whom I was lodging—served me dinner and chatted and teased with me. When I came home after classes for tea—that very afternoon, mind you—they told me she was dead. The cholera had struck her down a few minutes after I had left the house. They had buried her within an hour, for panic held everyone in those days. But I would not believe it." Stanton struck the

269

palm of his hand with a clenched fist. "I simply would not believe it. Do you know what I did, ma'am? I went out with two young friends of mine and opened her grave and looked at her dear face to make sure she had not suffered the awful agony of being buried alive. But" —he began to tremble again—"she was past help. She was dead."

He sat silent for a few moments before he spoke again.

"On a New Year's Day, ma'am, just after my twenty-first birthday, I went to Cadiz, a little village in Harrison County, and entered into law partnership with a brilliant and wealthy youngster named Chauncey Depew. That very first autumn I bought a house in Cadiz and then went to Columbus, walking twenty miles in fresh-fallen snow and riding the rest of the way to claim a girl who had waited for me three years. Her name was Mary. . . .

"Her name was Mary Lamson," continued Stanton, his voice shaking. "She was an orphan and I loved her completely. For our wedding journey we drove one hundred and twenty-five miles on the stage sleigh from Columbus to Cadiz in a marvelous fall of fresh snow, over rolling hills mantled in white, through quiet, sunny woods, by flashing streams half covered with ice. It was the brightest, sweetest journey of all my life. You know, Miss Carroll, I never could control or limit my adoration and affection for Mary. Well—I worked terribly hard. In 1840 my daughter Lucy was born and a year later she died. Later on came a fine boy and Mary insisted on naming him Edwin."

Stanton, now in the full flood of these memories, absently rubbed the side of his face.

"My wife died in childbirth in the spring of '44, ma'am," he said simply. "I could not believe it. I would not. I knew if I did my heart would stop beating. The family wished to dress Mary in black and I would not let them. I told Miss Elliott, our seamstress, 'She is my bride and shall be dressed and buried as a bride.' And so, at last, she was."

He had begun to weep. But the catharsis of speech, the pouring out of these long-submerged memories, was bringing about a profound change in Stanton's appearance. He regained control of himself, suddenly sat up, quite erect, borne along on the aroused currents of his mind.

"I'm almost through, ma'am," he said humbly. "You are right. It somehow relieves me to talk of these things. But there was one more blow to endure. Less than two years after Mary's death my fine brother Darwin—he was a doctor and an assistant clerk of the House of Representatives—fell ill of a fever in his Virginia home across the river, just opposite Steubenville.

"He lost his mind, took one of his own lances and severed the femoral artery, and bled to death in a few moments in the sight of our mother. I was called late at night and told only that Darwin was ill. When I got there and saw what had happened, saw Darwin on his bed in a great pool of blood and Mother shrieking and prostrate, I could not stand it. I could not. I remember rushing wildly from the house, running into the woods, without hat or coat, determined to do away with myself. If I had had a weapon I would have. All during that terrible flight I felt as if Death were breathing on everything I loved, as if Death were determined to destroy everything I cherished, as if Death had struck down the only dear ones that had made my life worth while. And then, pursuing me wildly through the woods, Death glared down on me, its last victim, and flung its cold folds about me, and froze my heart and said to me, 'Come.'

"After that I remember nothing until the next morning, when I woke at home. Two old friends, Will Brown of Holliday's Cove and John Knox, told me they had chased me in the woods for an hour and found me raving and calling on Death to take me away. Sometime later I took Mother and Darwin's widow and three children into my house and we lived there as one family while I tried to support and comfort them."

Stanton sighed deeply. Anne, who had listened to this appalling recital, unable to say a word, saw that his account was nearly finished. His eyes were clear and bright as he turned to her, though he seemed drained of all energy.

"It was twelve years before I married again," he said. "I married the lovely daughter of a Pittsburgh client of mine. Her name was Ellen Hutchison. But before I married her, Miss Carroll, I had one very painful duty to perform. I went back to Steubenville to burn Mary's letters, two great chests of them. I remember placing them all in a grate, in neat piles, while our old gardener, Alfred, now aging, silently watched me. Three times I tried to light a match and it finally fell from my hand. I said to Alfred: 'I am required to burn these, Alfred, but I cannot do it. I cannot. You light them for me, please.' And I began to weep. Alfred finally lighted them and turned his back on me. I thought he was reproaching me, that he felt I should not burn them, but when he turned around the poor old man was crying as if his heart would break."

Anne was close to tears herself. She cried out:

"Don't, Mr. Stanton, *don't, please!* Oh, I wish you hadn't told all this. I wish you hadn't!"

As she spoke an astonishing change took place in Stanton. He rose to his feet and began to pace the room, once more nearly oblivious of her. He began to speak rapidly, his voice hard, pushing through

271

the underbrush he had cleared so thoroughly, pressing on to the present.

"You are right, madam, to make me talk of these things. By heavens, you are right. For I think in some way these matters do bear upon my present situation. The reason I find my position so intolerable is this—that I, a man who has known and seen and lived face to face with death since boyhood, must now on a colossal scale be an instrument of death myself. Something of all this may lie in the horrible remorse and guilt I feel in discharging my harsh duties. I have to play slave to Mars, who is but another aspect of Death. Upon me falls the duty of raising armies, marshaling thousands of boys, many of whom are sons of friends of mine, and hurling them into the arms of death. You think this is easy? You think it merely the discharge of official duty? A thousand times no. It is a hateful, horrible, bloody, death-dealing task. It is a great and supreme irony of fate that I who hate death now have to dispense death to others on such a scale."

"I have many enemies, ma'am. Trust me to know what they say of me—that I am brutal, arrogant, without heart, cruel, unjust, born to intrigue, that I despise my betters, hate my equals, have contempt for my subordinates. But do you know what it means with my background to stand in the midst of chaos and hurl thousands of men to sure death?"

He sighed. "Every Friday I must prepare a list of Army executions —scores of boys, seventeen, eighteen, nineteen, or twenty—boys to be shot to death—shot for sleeping on duty, for desertion, for creeping back to ones they love after having been thrown into an outrageous kind of life for which they have not the slightest aptitude or preparation."

His whole body seemed to sag as he sat down again on the couch.

"Every Friday I have to go through this horrible business. One hundred and three lads shot to death last week, on my orders, and eight months ago they were ploughing furrows, clerking, living in their homes, with their families. I, God help me, have to sign their death warrants. Mr. Lincoln will not do it. He calls each Friday 'Butcher's Day,' and not a week passes that he does not come over and pull out and destroy warrants of execution and plead with me to reprieve dozens of others. I cannot. Such kindness to cowards and malingerers is cruelty to the Army, for it encourages the bad to leave the brave and patriotic unsupported.

"Thus," said Stanton bitterly, "Mr. Lincoln builds about him the legend of a kind heart, though in this matter he is actually most fearful that these executions will discourage recruiting, while I am portrayed as a very vulture of Death waiting to tear these erring young from their parents' arms. Every week I am forced to face an army of shrieking, grief-stricken women whose husbands, sons, and lovers I have murdered. I am the monster of this war, the messenger of Death. And God help me, it is something I can hardly go on with.

"One more word, ma'am," Stanton said earnestly, "and I'm through. I know I've tried you beyond endurance. But on top of all this, knowing what should have been done all these months and unable to do it, knowing there is treason in the Army, treason at home, treason among men and women who wish to line their pockets and bring this war to a close at once, at any price, I have to deal with generals I don't trust, with contractors who think nothing of selling defective weapons to these boys who will die with them in their hands. I have to deal with politicians and riffraff to whom this Union is nothing but a word to spout on a platform—while the rank and file of our humble patriots are cheated, lied to, and exploited.

"That is why I leaped at your plan, ma'am. I saw in it a will to *act* equal to my own. But that in such a situation I should so disgrace myself as to attack you personally the other day! I beg you to forgive me. Can you accept what I have said—and remain my friend? For I'm yours, ma'am, as long as I chance to live."

She knew well what she wished to say but knew no way in which to say it. To dissect political, social, and legal matters was one thing. But to lay bare a human soul was another. To her every man and woman had a sacred façade that should, so far as practicable, remain inviolate. And to have the creator of such a façade, and at her express invitation, ruthlessly tear it down, not only frightened her, but—and this was even more relevant in the present situation—it left her wordless and embarrassed. Her sympathy and affection solved the problem for her. Completely without intent or self-consciousness, she went to Stanton and put her arms about him.

"If I had only known this, Mr. Stanton, I would never have been the fool I've been. I've had no idea of what you've had to bear. You give so little outward indication of the kind of burden it is." But she thought of many little signs she had indeed noted and never correctly interpreted. "I could not begin to understand what happened the other day. Now it is completely explained—and, once explained, is waved away and forgotten. You terrified me at first with your revelations, but——"

"No, no. You were right," interrupted Stanton, holding her hands and smiling for the first time. "It has lifted a tremendous load. God bless you, ma'am, for hearing me out. You have no greater admirer anywhere than I, and I pray we now have an understanding that will last—and I am sure we do. You have helped me enormously."

273

He got up, still very pale but much more composed.

"Ma'am, I want you and Evans to dine with us Thursday a week. I want you both to meet Ellen and the children—and forget for once the ogre I am on public exhibition."

She walked with him to the yard where his carriage was waiting.

"Do get some rest. Do get some sleep, Mr. Stanton. You are quite exhausted."

"I will, ma'am. I am all right now, and at ease in my mind for the first time in ages. I will sleep. I know it."

After Stanton's carriage had disappeared she was still standing there shaken and staring when Evans saw her from the window of Tucker's office and hurried to join her. She told him all that had happened and he shook his head wonderingly.

"That clears up a lot," he said. "Many of us have never been able to figure him out."

"I can't stand prying into a person's heart like that, Lem. I feel so helpless. Do you suppose Mr. Lincoln knows anything of Mr. Stanton's story?"

"He may. He once told me Stanton had endured some early experiences very close to his own. And Lincoln don't admire a man without reason. He likes Stanton a lot and calls him 'Old Mars' to his face." Evans smiled. "Did you hear what the President said about the last batch of complaints against Stanton?"

"No," said Anne curiously. "What was it?"

"Why, Mr. Lincoln told a group of senators howling about Stanton's highhanded methods that Stanton reminded him of an old fire-eating Methodist minister out West who got so excited jumping up and down exhorting his flock that the folks used to put bricks in his pockets to keep him on the ground. Uncle Abe grinned and said, 'Well, gentlemen, no bricks for the present. I guess we'll let Stanton jump awhile.' "

Anne laughed for the first time that day. But late that evening, as she lay sleepless, Stanton's story again overwhelmed her. Sympathy and horror had split open dark recesses of her mind that she had not known existed. She had looked into these dim regions once and unforgettably. But she did not wish to look again. In the darkness of her room she whispered to herself, "What horrible, ghastly, frightful things really happen to people. And hardly a soul ever knows. Hardly a soul ever knows."

33

A FEW DAYS LATER STANTON CALLED SENATOR WADE to his office and invited Anne and Evans to sit in on the meeting. The Secretary showed no signs of the emotional ordeal through which he had passed. He was his old bustling, confident self.

"Well, Ben," he began, "we should be making strides in the West, but there's hell to pay. I want to show you what threatens this Western campaign behind the scenes."

He slapped a sheaf of papers on the table.

"These are telegrams from Colonel Scott in the West. You recall our original plan was to have a simultaneous drive on Richmond. Well, sir, for a month Scott has been pleading with McClellan to send one hundred thousand veteran troops West from the Army of the Potomac. So have I. But Mac won't hear of it. Scott is now begging for fifty thousand or even thirty thousand men. Mac will not send them." Stanton's voice rose. "The man baffles me."

Thoroughly angry, he got up and stood over his desk.

"Time and again Scott has implored McClellan to go to Cincinnati or Louisville to confer with Halleck and Buell and iron out these separate commands so we may push three hundred thousand troops up the Tennessee. I myself have pleaded with the general. I've asked him at least to appoint a single commander in the West, so that we won't lose all we've won. He refuses to do that either."

"But why not?" demanded Anne angrily.

"I'm not sure," said Stanton slowly. But he corrected himself. "Yes, I think I am. Mac is deadly afraid of competition in command. To place a single man in charge of the forces in the West might be to name his own successor. He, too, suspects that the West is the real battlefield. A victorious general out there with a single command might threaten his whole authority. In this respect the rebels have the advantage, with a unified Western command under Albert Sidney Johnston.

"Mr. Lincoln has done all he could," Stanton continued. "McClellan never obeyed his executive order to move on February twenty-second. By refusing to do so he has endangered the government's whole program East and West. To punish him, Mr. Lincoln, on March eleventh, issued his Special Order No. 3 relieving McClellan of all commands except the Department of the Potomac. The President ordered that the commands of Halleck and part of Buell's be consolidated under Halleck, and he set up a new Mountain Department in western Virginia under Frémont. But that didn't settle the problem —and Mac is raging at both Lincoln and me."

Wade was aroused.

"Why don't Grant go ahead and move on Corinth instead of sitting two weeks at Pittsburg Landing?" he demanded.

"I don't know," replied Stanton wearily. "He has about forty-five thousand men. But he says he's waiting for Buell. The gist of it is," he went on in tired exasperation, "we can't get Halleck to accept Evans's Richmond reports or Miss Carroll's St. Louis estimates of Johnston's army. Yet somebody's got to move out there soon, and McClellan won't lift a finger to give them a push. The great double plan we had is falling apart. Meanwhile Grant is in a somewhat dangerous position."

"Well, Mr. Stanton," commented Anne, "the Western armies still have their golden opportunity. Once you beat Johnston at Corinth, you can take everything south to Vicksburg and east to Atlanta—New Madrid, Island No. 10, Fort Pillow, Memphis."

But their discussion soon ended and everyone left feeling discouraged and frustrated by the lack of action.

That evening Anne sat down to write Stanton her conclusions in a long letter.

"I've got to tell him," she said to Evans later as he read her final draft, "that the failure to take Island No. 10 does not surprise me. Eads's gunboats are not well fitted for the taking of strong batteries on the Mississippi."

Evans had been penciling minor changes in her letter.

"Let's put it bluntly—like this," he said. " 'Had our victorious Army, after the fall of Fort Henry, immediately pushed up the Tennessee River and taken a position on the Memphis and Charleston Railroad between Corinth, Mississippi, and Decatur, Alabama, which might easily have been done at that time, every rebel soldier in western

Kentucky and Tennessee would have fled from every position on that railroad.

" 'Had Buell pursued the enemy in his retreat from Nashville and taken a commanding position on that railroad between Chattanooga and Decatur, *the rebel government at Richmond would necessarily have been obliged to retreat to the cotton states.*' " Evans added impatiently, "They've got to be hammered with that. I'd end it right here, Anne: 'I am fully satisfied that the true policy for General Halleck is to strengthen Grant at once and enable him to seize the Memphis and Charleston Railroad, as it is the readiest means of reducing Island No. 10 *and all the strongholds clear to Vicksburg.*' I think that does it," concluded Evans.

She nodded and he went out to mail her letter.

But in the days that followed she thought often of Stanton's warning that Grant's position might be unsafe. All during March she had plotted on her maps the disposition of Grant's forces, now strung out in a region of desolate swamp on the western side of the Tennessee River about Pittsburg Landing. Dispatches coming now from this area were causing a steadily rising tension around the War Department.

The site had been selected simply as a general rendezvous for Union forces. General Lew Wallace with another Union army was at Crump's Landing, a few miles down the river to the north and opposite Savannah, a small Tennessee River town where Grant had his headquarters. Buell, at last en route from Nashville, was due at Savannah on April 8. The whole force was then designed to move on Corinth in Mississippi, some twenty-odd miles away to the southwest, and there defeat Johnston and seize the Memphis and Charleston Railroad.

On Saturday night, April 5, Anne dined alone. Evans had been gone more than a week, accompanying Colonel Scott to the West, and he was now somewhere up the Tennessee. Only an infrequent sufferer from nerves, she was surprised by her anxieties and felt that she could not bear the solitude of her rooms a moment longer. She called on Caroline only to find that Caroline was attending a Sanitary Commission meeting. She decided to drop in at the telegraph office and then go home to bed.

There was a curious atmosphere at the War Department, of which she became aware almost immediately. Stanton was in an ugly humor. Mr. Lincoln had just left. She listened to several officers arguing heatedly over a number of errors made in the tangled web of Western command. They were alarmed over the loose disposition of Grant's and Sherman's armies near the Corinth road.

277

Her anxiety increased as she studied the telegraph file. The Army's scattered positions, all unentrenched, frightened her, and her fears were confirmed when an officer said loudly, "Colonel, if I were in Johnston's shoes I'd call ourselves wide open."

Copies of several telegrams from Grant and Sherman to Halleck in St. Louis attracted her attention. Both generals had just assured their commander that they expected no attack or anything like it on their positions.

She was amazed by these dispatches and called them to Stanton's attention.

"I read 'em," he said impatiently.

"They're idiotic," she began heatedly.

Stanton, tired and angry, pounced on her. "Are you contradicting the judgments of trained generals who happen to be in the field, ma'am? If so"—he salved his rancor with a wry smile—"perhaps you'd better put on a uniform."

"I'd like nothing better," she retorted. "Every man in this room senses a dangerous situation. I admire Sherman greatly, but these telegrams—these are the words of fools."

Stanton relented. "I don't like their attitude myself," he said softly. "I don't like it at all."

She lingered until midnight, depressed by and impatient with the obvious confusion of command and the lack of ordinary precautions revealed all the way from St. Louis to Washington. Then she went home to bed. At seven in the morning a thunderous knocking on her door awakened her. It was Stanton's coachman, a free Negro named Dan.

"Ma'am, can you come over at once? I'm pickin' up several officers. There's a terrible battle on. General Sherman's whole army, ma'am, was swept into the river three hours ago. I done took Mr. Stanton to his office at five o'clock."

In the telegraph office she found a silent crowd of officials, headed by Mr. Lincoln, crowding about the chattering instruments. Stanton, red-eyed, in his shirt sleeves, his tie and collar removed, threw incoming wires from him as if they were white-hot and blistered his hands. The news was appalling. Forty thousand rebel recruits under General Johnston had moved entirely unobserved—for no Union scouts were even in the field—out of Corinth, had marched eighteen miles north, camped a full day, quite undiscovered, only two miles from the main Union force, and had between three and five on that Sunday morning ripped through the unentrenched Union lines, rolled shotted cannon to the very openings of Sherman's tents crowded with sleeping men,

278

had brushed Sherman's men aside in a hail of lead, and now seemed about to hurl the whole Union Army into the Tennessee River. Panic and hints of disaster crowded every telegram. Not a word had come from Grant. He was not even there. He could not be found. He was reported lying drunk at his Savannah headquarters, miles away.

Thus, in terror, panic, and dismay, began the terrible battle of Pittsburg Landing near Shiloh Church. All during the day Anne sat silent and white-faced in the bedlam of the telegraph office, trying to penetrate without success some of the terrible truth that might lie in the welter of conflicting reports that poured into the office where Stanton and his staff, first shocked, then amazed, then frightened, could do nothing but read and wait and ponder the fantastic imponderables of war.

At seven that evening she went to the Wades' for an hour's rest. Caroline and Wade returned with her to the telegraph office. A fever of excitement, stimulated by the wildest of reports, had transformed the place by nine o'clock. News had come in that Buell's forces had been ferried across the river late in the afternoon just as eight thousand of Grant's panic-stricken raw recruits were cowering under a bluff by the river and thousands more were trying to swim the icy stream. The wounded, lying on the bank awaiting transportation that had not appeared, had been trampled by those in panic, by new forces arriving, and by officers clubbing stragglers back into the fight. The last wires from Paducah, shortly after eight, reported that Beauregard had called off the exhausted rebels and refused to order another attack.

Stanton, rushing past her, caught her eye and shouted, "Good news, ma'am! Albert Sidney Johnston was killed late this afternoon."

In the strange web she had helped weave, the fate of Johnston shocked her immeasurably. In a single, vivid vision all her meetings and talks with the general's kinsman, Mr. Johnston of the St. Louis Mercantile Library, flashed before her. Try as she would, she could not evade a weight of depression, almost guilt, as if she shared in the responsibility for the death of this gallant officer. Even Ben Wade could not cheer her up when, shortly before midnight, he announced excitedly, "The Army is holding, ma'am. By the Lord, I think we've pulled a victory out of this mess."

She could not rejoice. She went home, slept badly, came back to the office next morning, and remained there. In midafternoon came the great news that Grant, in final charges, had swept the field. But in the very midst of the office celebration over this announcement came a simple telegram from Colonel Cameron at Paducah containing the first rough estimates of casualties on both sides. This telegram arrived with all the effect of a bombshell, for no one had half guessed the

279

actual slaughter and panic that had occurred. By late afternoon of the first day, said the dispatch, Grant had only seven thousand effective fighters left in all his armies. Altogether, some twenty-five thousand raw recruits on both sides, farm boys and officers, were killed, wounded, missing.

Before this blast from the West, the jubilant groups dissolved.

Buell, it appeared, had saved the day. But he could not save the enormous number of dead, mutilated, wounded, and dying, lying motionless or writhing in muddy swamps, floating by the scores down the muddy river, piled in heaps through the rain-drenched woods and by the bloody riverbanks.

Stanton sat speechless in a low chair, rubbing his hands together, from time to time mopping his pale face with a handkerchief. She heard Major Eckert, superintendent of telegraphs, say, "On your peril, don't show that to the President tonight. Not until morning, or by God I'll make trouble for someone."

Wade, too, talking in a low voice to Anson Stager, seemed thunderstruck. When Caroline crossed the room to talk to her, Anne gave up.

"Take me home, Caroline. I feel sick."

34

THE SHOCK OF SHILOH PARALYZED THE LAND. THE white horsemen of Death rode up to cabins and mansions, hamlets and cities from Maine to Missouri, and the casualty lists appalled the world. Never again was it the same war after Shiloh. Gone were the parades, the glib slogans, the academic discussions of plans and campaigns.

Two great armies of raw inexperienced youngsters, the average age far under twenty years, had collided in a maze of mounting blunders, in a remote stretch of swampland no tyro would have selected for battle. There they had fought and fled and rallied and held their ground with a hot heroism and a mounting thirst for blood that astounded veteran officers. There they had butchered one another's brigades until the press and public realized to their collective horror that no such battle and no such slaughter had been known before in the nation's history. This had been the bloodiest struggle yet known in the Western Hemisphere and one of the greatest and strangest battles ever fought on the American continent.

For three days the endless lists of dead, dying, wounded, and missing poured into the homes of the people. And then these people rose in their fury, and the fury of the land broke on Grant, and a little later on Lincoln.

When it was discovered that Grant had been eating breakfast in the Cherry Mansion at his Savannah headquarters hours *after* the battle had begun, and that Sherman had been caught completely by surprise; when it was published that neither Grant nor Sherman had anticipated any attack, or had entrenched, or sent out scouts, or even established liaison among the various camps; when it was learned that all these

281

boys had died in vain and Shiloh was a rout and a disaster saved in the nick of time by Buell's fresh forces, and that Buell had disregarded Grant's orders and thereby luckily arrived a day early, the wrath of men and women, of the bereaved and mourning, achieved new heights. Grant was reviled. The press shrieked for his removal.

The fact that Grant had fought, and fought doggedly, was forgotten.

Evans walked into Anne's parlor shortly after nine on Friday evening. He was a very different man from the easygoing imperturbable creature who had left Washington a fortnight ago. He had come directly from Shiloh. An invisible hand seemed to clutch her heart as she looked at him. He had lost weight, his color under his usual tan was sallow, and there was an almost haggard line to his flat cheeks. "Oh, dearest," she cried softly, her eyes filling.

He took her in his arms, holding her close, and kissed her fiercely.

"Do you want to tell me about it, Lem?" she asked finally.

"I guess I'd better—a little, at least," he answered in a lifeless tone. "I can't convey much of it to you," he said, sitting on the sofa and drawing her down beside him. "You can't convey to anyone the nature of such an experience. I guess it was both the suddenness and the size of it that staggered everybody. But in certain places—— Anne, there was a cocklebur meadow in front of Sherman's artillery where Beauregard had sent Cleburne's Brigade across time after time. . . . Sunday night I went out with a handful of Grant's surgeons and looked it over. We estimated ten thousand men—think of it, ten thousand!— lying in that single field not more than a mile long by half a mile wide. Old grass, set afire by gun blasts, had burned over half the field. . . . Here, I almost forgot. This is Pilot Charley Scott's account. He was going to mail it, but I brought it with me."

She took the letter but made no move to open it.

"Lem, you're safe," she said wonderingly. "I was so afraid. . . ."

Then sharply, angrily, she said, "What in God's name happened to Grant and Sherman?"

He shrugged, looking a little at a loss for an answer.

"I don't know. They just didn't think anything would happen. In any other army they'd be cashiered for what happened Sunday. On the other hand, they fought like devils once they saw the situation— Sherman especially, He had a bullet through one hand, four horses shot dead under him. He had to drop back all the time, but his line of boys never broke once.

"The first we knew something was up was when we were all having breakfast with Grant and John Rawlins at Savannah, nine miles north of Pittsburg Landing. Charley Scott went to an open window and listened. Suddenly we recognized the sound—artillery, a long way off, then a dull roar that never stopped. Grant got up, pale as paper, and spilled his coffee. It was the first time I'd seen him like that. He snapped out, 'Boys, that means business. Come along.'

"It was two hours before we reached Pittsburg Landing. And Grant was badly rattled. Everyone could see it. He had no idea what to do. And then I really understood—neither he nor Sherman had had the ghost of a notion that Johnston would move out of Corinth and fight. They had no command in the field, no battle plans, no liaison—nothing!"

Evans paused, took out a cigar, and lighted it.

"After you've said that," he went on, puffing away, "Grant managed to do a whacking good job. He and Sherman are a team. There's no doubt about it."

"You know that yesterday Mr. Lincoln proclaimed a day of special Thanksgiving, don't you?" she asked.

"So I've heard," Evans said gloomily, "but I can't get those two days out of my mind."

He went on to tell her many curious things about the battle—how Colonel Appler of the Fifty-third Ohio, far out in front, had sent word to Sherman at four in the morning that a large force was approaching, and Sherman had lost his temper and sent back a message, "Take your damned regiment back to Ohio. There is no enemy nearer than Corinth."

A boy, wounded and sent to the rear, came back in fifteen minutes, crying, "Captain, for God's sake, give me a gun. This damned fight ain't got any rear."

"Monday it was all over," concluded Evans. "Lew Wallace's men came up in the morning—they'd been lost all day Sunday trying to find the battle—and in midafternoon Grant gathered up what he had, threw it at the rebels in a final charge, and the two-day hell was over. But to me, Monday night was the worst. All through the woods for miles, along the sunken road where Prentiss stood, by the peach orchard where Hurlbut had piled thousands of dead rebels, all about Shiloh Church, clear to the bluffs and the river, there was nothing but a wave of sound, of moaning, crying boys, and above that the slash of hail cutting through the last of the torn branches and peach blossoms. And nobody to help them, for those who could fight had to sleep."

When they talked to Stanton the following day their spirits lifted a little. The Deep South had been ripped wide open. Fresh armies were pouring up the Tennessee.

283

Mr. Lincoln's proclamation on April 10 celebrating these triumphs gave impetus to another clamor in Congress for the author of the Tennessee plan. On April 14 Vice-President Hamlin arose in the Senate and announced that after long search he was sure Flag Officer Foote of the Navy had first proposed the Tennessee campaign. Nobody believed him.

Meanwhile the capital was in worse than an uproar, for it was now thronged with bereaved mourners, with wives, mothers, families, and weeping relatives seeking news of the dead or missing and hotly determined to question every man in the several trainloads of wounded brought all the way from Shiloh to new hospitals in the city.

Deeply moved by these sights, Anne and Evans were walking along the Avenue one morning when they met Colonel McClure. The handsome burly Philadelphia editor stopped to talk with them. After several minutes Evans asked, "Colonel, have you any idea what's going to happen to Grant? I see he's lost his command again. Is he through?"

McClure's eyes narrowed. He frowned and said shortly, "No. The President is going to keep him."

"How do you know?" asked Anne curiously.

McClure was silent a while, as if reluctant to reveal a confidence. Finally he shrugged.

"Because he told me so," said McClure. "I called on Mr. Lincoln only last night, acting as a spokesman for some of his closest advisers who believe as I do, that Grant is a calamity. I urged, demanded, and pleaded for Grant's removal as the only thing to restore confidence in the White House and the country. Well, it did no good at all. Mr. Lincoln politely allowed me to talk myself out. He just sat before the fire with his feet clear up on the marble mantelpiece. When I thought I had him, I stopped. It was all of two or three minutes before the President got up, looked at me as if I hadn't been there, and shook his head violently. You could have heard his voice upstairs. All he said was:

" 'McClure, I can't spare this man. *He fights.*' That is why," added McClure, tipping his hat and passing on, "General Grant will be around a while longer. Good day, ma'am. Good-by, Mr. Evans."

35

ANNE BEGAN, DURING THAT SPRING OF 1862, TO FEEL
the strain of concealment—a twin concealment that veiled most of
her professional activities and all of her personal life.

Moreover, her increasingly close association with the President
added to the strain she was under. Quite without her realizing it at
first, her discussions and debates with him were affecting her profoundly, undermining old and supposedly solid convictions, softening
the sharp edges of long-held opinions, plunging her into thoughtful
silences that cut increasingly into the brisk gay volubility hitherto so
characteristic of her.

Evans, too, was undergoing change. He was a man of immense
physical strength and endurance. But he was also a man of high
sensitivity. As he watched the endless casualty lists filled with the
names of men and boys from Texas that he knew well, much of his
natural exuberance fled. A note from his brother, Dr. William Evans
of east Texas—a brother from whom he was all but estranged by the
bitterness of their political differences—curtly informed him of the
death of Dr. William's son and his own favorite nephew, John David-
son Evans, killed in action with the Confederate Army. The expression
of the scholar that Anne had often noted in Evans's features now
deepened and mellowed. A brooding quality crept into the clear brown
eyes.

These changes in Evans gave him a new dignity and distinction so
noticeable that Wade even teased him about it one evening. Studying
him across the supper table, the old senator had exclaimed:

"Evans, you'd better not invade Richmond again. Did anyone ever
tell you you're getting to be a dead ringer for Robert E. Lee before
he grew that beard of his?"

There was a general laugh and Wade added, "That's a compliment. I knew Lee well several years ago. Colonel Lee, then. A fine man and a handsome one. With little understanding of politics, more's the pity, or he'd never have gone South. Now if you and Lee——"

And Wade had continued his teasing.

As for Anne, Evans increasingly fascinated her. Their relationship was quite chaotic and in normal times would have been wholly unendurable. He was away for weeks at a time. He usually returned quite unexpectedly and they snatched a few days together—days of stimulating discussions or silences shared in reading or study. Their refuge was Trenthan with Sallie, or Cambridge with her father, where in brief interludes they enjoyed all the informal, secure, pleasant family life she intended to create for Evans and herself someday.

The solid affection between them was the rock on which she stood and battled other forces surging about her.

And he became for her not only a devoted companion but a stimulating consultant who edited and rewrote many of her papers and writings for the press. He was gay, teasing, playful, serious, and humanly irritable in turn. Under strain Evans's high-strung nerves and volatile temper occasionally made him blunt and direct. Sometimes his sarcasm hurt. He had an uncanny ability to ferret out false logic and false premises.

"Your feelings are right, but your thinking's rigid," he often told her. "Nobody can be as right as you sometimes think you are. Loosen up, Anne. Listen to Mr. Lincoln a little more," he would add a bit maliciously, aware of her tendency to dominate discussion and aware, too, that the President was making greater inroads on her thinking than she realized. Occasionally he really hurt her with his thrusts.

"For God's sake, Anne, you're dealing with people—not legal briefs," he would exclaim, looking over some of her more opinionated outbursts to the press. "Get off your high horse. You take people personally and most successfully in your social life. You know them, understand them, sympathize with them. Write about 'em the same way."

She kept her temper, tried, and often succeeded.

On the other hand, Evans often stood in genuine admiration and awe of Anne. He was primarily an analyst and able critic. And the creative side of Anne always amazed him. He was a brilliant interpreter of laws and ideas, an able student of military matters, with one sharp eye forever on the social struggle. But he was never able to take familiar elements and from them, through the magic alchemy of the mind, produce new, startling, or revolutionary conclusions. And this

286

Anne, under sufficient stimulus and at important crises in her life, was able to do.

She also confounded him with her femininity and with her easy frank association with men and women with whom he often thought, in moments of superficial speculation, she would have nothing at all in common. Her cheerfully disordered rooms, full of military maps and papers and piles of franked documents tossed everywhere, were frequently crowded from four in the afternoon to midnight with an astonishing variety of callers, chatting, laughing, drinking tea, or staying for a hastily assembled supper. In these social encounters he saw in Anne a warm, generous interest in others so genuine that even those who most differed with her had to fight to overcome her magnetism.

He recalled Thurlow Weed, invited to discuss some matter with Anne, and Weed's laughing refusal:

"Not today, Mr. Evans. She'll change my mind in five minutes. Tomorrow at five. I'm going home to fortify myself and I'm bringing along the ablest lawyer I know to prop me up."

He was also impressed by the manner in which Anne had fought her way out of a slaveholding background steeped in conventional tradition and exclusively Southern associations. She had discarded all these feudal ties one by one and now found herself allied with the most vigorous prosecutors of a war against her own kind. Senator Sumner had commented on this phase of her career:

"Miss Carroll has had so much more to overcome than any of us, Mr. Evans. I absorbed my convictions with the air I breathed. Miss Carroll has had to fight to find hers. That is a superior achievement and you must remember it."

Evans had teased Anne one evening about her incessant letter writing. An Indiana representative, unaware of their close relationship, had said to Evans, half jokingly, half complainingly:

"She's a confounded nuisance at times, sir. I run when I see another letter from Miss Carroll. She must operate a letter factory. And she's always demanding I *do* something."

Evans had related this as a mild pleasantry and was taken aback at the quick anger that flared in Anne.

"How else can I work or make my weight felt?" she had snapped. "Letters are the only real weapon a woman in my position has. I can hold no office. I have no official status whatever. I'm constantly regarded as on sufferance, on trial, as any woman must be who competes with men. My brain is my only capital, and more often than not men don't want me to invest it in any of their precious projects. I know I'm a nuisance. I *have* to be. I have to pound and pound incessantly at every crack and cranny I can find. They're not numerous for any woman, Lem, let me tell you. And for two years of work I've not received one cent of compensation."

For once Evans had no ready retort. He thought of the solitude and concealment of his own professional life. But all his relatively high fees from the State Department were paid promptly. Again, and quite poignantly, he saw beyond what she had stated—that the dearest concerns of her life and all her most vital interests were continually forced into a shadowy hidden world increasingly hard for her to endure. The very next day he had gone to the War Department and raised a row over her unpaid accounts. That at least he could do for her. Stanton had shrugged his stocky shoulders.

"We'll do what we can, Evans. But she has no written contract. And the unpaid accounts of this department alone amount to nine millions, many of them dating from before the war."

Now, in late spring, with fresh foliage and new grass making green the ugly winter face of the capital, Evans saw something else. He said to her one night, "You'd better get ready for your second campaign, Anne. Do you realize what you're in for?"

"I haven't an idea," she said cheerfully. "What are you talking about?"

He was looking at her a little grimly.

"Don't you realize your Tennessee campaign has ripped the lid off the slavery question and thrown the whole problem into Congress where everyone's ducking the issue or dancing about on a red-hot stove?"

"You think these slavery debates are a result of the Tennessee campaign?" she asked in astonishment.

"What else?" he retorted. "You thrust a Union Army into the heart of the slave belt in a matter of weeks. It's lanced the huge sore everybody's been trying to treat with shinplasters—and the poison's pouring out. What are you going to do about it?"

Evans's line of reasoning had never occurred to her. It jarred her, as so many of his ideas did. He went on ruthlessly, outlining the situation to her.

"This fear of facing the slave issue is reflected all over Congress. I feel it myself. Take the Army's inaction around Washington. I don't openly assert that McClellan is a traitor—but in my opinion he is. The Army of the Potomac has been paralyzed by political pressure ever since its inception. Are we now discussing military plans after these victories, or how to smash rebel armies and destroy the rebellion? Not at all. We're in a panic. Negroes are pouring North in a flood. *What*

288

are we going to do with 'em? That's what is killing us. Even Mr. Lincoln is still trying to pretend this war isn't over slavery. But Congress knows better."

Anne smiled and Evans turned on her.

"What's amusing about it? What is your own point of view? You've opened Pandora's box with this Western campaign. Charles Sumner sees this clearly. The senator now hammers Abolition, complete freedom for blacks, death to the slaveholders, and shouts this from the housetops until even Mr. Lincoln wants to hide in the White House cellar."

"But, Lem, you know what I think." Patiently she restated her own attitude—that with the war soon over and the Union re-formed on constitutional grounds, the people in the several recovered Southern states would be glad to agree to gradual compensated emancipation, as Mr. Lincoln had recently urged.

He brushed her familiar arguments aside.

"Suppose the war don't end soon. Suppose the South goes on the rampage. Here's Halleck inching toward Corinth, McClellan floundering about the Peninsula, the whole works bogging down."

She showed him her letters in the New York *Times* upholding Lincoln's stand, one of them published on the same day, March sixth, that the President's compensated emancipation proposals were made public. But Evans tore them apart.

"Colonization of Negroes be damned!" he said roughly. "How can you join in this nonsense? In ten years, with a fortune expended, not four thousand blacks were colonized in Liberia. Why should they be colonized? You profess freedom for Negroes. Did you ever *define* that freedom? *What kind of freedom do you suppose it is going to be?* It's either full freedom in every sphere—social, economic, or political—or it's no freedom at all. Can't you understand that?"

She winced at his words. He had a talent for finding any weakness in her arguments.

"But what am I going to do?" she cried. "I'm gathering all sorts of data on Central America—New Granada and the Chiriquí coal fields and other areas that might provide large colonies for Negroes. You think this is nonsense?"

He evidently did. They argued heatedly in the worst quarrel they had stumbled into.

"Don't look at me so, Lem," she pleaded finally. "I can't bear it. What you and Sumner demand means violence, more death, more destruction. Solutions to a problem like slavery take time."

"No," said Evans angrily, "that part of you that fears to face these truths said that. Time won't wait. Every Yankee has tried to avoid or

289

wait out this struggle for years. What did it get them? The most colossal war in history. Even now, most of the North feels as you do. They are being pulled into a bloody swirling pool of immediate decisions—and, God, how they hate it! Look at your pompous friends in the Cabinet wasting hours on childish measures that will never be undertaken."

"They're not childish," she retorted. "Mr. Lincoln himself believes in them."

"I doubt it," said Evans coolly. "If he does, he's badly mistaken. Even Wade's getting infected. I told him the other day the Army had some tough battles in the offing. He looked at me as if I'd reminded him of some trash in the back yard of his Ohio home. 'Battles, Evans? Right now I'm more worried over confiscation and who's going to run reconquered territory than anything else.' But this war isn't won by a damn sight, my dear, and you may have to eat a lot of your own words one of these days."

It was a violent quarrel, though not a serious one in a personal sense. For a long time afterward the words of Evans haunted her. She began a series of conversations on the same subject with the President. He almost paraphrased a remark of Evans.

"The Army of the Tennessee, ma'am, has smoked out the slavery issue and flung it before the nation. What we are going to do about it, I don't know."

Nor did anyone else know, she thought. For Negroes were pouring North in a flood, hanging in hordes on the coattails of every regiment, crowding Northern cities, confronting the fervent Messiahs of freedom, and confounding them by their actual presence.

Day after day she sat in the House and Senate galleries listening grimly to the frightened outcries of these Yankee defenders of freedom and democracy. Shouted Representative Cox of Ohio to a colleague who had dared favor limited emancipation of the slaves:

"But how long would it be, sir, before the manly, warlike people of Ohio, of fair hair and blue eyes"—Mr. Cox had long black hair and brown eyes, but no one bothered to mention this—"would become completely degenerate under the wholesale emancipation of the blacks favored by my colleague? No, sir, free Negroes cannot exist in this country without its ruin."

At a time of increasing doubts and self-searching, Anne was especially grateful for several solid tributes. A long paper on Negro colonization she had prepared for the Cabinet at the President's request had brought a warm letter of approval from Attorney General Bates.

A few days later Congressman Mitchell of New York had written to tell her about Mr. Lincoln's meeting with a congressional committee, followed by a study of her report. "Mr. Lincoln," wrote Mitchell, "was most enthusiastic and told us, 'This Anna Ella Carroll is the head of the Carroll race. When the history of this war is written she will stand a good head taller than ever old Charles Carroll did.' I thought you might like to hear this."

But praise from a far different quarter, wholly endorsing her military concepts, excited her even more. She burst in on Evans one evening following her return from New York, where she had been conferring for several days with various editors.

"Lem," she cried excitedly, "Mr. Greeley gave me the most remarkable article on the Tennessee plan. I'm quite set up. You must read it."

Evans laughed at her jaunty expression. "Has Horace solved the war again?"

"It's not by Greeley," she retorted. "But one of his former correspondents wrote it. It's a brilliant piece by a German named Karl Marx, now living in London. He wrote it for *Die Presse*, a Vienna paper."

"Is that the chap who wrote a series for the *Tribune* on revolution and counterrevolution in Germany a few years ago?" asked Evans.

"That's the man," said Anne. "Charles Dana lunched with us the other day and told me that he first met Marx and a friend of his, Friedrich Engels, in Frankfurt—oh, about ten years ago. Dana was then foreign editor for the *Tribune* and signed Marx on the spot. He was most impressed with both men. Engels is a military expert, and Dana says he writes most of Marx's military analyses. At any rate, here's Marx's article in *Die Presse,* dated March twenty-seventh, on the American Civil War—and it's all about that campaign of ours. Dana had it translated for me. Listen to this . . ."

It was a long, thoroughgoing article which stated that the Tennessee campaign was the springboard by which the North might win the war, that it opened up the only strategically sound avenue of attack, and that if the campaign were promptly followed by a smashing attack through Georgia to the sea and up the coast to Richmond the war might be won in a matter of months. After Tennessee, Marx maintained, Georgia was the final key to the collapse of the Confederacy. Several passages greatly excited Anne.

" 'With the Tennessee campaign,' " she read, " 'the war now takes on for the *first* time a *strategic character. Only with the victorious advance into Tennessee did the movements of the Western army become important for the entire theater of war.* The decision of the campaign belongs to the Western army, now in Tennessee. Should McClellan's "Anaconda" plan, however, be followed, then, despite all successes in particular cases and even on the Potomac, the war may be prolonged indefinitely, while the financial difficulties, together with diplomatic complications, acquire fresh scope.' "

There was much more that Anne read excitedly.

"Lem," she exclaimed when she had finished, "Stanton should paste that article in his hat. And I never felt so set up in my life. Greeley told me in that squeaky voice of his that he's always admired Marx's political views and had based many of the *Tribune's* leading editorials on Marx's analysis of events. But how does he know so much of the military side of the war?"

"Engels, probably," said Evans. "The President gave commissions to a number of German Socialists, who correspond regularly with Marx. Weydemeyer told me that in St. Louis. Marx is probably well informed."

They discussed other news she had, including a report that Lincoln and Stanton had hired Charles A. Dana away from Greeley and intended using him as their own personal observer on military matters in the West. Anne opened a letter from Sallie in reply to an invitation of her own with the news that her sister would arrive from Trenthan the following day for a week's visit. When she finished Sallie's note she glanced up to find Evans looking at her quizzically.

"Sweetheart," he said mildly, "you're probably floating around in the clouds this week—and I can't wonder at it. But you're going to find a storm up there. And Uncle Abe wants to see you. I promised to deliver this personally."

It was a note from the White House in the President's hand.

DEAR MISS CARROLL—Can you dine with us informally tomorrow (Wednesday) shortly before seven? I have certain matters to discuss with you afterwards.

Your friend,
A. LINCOLN

P.S. Mrs. Lincoln would like you to come early, if you wish, so she may show you her flowers.

A. L.

She looked at Evans very solemnly and then laughed.

"Lem, there's no rest for the wicked. I'm afraid I'm being put to work again."

36

ON THE FOLLOWING EVENING SHE FOUND MRS. LINCOLN, with Tad, waiting for her on the first floor in the Red Room, always called "the living room" by the family. Mrs. Lincoln, dressed in mourning for Willie in a handsome gown of black watered silk, sat on a red divan with a pile of newspapers beside her. She was looking much better and her blue eyes sparkled a greeting. Her brown hair was brushed back in simple waves that showed only traces of gray.

Tad, a fresh-faced youngster of nine, wearing a blue suit trimmed in semi-military fashion, was on the floor busily cutting out large colored figures of uniformed soldiers from a magazine.

Mrs. Lincoln welcomed Anne cheerfully and after a few moments led her downstairs to the conservatory, a great glass-enclosed structure jutting westward from the lower quarters of the White House. Mrs. Lincoln had a passion for flowers and plants which Anne shared. Suspicious of many of her husband's feminine friends, Mrs. Lincoln had finally been won over by Anne, partly by her frankness and honesty, but in large measure by Anne's gift to her of a superb early London edition, with many colored plates, of *Species Plantarum* by the renowned Swedish botanist, Charles Linnaeus. After that evidence of their mutual interest the two women got on famously.

They spent half an hour enjoying the conservatory before they returned to the Red Room. Mr. Lincoln had come in and was quietly reading. Smiling, he rose to greet them.

"Good evening, Miss Carroll. I trust you've a good appetite. And what have we got to eat, Mother?" he asked Mrs. Lincoln.

"Surely you ought to know, sir," replied Mrs. Lincoln jokingly. "You overruled my roast lamb this morning, so we have roast beef again."

Mr. Lincoln grinned.

"Let it be again and again, as far as I'm concerned." He turned to Anne. "Mary's found a market with the finest roasts I've ever tasted. Come along, ladies, I'm hungry."

His towering figure led the way to the small, unpretentious family dining room where a bright fire was burning briskly at one end, and two white waiters were standing on either side of the serving door.

The dinner was plain, substantial, and excellent, with a thick soup, a delicious roast of beef, browned potatoes, fine small peas, apple jelly, and mince pie and ice cream. Mr. Lincoln ate heartily. He was in almost a gay mood and regaled them with tales of the day's callers, including a delegation of Sioux Indians who wanted permission to camp by the Monument for two weeks. Mrs. Lincoln began to tease him about his early and bloodless adventures in the Black Hawk War years ago, and soon both the President and his wife were competing with one another in accounts of their early life in Kentucky and Illinois. The President finally pushed back his chair, stretched out his legs, and reached for an apple from a big bowl in the center of the table. As he munched away happily, Mrs. Lincoln said to Anne:

"He eats barrels of them—I always order them ahead. Just now he won't touch anything but upstate New York apples. Mr. Seward sent him these a week ago and Mr. Lincoln ruins all his clothes by carrying them around in his pockets."

"Seward should have been a salesman," laughed Lincoln. "He keeps pushing me to come up to Auburn for a stay. Even has some land around Owasco Lake he'd like to sell me. He wants me to run down to a place called Ensenore and drive around the lake region—Otisco and Skaneateles are his favorites, I believe. He says they're as fine as anything in Switzerland. He kept insisting I come in the summertime. I said, 'What's the matter with your winters up there, Mr. Secretary?' Seward looked mighty pained and told me, 'Mr. Lincoln, in wintertime that country just plain ought to be evacuated. Eskimos would freeze overnight up there.'"

After a little while Mrs. Lincoln stood up and said with a smile, "Miss Carroll, Mr. Lincoln warned me he was snatching you away on business tonight, so I've arranged to go over some clothes with Mrs. Keckley. Don't let him put you to work until you're rested. I understand you've done far and away more than your share. And if you can drive to the Soldiers' Home with me Friday, I'd love to have you. A number of ladies are taking baskets and dressings along at that time. Would you care to join us—about three?"

Anne accepted with pleasure and paid Mrs. Lincoln her respects before that lady left. A little later she and Mr. Lincoln walked thoughtfully down the corridor.

"Let's go to the living room," he said eagerly. "That study got on my nerves today. It was nothing but a confessional for sinners—and I didn't absolve most of them."

In the glowing warmth of the Red Room he picked up a paper Mary had left and scanned it rapidly. Anne seated herself in a deep chair by the fire and watched his absorbed face. Suddenly he put down the paper and began to talk, disjointedly at first, in his familiar habit of thinking aloud. He discussed many things, the slowdown in the Western campaign, the renewed rise of the secession spirit in the Northwest, the growing revolt against him in Congress and the country, and always, always, he came back to the problem of the slaves. As he spoke his face darkened, his temper rose steadily.

"Another potential danger, as I see it," he said, "lies in the Army of the Potomac. I will now speak more frankly than I have to anyone, and not a word of this is to be even hinted at outside this room. I am patient with McClellan, ma'am, to the point of torture, because I have to be. This man is proud, popular, and commands an immense following. Above all, he is a Democrat, and I say this, with all due regard to his military ability, he is politically in a situation that could lead to an alliance with the rebels in Congress who don't like me or my works. I do not say this *is* the case. I say it conceivably might be. The general's inaction in the East has already undermined our victories in the West. There is no support at all for the Western armies from the commanding general."

Mr. Lincoln got up and stood before the marble mantel, his hands behind him. His face was the face of a warrior, stern, hostile, determined.

"But the political rebellion we face must be obvious to you. Many men on the Hill are determined to vest the powers of the Chief Executive in Congress. *And I will not let them do it.* I intend, as President, to direct the reconstitution of the recovered states. The South, as it is reoccupied, is going to function under the shield of the Constitution and the authority of the President, or by the Lord Almighty I will step out of this office. And now Charles Sumner of Massachusetts, I understand, is to lead the charge against this office."

He was greatly excited, but his voice became calmer as he went on to show that major decisions on the slavery issue would, out of military necessity, have to be faced very soon.

At this point Mr. Lincoln paused and gazed at her fixedly.

"Miss Carroll," he said, "I want you to prepare a paper which will answer Sumner's arguments in the Senate.

"I wish this paper," he continued, "to reflect *my* views and my views alone, as I know you disagree with me on some points. I would

295

separate the paper into such divisions as will provide a clear definition of the relationship of the national government to the revolted citizens. I would present detailed proof of the lack of vested powers in Congress to issue executive orders dealing either with the emancipation of slaves or their confiscation as private property. I would add a summation presenting the Constitution, aided by the President's war powers, as the only hope and shield of a restored nation. Is that clear?"

"Perfectly," she replied.

Mr. Lincoln glanced at his watch and she thought the interview was over. But he began to talk again. As she listened she realized that the slave question obsessed him fully as much as it did her and others. She remembered Evans's acid remark, "The slaves will win their freedom long before we win this war." Mr. Lincoln was now discussing that very point.

"Miss Carroll, I want to warn you that on the subject of slavery right now no one can be quite sure of anything. I've had to feel my way. You know John Bigelow, squinting at me from our Paris Consulate a while back, wrote to Thurlow Weed about my 'slows' and yelled, 'Why don't Lincoln shoot somebody?' Weed told me about it, and I said to Weed, 'Maybe I should, but in God's name *who?*' "

Mr. Lincoln went on, examining the whole issue, turning it inside out and outside in, thinking aloud. He told her of a visit from Henry Ward Beecher.

"I told Beecher in this very room," said Lincoln half humorously, "that defeat for us in the field makes everything seem wrong. He came right back at me. 'Let the administration honestly seek to destroy slavery, Mr. President, and you will have no enemies left, and no rebellion left.'

"But," added Lincoln impressively, "when Beecher said those very same words in the Cincinnati Opera House a week later they mobbed him. 'Hang the nigger! Lynch him! Kill the dirty Abolitionist!'—and so on. They tell me eggs struck Beecher in the face. Well, when I have received Negroes in this house there have been riots in Northern cities. Pictures of me have been torn from walls and hurled into gutters by families of soldiers in our armies."

The President struck the table top with the flat of his hand.

"When the North believes slavery to be the issue of this war, when they are ready as a people to fight and abolish that slavery and wish me to do it, I will do it. But the time is not yet.

"By and large the people of the North, Miss Carroll, are *not* anti-slavery. They don't give a damn about it, if you'll pardon frank words. They desire only quick victory and the restoration of this Union. To understand this you have only to listen every day to the powerful men who come here and argue this with me. These men come from New York, Ohio, Michigan, Wisconsin, Iowa. One and all, they are terrified that slavery will be made *the* issue of this war. There is wide hysteria and single, triple, and multiple hates on this issue that have to be weighed. The problem drives me quite crazy at times."

He was silent a moment and then continued earnestly:

"The Army, officers and men, as a whole, cares nothing about slavery. Our forces are only beginning to get mad because they have begun to suspect they've got to fight. If I humored the Abolitionists at this moment half the soldiers in the Army would fling their guns in my face and go home. What I fear now is this rising demand for vengeance. It's burned the air since Shiloh and Grant's statement that only 'conquest' of the South could now win the war."

He went on to discuss the steady sharpening of the slavery issue—new editions of *Uncle Tom's Cabin;* Harriet Beecher Stowe at her home in Maine receiving a pair of Negro's ears, cut off and mailed to her in a box; new books adding fuel to the flames, such as *The Uprising of a Great People* by the French liberal, Count de Gasparin, and Lydia Maria Child's volume on the liberation of Negroes in the West Indies.

"This cry for vengeance frightens me," said Mr. Lincoln. "We now have 'The Battle Hymn of the Republic,' a truly grand song but a thunderous one. And have you heard Holbrook's flaming hymn with a text from Isaiah, 'The day of vengeance is in mine heart, and the year of my redeemed is come'?"

He shook his head sadly.

"That won't do at all. And now Mr. Garrison, who once burned the Constitution, cradles that document to his bosom and thirsts to wade in Southern blood up to his horse's neck." Lincoln concluded dryly, "If Mr. Garrison *had* a horse and *were* in the field he might feel differently."

As Lincoln continued with his remarkable soliloquy an odd sense of unreality swept over Anne. It seemed to her, as he talked, that her own stature continually diminished; that as he neared the end of this discourse she was like a little girl who had been quite sure of a small stream she was exploring until this tall man by the fire had taken her by the hand, led her to where the stream merged into a large river, and on to where the large river flowed into a greater stream, and on still farther until they came to a spacious harbor. And yet the journey was not completed and he pressed on until she stood at last on the shores of a boundless sea over which he gazed with all-seeing eyes and described to her its character and the many shores, dim and distant, unseen, unimaginable, that bounded it.

A strange thing happened. The Red Room became another room,

many times more familiar, like some well-loved scene vividly remembered. She was conscious most of all of the brisk fire, the brass fire rail, the tall man sprawled in a big armchair with one leg over an arm rest, and herself sitting quietly with a sheaf of papers in her lap.

Then in a revealing flash it was as though the years had fallen away and she was a child again. A child at Kingston Hall, in a yellow smock with a pad and pencil on her lap. Her father was sitting by the fire and the brass fire rail, pouring out his mind, laying bare his wisdom and his confusion, his sympathies, his doubts, and his faith.

Her vision became painfully real. So real, in fact, that she saw Thomas Carroll before her, with his slender patrician features, his cool gray eyes, his tender ironic smile and precise bearing; Thomas Carroll, so different from this homely man with the tangled hair and coarse beard who slouched down in his chair, talking as if to himself.

For the first time in her life Anne looked deeply inward into the very source springs of her own impulses. And she caught a shadowy glimpse of the powerful, driving pattern of her life.

She was so absorbed by her discovery that she did not see Mr. Lincoln look up and catch the pallor of her face.

"—and once people are united," he was saying, "you can push mountains aside like molehills. Let the North get behind this issue. Let it wish to get rid of slavery. Let it realize it has to fight this war to a finish—and on none of these matters has it begun to get united, Miss Carroll—and we'll see some real light. Then we can move."

He drew out his watch abruptly.

"Great Jehoshaphat!" He grinned guiltily. "Do you know what time it is, ma'am? It's after eleven. Why——" He looked wonderingly around the room and then laughed ruefully. "Why, I was to see Eckert, Chase, and a whole raft of fellows tonight. And you must have had your plans too. I guess I've imposed a lot on you this evening, ma'am, and——"

But she got up quickly and came close to him. Mr. Lincoln was struck by the odd brilliance of her eyes and saw, to his surprise, that they had filled with tears.

"Mr. Lincoln," she said hesitantly, "you have shown me something tonight, perhaps quite unwittingly. You have often mentioned my decided views, my sureness of mind. But tonight, as I listened to you, these seemed nothing but the pretensions of a clever child. I would give whatever abilities I have, I would sell my soul for one ounce of the terrifying patience you possess, one ounce of your understanding and insight. I——"

"Why, bless you, don't take it so solemn," said Mr. Lincoln, his eyes alert and full of a quizzical curiosity. "I'm pretty cocky about a lot of things, ma'am." His eyes twinkled. "As cocky as you are. But not on this question of the blacks."

"It's not that," she exclaimed. "I'm just beginning to realize that on any matter we discuss you make me *see*—you make me see so much I never imagined even existed. And I'm profoundly grateful for this. . . . I'm not going to bed," she added with cheerful defiance. "I'm going home and digest everything you said here tonight."

There was much more she wanted to say, but she did not know how to say it. The President smiled broadly.

"You go to bed, Miss Carroll, and do all that digesting tomorrow. Just one word, however. Did you ever stop to think that every good rule works both ways—and that I've learned a whole lot from you? Think about that when you feel too modest."

She walked all the way to the Washington House, something she rarely did at that time of night. But she was quite unable to dispel the mood of the evening and she wondered what she could find to talk about with Sallie in her present state of mind. When she reached her rooms she found her sister, her blue eyes and pert face crowned with a cloud of fine auburn hair, leisurely sewing before a brisk fire. Sallie jumped up and embraced her affectionately.

"Anne, you're becoming a night owl! Do you know what time it is? Judge Evans and I had a delightful time at Varini's concert. But he left ages ago. And what——"

She paused, struck by the rapt look on Anne's face.

"Anne dear, you do look dreadfully solemn. Is anything the matter?"

Her sister did not reply, and Sallie wonderingly helped her off with her cloak. Anne drew her chair close to Sallie's and absently seated herself. Sallie, quick to sense her sister's moods, patiently waited.

Anne drew a long breath.

"Sallie—something very strange happened to me tonight."

37

ANNE TOLD HER SISTER AS MUCH ABOUT HER EVENING
with the President as she was free to report and Sallie listened, fascinated. When Anne came to the curious feeling—almost vision—
she had had, Sallie looked startled.

"I can't imagine what happened," Anne concluded wonderingly.
"It was partly the room, I think, with that handsome brass fire rail
that so reminded me of Father's study at Kingson Hall when I was
a little girl. But why should I have felt so upset? For a few moments
I had the queer feeling that I've been doing the same thing over and
over all my life. I'd never thought of such a thing before, Sallie."

Sallie not only understood her sister thoroughly, she also had a
remarkably clear memory and intuitive talent for analyzing behavior
uncritically.

"I've thought of it—often," she said slowly.

Anne glanced at her in surprise. "What do you mean, dear?"

Sallie evaded her eyes and looked into the fire.

"Pet," she said after a long silence, "would you mind very much
if I asked you a most personal question?"

"You know you can ask me anything in the world."

"Then," Sallie said quickly, "why don't you marry Judge Evans—
now, at the earliest possible moment you can agree on?"

Anne blushed.

"But, Sallie, what has such a question to do with what I've just
told you?"

"Perhaps a very great deal," Sallie answered quietly. "And"—she
laughed lightly—"you haven't answered it yet."

Still blushing, Anne began rather defensively: "Sallie, Lem and
I understand one another completely. And we intend to be married

the minute we're free to. But right now both of us are terribly involved in confidential, important work. Just as soon as my work for Mr. Lincoln is over, as soon as Lem is through at the War Department—you can help with the arrangements for our wedding." She smiled at her sister brightly, as if to overcome any arguments. Then she added almost as an afterthought, "Besides, Mr. Stanton has asked us to postpone our marriage."

Sallie's face was inscrutable.

"Indeed! So Mr. Stanton decides your most personal affairs for you! And you let him."

"But, Sallie," Anne protested, "I didn't at first. Then he made me see that if Lem and I were married it would enormously complicate ____"

"Complicate fiddlesticks!" Sallie said impatiently. "Well, I never ____" Then she stopped and started again very quietly: "Anne dear, you began this conversation—and as long as you did, I wonder whether you'll let me say something, even if it makes you angry and I have to apologize when I'm through."

"Let you! I *want* you to help me understand what happened this evening. It was very disturbing—as though the past had suddenly risen to haunt me, as though____"

"Perhaps it has," interrupted Sallie gently, "perhaps it should."

"But I don't see what all this has to do with Lem," Anne insisted. Definitely there was some connection in Sallie's mind, and she was determined to find out what it was. "Tell me, Sallie," she demanded.

"Dear," Sallie began slowly, "this isn't easy and I'm not sure where to begin, or even whether I really should try to explain. . . . You know I've always loved you, admired you, disagreed with you about lots of things, especially politics, and—been just a bit jealous of you too. Now don't protest," she warned and smiled, "every one of us is jealous—and terribly, terribly proud of you. And remember, my life is different from yours and I've had plenty of time to wonder about you ever since I was a child and watched you plunge into a world completely strange and mysterious and foreign to me—to most of the family, I'd say. Living quietly in the country as I do with Tom and the children and seeing so much of our own family, I've thought a great deal about you, Anne dear. And sometimes you frighten me, pet, you really do."

"Frighten you? Why?" Anne asked sharply, sitting up, very alert.

"You frightened me tonight, Anne—because your experience with Mr. Lincoln, remembering Father and Kingston Hall, confirms something I've had in mind for a long time—ever since you went to work for Governor Hicks. Look, dear," said Sallie, floundering a little, but

301

determined. "Now don't interrupt me, even though I seem to be a long time getting to the point; all of this is part of it. You may as well know that your admiring but very curious young sisters have wondered why you haven't married——" She headed off Anne's gesture of protest. "After all, you cut quite a swath in Baltimore and you really had the pick of everyone's beaux——"

"But I didn't want to marry until I was ready to," exclaimed Anne. "Is that so strange? Loads of women never marry. Anyway, I always had too much to do."

"You always *managed* to have too much to do," Sallie said pointedly.

"What do you mean?" demanded Anne in a tone of affectionate exasperation.

"Just that," her sister said calmly. "Your life follows a pattern, and that's part of it. Apparently you've never stopped to realize that you *have* been doing the same thing all your life—that you've attached yourself to one distinguished man after another, worked for each of them until you were too busy to have time for any other man—and I think, what's more, without being conscious of it, you've been very careful to choose men who were not eligible to marry you."

"That's sheer nonsense," Anne retorted indignantly. "You're letting your imagination run away with you."

"I don't think so." Sallie's bright eyes were fixed on her sister. "I've tried to dismiss the idea—but even your own story tonight supports it. First, there was Father. You were his favorite and you adored him. He spent more time with you than he did with any of the rest of us. He taught you law, he taught you politics, and whether he meant to or not, he made it possible for you to take your place in a man's world. You must have been a lot smarter than the rest of us. Father once told me that when you were very little he realized that you weren't just precocious—you were destined for something exceptional."

Anne sighed in irritation. "I wish I'd never let you get started, Sallie."

Sallie ignored her. "And then there was dear old Dr. Breckinridge after you went to Baltimore. You surely must remember how disappointed you were when Father left politics and how determined you were to leave home and do something. At eighteen, pet, you were rather terrifying. There you were, equipped for a political life and also the belle of the county, to say nothing of your social life in Baltimore."

"I was restless," Anne explained.

"Whatever it was, all at once, over Mother's protests and Father's reluctant permission, you were off to Baltimore—alone—to earn your living and restore our fortunes, I suppose. The neighbors thought it a scandal. We all thought you quite mad. Ada and Mary and Thomas and I sat up all night talking about it.

"And what did you do, Anne, once you'd left home—and this I want to impress on you, dear. First, you became the devout young protégé of Dr. Breckinridge. But in no time at all you apparently found the church just a little too quiet—and you attached yourself to Henry Clay. You said yourself you worked like a dog for the senator. You were determined he should become President. And when he didn't you were actually sick for weeks. Then quite suddenly you were sounding the praises of Millard Fillmore, and soon after that, Tom Hicks, Father's old friend. Before we knew it you'd started a press campaign that placed Hicks in the governor's chair—where Father had once sat."

Some deep, dim comprehension stirred in Anne. She was sitting up very straight, watching Sallie intently.

"Go on, Sallie," she said, strangely subdued.

"You became the close friend, the confidante—in fact, the colleague—of Governor Hicks. And I remember you used to tell me you'd ask yourself what Father would have done and then advise Hicks to do it."

"It was good advice," observed Anne.

"That's not the point," Sallie said emphatically. "What I'm trying to say is that once Father gave up political life you were terribly disappointed—I think you'd wanted to see him in the highest office in the land—and then you jumped right into his shoes. I—I think you've been wearing them ever since.

"Your next personal and political conquest was James Buchanan —at least for a time—a bachelor, years older than you. I remember you thought it quite laughable when he proposed to you."

"It *was* ridiculous. He was old enough to be my father——"

"Exactly," exclaimed Sallie with almost grim satisfaction. "But *why* was it so ridiculous? He was devoted to you and could offer you everything."

"But——"

"But," continued Sallie smoothly, "I maintain, pet, that you arranged most adroitly that none of these men you worshiped and for whom you worked so hard *was* eligible for marriage—at least in your own mind. It's as if you carried a precious little image of Father about in the pocket of your petticoat, and when any man advanced, or became bold, or actually proposed to you—and I've no doubt many did—you quite unconsciously compared each of them with this image

303

and invariably found each one wanting. For you always said you'd never met a man to be compared with Father. And if that wasn't enough protection," Sallie added, studying Anne's expressionless face, "whenever the chase became too warm, you always found a convenient political crisis, a new problem, an overpowering cause into which you might fling yourself."

"And where does Harry fit into this clever little picture?" Anne asked triumphantly. "We were very much in love."

"That's what you both said, but I never believed it. I think each of you represented something to the other which you were afraid of losing. I'm not sure what it was you represented to Harry—sureness of conviction, insight, a sense of reality.

"As for you"—Sallie hesitated, not quite so sure of her ground now—"I think Harry was a symbol of the South you used to worship. Your sudden affection for Harry puzzled me at first—such a match could never have lasted. But think of when that happened—just as war was in the offing. You were very much involved with Northern men. Then Mr. Lincoln was elected and you were panicked because you foresaw what has since happened. But there was Harry waiting for you—ardent, proud, charming, cultivated—personifying everything that you longed for the South to be."

Sallie looked at her sister. Anne's face was still and white, and for a moment Sallie faltered, then forced herself to go on.

"In getting engaged to Harry, Anne, you tried to return to the South, the Southern world, that you had given up when you were a child. You couldn't do it, and I think that explains the violence of your quarrel with Harry, because it wasn't just Harry you were fighting against. You must have seen that you were caught—caught between two worlds—and that you had to choose a new, strange, and, as you told me tonight, frightening world. That is why you tore into poor Harry, even struck him—something you've never dreamed of doing before or since to anyone."

There were tears in Sallie's eyes and she laid one hand affectionately, almost imploringly, on Anne's rigid arm.

"Perhaps Father was responsible for tearing you away from the South. You remember the sensation he caused when he came out for Jackson, when he insisted the common people were paramount and warned Calhoun and other Southern leaders that war and ruin lay ahead if they persisted in their policies. . . . Anyway, you and he see and detest a South I cannot begin to see or understand. You feel you must do something about it, and yet you are torn. Am I not right?" she asked pleadingly, alarmed now by Anne's strained expression.

Anne looked at her, a strange remoteness in her eyes, as though she were at last recognizing a distant landmark.

"You've shown me a side of myself I never dreamed of, Sallie. I can't quite take it in yet. I want to say you're mistaken, but I can't——"

"Then don't you see, Anne, how the rest follows? Once you'd rid yourself of Harry and Mr. Breckinridge—of your Southern ties—you moved into a different world, but you took along with you your familiar formula. Two years ago it was Mr. Seward you worked for. Now as high as you can go, it's the President himself.

"It's a pattern you've clung to all your life, pet," Sallie repeated, "since you began with Father. And you—you've got to break it before it's too late. You *must*, or nature will have its revenge." Sallie's voice was trembling. She took out a handkerchief and wiped the tears from her eyes.

"Are you angry with me, Anne? Please say something," she begged after several seconds had passed.

Anne shook her head wonderingly. "Of course not. But how on earth do you know me so well?" She looked curiously at Sallie. "When did you first start to think of all this?"

"When you first went to Baltimore. It changed you so."

"No," said Anne soberly. "I changed before that. I changed when Mother died. Until then I had taken everything for granted. And suddenly I felt as if I had been swathed in lovely veils and some harsh hand had torn them all away. I—I understood all at once what women had to face in this world today. But in Baltimore I saw freedom—and to Baltimore I went."

Her eyes brightened. She added reassuringly, "But, Sallie dear, I *have* broken this—this queer pattern you have made so convincing. I've found Lem, and I love him."

"Then for heaven's sake marry him. You must see now why I asked that question at the beginning."

"You're not implying that I'll find some excuse not to marry Lem, are you?" Anne asked indignantly. "I've told you I love him. He's the first man I've ever really loved. I didn't love any of those others."

"No, no, I'm not saying you won't marry Lem," Sallie said quickly, and then was silent. You've gone quite far enough, too far, she told herself, and yet one final thrust of fear for her sister's happiness made her add slowly, "But I'm afraid, pet—I do fear that at times part of you resists, part of you invents or finds reasons why you shouldn't marry Lem just *now*. You've even taken Mr. Stanton's request seriously. But Mr. Stanton isn't Father.

"Oh dear," she sighed. "I haven't any right to talk this way to

305

you, but I want you to be happy. We all want you to be happy. And we like Lem, and if you love him we want you to marry him."

Anne suddenly put her arms around her sister and kissed her fondly. "I fully intend to, dear."

But Sallie's eyes filled with tears. "Then marry him at once, pet. I'm so terribly upset because I adore you, I want you to find happiness—and these terrible times divide us so."

"They can't and they won't divide the Carrolls—nor Lem and I," said Anne firmly. Holding Sallie's hand in both of hers, she leaned over and gently touched her sister's hair with her lips.

During the following days neither of them mentioned their conversation again. Sallie had shopping to do for the house and the children and Anne accompanied her, even allowing Sallie to persuade her to order two dresses for herself to be made by a new seamstress of whom Sallie had recently heard. Caroline Wade gave a small tea in Sallie's honor, and one of Tom Cradock's cousins gave her a dinner.

They were gay and carefree so far as it was possible to be in the spring of 1862, and Anne found herself enjoying the interlude. Then Sallie went home to Trenthan and as Anne turned back to her work she realized that her sister's penetrating observations had unsettled her more than she realized.

38

THERE WAS THUNDER IN THE SENATE A FEW DAYS later. On a mild May morning Charles Sumner of Massachusetts rose to deliver a slashing attack on the administration, a major address summing up the advanced position of the radicals.

Seated in the front row of the Senate gallery beside Lem, Anne was aware of a new self-consciousness with him which was part of her general feeling of unease. Unintentionally Sallie had shaken her assurance. And as she listened to Sumner she also felt, for the first time, a lack of confidence in her political conclusions. New currents of thought, swift and changing, seemed to be undermining the position she had taken a few months ago and had thought so safe.

The distinguished senator from Massachusetts, impeccably dressed, towered over his desk, his large expressive face topped with a handsome mass of briskly curling hair. There was an aristocracy and assurance in Sumner's bearing, his voice, his whole manner, which commanded the immediate attention of the most disinterested. He had not spoken six words before Lincoln's comment about him flashed through Anne's mind: "Charles Sumner is my idea of a bishop."

Sumner, without preamble, had plunged into an impassioned demand that Congress declare immediately its powers in respect to slavery and the war; that it assume a revolutionary role in grasping active direction and control of all legislation concerned with the war; that it legislate, confiscate, and emancipate as it saw fit. His speech was a brilliant plea that Congress assert itself over the President, drop all pretense, and turn the whole war into a relentless revolution on behalf of free labor and the people.

Anne was worried as she sensed that the galleries, indeed a great

307

part of the Senate, were thoroughly in accord with Sumner. And to unleash a revolution instead of a carefully conducted civil war, Sumner issued a ringing demand "that Congress should not fasten upon itself *the restraints of the Constitution.*"

"The rebels," he thundered, "have gone outside the Constitution to make war upon their country. It is for us to pursue them as enemies outside the Constitution, where they have wickedly placed themselves, and where the Constitution concurs in placing them also."

Everyone had come running to hear Sumner. Evans watched Anne as she sat in her favorite position—well forward on the hard, narrow bench, her auburn-blond hair brushed back under a small blue-and-white bonnet, her chin cupped in her left hand, her right hand grasping a pencil poised over a pad in her lap, her blue eyes fixed unwaveringly on the tall man in the aisle below her.

She had begun with Sumner's first words to make notes rapidly and easily in Benn Pitman's shorthand, which was all the vogue. Once she looked away from Sumner and caught Wade, almost directly below, frowning up at her. She nudged Evans and whispered, "I'm going to catch it. Ben Wade knows I'm taking notes."

Sumner wound up his long speech by repeating his angry demand that the Constitution and the President yield before the crisis to the powers of Congress to legislate in that crisis. She was thoroughly aroused and said to Evans as they walked down to the rotunda, "Any child can answer that part of his speech."

"You'd better not answer it like a child," said Evans grimly. "The people generally will support that speech. It is damned persuasive."

In the vast and crowded rotunda they met Wade hurrying toward them, great excitement in his expression and manner.

"What did you think of it?" he asked. He was studying Anne intently. "I think that will pull the White House teeth for a while." He caught sight of Anne's pad and pencil and added sharply, "Are you actually preparing to reply to that masterpiece, ma'am?"

"I am, Ben. Why?" she asked casually.

An expression of anxiety crossed Wade's big, bluff face.

"Don't do it, Anne," he said earnestly. "You'll only muddy clear waters. That speech voices the considered battle cry of the most formidable alliance ever formed in this chamber. Congress *must* take the reins in handling the reoccupied South, and it is going to do so."

She turned on Wade so fiercely that the elderly senator stepped back a pace.

"Ben," she exclaimed in a cold, quiet voice, "I am your devoted friend. But you amaze me. You dare to stand there and tell me this Congress proposes to toss the Constitution out the window and usurp

308

all the vested powers of the Executive and then order Mr. Lincoln to sign the measures you create and enact in a field that is exclusively his. Well, it's damnable nonsense! I knew more constitutional law at ten years of age than Charles Sumner has forgotten in forty years."

"You let your conceit run away with you, madam," said Wade harshly while Evans pulled vainly at her arm, appalled by this sudden quarrel.

"My knowledge doesn't run with it, Ben," she retorted. "You and your committee have done invaluable work. And often you've been an infernal nuisance to Mr. Lincoln. There is only one driver's seat in this nation, Senator. It is located in the White House. The man in that driver's seat is the President and his name is Abraham Lincoln. And no clique, no cabal, no unconstitutional advice by Sumner and all his scheming adherents is going to whittle down his power to *command*. Can't you understand that?"

Wade was furious. His angry eyes glanced down at the pencils in her hand. A vast suspicion dawned on him and his dark eyes became hostile slits.

"Did Mr. Lincoln send you up here?" he demanded. Anne threw all caution to the winds.

"He certainly did. He personally requested me to answer this man. But he had no need to. Believe me, I would have answered this emotional bosh myself. And I advise you, Ben, to go down to Shillington's bookstore, buy a copy of the Constitution for fifteen cents, and read it this afternoon. And now, good day, Senator."

They left him standing in the center of the rotunda, flushed and furious, glaring after them.

"Whew!" said Evans as they walked down the great main steps onto the graveled walks. "For God's sake, don't do that, sweetheart. Ben Wade is one of your best friends. You hurt him terribly."

"I can't help it," she exclaimed, wanting to laugh and cry at the same time. "Ben's got to understand my position. If he's still angry with me tomorrow, I'll apologize. I really will."

"You may have to," said Evans anxiously.

"You men exasperate me," she retorted. "You're always bleating about the Constitution. But Sumner just tore up that document in the Senate's face and everyone applauded. You are all going too far——"

"You mean," interrupted Evans sharply, "we are all going *beyond* your hairsplitting legal stand, and you're not quite sure what to do about it. The parade has taken a left turn—and you don't think you can follow it. Isn't that it?"

"Lem!" she began heatedly, and then fell silent. Sumner's speech had greatly upset her. Worse than that, it had confused her. And Evans seemed to guess as much. He added more gently:

"History has a habit of making hash of the law. That's why I think Sumner voiced the feelings of the people pretty accurately today."

Again she had no ready retort and was exasperated by the sense of uncertainty and insecurity that assailed her. She finally said a little acidly, "I'm going to work at once. Will you help me?"

"I don't think so," replied Evans blandly.

She was so hurt and astonished that she actually stammered like a schoolgirl. "You—you—you mean you don't wish to aid me or make any suggestions at all on my paper?"

"That's it," said Evans with a smile that softened some of the harshness of his words. Almost childishly she had taken it for granted that he agreed, at least generally, with her reaction to Sumner's speech. But she saw her mistake. His usually relaxed body was suddenly tense. There was an angry light in his eyes that reminded her very much of Sumner himself.

"No, I will *not* help you," he said clearly. "This is *your* paper— and perhaps Mr. Lincoln's. And I doubt if I'll agree with a word of it. Wade is right. Thad Stevens is right. Chandler is right. And Sumner," he said ungrammatically, "is the rightest of all. If Congress wants to string up Southern planters on telegraph poles from here to New Orleans, and over the President's veto, I'd go out and help 'em with a mile of rope myself. You and Mr. Lincoln will find yourselves mistaken. I believe in the issue, not the law."

She was badly shaken by Evans's reaction. For his driving intellect and analytical powers she had great admiration. And she respected most of all his ability, at important stages in his development, to reverse completely some of his dearest convictions in the face of hard logic and facts. No wonder political parties and Evans rarely remained united. He had never been a "joiner." He never would be.

Rather nervous and ill at ease, she ranged through her law library alone, hunting down references and authorities as she developed the outline of her paper. From her shelves she took the leather-bound volumes of Rutherford's lectures; digests of Grotius, the lawgiver of nations; the commentaries of Chancellor Kent, Wheaton, Manning, and many others; the works of the noted Swiss jurist, Vattel; marked copies of the *Congressional Globe* with all of Sumner's speeches carefully annotated; the proceedings of the United States Supreme Court, with marginal comments in her own clear hand.

Her paper, completed a week later, was ponderously titled: *"The Relation of the National Government to the Revolted States Defined.*

310

—No Power in Congress to Emancipate the Slaves or Confiscate Their Property Proved. The Constitution is the Only Hope of the Country."

No one ever called it all that. It was known simply as "The Reply to Sumner."

In her clear bold handwriting she opened her argument by first tracing in great detail the various struggles between the executive and legislative branches of the government. Next she attacked bitterly the repeated attempts of Congress to wrest the delegated powers from the Chief Executive. Then she turned her attention to another senatorial colleague who had argued that "there is no limit over the power of Congress, it is *supreme,* and the ordinary provisions of the Constitution must *yield* as resolved by the Congress." She attacked such statements by asserting:

"I do not charge that there is a conspiracy in Congress to grasp the sword and overthrow Republican institutions, and establish upon its ruins a legislative despotism. But certain it is that unless this claim is rebuked by the country, it will end in one. The annals of the world record no instances where the usurpers of power have ever, voluntarily, laid it down."

At last, with a timidity new and strange to her, she handed the final draft of her paper to Evans one evening. When he had finished he came over and kissed her, and she thought for a moment she had won her little duel with him. Then he shook his head.

"Anne darling, from a strictly legal point of view, it can't be refuted. It obviously sums up the President's position *today.* Don't worry, he'll like it tremendously. But *tomorrow?* It won't hold water. Uncle Abe is too damn slow. Congress is now going ahead with its own plans to remake the South. They won't wait."

"Do you mean to say you think Congress can abolish slavery by edict if they so desire?" she asked.

"Why not? Believe me, if Lincoln won't, Congress will. You'd better tell him that."

Anne looked horrified.

"But that isn't the law," she protested.

"Maybe not, but it's the issue," retorted Evans. "Look here, Anne, you'd better realize that these battles between the President and Congress aren't always the world-shakers you're inclined to make them. There's another force behind them all—the voters, the people. If folks back home think the President too slow, too backward, or too despotic, they'll try somebody else. The same with Congress. If Congress bucks the people too long, they're tossed out. Sometimes we have a strong President who rules Congress—and sometimes we have

311

a strong Congress that rules the President. What's it prove? The people, if they want to, can get either the White House or the Hill to get something done. This legal hairsplitting of yours is useful, but it's beside the main point."

"But Congress has no right to decide the slavery issue," she insisted.

"Just the same, they're going to do it," said Evans cheerfully. "You can't feed these blacks freedom through an eye dropper. And freedom for slaves is now being forged into a mighty military weapon. Did you hear what Sanford, our minister in Brussels, wrote Seward last week? 'All Belgium now realizes that this is a war for *free labor*.' Uncle Abe has got to act fast. And six months from now I'm going to make you read this paper of yours all over again. You won't believe you wrote it."

Worriedly she carried the first copies of her "Reply to Sumner" to the President early Monday morning. He had just finished breakfast. She felt utterly exhausted and sat with her eyes closed while Mr. Lincoln slouched down in his old rocking chair and read swiftly through her paper. When he was through he sat back and looked at her, a shade of anxiety in his eyes.

"You're tired out, aren't you, Miss Carroll?" he said almost accusingly.

"I'm afraid I am," she agreed. "Is it—is it all right?" she asked.

"I wouldn't say just that," he said slowly. "The fact is, Miss Carroll, I've about run out of bouquets for you. I would not change this if I could. I would add nothing to it, take nothing away." He paused, looking at the pamphlet in his lap. "I only wish Charles Carroll might read this. He would have been mighty proud of you. . . . How many copies did you order?"

"Five thousand," she replied, feeling much better for his words.

He looked dismayed. "Why, that wouldn't get around this town. You tell Polkinhorn we want fifty thousand as fast as he can run 'em off. The bill will be paid, this time by the State Department."

"Fifty thousand!" she exclaimed.

"Yes, ma'am," said Mr. Lincoln harshly. "It is my answer to Charles Sumner, my answer to Congress, and my answer to the country. It is to go at once to every member of the House and Senate and to every federal official at home and abroad. Sumner raised my blood last week. I am going to send this paper farther than I did your blast to Breckinridge and with even more effect. . . . I beg pardon, ma'am, but are you feeling unwell?"

For the first time in her memory an attack of giddiness had seized her and she had leaned her head back and closed her eyes just as

Mr. Lincoln glanced up at her. He came to her side and took her hand.

"Now look here, Miss Carroll," he said quickly, "this won't do. You've put about a year's effort into the past five weeks. I got a look at your military memoranda to Stanton. Why don't you run away and hide on that Eastern Shore of yours a bit? It's spring," he went on, an odd note of sadness in his voice, and he added whimsically, "Even you and I can't fight this whole dang war by ourselves. Make that young man of yours take you out in the air. Will you?"

"He's already suggested it," she replied. "I hadn't thought of it, but both you and Mr. Evans have commented on my fatigue—so I must be tired."

"So Mr. Evans is trying to pry you loose too?" said the President quietly. "How are you two getting along?"

His eyes were bright with amusement and more than a trace of curiosity and he laughed a little at the full blush that colored her pale cheeks. It was all she could do to look him in the eye, but she did and said frankly:

"So well, Mr. President, that we plan to marry when the worst of this is over."

"Is that a fact!" exclaimed Mr. Lincoln with real delight. "Well, I do congratulate you both. Evans is a man after my own heart—quiet as a cat but with more brains and integrity than I've seen in a long time. Is it a secret?"

"I'm afraid it is," she said smilingly. "Only Mr. Stanton knows and he's asked us not to spread the news for the time being."

"Old Mars knows everything before I do," grumbled the President good-naturedly. "So he's playing Cupid in the dark, is he? Well, I wish you every kind of happiness, ma'am. You tell us all to go to blazes for a couple of weeks—and you *rest,* Miss Carroll. That's by order of the President," he added with a laugh, and escorted her to the door.

After leaving the White House she drove to Polkinhorn's printing shop, gave him the President's minor corrections on the Sumner pamphlet, then shopped a little, lunched with Caroline, and drove home late in the afternoon, frightened by the utter fatigue that possessed her. Her momentary elation over Mr. Lincoln's reception of her paper had now deserted her. She found Evans in her parlor.

"Can you tuck that mind of yours away for two weeks, Anne? Good!" he exclaimed as she nodded wearily. "Because Judge Trent has invited us down for a visit at his cottage on the Choptank for a fortnight. You're going to eat, sleep, play, do anything your heart de-

313

sires. But no newspapers, telegrams, and nobody but Stanton is to know where we are."

He was startled by her lack of response. She finally managed to say, "That will be heavenly, Lem. I'm—I'm really exhausted."

She closed her eyes and swayed. Evans took a single long step and held her in his arms.

"Dammit, girl," he said tenderly, "you can't keep up this pace. You're going to bed and not stir until I give the word."

He lifted her up. Her arms slipped round his neck and her head rested against his shoulder. He carried her into her room and laid her gently on the bed.

"All right, Doctor," she murmured. "I've no objections at all. I'm so tired, Lem, so terribly, terribly tired."

39

THE NOTORIOUS INDIFFERENCE OF NATURE TO THE affairs of man was conclusively demonstrated to them during their stay with Judge Trent, who owned a secluded but accessible haven only three miles from Cambridge.

They slept long hours and ate ravenously. They rode, walked, rested, and on mild days often drifted about on the Choptank River in the judge's green rowboat. Occasionally Judge Trent joined them. More often he lay supine and supremely comfortable in an old blue hammock with an unopened book slowly rising and falling on his broad chest.

They dreamed and planned together, and the war receded like summer thunder on some far horizon.

This paradise lasted for three weeks. Then they packed up reluctantly, bade a grateful good-by to Judge Trent, and drove to Walnut Landing to spend a final week end with Dr. Thomas Carroll and Peggy and a rapidly increasing brood of gay children. Anne's father came down from Baltimore and, for a few brief days, the pleasant life they had all once known together seemed permanent and whole again.

On a Monday afternoon they arrived in Washington. They returned full of new energy, full of health, spirit, determination, and fresh faith.

And they returned to chaos.

For the military record of that late spring and summer of 1862 was a mournful and tragic one. Time and again golden opportunities to bring a quick end to the rebellion were tossed into limbo. The great double attack envisaged by Mr. Lincoln and the War Department, and based on Anne's plan, bogged down East and West. In the

West great blunders were made that one would not think a child could commit. The Army of the Tennessee, having inched forward twenty miles in thirty-one days under that scholarly snail, Halleck, came to an ignominious halt before Corinth, where the generals then dispersed their forces all across Mississippi, Alabama, and Tennessee. They were merely holding onto a deserted stretch of hinterland when they might have had every great Southern citadel for the taking.

The Eastern half of the great pincers movement collapsed completely with McClellan's disastrous Peninsula campaign, insisted upon by the general against the advice of all of his political superiors and many of his own staff.

Stanton, enraged by these incredible doings, had embarked on a scheme of his own. In one hundred days he had organized and manned a swift fleet of Ohio River steamers and steam rams under Commander Charles Ellett. Stanton had moved this fleet west and south a thousand miles and, with no co-operation at all from the Navy, destroyed a rebel fleet and forced the fall of Memphis on June sixth.

But there was chaos in all these commands.

At any time between the first of June and the middle of July a force of twenty thousand men, co-operating with the fleets of Farragut and Davis, might easily have taken Vicksburg and saved a whole year of death and disaster in this quarter. The Union could have seized Mobile, Chattanooga, swept on to Atlanta, fought its way north to Richmond. The war could have been won in months.

Of this critical period the chief protagonist, Grant himself, fully confirming Anne's strategy and conclusions, wrote to the Department:

> If one general who would have taken the responsibility had been in command of all the troops west of the Alleghenies, he could have marched to Chattanooga, Corinth, Memphis, and Vicksburg, and as volunteering was going on rapidly over the North, there would soon have been force enough at all these centers to operate offensively against anybody of the enemy that might be found near them.

It was not to be.

Halleck was called a "military imbecile" by Commodore Foote in an official dispatch to Secretary Welles. Stanton, too, blundered badly. He had also lost his assistant, Tom Scott, who resigned on June 1 to return to the Pennsylvania Railroad. Sure of quick victory, Stanton abruptly halted all recruiting in the North, bringing down on his head the justified wrath of the generals and instilling a feeling of blind overconfidence in the apathetic supporters of the Union cause. On the approaches to Richmond, in the swamps of the Chickahominy, McClellan, already conniving with political Catilines from the North,

316

begged his friends to find him "some peaceful occupation," preferably in New York. His great army was blasted in battle and wasted away in sickness and fever.

The rebel forces, so thin and meager a month ago, were now swelling and massing in the East. The Confederates had taken full advantage of the Union paralysis in the West. Every man who could be spared was rushed eastward to Richmond and placed under Lee and the most brilliant array of military talent ever developed in the nation.

It was catastrophe, pure and unadulterated.

How deeply Mr. Lincoln felt about all this, Anne did not realize until an afternoon late in June when she and Evans sat talking with Secretary Seward in his study. Seward was rushing to New York the following day to aid Eastern governors in raising new regiments to stem the debacle. As they rose to go Seward reluctantly drew a letter from his desk marked "Private and Confidential." It was from Mr. Lincoln.

"I think I run no risk of breach of confidence in showing you this," said Seward. "It is a remarkable letter and in my opinion should never have been written. It will not be entered in any file or shown to any clerk in the department. It is an appeal for another one hundred thousand troops to end the war, but it is also a frightening revelation of Mr. Lincoln's state of mind. Let me read you this one paragraph. The President writes: 'I expect to maintain this contest until successful or until I die, or am conquered, or my term expires, or Congress or the country forsakes me; *and I would publicly appeal to the country for this new force were it not that I fear a general panic and stampede would follow, so hard is it to have a thing understood as it really is.*' "

Silently they read the rest of the letter and handed it back to Seward.

"I suppose," said the Secretary, "that Mr. Lincoln intended I should show this to the governors in hastening their efforts to save the situation. But I am not going to do so. They are already in a panic."

On their way home Anne listened to an outburst from Evans on the conduct of the war. But it only aroused her own temper and finally she turned on him.

"You're only half right," she said angrily. "Do you think blunders are confined to the North? Mark my words, Lem, half the South will fight this war fanatically. The other half will shirk it miserably. They'll dodge conscriptions, taxes, levies, and tell the Richmond government to mind its own business. Their mountains are already filled with deserters. I would estimate almost a third of the South is still loyal to the Union. The South united? That's nonsense.

317

"The fact is, Lem, their precious doctrine of states' rights is already a dagger thrust deep in the back of the South."

Meanwhile her "Reply to Sumner" had been widely circulated, widely read, widely discussed. It was recognized as the President's official reply to Sumner and other critics of his office. It piled new tinder on the fresh fires now raging in House and Senate on the eternal slavery issue. Wondering what Sumner himself thought about her paper, she was delighted one morning to encounter him in the Capitol rotunda and he hailed her pleasantly.

"Miss Carroll," he said after his greetings, "I read your paper carefully and I wish to congratulate you on a very brilliant piece of work."

"Well, Senator," she replied warily, "I appreciate your comment, but I'd much rather hear what you really thought about its contents."

He threw back his big handsome head and laughed easily. His tall figure was clad in a dark blue broadcloth suit, patent-leather shoes, a doeskin vest, and a voluminous silk polka-dot stock. A graceful blue cape edged with scarlet was tossed carelessly over his broad shoulders. Both hands grasped a gold-headed cane as he smiled down at her.

"Well, I'll concede this much readily," he said warmly. "You made the most persuasive presentation of the President's own conception of his position that could possible be made. And you might like to know, Miss Carroll," he added with sudden emphasis, "that I thought quite enough of your paper to send it along, with other able pamphlets of yours, to the files of the Harvard Law Library. You know, my dear friend, you have great ability and a fine legal mind. You should practice law."

"How could I?" she asked simply.

His handsome face flushed. One of his hands reached out and grasped hers.

"That was inexcusable of me, though it was meant as a compliment," he said gently. "We've more than one slavery to fight, Miss Carroll. More than one. But I do want to tell you that, though we differ in some things, I have nothing but complete admiration for you as a person."

Sumner hesitated a moment. Then his eyes twinkled.

"You won't believe me, Miss Carroll, but I suspect you're only a few laps behind these doctrines you profess to detest. If the war were over today I might modify my stand somewhat. But the war continues —and I should like to hear *your* point of view a year from now."

By the end of August 1862, destiny had dealt all but a deathblow to the panic-stricken capital. The Army of the Potomac had been

318

pulled back from the Peninsula. A hurricane was sweeping up from the South—a hurricane led by Lee and moving rapidly on Washington and all Maryland. In the West a Confederate general, Braxton Bragg, striking northward in a series of brilliant raids, threatened to reconquer all Tennessee and Kentucky, and threw fear into every state north of the Ohio.

Where the Tennessee plan had not collapsed it remained in complete abeyance, while in the East the administration sought to retrieve McClellan's disasters that had paralyzed the Union on both flanks.

Swept into the void were all the pretty little schemes of Negro colonization that Anne and various Cabinet members had discussed. Gone were all the roaring debates in Congress, all the wordy hairsplitting on constitutional law. In the face of these military disasters Anne revealed a quality of quiet patience that impressed both Wade and Evans.

"They'll come back to the Tennessee plan. They'll have to," Anne insisted whenever they discussed the matter.

Others were not so sure. Stanton said to her one night, "There are some in the Cabinet who think the war all but over, ma'am."

The Secretary took off his glasses and carefully polished them. "I'm quite beyond wrath, ma'am. I am profoundly saddened by all this. I simply do not understand these military men. A month ago McClellan's father-in-law and Chief of Staff, General Marcy, told me that unless certain things were done and McClellan given perfect independence he would have to surrender his army to Lee!

"There on my desk is a most private note from General Pleasanton, a devoted partisan of McClellan, begging my permission to strike at Richmond over the general's hand. He claimed that two Army corps could take Richmond in forty-eight hours. Well—McClellan's magnificent army has since collapsed."

"What are you going to do?" she asked.

The Secretary fished another document off his desk and gave it to her.

"Madam, as you know, McClellan is no longer the general in chief and sits sulking at Alexandria. Halleck has taken his place, and Pope with his Army of Virginia is now on the point, I believe, of destroying Jackson's forces in a great battle that may yet turn this tide. Therefore, I am now ready to dispose of McClellan altogether, something I should have done long ago. Read this."

It was a biting document denouncing McClellan in blistering terms and demanding his immediate removal from any command. She was secretly appalled by its tone.

"Has the President seen this?" she asked.

319

"He has," replied Stanton. "We have been discussing it all day."

She saw that Stanton, Secretary Chase, and Secretary Smith had already signed the round-robin letter. There were blanks waiting to be filled.

"My lord," she said in a low voice, "what did Mr. Lincoln say?"

"He does not want to release it. He says it will set a hundred thousand copperheads to biting and he has had enough of that already. But once Pope wins his victory, I think he will consent to it."

"It is a terrible indictment," she said.

"And a true one," retorted Stanton. "In my opinion, this cowardly idiot has worked harder for the South than some of Lee's own generals. With the paralysis of your plan in the West, McClellan's Peninsular failure has unleashed an avalanche on the capital. Everything now depends upon Pope."

The answer came all too soon. Twenty-four hours later General Thomas J. "Stonewall" Jackson caught Pope's army completely unprepared and in those last black days of August hurled it into oblivion at the second battle of Bull Run. McClellan, unwilling to lift a finger, sat with a small force at Alexandria and in letters to his wife secretly exulted at Pope's defeat.

But the crisis was not really reached until September second. While Evans ran about town ransacking armories and ammunition dumps with hastily drawn requisitions, Anne remained at the telegraph office, reading the reports of demoralization and chaos. Jackson's men had cut most of the Army's wires to Virginia. All day long the building clattered to the rush and departure of harried officers, pale clerks, and frightened officials. Toward six o'clock Evans joined her. She hurried him out of the building.

"I want you to take me over to the White House, Lem. We've heard from Major Eckert that a terrible quarrel has been raging in the Cabinet. Stanton grossly insulted Mr. Lincoln, and a messenger who took dispatches there told us a genuine brawl was going on. I'm going to find out about it from someone."

They joined a worried group waiting in the main hall of the White House. As luck would have it, the Secretary of the Treasury was the first person to emerge from the Cabinet room. He was almost running for the front door when Anne interrupted him.

"Mr. Chase," she exclaimed, "can you take us along? I must talk to you."

Chase looked positively frightened.

"My God, not here," he whispered. "Get out of here at once. Get in my carriage. I'll drive you to my home."

320

Later, in his study, Salmon Chase told them what had happened. He spoke with his usual composure, but his handsome white face and blinking eyes told them of the strain he was under.

"Well," he said accusingly to Anne, "your Mr. Lincoln has brought about a national calamity this afternoon by putting that imbecile McClellan back in command."

Evans asked quietly, "Are you at liberty to discuss what happened this afternoon, sir?"

For a few moments Chase looked directly at them without replying.

"I suppose not," he said at last, "but I am going to exercise that liberty just the same. I've never seen such a disgraceful situation in my life. The navy yard now has a large steam yacht ready to take off the President and his family at a moment's notice."

He paused a moment, looking out the window, his eyes seeming to re-create the tempestuous scene he had just left.

"I never hope to engage in another such Cabinet storm in my lifetime. Just as we had assembled, and before the President arrived, Mr. Stanton rushed in with murder in his eye. I firmly believe if Mr. Lincoln had been present he would have been assaulted. Stanton was in a towering rage, howling he had been undone behind his back by the President's order, of which he had just heard, putting McClellan in charge of the troops around the city. Then Mr. Lincoln appeared. I asked him if he could confirm what Stanton had just reported about McClellan. To our shock, he said he could, that, in his own words, he 'had set him to putting these troops into the fortifications about Washington.'

"Mr. Stanton, almost apoplectic, said that no one now was responsible for the defense of the capital; that the War Department had known nothing of the order, that it was a stab in the back; that as Mr. Lincoln had given the order himself General Halleck would now consider himself relieved from all responsibility; that, furthermore, McClellan could now shield himself if anything went wrong."

Chase drew a deep breath.

"I then jumped into the argument and told Mr. Lincoln any Engineer officer could do the work around Washington as well as McClellan. We all began talking and shouting at once. Mr. Lincoln thereupon got in a terrible temper, shouted at us, and told us flatly he would gladly resign his plan—several were shocked because in all the uproar they thought he said 'his place'—but he still could not see who could do the work wanted as well as McClellan.

"But Stanton and I kept hammering at him, naming Hooker, Sumner, and Burnside as more effective in the emergency. The President then calmed down, but he said emphatically that the order

321

was his and he would be responsible for it to the country. There were more angry words, many of which I will never repeat to anyone, and just before we broke up I told the President that his putting McClellan back in an important command would prove a national calamity. And God help us, so I believe."

Finding Chase becoming too angry for further discussion, Evans and Anne soon left.

Almost hourly the frightened population of Washington expected to hear the guns of Jackson thundering up from the south. But Evans told her that spies and secret service reports stated that Jackson's forces were striking northwestward along an inland course parallel to the Potomac.

"He is going to try to break into Maryland," said Evans. "He won't bother with this town." The next few days verified his prediction.

One morning Anne accompanied him to Seward's home on F Street to discuss a slight legal dispute the Secretary was having with Stanton's ordnance men. Seward, after disposing of the matter, talked in a desultory manner for a few moments, then got up with his eternal cigar and went to a silver salver on a small hall table, returning with a card in his hand. There was an odd glint in his shrewd eyes and he waved his glowing cigar at the bit of pasteboard.

"Do you know whose card this is? Do you know what's going on?" he demanded in his rasping, husky voice.

Without waiting for a reply he continued: "This is George Brinton McClellan's calling card, left this morning. I'll give the devil his due. Three days ago McClellan heard Lee and Jackson were heading to cross the Potomac near Harpers Ferry and intended to dive straight through Maryland into Pennsylvania. He told me this in person and I took him at once to Halleck. We routed the old boy out of bed after midnight. Halleck pooh-poohed the whole idea, told Mac to go to bed and forget the whole business, and he himself promptly followed his own advice.

"Wa-all," said Seward with a touch of his upstate drawl, "yesterday little Mac, without saying a word to anyone—mind you, he has no real command beyond responsibility for the capital's defenses—gathered the whole Ninth Corps on the Seventh Street road, sent off the Second and Twelfth Corps to Tennallytown, sent the cavalry to Poolesville, and still other corps off yesterday and the day before."

Seward flicked a long cylinder of white ash on the floor, and his lean seamed face broke into a smile. He said to Evans, "Nobody had any idea of this, Stanton least of all. This morning McClellan, dressed like a major-domo at the Astor House, white gloves and all, took three of these calling cards, got his staff together, and galloped over to the White House, then to the War Office, finally to my home, dropping his three cards on the way. A typical gesture blended with impudence. Then he tore out of town to lead the whole damn Army against Lee somewhere around South Mountain, about sixty-odd miles northwest of us."

"You mean," said Evans, "the general had no authority for these moves?"

"None whatever beyond the refurbishing of his self-esteem," said Seward genially. "What do you make of it? You urge, threaten, and implore this man to fight—and he sits in the mud and yells for more men. Fire him, disgrace him, and he seizes upon a defeated army, and before you can say Jack Robinson goes rushing pell-mell after the man we've been trying to get him to lick for over a year."

Seward coughed and smiled grimly. "He must have a strain of mule in him. We should have ordered him *not* to move out of Washington a year ago. He'd have been in Richmond in six weeks."

They thought all these developments quite as fantastic as anything that had occurred. But two days after McClellan left town Evans hurried to Anne's rooms from the War Department with a batch of papers in a dispatch box.

"Read these, dear. We're to be at Mr. Stanton's office in an hour. The President, with Chase and Wade, are coming along to talk them over."

"What are they?" she asked faintly, staring at the dispatch box.

"Statements from the West," said Evans, "that make the Potomac look like some peaceful river in paradise. Governor Morton reports to Stanton that with the collapse of your Tennessee campaign the Northwest is again on the verge of secession. They want to leave the Union *now!*"

A grim dejected group gathered in Stanton's plainly furnished office that afternoon. Mr. Lincoln came in late, his face lined and worn, the color of yellow parchment. He and Stanton scarcely exchanged a word, the latter's inscrutable liquid eyes gazing mournfully at a huge inkstain on the rug. Wade was in a bitter mood. Stanton came to the point at once, his voice soft and threatening as it always was when he was trying to hold his temper.

"Governor Morton," he said with obvious irony, "in the course of some thirty letters has succeeded in making one thing plain: 'Another three months like the last six,' he writes, 'and we are lost—lost.'"

For half an hour there was an aimless, dispirited discussion of possible measures. Mr. Lincoln had said nothing, all the time playing with his watch chain, moodily staring out at a clump of fog-shrouded trees. But he suddenly electrified them by remarking, as if to himself, "Let's look at this mess, piece by piece. McClellan, who ain't even supposed to be where he is, is perched near South Mountain about to fight a great battle. What will happen if he loses, I'd rather not say."

His swarthy, sallow face turned toward one, then another. His eyes, for all their fatigue and strain, glowed a little as if from a slow spark of grim humor.

"But there's more than one way to bell a cat, even when you're running for the woods," he said slowly. "There's been a friend of mine from Illinois stalking me for eight weeks. He's John McClernand, a general from my home state up from the ranks. Now John don't like West Pointers. He claims that clique has brought on more trouble for us than the politicians. When I got wind of Morton's letters here and read 'em, I up and told John one day, 'General, if the folks in Indiana, Illinois, Wisconsin, and Iowa don't like the way we run this war, and if they want the Mississippi, why'n hell don't they go right down the river and take Vicksburg themselves, and why don't *you* lead 'em?' "

Mr. Lincoln sat up, his hands on his knees.

"The short of it is, friends," he said forcefully, "the general jumped at it, wanted to get going right away. He's widely known and listened to out there. Now in order to get Miss Carroll's plan going again I propose, with Mr. Stanton's approval, to let McClernand recruit his own army in the Northwest, stamp down the riots and secession meetings now going on, and try his luck down the river. He'll draw off steam. He can't do any harm—and I'll wager here and now that when Grant and Sherman get wind that McClernand is under way they will jump for Vicksburg twice as fast."

A long astonished silence greeted this remarkable proposal. Several of those present doubted its wisdom, but no one dared oppose it.

"Has General Halleck been consulted about this?" asked Evans innocently.

Mr. Lincoln pulled his nose reflectively.

"He has not. And I don't think he will be," he said finally in a tone of voice that did not invite further discussion. "Miss Carroll, have you anything new to contribute on the Vicksburg situation?" he asked mildly.

"Nothing whatever, Mr. President," she said a little stiffly. "I believe my old ideas are still new—for no one has yet tried them. I still repeat that Vicksburg cannot be taken by the combined fleets of Davis and Farragut, or twenty other fleets. It will *have* to be taken by the occupation of Jackson, Mississippi, and by that means alone."

"Yes," said the President patiently. "You've told us that before and I don't doubt its wisdom. But we are all civilians here. Even as Com-

324

mander in Chief, I do not dare upset the calculations of trained military men without allowing them to try their own conclusions. But if you'll condense your reflections on this matter in a final letter to Mr. Stanton—we will see what we can do with Grant this time. And with John McClernand breathing down Grant's neck from the Northwest—something ought to happen."

Complete silence greeted these observations, and the President, obviously nettled, got up to go. There was an angry expression on his face.

"I advise everyone here to pray for McClellan's success," he said grimly. "The safety of this Union may rest upon it."

The others did not linger after he had gone. The atmosphere in Stanton's office was explosive.

"Just to coin a chaotic metaphor," said Evans as they walked slowly homeward, "there's the Gordian knot in a nutshell. If the military command collapses, stir in a couple of political coup d'états, and add a pinch of improvised action over the heads of all concerned. By the time these measures won't work, the former generals have been propped up, sewn up, and restuffed, and the whole damn machine starts over again." He spat disgustedly. "But Lord Almighty, Anne, what a way to run a war!"

"How else would you run this one?" Anne demanded heatedly. "You're analyzing too many paper reports, Lem. Furthermore, you aren't charged with any of these crushing responsibilities. Believe me, when it comes to holding an unwieldy, divided mass of confused people together, and giving that mass time to breathe, to use its collective arms and legs, and finally, God grant us, its brains—there is no one who comes within miles of Mr. Lincoln."

He looked at her in thoughtful surprise.

A few days later the victorious news of the battles of South Mountain and Antietam thundered into the astonished capital which, for months, had wavered between elation and despair. Over the hills of western Maryland, by Sharpsburg, Antietam Creek and a little Dunker church, and for miles around, some two hundred thousand men and five hundred pieces of artillery roared and rocked the countryside. September 17, 1862, was the bloodiest single day of the war. Almost twenty-five thousand dead and wounded carpeted the fields and woodlands. And when this memorable battle was over Maryland, Pennsylvania, and the East had been delivered from the threat of rebel invasion and Lee's battered forces had to retreat across the Potomac.

40

ON MONDAY MORNING, THE TWENTY-SECOND DAY OF September, the President, though furious at Lee's escape from McClellan, seized upon the undoubted victory at Antietam and released his first draft of the Emancipation Proclamation, to take effect January first, to the press of the nation.

The proclamation rocked the country, shook the souls of men across the nation. One million copies of it, paid for by John Murray Forbes, a wealthy Abolitionist merchant of Boston, were to be distributed throughout the South.

The proclamation was aimed at Europe as well as the North and South. And in the South a bitter fury burned the very air.

To Anne the Emancipation Proclamation came as a stunning shock. She had fought against it. She had pleaded with Mr. Lincoln to veto every form of emancipation, convinced that the South, once its rebellion was put down, would at last resolve the problem itself by constitutional means. But in one stroke a world of her outworn beliefs and stubborn convictions, subtly and steadily undermined by the President, now crumbled about her, collapsed like a house of cards which this tall, gaunt man with the anxious eyes had finally flicked apart with an impatient finger.

If Anne had needed any further evidence that a crisis in all her convictions was at hand, the Emancipation Proclamation provided that evidence. The thunderous symphony of war was playing a far different tune than she had anticipated.

A few days after the President's momentous announcement she had pleaded a headache when Evans invited her to attend an informal conference with Wade and several members of his Committee on the Conduct of the War. Evans had looked at her quizzically.

"You never had a headache in your life, sweetheart."

He was on the point of saying something else. Instead, after asking her to wait up for his return with Wade, he left her rooms almost hesitantly, with a worried expression in his dark eyes.

A headache, she reflected after he was gone, *was* a childish, time-worn excuse. But in every way the mood that had been growing upon her in recent weeks was far more of a headache than anything she had experienced. It was a spiritual headache, a soul-shaking headache, a congestion of unresolved questions without answers, of far cries and mocking echoes, of proddings of mind and heart that found no satisfaction anywhere.

She sat alone at her desk and thought of Mr. Lincoln and of many things he had said and left unsaid. For the man in the White House now haunted her. Why had he signed that proclamation?

And the man in the White House, she reflected, by the very nature of the revolutionary act he had issued, now placed her in an impossible position. Her dilemma, in essence, was very simple. She was a Southerner. All her labors for the North were labors for the preservation of a Union that would bring the South back to the shelter of the Constitution through legal forms and by legal methods stated and implicit in that document. Further than that she could not go. Had the military strategy she proposed been aggressively followed up, her principles might have been maintained. But unforeseen disasters had shattered these principles and flung them to the wild winds of chaos and revolution.

She had no illusions as to what now threatened. The North was slowly rising, like a colossus wakened from sleep. She saw in a flash that violent and revolutionary methods of waging this war were being proposed and would soon be adopted. She felt that all she still held dear in the South, all values, social standards, the whole structure of society as she had known it, was to be smashed.

The outright confiscation, emancipation, call it what you would, of four billions of private property—that is to say, four million slaves—spelled ruin, nothing but ruin to the South she still sought to save.

She simply could not follow this road. She could not, and she would not. It was as simple as that.

She was sitting at her desk, her head in her hands, trying to digest the decision confronting her, when a voice behind her made her jump.

"What's the trouble, Anne? What in God's name is the matter?"

Evans, with hardly a sound, had re-entered her parlor and was looking down at her. His face was solemn as he saw her drawn face and startled expression.

"Why—why did you come back?" she managed to ask him.

327

"I reckon I had a feeling you needed me. You're in trouble. What is it?"

She got up, walked across the room, then with evident reluctance turned and faced him.

"Lem," she said in an expressionless tone, "I'm through. I'm leaving Washington. I can't go on." She added a little breathlessly, "I don't think I can ever marry you. I don't think I should."

Instead of shock, an expression of mild interest and curiosity flickered across Evans's features. He pulled over one of her rosewood chairs, sat down carefully, and motioned to the divan close beside him.

"As bad as that? Sit down, Anne—please—and tell me all about it."

Quite mechanically she obeyed him. She began talking, still in the same expressionless, almost wooden voice, as if reciting a lesson she had been at great pains to learn. Only the twisting of her hands now and then revealed the stress she was under. Evans listened carefully.

"Lem, I—I was going to suggest this week that we be married at once. That after all there was no real reason why we should delay a day longer. Now I cannot. The whole thing is impossible."

"Why?" The tone of his voice told her nothing at all.

"The facts are—and I must face them," she said violently, "I cannot go on with these radicals, these red Republicans. I cannot endure these men any longer. I can't stand what Wade, Sumner, Stanton, Stevens, and Chandler—yes, and Mr. Lincoln too—now propose to do. I will not take part in the violent, revolutionary acts now proposed. I will not endure seeing the South torn apart by Abolitionists thirsting for vengeance and tossing the Constitution out the window into the bargain. I won't see the whole structure of Southern society ripped to pieces to make a Northern holiday for a pack of Northern pirates. I wasn't born for that."

"Weren't you?" asked Evans softly. He added in a slightly sterner tone, "Let's omit the high-sounding phrases, Anne, and talk this over very simply. It means a lot to both of us—and a very precious part of my life to me."

Something in his expression put her on her guard. This, she thought with a start, was becoming too idiotically like a prelude to that strangely similar and shockingly violent scene with Harry so long ago. But this time the situation was incredibly reversed, and she was the Southerner. The idea frightened her. She said slowly:

"I don't think we should talk about it now, Lem. I'm not feeling well. And I'm very much afraid you may think me cowardly. But I've just decided to sever all my associations with this government, to stop my activities at once. And feeling as you do, with the duties you have to perform, I—I don't see how our understanding, our intentions can endure in the light of—of my decision."

"Before you consider it a decision," said Evans encouragingly, almost impersonally, "let's look at it. Perhaps you're only speculating. We'd better have this out right now, Anne. What do you want to do—retire to Castle Haven with your knitting, tell us all it's good-by, you were mistaken, events have leaped out of your neatly fenced lane—and you wash your hands of the whole affair—and of me? Is that it?"

Her throat suddenly felt tight. She forced herself to say, "That's cruelly put. But——" She could not go on.

Evans finished her comment: "But something like that, eh? Well——" He sighed deeply and leaned back in his chair as if pondering how to say what had to be said. "Let's put it my way first. Then we'll look at it your way. You say there are facts you've got to face. I agree. They've been coming on fast, haven't they? The trouble is, you're looking *backwards*—at the *wrong* set of facts. You must turn around and look at a lot of big, fat, bulging facts right in front of you, facts you haven't even caught sight of yet. Once you do that—then we can talk."

"I don't understand you."

"I'll try to explain. And for the time being, let's leave our personal feelings out of this. They'll solve themselves if other things are made clear. I might suggest that you've lost your nerve. But it isn't as simple as that."

"It isn't a question of courage at all—it's a question of conviction," she said vigorously.

Evans nodded. "That's right. But it's tougher than that. It's a question of giving up old convictions and finding new ones you can live with—and believe in. Isn't that it?"

She said reluctantly, "In a way," and then burst out, "But I can't give up my convictions. I've lived with them all my life."

"You've dumped some of them before," observed Evans mildly, "though it's always been an extremely hard thing for you to do. Let's see what's blocking you now."

"For heaven's sake, Lem," she exclaimed heatedly, "don't sit there like a schoolteacher reading me a lesson. What right——"

"Look," Evans interrupted, "I have a right. I love you. I want to marry you. And I've been all through this mill myself. I have to show you something, and I'm not sure I know how to. But you'll be in a damn tragic situation, Anne, if somebody doesn't point it out. I think what it all amounts to is that—the war's getting out of hand. Your precious South is about to be placed out of bounds to any constitutional appeals. With your legal mind, you can't stand that." Evans leaned forward, his hands clenched on his knees. "But a roaring revolution is on us, Anne—a hell of a revolution. Everything we can lay our hands on—Negroes, Negroes with guns in their hands, emancipation, military conquest, the sacking of cities, farms, plantations—all this is now to be hurled at the South. As Thad Stevens points out, the Constitution is dead. The rule of war applies. You can't endure that. Your neat well-ordered legal mind, with all provisions carefully provided for, won't go along."

Evans stood up suddenly and almost shouted at her, "Well, you'll have to go along with it! You've not only got to endure it—you've got to face it, embrace it, and fully support it all!"

Her face went white.

"Lem!"

Evans looked down at her, his eyes blazing.

"You can't cut and run. You've got to stand by your beliefs! You've got to face up to the consequences of your own acts. Don't you understand that?"

"My beliefs! My own acts!" Her face registered blank astonishment.

"Good God!" said Evans almost to himself. For a moment he looked at her in sheer exasperation. "Look here, Anne, can't you understand?"

He searched savagely for words, then said explosively, *"You're a woman with a sword*—a terrible sword you know how to use. But look at what you did. Then examine what you're doing. Wittingly or not, you allied yourself with the most rabid prosecutors of this war—Wade, Stanton, and their supporters. Nearly a year ago you gave them the greatest weapon imaginable—a practical military plan that stabbed the South to the heart. And now you want to file down that sword, shatter it, throw it away, because, politically, you're panicked by what's happened. A year ago you begged for action to head off those secessionists who would betray the Union. But now that others have taken that violent action you urged—others who won't abide by your little legalisms—you want to step out of the storm. The Army of the Tennessee, *your* army, smashes a large part of the South, liberates thousands of blacks.

"And good lord, what have you done ever since Shiloh? Bombarded the President with feverish pleas to stop the Abolitionists. You've implored him to veto emancipation in the District and everywhere else it's been proposed. You told the Army where to strike. But then you turn around and beg the President not to antagonize the South too much, to confer with their delegates, let them snuggle safely into the Constitution again and settle slavery at their leisure, doubtless on their

330

own terms. Well—it's idiotic nonsense and a damnable contradiction I wouldn't have believed you capable of!"

"How can you talk to me like that? My military work and my political activities are two very different things."

"You're dead wrong. One merely supplements the other. You can't or won't recognize that—and you must. It's the heart of your problem. You believe in striking to the heart of a problem in military matters. But you hate the same procedure in politics."

They confronted one another like two opponents searching for a hold. They were both furious. And both were a little frightened.

"In politics," she protested violently, "I worship the law. I've always prided myself on possessing a liberal mind. I've always been a liberal."

"A liberal? God in heaven, what is that?"

His voice was sharp, full of biting sarcasm. The crack in their relations was becoming a crevice. The crevice was becoming a gulf. Though shocked by the realization of this, Anne said angrily, "I won't stand for your tone of contempt, Lem. You disapprove of liberals?"

Evans's mouth tightened.

"Thoroughly. In parlors or lecture halls they're pretty harmless. But in any theater of action—I detest 'em."

"In God's name, why?"

Evans was silent a moment. He, too, was suddenly aware that this quarrel might burst its banks and overwhelm them with rising violence and unpredictable results. He said more composedly, "Maybe 'liberal' isn't the right word. A lot of able people work under that label. But I'm talking about you and me—and what's been the matter with us. Let me tell you my definition of these straddlers—these people who sit on two chairs—and why their way is not for you." He searched a moment for words.

"The people I'm talking about," said Evans slowly in a voice harsh with hostility, "are persons of fine emotions, sound sensibilities—and seldom any guts. These well-wishers, these straddlers, these liberals know the right road to take. They are always shouting for others to take it—but they never take it themselves. I know. I was once one of them. All middle-roaders, in my opinion, share one characteristic. Each one has his price. I'll grant you a few exceptions—a handful of able liberal-minded legislators in House and Senate who've stuck to their guns. I know others who fight well if the issue isn't too crucial. But you can never depend upon these people in a real crisis. You never know when they'll break and run.

"To prove this, let me ask you something. Where are all the liberals, the compromisers, the tolerant, the so-called men of good will of the past decade? *Where are their works?* Where are *your* friends in that camp—the friends you once worked with? They've run to cover. They're gone, forgotten. And you? You're working hand in glove with a bunch of militant radicals who will go to any extreme to win this war. And two years ago you detested every one of these men, with the possible exception of Wade."

This was bitter truth. She could not deny it. She was trembling with anger, but he would not let her speak.

"Just one thing more. What is the inevitable course of these people who always think there's an easy way out? It's a curious one. As long as such a person stands above the crowd, he feels safe. As long as he can *talk,* he has confidence. But when he has to *act*—he's through. He demands that those behind him *advance.* But the moment they do so he begins his own retreat. Your straddler can't stand *action,* for action means conflict, danger, peril to self. Even men as big as Clay and Webster were often timeservers. They sold out the people time and again at crucial moments. You know that."

"You're ruthless and hatefully extreme," she protested. "Many of these men did valuable work, great work, without resorting to un-bridled violence."

"You may think so. I don't. They simply staved off a final account-ing—and the debt is now to be paid in an ocean of blood."

"Then who *are* the rash spirits you so admire?" she asked bitterly. "The men who advocate violence, destruction, and the ruin of the innocent that such doctrines embrace?"

Evans was trying to hold his temper and having a difficult time of it.

"I'm trying to get you to look at facts. Who wields power, terrible power, now? You know the answer. The hated radicals are in the saddle. The red Republicans are in control—with the despised Abo-litionists breathing down their necks. Why is that? You and I fought these people for years. The answer is simple. These people faced the real issue long ago. You and I didn't. They never compromised. You and I compromised for years—anything to save the South and stave off this collision between slaveholders and a free people.

"For thirty years, Anne, the Abolitionists were a despised handful, mobbed, tarred and feathered in *Northern* cities, hanged—hanged in person and effigy. But from the first they stated boldly their stand and their purpose. No dealings, no compromise with slaveholders! They were out to smash the slave power; in a word, to smash a powerful form of society that flourished in almost half of this nation. Lord, how I used to hate 'em! Old Garrison was my idea of the devil himself. I fought them. So did you. Even Mr. Lincoln tried to fend them off.

He is going through his own hell in this dilemma. He had to issue that proclamation. We all have to admit we're wrong, that *you* are wrong. *And by your own military genius, Anne, you've blown your political world to hell and gone.* It's sheer irony—but it's a fact."

"And just when," she asked with cold sarcasm, "did *you* cross this Rubicon you consider so vital for me?"

To her astonishment Evans suddenly laughed.

"That's a fair question. I'll tell you. When I was in the House I used to play cards a lot with Thad Stevens. A damned skillful player, too. Well, in one all-night session at the Card Club I took almost five hundred dollars away from Thad. When we threw down our cards at dawn Stevens downed another brandy—he'd had a lot. Then he grinned at me and pulled out a parcel of clippings. 'Mr. Evans,' he said, 'I need a little revenge. Let me read you something.' He read me a nonsensical hairsplitting defense of slavery combined with a mild censure of Southern planters. I stopped him. It made no sense at all. I said to Stevens, 'That's sheer drivel, sir. What ass wrote it?'

" 'I'm talking to the ass who uttered it,' Stevens said pleasantly. 'You spouted three hours of that in the House one morning and I damn near shot you. Now, sir, let's walk down the Avenue and talk.' "

Evans was much more his old self.

"We walked and talked till the sun came up. Old Stevens thumped along on his lame leg, his wig askew. He was full of brandy—but his mind was sharp as a steel trap. He tore me and my beliefs to bits, pointed out one terrible contradiction after another. He told me to get my guts up in my head where they belonged—or go to digging ditches. We drank for another hour."

Evans paused and added solemnly, "Then I went home and burned every damn speech I'd ever made—and I had a very pretty collection. For a few days I wanted to kill Stevens," said Evans explosively, "But he taught me a lesson I never forgot."

She was frightened by his now forbidding expression and tried to take a stand.

"But you want to pull down a whole social structure to right a single wrong!"

"Why not," exclaimed Evans, "when that society rests on that wrong?"

"You—you wish to turn the South over to the mercies of the Negro?"

"The mercies of the Negro," said Evans, "can't be worse than the tyrannies of their masters. And stop these generalities, Anne! What's this precious social system you're so concerned about? It's nothing but the feudal strangle hold of four hundred thousand damned planters on the wealth, the labor, the entire production of the South—backed by Yankee dollars and Yankee banking houses."

His anger rose again like some quick tide.

"Smash that power! Colonize the planters, if you want to, in Liberia or your Chiriquí coal fields. Or string 'em up! It makes no difference to me. *But get rid of them.* Hand over five or ten acres of land and a mule to every black and white who wants to work. Enforce his political rights, and instead of chaos you'll have a new nation. . . . But you—you won't pay that price."

"I certainly won't," she cried. "I wouldn't have believed this of you, Lem. You're nothing but an anarchist. You—you're worse than the most rabid, hateful Abolitionist. Worse than Mr. Phillips!"

He fairly leaped at her words.

"Wendell Phillips? Do you know what *he* said? He told a screaming crowd the other night that the broad mass of people need only know the first two lines of the Constitution—'establish justice and secure liberty'—to know what to do. He shouted that the people have waited too long, apologized enough, eaten dirt enough for bankrupt statesmen; that they have now got their hard hands on the neck of a rebellious aristocracy, and in the name of the *people* they mean to strangle it!

"Phillips tore the South, its feudalism, its slavery, to pieces. He wound up with his battle cry, 'Death to the system, death or exile to the master, is our only motto.' That, my dear girl, I've been forced to believe. And that is what *you* are going to have to believe."

Anne shivered. She cried angrily, "Never! Never will I accept such a horrible doctrine, Lem. And now stop it. Let me alone."

Evans looked at her thoughtfully. His anger was subsiding. He knew that violent arguments of this kind seldom won converts. He knew Anne was stubborn, usually sure of herself, and that her convictions were deeply rooted. He felt, in fact, that he had already lost his battle with her. But he would not give up without another word.

"Anne, what you refuse to recognize, what you will not face, is that these Southern traitors you hate rely on one great power. That power is slavery—exploitation of man by man, of man's labor, produce, his very life. You won't consent to the destruction of that power, for this means the destruction of Southern society as you know it. Just the same, that whole system is going to be destroyed.

"And Phillips showed me something else the other night I'd never thought about—that the fight against slavery, the organization of free labor, the battle against child labor, the fight for women's rights, the struggle against capital, for education, for equal liberty are all one struggle indivisible. If we could all see that," added Evans, "if we formed one front in such a fight"—he shrugged—"it would be won

334

tomorrow. But you see a piece here, I a piece there, and someone else still another bit of the puzzle, until we are all at loggerheads with one another, while the masters of us all remain undisturbed."

Anne suddenly wilted and burst into tears.

"I hate you for this, Lem. You've no right to bait me like this, to try to force me to accept a hateful point of view that I could never believe in. I don't wish to see you again for a long time, if ever. I cannot stand such harshness, such—such hatred that, coming from you, seems almost personal."

Deep conflict was mirrored in every line of Evans's face. He wanted to take her small tearful body in his arms and deny for the moment everything he had said. But he could not. He said harshly, "By God, you must see this or we *are* through. You must accept the reality of events, the lesson of events." He added quietly, "For both our sakes, for both our lives, you've got to do this."

Without another word he strode across the room and left, slamming the door with a shattering crash that numbed her heart.

She walked without thinking to her desk and stood there, caught between tears and rage. She picked up a handsome glass paperweight and flung it on the floor, then walked up and down the room in such a conflict of inner forces that she felt it would literally tear her apart.

For an ancient fear undermined her mounting rage. A fear compounded of Sallie's insight and the riddle that Sallie had presented— the riddle of herself. If only this savage quarrel with Evans did not remind her so horribly of her quarrel with Harry. For a brief moment she understood Harry's violent reactions on that occasion. They were so similar to her own now. And again this idea frightened her. There was a terrible repetition in her relationships with men she worshiped and with the only two men she had loved. Where, where was the fault?

For almost an hour she sat at her desk without moving. Once she rose and trimmed the failing lamp. Out of all this welter of discussion, ideas, cross-purposes, and crumbling convictions one stark fact finally confronted her. She was about to deny herself the one man she loved profoundly, completely. She was about to throw away what she now knew was fate's final opportunity to solve this riddle of her life. She had tossed away such an opportunity once before. But if she did it now every instinct told her Sallie's worst warnings would be realized. She would destroy the only part of her life that really mattered. The reality of events? She remembered another warning, something Evans had said. "There are times when one has to accept events, accept reality, or go under."

Finally Anne picked up her pen, placed several sheets of fresh paper before her, and began to write.

335

It was well past midnight when Evans, looking thoroughly upset, again hurried down the hallway of the Washington House with Ben Wade just behind him.

He knocked softly at Anne's door, but there was no answer. Evans turned worriedly to Wade.

"I'll never forgive myself for this, Ben. I hurt her terribly. I said some outrageous things. For God's sake, help me to undo this damage if you can."

"You think she's gone to bed?" asked Wade anxiously.

But Evans had seen a crack of light under her door. He gently turned the knob. The door opened and both men hesitantly entered Anne's parlor. The green-shaded lamp shone pleasantly on the big desk. But Anne's chair was empty. Then Evans saw her and motioned to Wade. In the dimness of the far side of the room she was lying on the couch, fast asleep, in a curiously defenseless position of utter fatigue, one arm lying easily on the deep blue upholstery. But some impulse first made Evans cross to her desk and examine the papers there. Wade looked over his shoulder.

Several pages with the heading, "A New Program," were covered with her strong, breezy handwriting. Both Evans and Wade read carefully what was written there. It was the plan for a series of articles for fifty newspapers in the North. It was also a new declaration of war, a new declaration of faith by Anne.

Evans, his dark eyes alight with astonishment and excitement, fastened again and again on certain sentences: "This war, once a limited rebellion, is now a great revolution in fact and should be fought as such. . . . The Congress may declare all the black race *citizens* with *all* the rights and privileges of citizens, and may retain them upon the soil and make them its *proprietors*. . . . Land is the solution of race equality and civil reform in the South. . . . Land equality and race equality should be enforced, wherever necessary, by federal bayonets, until a new and far juster society is founded in enduring form. . . ."

There was a great deal more, but Evans had read enough. Placed carefully on her papers was a copy of Senator Sumner's great speech of May 16, 1862. On it Anne had penciled a brief message in large flowing letters:

"Events win, Lem. I accept them. I think it's time! You were so right, and so was Charles Sumner. And I love you dearly."

Evans took a deep breath. His hands were shaking. He looked at Wade, and Wade's eyes were eloquent.

"Good God," said Evans softly, "she's done it! She's done it! She's made the shift!"

Wade said nothing. He was staring solemnly at her desk as Evans walked toward the couch.

"Anne!" he said loudly, and moved as if to waken her. But Wade quickly turned, motioned to him, and shook his head. Both men stood awhile, looking down at the white tired face, but a face composed, firm, and beautifully serene.

"No," breathed Wade at last, "don't waken her. That cost her something. Let her sleep."

41

THE CATHARSIS OF ANNE'S QUARREL WITH EVANS
brought them closer together than ever and enormously strengthened
their respect and understanding of one another. Wade, when he heard
the full story, presented Anne with a handsome Sheffield silver tea
service. Attached to the beautifully engraved salver was a small card
which said simply, "To a gallant lady from two very contrite gentlemen," and it all aided greatly in restoring their old intimacy.

Moreover, there was new steel in Anne, a new attitude, as the war
roared into more violent phases in both political and military realms.
Wade was immensely impressed by the fresh patience and fortitude
Anne revealed in the face of disasters piling up everywhere and the
apparent collapse of the Tennessee plan.

"They'll come back to it. They'll have to," she insisted whenever
they discussed the matter, and on that simple statement she took her
stand.

Fortified by this new faith which had cast out the last major contradiction in her attitude toward the war, Anne began to concentrate on
the stubborn military impasse at Vicksburg. She had changed her
political clothes, but on the subject of Vicksburg, from first to last,
she refused to back down, hammering home with sometimes exasperating insistence her original plan.

With Evans's help she prepared a long letter and an elaborate map
for Stanton. Again she blasted the decision of Army and Navy authorities to reduce Vicksburg from the river, stating they would never
succeed. She pleaded with them to take the town of Jackson and the
railroads in the rear of Vicksburg.

*"The occupation of Jackson and the command of the railroad to
New Orleans would compel the immediate evacuation of Vicksburg."*

338

She also advocated an immediate fleet attack on Mobile in order to prepare the approaches to Georgia, and she went into great detail as to the forces needed to make these moves. After she had delivered these documents to the department she said to Evans, "Lem, I assure you, I'm not obsessed with my own ideas. But on this I know I'm right. Taking Jackson first is the only way to get Vicksburg. If they try any other method they invite disaster."

Vicksburg—Vicksburg—Vicksburg.

It was a refrain that hammered at her all during the long fall and winter months. Early in November, Stanton showed her a telegram from Grant to Halleck, now in Washington commanding the armies, saying that he proposed to move at once on Jackson by the Mississippi Railroad. Weeks later she found to her dismay that Halleck never even replied to Grant's proposals. Grant finally went ahead on his own authority, but by that time, because of winter rains and impassable roads, the attempt on Jackson had to be abandoned.

But something had been accomplished that fall. The President's scheme to head off secession in the Northwest had succeeded. His appointee, General McClernand, with an entirely separate command of thirty thousand men under a special commission from Mr. Lincoln, was heading down the river. The Northwest was saved.

Meanwhile, letters from Captain Scott, on the steamer *War Eagle* before Vicksburg, poured in on Anne's desk, full of gossip, the pilot's picturesque speculation, and military information. Many of these letters she turned over to Stanton.

All through the winter Scott related in his own inimitable way the devices by which Grant and Sherman and the river fleets probed the swamps, rivers, bayous, and rear works of the beleaguered city.

But in early spring she sensed an exciting change in Scott's letters. Evans, studying them carefully, remarked one night, "Sweetheart, something big is coming off."

Something big did come off. With stunning suddenness a stubborn stocky man who had wallowed through blunders and plodding mistakes, most of them made by his superiors; a man who had fought doggedly and tempered himself for months in blind proddings about Vicksburg, became with incredible swiftness a great general who forged a thunderbolt destined to rock the Confederacy.

On May 7, 1863, Grant, having distributed five days' rations to his troops, cut loose from Grand Gulf and every base of supply and flung his entire army in the direction of Jackson, the state capital. Further to confuse the enemy, he sent Colonel Grierson and a thousand men on a whirlwind cavalry raid through the state, cutting three railroads to pieces and isolating the city on three sides, north, south, and east, just as General Joseph E. Johnston hoped to rally his army there. It never occurred to the rebels that Grant would abandon his supply lines, and they wasted a week trying to cut behind him and destroy the non-existent lines.

Anne, and Evans when he could find time, haunted the telegraph office, often until three and four in the morning. And Stanton was almost delirious with joy at the news.

One week after he left Grand Gulf, with rebel troops rushing about the state of Mississippi trying to locate him, Grant defeated Joseph E. Johnston and on May 14 hoisted the Stars and Stripes over the city of Jackson and went to bed in the very house Johnston had slept in the night before.

"Well!" shouted Stanton to Anne through a mouthful of sandwich he was munching. It was late at night and the telegram had just come in. "There you are, ma'am. The Army's at last where you wanted them last fall. Vicksburg is finished."

There were more victories—at Champion's Hill and Black Hill—and Sherman's rapid advance threw the whole Yazoo River territory, with guns and stores, into Union hands. She did not know until later that Sherman, in excited astonishment, had ridden out to the river bluff he had tried vainly to storm from the water five months ago and remarked to Grant, "Till now I never thought this movement a success. But this is a success if we never take the town."

The campaign, suggested by Anne and beautifully executed by Grant, was a classic. Vicksburg was no longer the unapproachable Gibraltar of America. It was just eighteen days since Grant had crossed the Mississippi, eleven days since he had left his base at Grand Gulf. In those eighteen days he had marched two hundred miles and, by the novelty of his movements, disconcerted and separated forces much larger than his own. With a loss of not more than five thousand men, he had defeated two armies in five battles, taking nearly one hundred cannon and destroying or capturing more than twelve thousand of the enemy. And, to crown it all, he had solved the apparently insoluble problem of investing Vicksburg.

"To find a parallel in military history to the deeds of those eighteen days," said one commentator, "we must go back to the first Italian campaign of Napoleon in 1796."

Vicksburg began to crumble at once. In less than two months of futile maneuvers by the enemy, Grant's forces entered Vicksburg and on July 4, 1863, planted the flag of the Union over the surrendered city. It was the greatest single victory won by an American army since the founding of the Republic. At the same time, in the East the Union forces under General Meade, in hard-won battle at Gettysburg, had

340

stopped Pickett's gallant charge and turned back Lee's deepest penetration into the North.

Washington and the nation went wild over the double victory. On July 4 Stanton rushed about the War Department like a madman, crowding the wires with emotional and congratulatory telegrams to all concerned.

"There's your general, ma'am," he exclaimed to Anne as she read Grant's final reports on his desk.

"And you had better not forget Sherman either, sir," she warned him gaily, aware of his prejudice against the man.

Stanton laughed and then said quickly, "You first suggested this campaign on Jackson last October, didn't you?"

"No, Mr. Secretary, I first suggested it last May, a year ago."

Stanton looked incredulous. He went to his files and returned with a letter in his hand.

"But I have it here, ma'am. It is dated October 5. You wrote then, and I am quoting your letter directly, 'The most economical plan for the reduction of Vicksburg now is to push a column from Memphis to Corinth, down the Mississippi Central Railroad to Jackson, the capital of the state. *The occupation of Jackson and the command of the railroad to New Orleans would compel the immediate evacuation of Vicksburg,* as well as the retreat of the entire rebel army east of that line,' and so forth."

"Mr. Stanton," said Anne with an edge to her voice, "if you will go back to your files and find my letter dated early in May 1862, the fourteenth, I believe, over a year ago, you will find I said exactly the same thing at that time."

Stanton looked owlishly at her, then without a word returned to his files, rummaged about a few moments, and drew out several letters she had written. He handed them to her.

"Suppose you find it for me," he said, watching her closely.

"But it's right here," she retorted, and began to read from the first letter she had opened. "At that time I advised you twice to take Vicksburg and Memphis when they could have been had for the taking. And then—here it is. This is what I was referring to. I said, 'I think the enemy will retire southward from Corinth, Mississippi, and go down the Mississippi Central to Jackson. *The battle that compels the evacuation of Vicksburg will eventually have to be fought there.'* "

Stanton almost snatched the letter from her hands and read it carefully. "You're right," he said shortly, and placed the letters in his files without another word. He acted, indeed, as if he had no wish to discuss the subject further. He went on to other military affairs.

"Mr. Lincoln is sick," he said somberly, "over Meade's letting Lee

341

get away after Gettysburg. General Haupt ran down here on a special engine and begged us to get Meade going again. And when Lincoln asked Wadsworth, who was also there, 'General, why wasn't Lee stopped?' and Wadsworth replied, 'Because nobody went after him,' I thought the President would explode. He just looked sick, dropped his hands on his knees, and yelled, 'My God! My God! What is the matter with us all?' "

"Mr. Stanton," she said urgently, "that has *got* to be avoided in the West. Grant knows what to do. Give him authority and he'll end this rebellion in six months."

"We're going to try to," said Stanton. He added seriously, "But it's about as easy to give orders to Lee as to try to get co-operation from Halleck."

The war roared on. The great single co-ordinated plan originally projected by Lincoln, Stanton, and Colonel Scott had split into huge fragments, into a dozen bloody campaigns swirling across as many states. For after Vicksburg and Gettysburg jealousy and disunion again dammed the surge of Northern victory. And now Halleck peremptorily refused both of Grant's requests—to capture Mobile and confer with Farragut at New Orleans.

The truth was that Grant's stunning successes, while he was still under heavy criticism, had shaken Army Headquarters in Washington. In the Army's opinion, Gettysburg had sealed the fate of the South—and in this estimate of the situation the military were almost fatally mistaken. For all through the late summer of 1863 Grant's hands were tied by Halleck and the exhausted Confederates began to build and lay new plans. Not a Union move was made toward Mobile or any other vital point. Rebel troops and supplies under Longstreet were rushed unmolested into Tennessee. Jefferson Davis himself went West to confer with Braxton Bragg and survey the vast double bastion of Chattanooga and Chickamauga.

All these events, combined with an indefinable tension in the air, convinced Anne that the real crisis of the war was in the immediate offing. It came, out of near disaster, and with startling suddenness.

Late in September 1863, General Rosecrans and the Union Army of the Cumberland, defeated at Chickamauga, were driven into Chattanooga, Tennessee, and surrounded by large rebel forces. The War Department had taken the news stoically, but one evening Stanton's rooms erupted in violent action. Orderlies ran in and out, were sent scurrying to the homes of Cabinet officers and to the Soldiers' Home where the President was staying. It was long past midnight. Stanton's message to the President and Cabinet was no request. It was a peremptory command.

"The Secretary of War wants to see you at once at the department."

In half an hour Mr. Lincoln, the entire Cabinet, Halleck, and many staff officers had filed sleepily into the reception room where Stanton stood at his high desk. Evans accompanied Colonel Eckert there. And Stanton, sketching a great disaster in the making, read to the startled group a whole series of telegrams, each one more urgent than the last, from Charles A. Dana, the President's observer at Chattanooga. The Army of the Cumberland, reported Dana, was on half rations and without fuel. Horses were starving to death by the thousands. General James A. Garfield stated that another ten days would destroy the Army and give the rebels the whole Western gateway that now controlled the Confederate hinterland and protected Richmond and the East. Neither Dana nor Garfield were alarmists.

The President finally spoke.

"What do you propose to do, Mr. Stanton, if it is as bad as all that?"

"I propose," said Stanton, "to send twenty thousand veterans from the Army of the Potomac over the mountains to Chattanooga—and with your permission, I can do it in five days."

Mr. Lincoln looked astonished.

"I'll bet you can't get them out of their beds and into Washington in five days," he said sharply, and Halleck, rubbing his eyes, added irritably, "You can't make such a transfer in less than forty days, sir."

This enraged Stanton and a violent discussion took place, interrupted by the arrival of General McCallum, the director of military railroads. Stanton at once sought his support.

"If you have the authority, General, and plenty of rail transport—how fast could you make this transfer?"

"I can complete it in seven days—probably less," said McCallum promptly.

"Good! Good!" exclaimed Stanton delightedly. "I knew it could be done." He turned savagely on Halleck. "Forty days! Forty days, indeed, when the life of the nation is at stake!" He addressed McCallum again. "Go ahead, General. Get going. Begin right now."

The President flushed and stepped forward a pace.

"Just a minute, Mr. Secretary. I have not yet given my consent."

Stanton's reply for once was restrained and delivered softly. "Mr. President, it must be done. No other measures can save that army. Once the Army of the Cumberland is destroyed it can never be replaced. Chattanooga will be lost; Burnside's army perhaps lost; the cause of this Union set back for years. But twenty thousand men delivered at Chattanooga within a week will save the entire situation. I *know* this. And I will guarantee the safety of the capital. It must be done. I beg you to give me your immediate approval."

343

The President looked at the Secretary of War a moment, then smiled slightly.

"All right, sir. Go ahead. Let's see what you can do."

To Evans what followed was one of the magnificent performances of Stanton's remarkable career. McCallum left in twenty minutes for the Virginia camps on a special engine and within an hour was routing sleeping regiments from their tents. By morning locomotives and troop trains were piled up in the Washington yards. At dawn the railway managers, Tom Scott of the Pennsylvania, John Garrett of the Baltimore and Ohio, and S. M. Felton of the Philadelphia, Wilmington and Baltimore, arrived by special train. And at nine o'clock that evening the entire Eleventh Army Corps had rolled out of Manassas, in northern Virginia, bound for Washington and the West.

Train after trainload of troops and artillery, dispatched at half-hour intervals and stopping for nothing but wood and water, a great caravan six to eight miles in length, chugged over the mountains and thundered westward. Soup kitchens and cooks were tossed into baggage cars to feed the men en route. Ten boys, clinging to the car tops, froze to death in the cold of the high Alleghenies. But Hooker's entire corps made the unparalleled transfer in a little over five days.

Stanton, who had labored two days and nights without taking off his clothes or leaving the department, was stretched out on his sofa, a handkerchief wet with cologne tied round his head, when the office force rushed in and cheered him with the news.

On the day following the completion of this achievement Evans went West to join Tom Scott. The next afternoon Anne was summoned to Stanton's office. The Secretary was profoundly angry. His usually soft voice was sharp, high, and strained.

"Well, madam," he began abruptly, "I think we have saved the situation. But I also believe the crisis of this war is now at hand. I wish to tell you that in two hours General Anson Stager and I are leaving for Indianapolis by special train as fast as we can get there to confer with Grant. I am going to swear in your presence without any apology. I say God damn these leaders who will not lead, these blind braggarts who will not see. You know of whom I speak. We have had five different and equally idiotic commanders in the East in eighteen months! And I will endure no longer seeing these boys die by the thousands and their great victories tossed into a cesspool of incompetence and career rivalries.

"I brought you here, ma'am, to inform you that the Tennessee plan is to be restored and at last *executed*. I am going to put Grant in charge in the West over the heads and bodies of every damn superior

344

he may have. *He is our man.* He is going to execute the rest of that plan or I will have men, important men, shot for it. I dare not bring Grant to Washington. I believe even he can be poisoned by these rats around us. Hence I am going to him to tell him what we want. I'll be back here in five days to discuss the whole matter with you."

Stanton paced erratically up and down before his desk. Anne said nothing and the Secretary, looking at her reflectively, asked in a mild voice, "Well?"

"Mr. Stanton," she said simply, "from first to last Grant has been the one man who has fully grasped the solution in the West. And time and again he has been blocked by idiots who happened to rank him. He has no friends in court. You know that. Halleck is indifferent to him. McClellan has never had any use for him. Even Mr. Lincoln and the Cabinet know little about him. But this decision of yours now launches the last phase of the war. I'm sure of it."

The Secretary rose to accompany her to his door. In an unaccustomed gesture of familiarity he placed one arm gently on her shoulder.

"Miss Carroll, this time your great plan will be carried out. And Grant is the man who can do it."

42

IN THE DAYS THAT FOLLOWED STANTON'S WHIRLWIND visit to Indianapolis, Anne realized with a little shock that her role as an unofficial military adviser was at an end. No longer would she have to work over military plans and prepare long papers to convince people that those plans should be adopted. Her part was done, and now the last great phases of the drama were being hurriedly but carefully prepared. Huge armies were massed in and about Chattanooga, one hundred and thirty-odd miles from Atlanta, in the very area she had outlined two years ago as the vital key to the war. On both sides veteran commanders, tried in dozens of battles, were to lead their forces to new and final decisions.

Grant's command arrived in Chattanooga on the twenty-second of October, and Sherman surprised the rebels by speedily joining him there on November 15. Plans for a great campaign were at once begun.

Just ten days later occurred the most dramatic and spectacular battle of the war as Grant's army assembled in the Tennessee Valley before Chattanooga in full view of the rebel positions under Bragg on the towering fog-bound heights around them. In its very beginnings the battle leaped out of its planned framework and was won by the courage and joint impulse of common soldiers.

General Thomas's men had been instructed to drive the rebels from the rifle pits at the foot of Missionary Ridge and then halt there. But when this had been done with greater ease than expected, thousands of exhilarated men in blue suddenly began to storm up the steep slopes, up toward the invisible cloud-shrouded summit, without a single command to urge them on. Standing on a slight knoll in the valley, watch-

346

ing this incredible attack, Grant turned angrily on George Thomas.

"Who ordered those men up the heights, General?"

"No one, sir," replied Thomas proudly. "They're doing it of their own accord."

"It's all right if it succeeds," exclaimed Grant. "If it doesn't, someone will suffer."

But it succeeded in a wild and staggering triumph. As the men in blue tore over the summit of the supposedly impregnable Ridge, a panic demolished Bragg's seasoned army. Thousands of his men who had fought bravely in a dozen campaigns tossed away their arms and fled like frightened children. Bragg himself was almost captured and six thousand of his soldiers were taken prisoner.

The War Department in Washington, when this news poured in, became a madhouse of shouting clerks. Curiously enough, the Union victory at Chattanooga caused in the North a greater and more profound sensation than Vicksburg and Gettysburg combined. Some accurate instinct, some deep psychological insight, seemed to tell the masses of strained and anxious people that the right road had been resumed, that the summit of the long bloody hill of war had at last been gained and never again would be lost.

And Grant's star of military genius—though he had had little enough to do with the actual battle plans at Chattanooga, which had been prepared by Rosecrans and Thomas—now rode high, rode at its zenith, not to be dimmed while the war lasted.

Grant's greatest honor was bestowed upon him on February 29, 1864, when Congress revived the rank of lieutenant general, originally created for George Washington and borne only by him and Winfield Scott, gave the title to Grant, and thus finally set the stubborn fighter of the West above Halleck.

Grant first saw the city of Washington on March 8 and received his commission, the first genuinely earned great appointment of the war, before the President and the Cabinet. Afterward there was a roaring reception for him in Willard's parlors and Ben Wade, with Caroline, insisted that Anne and Evans accompany them there.

During the brief drive Evans gave them an amusing account of Stanton's first meeting with Grant at the Indianapolis depot. Stanton had arrived late while Grant, with Rawlins and his staff, worried about the approaching interview, waited on the station platform.

"And," said Evans, "Stanton bustled right up to Dr. Kittoe, Grant's staff surgeon, who's a pretty impressive old fellow with a big square beard. Stanton peered at him through his glasses, grabbed him by the hand, and bellowed, 'How are you, General Grant? I'd know you anywhere from your pictures.' That brought down the house," con-

347

tinued Evans. "Rawlins had convulsions and said to Kittoe, 'Well, Doc, I guess we'd better vamose. You're in charge of the Army now.' Stanton was terribly chagrined. But it was the best thing that could have happened. It broke the ice at once. . . . Well," added Evans more soberly as Wade's carriage drew to the curb at Willard's, "here we are."

In a milling mass of officers, politicians, diplomats, and their families on the second floor of Willard's, they had difficulty finding the new lieutenant general. Evans, from his height, spotted him in a corner and pushed a way through the crowd. Finally all four of them halted a moment, lost in wonder at their first glimpse of the man. In a sea of black broadcloth spotted with uniforms stood a short, round-shouldered man in a general's tarnished uniform, with three bright new stars on new shoulder straps freshly attached to the faded blue tunic. He looked as if he had strolled in from a cornfield. There was no stature to him at all. He had rough light brown whiskers, blue eyes, a rather scrubby look. He stood negligently, awkwardly, only half listening to some pleasantries from those about him.

Wade waited until there was a lull in the conversation, then strode forward and introduced himself and his guests. Grant's eyes brightened when he saw Evans.

"—and Miss Anne Carroll of Maryland, General," Wade was saying loudly, completing his introductions.

Grant swung around and looked curiously at the short, graceful little woman with the blond hair.

"Miss Carroll? Delighted to meet you, ma'am."

Anne forgot her first impression of awkwardness and insignificance when she looked into Grant's keen blue eyes. His face, at first impassive, expressionless, showed amazing firmness at close range, and the straight, strong nose only accentuated the determination of his eyes. His heavy face broke into a smile as he looked up at Evans.

"Hello, Judge. I never thought to meet you here. I hope you've a better room than that fly-bitten bake oven at Cairo you had to sleep in."

Evans grinned reminiscently.

"I hope you have too, General. You've come a long way since Cairo, sir."

"About the longest way I could," said Grant stolidly. He turned to Anne, a quizzical expression on his face. "Miss Carroll, aren't you acquainted with my pilot, Charles Scott?"

"Yes, General," said Anne cautiously. "I've corresponded with him for some time. How is he?"

Grant laughed shortly and ignored her question

"You must have charmed him, ma'am. I never saw Charley write a line except to his wife and you."

She tried to change the subject.

"General, where's your cigar?" she asked smilingly. "I've never seen a portrait of you without one."

Again Grant laughed, a curious laugh far back in his throat, and his face scarcely moved at all.

"Ma'am, it's a funny thing how that started. I never smoked anything but a pipe until Donelson. Evans, you remember that old meerschaum of mine. I've got it in my baggage somewhere. But right after Donelson I couldn't find it and borrowed a cigar one morning when some press fellows interviewed me. They asked me what kind of cigars I smoked and I said I didn't know—this was the last one I could get. Well, ma'am, someone printed that—and in two weeks I had a thousand boxes of cigars piled up in the quartermaster's tent. They rolled in from all over the country—and I've been trying to make a dent in them ever since. They drive Rawlins crazy. He claims the rebels can smell me a hundred miles away."

During the evening, while Anne was talking with other friends, Wade had two long conversations with Grant. On the second occasion Evans joined them. Champagne and a buffet supper were finally served and the reception broke up.

After taking Anne to the Washington House, Evans walked over to Wade's home. Caroline had retired, and the senator led him into the living room. Both men lighted cigars and sat for a few moments in silence. Wade's handsome face had never looked more alive. At last he leaned forward in his chair and addressed the Texan.

"You know, I'm feeling better. I think Grant will help us get Anne credit. I didn't say much, but the general himself intimated that he suspected something of Anne's behind-the-scenes part in the Tennessee plan. His own pilot gave him a clue or two."

"Just the same, Ben," protested Evans mildly, "do you think the public parlors of Willard's, with Grant receiving on his first visit here, was the best place to begin your questioning of the general?"

Wade flushed a little but replied quietly, "I had to do it, and I said very little. But I had to find out where Grant stood on this. And he's all right. Do you know what he told me when he finally got my drift? He said that if, as I suggested, Miss Carroll had anything at all to do with the Tennessee plan, and if he stood in her shoes, he would raise heaven and earth to have that fact made known. For, added the general, 'at Forts Henry and Donelson, and every military man knows it, the South lost this war.' That's important, Judge, for we're in for a battle on behalf of Miss Carroll."

349

"I'm aware of that," said Evans a little coldly, "but——"

"Lem," said Wade pleadingly, "let's thrash this out right now. As I understand it, you and Anne plan to marry and I believe you hope to take her to Texas as soon as this conflict is settled."

"That's correct," replied Evans. "We'll marry as soon as I can properly sever my connections with the War Department."

"That means," continued Wade earnestly, "that as soon as this war is over you and Miss Carroll will remove yourselves from the city. And that, in turn, means we've got to move fast. It means that formal recognition of Anne's services must be planned *now* and the success of our every move assured."

"You think our claims for her will be fought so hard?" asked Evans.

"You know they will be," said Wade with some bitterness. "There's nothing harder to dislodge than an impression planted in the public mind. What do you think is going to happen when we present a full account of this woman's services and ask that the official records, let alone the flood of mental impressions, popular beliefs, press accounts, and the mouthings of thousands of satellites of powerful men, be altered accordingly? There aren't a dozen men in this city—let alone the nation—who have the faintest idea of what has really occurred. Man, we have a bitter battle on our hands." He looked sharply at Evans. "Have you finished that paper you were preparing for me?"

"I have it here," said Evans shortly. He drew from his pocket a small printed pamphlet entitled *The Material Bearing of the Tennessee Campaign in 1862 upon the Destinies of Our Civil War*. Drawing upon the War Department files, Evans had designed the document for use by Wade and certain senators and representatives whom Wade planned to take into his confidence.

For an hour the two men carefully discussed their campaign to organize in Congress official recognition of Anne's military record.

"I think we will finally have to get the President to initiate this," Wade said. "The House and Senate may not even take my word for what happened. The other day I realized this when, in strict confidence, I discussed our claims for Anne with General Logan. I showed him our records. And Logan was frightened. I could see it. He finally said to me, 'But my God, Wade, you claim so much for her!' "

"What did you say to that?" snapped Evans.

"I said to the general, '*Logan, we claim she furnished the information and strategy that led to the military movements now deciding the war*. That, in our opinion, is proved—and here are the proofs.' Logan just sat there. I knew what he was thinking. He didn't like it—but he had no answer at all."

"Then there's only one solution," Evans said, frowning. "Go to

Mr. Lincoln, Ben. Urge him to send at once the proper recommendations to Congress, backed by the Secretary of War, demanding national honors and full recognition for Miss Carroll."

Wade scowled a moment, then placed both hands behind his head and permitted himself the luxury of a smile.

"I guess that's it, Evans. And we still have time. What kind of honors would you suggest? Ever thought about it?"

Evans looked blank.

"Good lord, no. Not in concrete terms. All Anne wants is formal recognition of her military services—some resolution by both chambers that will set the story straight before the country. Even that old resolution of Roscoe Conkling's, presented two years ago, would do the trick with your story tacked on it. That's all we need."

"No, sir, no, sir." Wade cheerfully shook his head. "It's a lot bigger than that, my boy. If we were suddenly to make public only her solution of the whole Vicksburg siege, it would raise a furor. This has got to be done mighty carefully. . . . Has she been paid anything on her expenses?" asked Wade suddenly.

"Not a dime," replied Evans. "A few bills from her are lying on Stanton's desk—Chase's, too, I reckon—along with over forty-five million dollars' worth of other unpaid government accounts. She knows she'll never be paid. But by God, it's a disgrace. She has now spent around thirty thousand dollars of her own money. I know that for a fact."

Wade swore with his usual thoroughness and vigor.

"Did you know that Stanton, too, is completely busted?" he asked. "He had a fortune when he came here."

"No, I didn't," said Evans disgustedly. "It seems to me this damn government wears out its best people, pays them a pittance, and then tosses them on some dunghill."

"That's the way of all government," said Wade without emotion. His fingers drummed on his armchair. His dark eyes became thoughtful. "Riddle and I—that fine chap in the House from the Nineteenth Ohio District—were talking about the war only today. We talked about what fools most of us are, I suppose, when confronted by war in our own yard. I thought Seward was mad in '61 when he said the war would be over in sixty days. I went out to Ohio and solemnly told my folks not to believe Seward—I said the war would last at least six months."

Wade laughed without mirth while Evans stood up, smiling grimly.

"We were all wrong, Ben, every one of us. But I've got to go now. When you're ready to see Mr. Lincoln about Anne let us know."

"Judge, I wish to heaven I were twenty years younger and in your

351

shoes," Wade said unexpectedly. "You're a damn lucky man, Lem. You've got Miss Carroll, the finest woman in this country. You've got the biggest state in the Union to live in. You'll have, pray God, a time of peace ahead. You're lucky, too damn lucky."

"I know it," said Evans, suddenly humble. "I know it, and I never forget it. And if it ever came to a choice of location, Senator"—his voice became mischievous—"to hell with Texas, Senator. I'll take Miss Carroll and live anywhere. By the Lord, Ben, I'd even live in Ohio."

43

ANNE'S SUDDEN SHIFT TO THE CAUSE OF THE RADICALS
after the Emancipation Proclamation had plunged her into months of
hard work and difficult adjustments. In her new revolutionary role she
had been waging press campaigns proclaiming slavery as the issue of
the war. To the horror of several members of her family and many of
her old Maryland friends, she called for full recognition of Negro
rights throughout the South as the only stable cornerstone of peace.
With the same intensity as she had fought for the Tennessee plan, she
now fought for unqualified freedom of the blacks.

Her mail was sprinkled with threats ranging from unprintable
insults to pious warnings of eternal damnation from more devout
acquaintances thoroughly alarmed by her new faith.

But in this faith were tremendous compensations. She experienced
a new exhilaration in facing realities of the present and future instead
of holding desperately to legal tenets of the past. She was at last able
to take part enthusiastically in the full sweep of revolutionary events,
swimming with the current instead of against it. She found, too, that
many others were experiencing the same sensation. Her close friend
Chase, the dignified, sedate Secretary of the Treasury, but a determined champion of women's rights, put his finger on this spreading
phenomenon when he remarked to her over a cup of tea one day, "I
had been wondering a long time, Anne, how the Negroes would take
this Emancipation Proclamation. But when it was issued by Mr. Lincoln I felt as if I myself had been set free. Many others have said the
same."

She was among them. She, too, had noticed that the proclamation
had been celebrated with the wildest outbursts of emotion in many
conservative circles, where the participants in these celebrations had

353

been astonished by their own reactions. Most revealing of all for Anne was the discovery of a new freedom and relaxation in her relations with Evans. Driving home with him from a concert one evening, she commented on this.

"I feel a freedom I never enjoyed before, Lem. All this feeling of strain within myself has vanished." She looked up at him and smiled. "May I thank you for that hard spanking you gave me?"

"Whew!" laughed Evans, but his eyes reflected a trace of old fear. "Don't mention it. I was sure I'd ruined everything. The Evans temper is mighty short—right through the family. But tell me," he added curiously, "what really did make you change your mind?"

She shook her head.

"I was determined to toss everything overboard—even you. But when you showed me that awful contradiction between my military and political points of view—my whole case blew up." She laughed. "Even a legal mind is sometimes open to logic."

He pressed her hand.

"It was the last real hurdle we both had to take," he said, looking at her affectionately. "I had had a hard time of it myself. And I was terribly afraid you——" But he paused and then laughed and his dark eyes caressed her. "For two Southerners, sweetheart, we've come a long, long way."

She thought so too. They were both, she felt, awake to reality at last, aware of the real character of the war, and full of their new sense of freedom. The Emancipation Proclamation, she saw shrewdly, had freed whites quite as effectively as blacks. She winced as she remembered the wishful convictions on colonization she had once entertained. For Negroes, summoned by the Emancipation Proclamation, had been rushing not to colonies but to the colors of the Union.

One hundred and twenty-five thousand Negroes were now under arms fighting Southern whites. Plans for enrolling twenty more divisions, for arming half a million blacks, if necessary, were being considered. Stanton was pushing Negro recruiting everywhere, in spite of discriminations in pay and treatment. And now Grant, before taking command of the Army of the Potomac, had insisted on a Negro corps being attached to his command. They had fought under him with striking success in the West. She remembered a dispatch of Charles A. Dana from Vicksburg regarding the action of Negro troops at Big Black and Milliken's Bend. Dana had wired Stanton, "The African regiments fought gallantly. Black troops at Milliken's Bend revolutionized attitude of Army on Negroes here. Prominent officers are enthusiastic over their conduct and are all for Negro troops."

By early 1864 the fresh winds of freedom had stirred up a great

354

deal of oratory. Another woman, Anna Elizabeth Dickinson of New York, was also preaching the new faith with fiery eloquence. While Evans was away on a trip to the West, Anne had gone to hear her at a Freedmen's Relief Association benefit on January 16 and been surprised to see a young girl, just twenty-one, petite, quietly good-looking with chestnut curls bound close to her well-shaped head.

Miss Dickinson spoke in the House of Representatives, with Speaker Colfax seated at her right, Vice-President Hamlin at her left, and Mr. Lincoln on a bench in the foreground. The young girl's ringing contralto voice, her passionate sincerity and withering sarcasm tremendously excited her audience.

"I demand," concluded Miss Dickinson, "that this war be prosecuted until slavery lies dead and buried under the feet of the North, until its epitaph is traced with the point of a bayonet dipped in the young blood of this nation. We insist and require that territory wrenched back from the rebellion be used to underlay the development of the blacks in America into full citizenship, *with the ownership in fee of agricultural land.* South Carolina should be cut up into twenty-acre lots and as many Negroes settled on them as can be got there."

Anne never forgot the passion and conviction in her voice.

A week after Miss Dickinson's dramatic address Anne discussed with Mr. Lincoln the coming conventions and campaigns of summer and fall. She saw he was worried, almost ill, and uncertain of many things. For the Emancipation Proclamation, as many of the President's friends had predicted, had become a two-edged weapon—a powerful blow for freedom, but a great stimulant to angry, frightened Democrats in the North who had swept many states in the fall elections of 1862 and were now determined to unseat the President and place their own man in the White House in the next national election.

To Anne's shock and dismay that man, of all people, was George Brinton McClellan.

Aroused by the President's pessimism and McClellan's candidacy, Anne began shuttling about between Washington, Philadelphia, New York, sometimes Boston, conferring, listening, talking to important men and women whose support the President needed. New York disturbed her. The city seemed to believe the war won. It had little love for Mr. Lincoln. Shops and theaters flourished, and Anne attended many affairs where war news and the President were never mentioned.

But on May 5, 1864, the war again overshadowed all things. On that mild spring day began the bloodiest military enterprise in American history. Grant's Army of the Potomac crossed the Rapidan, en-

355

countered Lee, and began the carnage known as the campaign of the Wilderness.

In the same week Sherman's vast army moved eastward out of Chattanooga on the long hard road to Atlanta. Evans, who had been handling arms shipments for Sherman's troops, came back to town for a few weeks while they watched the jaws of the Union nutcracker begin to tighten around the Confederacy.

"It is a damned curious thing," said Evans abruptly one evening as he sat before her fire, "but do you realize this war is ending exactly as it was planned to end in the first year?"

"What are you driving at?"

"Why," said Evans in considerable excitement, "two years ago Colonel Scott organized the very kind of double campaign, based on your plan, that's coming off now. In the spring of '62 it was McClellan driving on Richmond and Grant scheduled to head east from the Tennessee Valley and Chattanooga. Two years later we've got Grant in McClellan's shoes and Sherman headed for Atlanta. And Grant and Sherman are the same two men who began your Tennessee campaign. It's an amazing coincidence—and this time the plan's going through."

There was no doubt this time that it was. Hate hung heavy over the land. Two halves of a desperate, riven nation were meeting in the final battles of a terrible war. Grant opened his Wilderness campaign on May 5 with one hundred and eighteen thousand men, and by June 14 his losses were a total of fifty-five thousand killed, wounded, and missing—almost as many men as there were in Lee's army when the campaign began.

And yet Anne and Evans watched new regiments pour through Washington so rapidly that Grant had as many men at the end of the campaign as he had had in the beginning.

At Cold Harbor, just outside Richmond, at four-thirty on the morning of June 3, came the holocaust in a frontal assault on the rebel works. In the first *ten minutes* of Grant's terrific attack no less than ten thousand men fell before the withering hail of rebel fire. The battle continued another hour. Not an inch of ground was gained. The rebel losses were much less than a thousand.

On the afternoon of the day of this battle someone told Anne that Mr. Stanton was alone in his office—had been alone for a long time. There she went and found him, sitting pale and rigid at his desk, staring into space. She had thought herself quite calm and composed, but even before she spoke to him she was suddenly aware that tears were pouring down her cheeks.

"Don't do that here, ma'am," said Stanton quickly. "It's much too late for any tears."

"Mr. Stanton," she said slowly, wiping her eyes, "Tuesday I rode up to Baltimore with Mrs. Lingard, who lost three sons at the Rapidan and Spotsylvania. The country cannot stand much more of this. Our cities are filled with women in mourning. They will not stand it."

"They have to," said Stanton softly. "This is what all we have done and planned has led to. Two years ago we might have had Richmond and all the South at much less cost by following a good plan. Today we are going to have to take it however we can, over mountains of dead boys, but take it we will."

He noticed she had begun to tremble and he added in a kindlier tone, "My dear lady, throw yourself into your labors for Mr. Lincoln. Don't haunt this office from habit and suffer more than you need to. Do you know what high officers themselves are going through? Do you know that for two weeks Rawlins, Grant's closest friend and Chief of Staff, has been assailing Grant for these awful assaults against entrenched positions? Rawlins told Grant to his face last week that these tactics were nothing but 'a murderous policy of military incompetents.' I suspect Mr. Lincoln feels so too. He is ill and heartsick. A part of our army before Richmond is almost mutinous over this slaughter, and General Warren, one of Grant's corps commanders, wrote me yesterday, 'For thirty-six days now it has been one funeral procession past me.'

"But by God, madam"—Stanton's voice rose and rang through the room—"this man Grant, who launched your own plan on the Tennessee, has not once stepped backward in six terrible weeks. He has done what no man has done before him. He has worn Lee to the bone. Rebels are deserting by the thousands. The mountains of the Carolinas and Georgia are jammed with Southern deserters, and no rebel provost marshal dares go after them. Many rebel states absolutely refuse to provide Richmond with another man. Grant wired me this week that Lee will never again dare fight in the open. I agree with him. I told you once before, and I say it again now, I am going to pour on men and more men, and ransack every Northern homestead for youngsters who can shoulder a rifle, and stamp out this rebellion so thoroughly that never again will traitors dare assail a free government supported by a free people."

She looked at him wonderingly, thinking of other moods, other occasions.

"How can you stand this," she whispered, "after what you once told me?"

"Because one learns to endure, one hardens—or goes under," said

357

Stanton harshly. "Mr. Lincoln showed me a sentiment Sherman had written him to the same effect, that bloodshed and destruction on a vast scale have become so common to him that the death of two thousand men in an afternoon now no longer upsets him as much as the wounding of a couple of sentries did two years ago. We have all changed, ma'am. Mr. Lincoln has changed most of all. He is ages older, centuries wiser. As for me, I have at last learned to live with death. I am accused of intrigues beyond number. I am reproached for sitting safely in this office and hurling young men out to die. Do you know the average age of these youngsters? Seventeen and eighteen! Some of them are only fifteen years old. Think of this!

"But all of us pay a price, ma'am, each according to his nature. I have paid mine. I cannot sleep. My health is shattered. I am bankrupt. I feel old, horribly old, and I am not yet fifty. Once this is over, I do not care to live much longer."

His large liquid eyes looked at her as if they were beyond further feeling.

"I think you had better go, ma'am, for I have a great deal to do."

Meanwhile, chasms yawned in the official family. At the end of May, in Cleveland, eight days before the Republicans' Baltimore convention, Frémont and other foes of Lincoln organized a party to insure the President's defeat.

Seated with Mr. Lincoln in his study on the morning after this Ohio gathering, Anne listened to a Cleveland citizen who described the event and said encouragingly to Lincoln that instead of thousands present there were only about four hundred.

The President grinned broadly, seemed struck by the number, and reached for the Bible on his desk. A moment later he read solemnly, " 'And every one that was in distress, and every one that was in debt, and every one that was discontented, gathered themselves unto him; and he became a captain over them: and there were with him about *four hundred men.*' "

This caused a great laugh and everyone felt much better.

But as Anne worked for Lincoln's re-election in Baltimore she watched fearfully the efforts against him organized by close friends of hers. There were rumors that Chase's followers would hire all the halls and prevent the Republicans from meeting in Baltimore and she had hot words with Henry Winter Davis over this. But finally Senator Morgan of New York rented the Front Street Theater, removed the scenery, floored over the parquet, and a convention hall was ready.

Two days before the convention she had a brief talk with the President and Henry J. Raymond, proprietor of the New York *Times,* the only Manhattan paper completely loyal to Lincoln. When Raymond had left, Mr. Lincoln looked out over the south lawn, his eyes half closed. Like Stanton, she thought he had aged greatly in a few months. Grant's holocausts had sickened him. He looked ill, his sallow face now a sickly yellow, the skin lined and loose. He rubbed his eyes as if he needed sleep, and she rose to go.

"Stay a minute, Miss Carroll. I like someone around with no favors to ask, and you can help me keep some of Indiana's political warriors at bay for a few minutes."

She sat down without saying anything. The President turned and looked at her gravely.

"Well, what do you think, Miss Carroll? You've been running around the country a good bit on my endless errands. And I thank you for it. But you've never ventured an opinion before me. Are you betting on the next President?"

"Yes, I am," she said slowly. "I—I think you'll win by a narrow margin."

"And your friend Judge Evans? Does he agree with you?"

He was looking at her sharply now and she blushed.

"Judge Evans is not quite so sure as I am," she said noncommittally, and the President gave a short laugh.

"Good for the judge. He always was an honest man. I tell you, Miss Carroll, four months ago I was pretty confident. Now I ain't sure at all. I think most folks have had enough of me. Sometimes I don't blame 'em. If Wall Street is an indication, I am pretty near through, for gold is going right on up."

"You've heard from the politicians, not from the people," she said forcefully. "I still believe the bulk of the people will see that you're nominated and elected. It has taken them time to understand you, to see what you are up to. But they do see it. In spite of the awful price they are paying, I'll stake my faith on them."

"Don't stake more than that," said the President humorously.

He got up, looking a little more cheerful.

"I'll call you to account for that statement next November, ma'am," he said, smiling slightly. "And now I'd better let the Indiana brethren in."

On June 7, with the casualty lists from Grant's defeat at Cold Harbor rolling through the land, the Republicans convened in the Front Street Theater of Baltimore. The bright light of her week had been a joyful reunion with her old friend and pastor, Dr. Robert Breckinridge, chosen as temporary chairman, supposedly at Lincoln's request. She had almost wept on his shoulder when the white-haired,

359

white-bearded, grizzled old war horse of Kentucky swept her into his arms on his arrival in Camden Station. Dining with her later, he listened to her fears about Lincoln and shook his head vigorously.

"Nonsense," he exclaimed. "He's going in again. I've got Kentucky under my belt, dear friend. Surely you can say the same of Maryland. You had it there once. But a pox on politics tonight. Tell me of yourself and your family."

Her old pastor was right, for in the days that followed the Baltimore convention became a Union convention, nominating Abraham Lincoln, a Republican, for the presidency, and Andrew Johnson, a Democrat, for the vice-presidency.

In November the President triumphed with a huge electoral majority and McClellan faded from the national scene with a paltry twenty-one electoral votes. But the popular vote was close enough to make Anne catch her breath. Mr. Lincoln's enemies were still legion.

Quite exhausted and aware once more that her amazing energies were not endless, Anne went to Cambridge to rest and at the same time to face a new and pressing phase of her own personal problems.

It was Caroline who first understood what Anne was going through. An affectionate, confident woman, she had dismissed Anne's tensions on her return to town from Maryland in late December as normal reactions to a long period of unrelenting work.

But Caroline was forced to look deeper. At the conclusion of one of her afternoon teas, when the two women were alone for a moment, Anne suddenly burst into tears. She quickly recovered herself but took Caroline's hand in a tight grasp.

"Caroline, will you walk with me while I get some air? I'm suffocating."

On this gusty afternoon the two women strolled about the bare grounds and graveled walks of the Capitol.

"You know, Caroline, I couldn't go on if I didn't feel the end of this awful war were near. I'm not designed for pretense and deceit—and I've had to practice both too long."

The senator's wife, thinking of Anne's professional activities, said a little too breezily, "But, my dear, so much of the work done in this town has to be carried out confidentially——"

"No, no, you don't understand," interrupted Anne vehemently. "To conceal one's work behind the scenes is difficult but bearable. But to maintain these fictions, this false aloofness in respect to one's affections and personal life month after month—I can't do it any longer!"

The urgency in her voice jarred Caroline. She said quickly, "But

360

surely, with the end in sight, you and Judge Evans are quite free to make your own plans."

"Not yet," said Anne simply. "Lem's been begging me to marry him and go to Texas at once. But Lem himself has so changed my mind that I can't leave until certain issues are settled."

"Anne dear, Ben has always insisted you drive yourself at too great a personal cost. I agree with him now, completely. You and Lem deserve all the happiness you can find. Why not marry him—and at once?"

"I can't," said Anne desperately. "I really must see some completion to this work of mine before I can let go."

The older woman glanced at her with worried concern.

"And suppose there is no end in the sense you mean?" she asked.

Anne looked very thoughtful.

"Several dear friends have said that to me at various times," she said slowly. "I never quite understood what they meant. But I'm beginning to."

"Moreover, you can't go on forever like this, depriving yourself of a personal life. Men don't. No woman should," Caroline said. "It's all wrong. For heaven's sake, do as Lem says. He's devoted to you. There isn't a reason in the world why you two shouldn't enjoy your life together. It's time you began to think a little bit about your own happiness."

"I know it," said Anne in a strained voice. "Yet everything I've fought for is coming to a head. If I married Lem now it would affect a number of vital projects I'm working on. It would——"

"But why, *why?*" interrupted Caroline, and then stopped as she saw Anne was close to some breaking point. Caroline did not pursue the subject. She walked silently with Anne to the Washington House. But when Ben Wade returned home late in the evening he found his wife alone, sitting very erect, waiting for him.

"Ben dear, get your brandy and sit down. I've something to say to you."

Wade caught the note of urgency in her voice. He poured himself a generous glass, drew up a straight-backed chair, and sat opposite Caroline, waiting attentively.

"What is it?" he asked quietly.

Caroline told him about her conversation with Anne. Wade looked very grave.

"Heaven knows if the War Department will ever pay her. Did you know she never made a written agreement with Colonel Scott at all—that he paid her the only sum she got from his own pocket? And since he's retired from the War Department there isn't an official contract of any kind to show for all her work for the department. She'll have to be patient a while longer. I intend to——"

"Patient!" Caroline was thoroughly angry. "Ben Wade, listen to me! That girl is killing herself. I'll pay her out of our own savings if I have to. But financial recompense isn't the point. I'm frightened about her, Ben. It's bad enough to hide her behind Mr. Lincoln's frock coat and advise her to be patient! At the proper time, I suppose, meaning when it no longer matters or won't upset someone's apple-cart, you men will coyly exhibit her, pass a resolution, and pay her a small tithe of what she deserves. But on top of this idiotic conceal-ment she's been forced to sacrifice all her personal life as well. No one should have to endure all this."

"What do you want me to do?" Wade asked seriously. "Mr. Lin-coln has told me time and again that he's determined to give her the highest honors. She won't have to wait much longer. And though I've never mentioned it, both Evans and I have bombarded the War Department with Anne's claims for over a year. But every depart-ment in this town is broke."

"Then for heaven's sake," blazed Caroline, "go to Judge Evans and tell him to take Anne out of this horrible town! Perhaps she can stand being a member of the Cabinet without any title and having her brains picked by every incompetent male in the government without even getting anything for it—but she can't stand all that and a com-plete denial of her personal life too. Do you remember what you said to me the other night when you couldn't sleep?"

"I said a lot of things," answered Wade dryly.

"You said, I remember, that no one had done so much for the country as Anne and no one had received so little for it or been treated so shamefully. You said you felt the injustice as your own; that the country, in its last extremity, was absolutely saved by her sagacity and labor; and that her services were so great it would be most difficult to make the world believe them. And you told me your own fear that the fact that all this great work should have been brought about by a woman might be quite inconceivable to vulgar minds. But then, Ben, you said you believed in the warm response of the people, and you were convinced that justice would triumph at last. You told me you'd fight for it to your dying day."

There was a long silence and each hesitated to break it. But finally Wade spoke.

"Yes, I did say all that," he said softly. "I believe it. And I'm sure we can get this incredible story to the people. But there is a great deal behind this terrible conflict, Caroline, that will never be told, and much that cannot be. I could name you a dozen persons whom

I consider great, who have played vital roles in this war, and you would recognize none of them. They are lost—they are leaves on a wild wind that has swept them into oblivion."

"Anne isn't lost!" flared Caroline. "You *have* her records. You *have* her witnesses. You have the power to *do* something about her."

Wade had never seen his wife so aroused. He started to speak, but Caroline added sharply, "Wait, Ben, I'm not through. For it isn't Anne alone that I'm so concerned about. Anne has made me realize that all women everwhere should be entitled to universal human rights, to work, think, and live side by side with men, and compete with men, if necessary, on the same ground. And don't think we can't do it!" snapped Caroline.

She paused for breath. Wade, looking at her with affectionate admiration, cocked his head a little and said jokingly, "Bravo, Caroline. But in that distant day—*who'll do the dishes?*"

But Caroline did not laugh. She did not even smile, and Wade felt there was something further he should say.

"You champion your sex most effectively, my dear," he began mildly. "But with all my admiration for Anne, has it ever occurred to you that there are times when she is her own worst enemy? It was necessary at one point to ask Anne to postpone her marriage a bit. But there's no real reason to prevent it now. And yet Anne can't see it. She won't let herself."

He got up suddenly, walked around the room, and sat down again. His serious eyes caught and held Caroline's.

"There's no good reason why she can't make the sensible decisions we think she should make. No reason, that is, that we and ordinary folks might *call* real. But Anne isn't ordinary. Destiny itself fashioned Anne. Destiny itself has woven its web about her. The *real* reasons for her decisions lie in herself. She has dedicated herself to a cause, performed great services in that cause. She will not rest until the success of that cause is assured. She has to do that. She cannot do otherwise. I once remarked Anne was married to her country. Unfortunately for her personal life, that is still the sober truth. *She cannot help herself.* First things come first with Anne, and her causes are first with her."

Caroline was frightened. But Wade's innate optimism reasserted itself.

"I don't like this kind of speculation," he growled. Then he smiled reassuringly. "She'll come out all right. If we can get those two married and pack 'em off to Texas, the rest of the puzzle will fall into place. In a few months you'll see this town rock with Anne's triumphs. There's no doubt about it."

363

Wade was so encouraged by his own remarks that he tossed off another half glass of brandy, picked up a magazine, and settled himself comfortably to read.

But Caroline, her hands folded patiently on her lap, her blue eyes thoughtfully fixed on nothing at all, sat in shadow, her mind revolving painfully on what her husband had said. For where she had only glimpsed before she now saw clearly the true nature of Anne's problem.

44

SPRING ARRIVED, THE SPRING OF 1865, A SPRING BURST-
ing with death and new life. And peace, instead of arriving on the
wings of a dove, swooped down like a hawk on the astonished capital.

Early Monday morning, April 3, Anne had walked with Evans
to the War Department from sheer force of habit. After he had gone
to work she wandered up to the telegraph office and sat there reading a morning paper. Warm fragrant air, smelling of fresh grass and
new foliage, wafted through the open windows. Next to her a young
boy named Kettles was operating the City Point wire. He suddenly
looked up at her with a grin.

"Something's up, ma'am. Fort Monroe has just switched City Point
on and told us to look out for Richmond. That's our operator four
miles outside the city. . . . Here he is now."

She watched the youngster copy down a short dispatch, then
stiffen in his chair, his mouth open. He sprang up without another
word, upsetting the table, instruments, inkwell, and everything on
it. He disappeared in the room adjoining the library and a few seconds
later Tinker, the cipher clerk, came running in and went to an open
window. Anne was about to speak to him when a friend of Tinker's,
entering the yard, looked up, recognized the operator, and called out,
"What's the news, Tinker?"

Tinker bellowed back, "Richmond's taken, Tom! General Weitzel
and a regiment of Negro troops marched in there at eight-fifteen this
morning!"

Anne never forgot the comical expression on the dazed face of the
man looking up at them. For an instant he was frozen with amazement. Then he rushed out of the front yard, yelling, his arms and

365

legs waving ludicrously. He shouted at the top of his lungs, "Richmond's taken! Richmond's taken!"

Tinker cried to her delightedly, "Weitzel and a parcel of Negro troops take over Richmond!"

Within what seemed like an instant screaming people appeared to leap out of the ground and the very walls and pour in a flood about the War Department, where every activity had stopped abruptly. Evans joined her and they eagerly watched the vast emotional eruption that exploded about the dingy building. Horsecars could not move five minutes after Tinker's friend had rushed into the street. Steam fire engines were hauled from their stalls, fired up, and left whistling in the middle of the Avenue. Cannon planted in nearby parks began firing wildly.

When the news of Lee's surrender at Appomattox reached Washington on a Monday morning just a week later, while the President still remained at City Point and Richmond, all business stopped, courts adjourned, flags blossomed everywhere, cannon thundered night and day. The land swarmed with laughing, crying, shouting people.

And on Sunday night, April 9, in a blaze of illumination and bonfires, Abraham Lincoln came home.

On Thursday, Washington went wild over the arrival of Grant, the shy, stoop-shouldered little victor. Stanton had turned the War Department into a controlled conflagration. The inner court was draped in a bower of silk flags blazing with color from the light of powerful lamps. In the center jets of flame gave life to the words: THE UNION: IT MUST AND SHALL BE PRESERVED. Beneath this motto a spirited American eagle grasped in its beak the single significant word: RICHMOND.

Every window of the department was lighted up. The façade was covered with flags, banners, evergreens, and corps badges. Over the balcony was a large semicircle of colored lights. Beneath this arc blazed in great letters the name: GRANT.

Thursday noon Evans came running to her rooms in great excitement. His face shone with triumph.

"Anne!" he cried and hugged her close. "It's come! Uncle Abe is back—and Stanton and Ben Wade cornered him this morning. It's all being arranged. Stanton won't stand for a moment's delay. You're to have a half-hour drive with Mr. Lincoln at four-thirty. Later we're to dine with the President, Mrs. Lincoln, and, I believe, Marshal Lamon. Great God, I'm busting with excitement!"

"What *are* you talking about?" she asked.

"Wake up, wake up," he shouted. "Wade has set the stage. Mr.

Lincoln is going to tell you his plans—we're all going to raise the curtain. You'll take your bow alone—as many encores as you wish—and then you and I are going to rush to the altar and then head for Texas as fast as we can make it."

She sat down, feeling suddenly faint. Watching her, Evans laughed and made an impudent face.

"You've got to face it, sweetheart. I've even telegraphed Pilot Scott. He'll be here tomorrow night to take part in the show."

She sat in silence for a few moments, her breath coming in quick gasps.

"Lem," she said like a child, "I want to hide. I honestly do. I'll tell you one thing—I will not be the only woman present today. Please see that Caroline is at the White House too. I'll never be able to go through this alone. And besides, she is my very dear friend."

"You'll have Caroline," promised Evans. "And you'd better get there early. Mr. Lincoln has an awful day. We'll all see you shortly after five."

He started for the door, then turned and came back, looking at her gravely.

"I was going to wait. But I don't think it's right to. There's something you should know—now." He hesitated. "Anne," he said simply, "Harry Heyward was killed with A. P. Hill outside Richmond the other day. Shot by one of Weitzel's scouts while reconnoitering in an exposed ravine."

Her face turned the color of chalk.

"When did you hear that?" she asked at last.

"Only yesterday. Eckert saw his name on some captured rebel casualty lists. He died gallantly, instantly."

So it had happened. So with the fall of Harry's cause, Harry himself had fallen. There were times when the force of destiny frightened her. This was such a time. She said finally, "If it had to happen, perhaps Harry would have wished it so. I—I don't think he could have endured what is to follow. And now, Lem," she added very soberly, "I'd like to be alone a little while."

Evans nodded. At the door he turned.

"Good luck, Madam General. And God bless you and keep your feet on the ground."

At four-fifteen she walked sedately up the White House drive and found Mr. Lincoln already waiting in his carriage and talking to Secretary Usher while a cavalry guard stood mounted at the gate. Mr. Lincoln raised his hat and waved his left hand in his familiar, informal salute.

367

"Good afternoon, ma'am. I'm mighty glad you're early. I skipped an appointment just now and have a rush of work before dinner. Step right in and we'll be off. Good-by, Usher, and tell Mary we'll be back by five."

The day was warm and sunny. After recent rains the lawns and vacant lots were yellow-spotted with fresh dandelions and blades of young new grass. Puddles shone like blue platters under a brilliant sky. And Anne found the President in a curiously gay and reflective mood as their carriage rolled briskly out Connecticut Avenue. He came to the point at once, looking at her a little mischievously.

"You seem to have survived the town's celebrations mighty handsomely, ma'am. More than I can say for our House staff. I've never seen so many swollen heads in my life, and the War Department's stripped—hardly a clerk able to crawl about. Can you stand more good news?"

She winced a little at this last phrase, for she was still thinking of Harry. But after a moment she managed to say:

"Mr. Lincoln, I just told Judge Evans I wish you and Senator Wade would handle this matter in your own way. We are all enjoying a tremendous victory. Why can't my affairs wait a while longer?"

Mr. Lincoln shook his head and noted with a smile the sudden shyness that had seized his companion.

"This matter, ma'am has already waited too long. Wade is breathing fire and brimstone down my neck. Not that I need prodding, ma'am. I agree with him. Now is the time to bring you forward. And I am going to do it at once. Now I want you to listen most carefully and I want to impress one thing upon you before your modesty conjures up objections. Suppose we leave you, as a person, entirely out of this, ma'am. I want you to think back, as objectively as you can, and try to realize that what we are about to do does not concern you alone. It is a matter of truth, of record, of fact, that vitally concerns many who have died in this terrible war."

"I don't know who it was, ma'am, but someone once said that history is nothing but the record of *known* facts. There are too many *unknown* facts about these last four years. Too many really fine and great spirits brushed aside, unnoticed and unknown in the struggle for victory. But you, at least, are not to be one of them. The records of this war, for the future, should be as honest, as complete, as we can now make them."

"What—what is it you propose to do, Mr. President?" she asked.

"I'm coming to that," he said gently. "More than once I've felt bad over having to hide you through this war. But I don't have to tell you that within the privacy of our official family I have spoken over and over again concerning your great services."

368

The President looked down at her and smiled over the secret they shared.

"Some of them have been curious, even puzzled, over my enthusiasm. With only one or two have I ever gone to the heart of the matter. Now, thank God, such caution is no longer necessary.

"Miss Carroll," he went on with increasing earnestness, "I propose to have Senator Wade, as chairman of the Committee on the Conduct of the War, call both House and Senate together sometime within the next fortnight. There I intend to make public, in a joint statement issued by myself and Stanton, as Secretary of War, a full review of your many services, with especial emphasis on your authorship of the Tennessee campaign; your suggestions and solution for the siege of Vicksburg; your help and advice on other military matters—with full recognition of the fine legal pamphlets I was fortunate enough to commission you to write.

"Your pilot, Captain Charles Scott, will be included in these honors as he richly deserves to be. I have no doubt, once the statement of fact is on the record, that the joint Congress will pass our resolution unanimously."

She said hesitantly, "No, no, Mr. President. That's far too much. I'd rather take orders any day than receive honors."

"Well, there is one order I had up my sleeve," he said quickly, heading her off. "But really it's not an order, just a favor I'm asking. In the time of peace ahead we'll all have our work cut out for us, for we've got to nail down the gains we've made in this war. I'd like to suggest, ma'am, that you go back to Maryland to carry the fight for emancipation and equal rights."

"That I can try to do," she replied. "That I *will* do."

"But not before"—and his homely face broke out into that infectious smile—"we've had our little ceremony."

"Mr. Lincoln, I—I don't think I have enough courage to be present on such an occasion."

"But you should be there. You'll *have* to be there," said the President, becoming serious again. "You owe it to your sex, ma'am. It pains me to see how little recognition the brave women of this war have received. There are so many of them, totally unknown. And these women have raised millions of dollars, nursed whole armies, labored mightily, gone into the field.

"Look at Clara Barton, and only a handful of people know of her great exertions. Women like her are passed over because they are women, and it is not right. For them alone you should be proud to stand up and receive these honors."

She hesitated only an instant.

369

"Very well," she said, her face glowing with excitement. "If you present it in that light, I can't refuse."

"That is not all, ma'am," said Mr. Lincoln cautiously, half turned on the carriage seat and watching her rapid breathing and the heightened color in her cheeks. "I wish you to permit me to present you in person to the Cabinet just prior to this joint session. And one thing more." He fumbled in an inner pocket and finally brought out a long sheet of legal foolscap and unfolded it. "I want you to read this, Miss Carroll, and ponder what I've said as to all you have done, as to the need to publish the *truth* and suitably to recognize that truth so that we may partially pay the debt owing to your sex whom you have represented so gallantly."

She took the paper with great reluctance, and saw that it contained but a single paragraph.

"Miss Carroll," said the President with great deliberation, "that paper is Stanton's doing. He insists upon it. He saw to it that General Edward Bragg was taken into our confidence, and the general himself wrote it. Stanton has said to me, over and over again, that the entire course of the war turned upon your ideas and suggestions made to Colonel Scott in that terrible first winter of the war. And now— please read it, ma'am."

The jolting of the carriage made her read very slowly. The single paragraph on the long sheet of paper was quite brief. It read:

Before a joint session of members of the United States Senate and the House of Representatives in Congress assembled, Greetings: Be it enacted that the sum and emoluments given by the Government to Major Generals of the United States Army be paid to Anna Ella Carroll from November, 1861, the date of her service to the country, to the time of the passage of this Act, and further payments of the same amount as the pay and emoluments of a Major General in the United States Army be paid her in quarterly installments to the end of her life, as a partial recognition of her services to the nation.

The date of the act was left blank.

She turned her head quickly, her lips half parted, and on them trembled words of protest. They were never uttered. For she was looking directly into the President's eyes, the deep gray eyes, the dull eyes, the sad eyes, the gay eyes, the humorous, brave, melancholy, cheerful, all-seeing eyes—and in them this time shone an expression she had never witnessed before. And as if he sensed what she intended to say, he shook his head very slowly, like an affectionate reassuring father.

"Not a word more," he almost whispered. "Not a word."

A curious thing had happened to Anne. Her delight, her excitement, her anticipation of this moment had suddenly vanished. For an odd

370

second or two she felt that she was on the verge of some new insight, some new vision. *Her* recognition? *Her* honors?

Then she experienced for a second time the sensation of shrinking in stature beside this man. The strange pattern of her life, her close relationship to the men she had worked for and worshiped—her father, Henry Clay, many others, and now this man—became clear to her in a different and poignant manner.

For what were these honors the President offered her but simple symbols, not alone of affection and understanding which she had had in large measure, but of appreciation and *acceptance,* acceptance of herself as a person, regardless of her sex and the limitations that society placed upon her. This man, this man alone among all those for whom she had worked, had given her these things freely, without stint, without qualification. And if, as Sallie had pointed out to her, she had sought the image of her father in each man she served, she had now, beyond any doubt, found that goal in the highest and most rewarding association of her life. And the measure of his stature reduced her own, not ignominiously, but in true humility.

Her father? This man, to his people, to a nation in travail, had been father to them all. He had worked with them, suffered with them, understood them, brought them through a time of decision, a time of death and bereavement, to the promise of health and the healing of old wounds.

Understanding this, and understanding it profoundly, she silently folded the paper and handed it back to him. For the moment she did not wish to see it again. She began to cry silently and bowed her head, for she felt she could not bear his comprehending gaze at such a time. But his very closeness to her made her fight to regain control of herself and finally she did so. When she looked up at him again he was smiling broadly.

"I guess that clears the air," he remarked calmly, as if all that needed to be said on this matter had been said. "And now, ma'am, let's enjoy the last of this fine air and sunshine."

371

45

ON THE MORNING OF GOOD FRIDAY, APRIL 14, ANNE and Lem attended the crowded services at the New York Avenue Presbyterian Church and prayed solemnly as the President's pastor, the Reverend Dr. Gurley, pleaded with those before him, and with others throughout the nation, to forego vengeance, give devout thanks for their victory, and ponder on Easter Sunday the meaning and the significance of the Resurrection, to the end that new life and new hope might be restored to a distracted Union after four crucifying years.

The services over, they sat quietly in a rear pew until the church was empty.

"Would you think it presumptuous, Lem," she asked him, "if we said a little prayer just for ourselves—for us both, and a new life together?"

He held her right hand and they knelt together for several minutes. When they rose she was startled to see tears in his eyes. Indeed, his dark eyes never seemed to leave her face all that solemn morning. In the vestry he said in an odd tone, "I feel very humble, Anne. I love you so much and I can't quite believe this nightmare is really over. It makes me want to walk warily."

They lunched with Pilot Scott at Brown's Hotel and found him a little more grizzled and aged, but resplendent in a dark blue suit and a massive new gold watch chain. Scott was as excited as any schoolboy. He had a thirty-thousand dollar claim on some cotton he held and the paper required Mr. Lincoln's signature. Evans had already secured him an appointment with the President that afternoon. Scott brought messages from many of Anne's friends in St. Louis, and after a vivid account of the situation there and of a new steamer in which he had bought a half interest, Scott dashed off for a session with a barber before seeing Mr. Lincoln.

Afterward Evans went with Anne to her rooms where she brought out a handsome new trunk filled with linens, lingerie, and new gowns Sallie had brought her from New York. With a shyness unusual for her she laid out these things for him to admire. Then for an hour or more they sat discussing their plans. They were to spend Saturday with the Wades and Easter Sunday at Trenthan. Everyone in the family and several neighbors from the Eastern Shore were to be there. Evans laughed as she ran through the guest list.

"It'll be worse than my first speech in Congress," he protested. "But you're going to promise me one thing, sweetheart. I'll do the talking. I'm going to break the news, make the announcements, and whet their appetites for what's being planned in this town. The Carrolls, for once, are going to listen to an Evans," he said to tease her.

"You're not fair," she cried. "It's that Texas self-sufficiency of yours, Lem, that piques the family. The Carrolls never like to feel there's anyone they can't do something for. And that air of indifference you sometimes wear"—she laughed in spite of herself—"honestly, Lem, you can be infuriating. When you first came to my house in Baltimore I wanted to slap you there in the garden. You were really impudent."

She was repacking her linens and he leaned over and kissed her hair.

"Why didn't you?" he drawled. "It was a very lovely garden."

When they went out at seven to dine at the home of Albert Riddle, Wade's intimate friend, the weather had turned cold, gusty, and raw, with low-scudding gray clouds, patches of fog, and chill brief showers that made everyone hug fires and seek the warmth of parlors and bars. They walked in a yellow murk relieved here and there by flaring gas jets and at last arrived at Riddle's in a world of mist and drizzle.

But inside Riddle's home were warmth and gaiety. Ohio friends were staying there and the Wades had promised to come over later. There was a huge roast, children, wine, and a pleasant crackling fire.

Eleanor, Riddle's oldest daughter, gobbled her dessert and rushed off to join an impatient young man who was taking her to the theater. Later on Riddle led them into the parlor and entertained them with accounts of his recent adventures with blockade runners while he was serving as a Union consul at Matanzas, Cuba. Lem, having fascinated the children with tall tales of Texas, was serving as a bucking bronco for two youngsters who insisted on driving him in opposite directions, whacking him over the ears with a folded newspaper against the amused protests of Mrs. Riddle.

While he was serving the sherry Riddle found the opportunity to bend over Anne and whisper, "I want to congratulate a very remarkable woman, ma'am. Wade has told me everything. I knew long ago he was hugging some secret, but I never dreamed its nature. We are going to work for you."

"You're too generous, Mr. Riddle. And Senator Wade, I'm afraid, has a very busy tongue."

"Oh no, he hasn't," protested Riddle. "In my opinion he kept his secret far too long. We are in for a battle. I have followed this war most closely, ma'am. I tell you from my heart that to me there have been two great geniuses of this war most disgracefully and damnably neglected. One is your charming self; the other is a man I worship, General George Thomas, who has never lost a single engagement of his own planning and, to my way of thinking, is responsible for much of General Sherman's success. I now have two causes I'll enjoy fighting for."

Shortly before eleven they were in the midst of a guessing game, and Mrs. Riddle was mildly insisting that the children should long since have been in bed, when they heard the front door open and a rush of confused footsteps pounding along the hall.

Evans, seated on the floor, looked up with an odd expression.

"I reckon somebody's in a hurry," he drawled in the moment's silence.

The door to the living room was flung violently open and Eleanor Riddle, her face deathly pale, her bonnet askew, her frightened eyes dilated enormously, screamed at them. The shocked face of her escort peered over her shoulder.

"Papa! Heaven help us! It's horrible! Wilkes Booth has just shot the President! Booth leaped down upon the stage and ran back of the scenes. A tall man from the audience rushed after him. The people have been panicked. Tom wouldn't let me stay. We hurried home as fast as we could. I don't know what's happening now."

The little group sat frozen in stunned disbelief. Riddle, seizing on her last words, said angrily, "If you don't know what's happening, child, don't talk such nonsense. Come in here. Calm yourself. Tell us what you *saw*. What is this incredible——"

But Eleanor swayed and her young man put an arm about her. He said in a loud voice that ended in a sob, "As God is our witness, Mr. Riddle, the President has been shot through the head."

Again there was that awful silence of unacceptance. But Anne, her eyes boring into the terror-stricken faces of the two young people, suddenly stood up and said with terrible quietness, "Oh, God in heaven, look at them!" Her voice rose to a scream. "Look at their faces! It's true! It's true! It's true!"

Evans scrambled to his feet and held her. The family crowded around Eleanor, as if to shake her story from her. But the girl sank on the sofa and moaned and sobbed. It was Tom, her young escort, who tried to tell them what had happened.

A night of horror and wild unreality had only begun. In the midst of Tom's account a neighbor, a former secretary to Riddle, burst in on them, even more distraught than either of the young people.

"Mr. Riddle," he shouted hoarsely, "lock up your house and guard your family. Or flee, sir, flee! All hell has broken loose. Murder is being done on all sides. The Cabinet has been slaughtered to a man—all of them! Seward is dead, his two sons slain with him. Stanton is killed. A man told my wife Chase and Welles were stabbed in their beds. Traitors have seized the town. There is blood running everywhere."

Evans stood with his fists clenched on his hips, his eyes blazing at this hysterical newcomer as if he would tear the truth from him bit by bit. Anne, her face the color of chalk, began to cry uncontrollably.

"Stop that. Keep quiet, Anne," commanded Evans.

Riddle, without a word, dashed into the bedroom and returned with two Remington rifles and a brace of Navy pistols. His hands were shaking.

"Here," he shouted to Evans, "take this rifle, sir. You and I are going to find out what this uproar is about. You, sir"—he turned on his trembling neighbor—"get your wife over here and guard her and my family until we return—until we return, do you understand? Tom, stay here with Eleanor, will you? Come along, Evans."

"Just a minute," said Evans sharply, and crossed over to Anne. "I want you to stay here, Anne. If there's anything to these insane reports none of us is safe. I'm going to the War Department and then to Seward's across the square. Will you be all right?"

Her staring eyes were fixed on some point past his shoulder. She seemed frozen, immobile. She whispered, "Yes, yes. But hurry."

Evans and Riddle ran out into the street. Riddle cocked his rifle and said tensely, "I'm going to Stanton's. It's only a block and a half. If I find nothing I'll come back here. If——"

But Evans was already running as hard as he could down New York Avenue. Riddle turned and dashed toward K Street.

At first the silent deserted streets reassured Evans. The mist was shredded by a light east wind. Not a soul was visible on the Avenue, and a ghostly moon seemed to sweep in and out of great banks of broken, scudding clouds. At the end of two blocks he said aloud between clenched teeth, "By God, it's not true. It can't be."

He burst into Lafayette Square, running down the middle of the muddy street past the north end of the Treasury and the squat State Department buildings, and cut across toward the White House grounds. Still the city seemed deserted and for an instant reassuringly silent. But just as he reached the sidewalk past the State Department he heard loud shouts and the clatter of sabers. Out of the east gate, from the stables behind the White House, thundered a troop of cavalry that raced eastward along the Avenue. White-faced officers, cursing and shouting, and men straining at their stirrups, gashing their horses with spurs, pulled at unbuttoned tunics and loose saddle gear.

Evans ran past the White House. Under wan gas jets fluttering in the portico he saw only a group of carriages and one or two coachmen. But across the square, before Seward's house, an excited crowd was milling about. Even as he neared the War Department building lights were beginning to flare in the upper windows. The long shadows of men running flickered among the bare trees in the grounds.

He dashed through the main entrance, past a company of hastily dressed guards with fixed bayonets. The hallway of the War Department building was filled with frightened clerks and white-faced officials. Evans ran upstairs. Eckert wasn't there and the telegraph office was in wild confusion. All circuits had been ordered temporarily broken. The capital was cut off. The tense operators were the only composed creatures in a sea of disorder. David Homer Bates, manager of the office, ran past him and Evans seized his arm. But Bates shook his arm loose and yelled at him, "I know nothing! But there's Colonel Eckert. He knows as much as any man."

Evans cornered Eckert, just coming in by the side door.

"Give me ten seconds, Colonel," demanded Evans. "What do you *know?*"

Eckert, breathing hard, had flung himself at a table and was writing furiously on a telegraph form. He did not even turn his head.

"Mr. Lincoln is dying," he said in a brittle voice. "Shot through the head by a goddamn actor. We believe Seward and his son, Fred, are dead. Some attempt was made on Stanton. We think everyone else is safe. But we don't know."

"Then the Secretary of War is not dead?" exclaimed Evans.

"He is not. An assassin called at his home, but the bell was out of order and the man left."

"And the President?"

Eckert shook his head.

376

"He's been carried to a room across from Ford's Theater. He still lives. Both Stanton and Welles went there in spite of warnings. But don't go there on your peril, Evans. The mobs are frantic. They are trying to burn the theater. But Stanton is in charge and Dana is with him. We've sent cavalry all over the town. You'd better stay here. The city will go mad within the hour."

But Evans shook his head and started for the door.

"I'm going to check on Seward," he called over his shoulder.

Half an hour later he was back. Outside the building the uproar had increased. The streets were full of the thunder of cavalry and militia patrols, of shouts, hysterical shouts, and men and women calling to one another. Eckert came over while Evans tried to get his breath.

"Nothing seems known," said Evans. "I got to Seward's——" He suddenly looked down with disgust at the rifle in his hand. "My God, am I still carrying this?" He stood the rifle in a corner by a bookcase, returned to Eckert, and with great effort tried to give him a coherent account of what he had seen.

"The Seward home is a shambles," he said slowly. "All the foreign legations have turned out in a panic. There are now four ranks of guards about the house. But Dr. Verdi told me he thinks Seward will live. The steel brace on his broken jaw suffered in that carriage accident last week parried the blows and may have saved him. Only one man seems to have done it all—assaulted Seward, beaten Fred Seward about the head, stabbed another son, Augustus, in the shoulder, knocked Seward's daughter down, stabbed Sergeant Robinson in the forehead, and pummeled a male nurse called Hansell. My God, who is behind all this? They've got the assailant's hat and shattered revolver. The man galloped off down Vermont Avenue. But Seward's home looks like a battlefield. There's blood everywhere—on the carpet, the stairs, the very walls. And God help us, it's true about the President. He is dying—if not dead already."

"I know," Eckert said brusquely. "Now stay here, Evans, and help with the dispatches."

While the War Department roared into action, a city disintegrated in a sea of frightening rumors.

Shortly after midnight conditions in the telegraph office abruptly changed. A taut, electric air of efficiency swept through the place. Every circuit was now functioning, handling a stream of orders from Stanton and Dana on Tenth Street.

Hours later Evans and Eckert took a breather, walking down the main sweep of Pennsylvania Avenue as far as Willard's. A cold steady rain had set in. The scene was incredible. A sickly, yellow dawn was breaking over the rain-swept city, driving back blackness and shadow.

377

Forlorn bunting and all the bright banners of victory hung limp and dripping in the raw air. Every few yards stood groups of whispering, stricken people, clothed, partially clothed, or with coats and cloaks pulled on over night attire, all ignoring the rain, all buttonholing one another, talking in low voices, some quietly weeping.

Up and down the Avenue thundered mud-spattered patrols, hacks, carriages, and phaetons carrying officials about the city. A huge and silent crowd had gathered about Willard's, reading scrawled bulletins pasted on ground-floor windows.

Far up the Avenue the still-illuminated dome of the Capitol shone with a ghostly glow in the growing light. Across the wide west portico a more intense oblong of light marked the eloquent transparency Stanton had ordered for victory, bearing the now terrible words, "This Is the Lord's Doing and It Is Marvelous in Our Eyes."

The great dome blurred in Evans's eyes.

"Let's go back," he said.

Another hour, an hour and a half went by. In the murky daylight inside the telegraph office the flaring gas jets looked ghastly. Rain poured down the dirty windowpanes. The office was now crowded but quiet, handling an enormous flood of orders, statements, inquiries, and outgoing material. Evans finished copying a long dispatch to Boston concerning military measures to be taken there. He leaned back in his chair and glanced up at the battered clock on the wall, the same clock that had ticked off every second of the war. It was exactly seven-thirty.

At that precise moment five horsemen tore into the yard facing the Avenue. Only one dismounted. A rain-soaked, towheaded youngster, his round face white, his blue tunic drenched, and his right sleeve covered with mud, ran up the steps two at a time, rushed into the waiting office, and without a word handed a slip of paper to Colonel Eckert.

Not a soul moved. They watched Eckert swiftly pen a brief dispatch and hand it to Homer Bates, manager of the office. Eckert stood up. His handsome face and strained eyes swept the room.

"He's gone," he said abruptly, and his words seemed to stab and rend the sudden silence.

Evans put on his coat, took up Riddle's rifle that he had placed against the bookcase eight or more hours ago—eight years ago—eight hundred years ago—and walked downstairs. In the lobby he found Riddle waiting.

"I took Anne home an hour ago," said Riddle. "Do you want me to go with you?"

Evans shook his head and silently handed Riddle his rifle. Then he went out into the yard and found a department hack.

378

When it finally stopped in front of the Washington House he got out stiffly, gave the driver a folded bill without bothering to look at its denomination, and walked blindly up the stairs. Milly opened the door of Anne's room and Lem thanked God that she was there. Milly had already put Anne to bed and she was about to get some breakfast for her. But instead Evans went down to the hotel kitchen and got fresh coffee and hot corn bread. Like some automaton he set out breakfast on the parlor table, then, hearing a slight sound, he turned to find Anne standing beside him in a rose-colored lounging robe. He was frightened by her expression. She came up to him and put both arms about his neck. He thought he had never seen her eyes so odd and empty. For several moments her lips moved before she could speak. When she did speak her words came with difficulty.

"It isn't true, Lem? It isn't, is it? Isn't it all just a ghastly, impossible dream? Tell me, Lem—has it all—all really happened like this?"

"It's true, sweetheart," he whispered. "It's true. And you've got to bear it."

She moved her head up until she was looking directly into his eyes, but, finding no hope there, she shuddered once and then, for the first time in her life, fainted. He carried her into the bedroom and laid her down while Milly, her face a mottled gray, moaned over and over, "Lord have Mercy—Lord God have Mercy——"

"Milly, pull yourself together," he said gently. "Take care of her."

Then he went out, closed the bedroom door, came over to the table, and picked up a cup of coffee, hot and steaming. But his hand was shaking and he had to put the cup down.

Abruptly he turned away and walked over to the long sofa by the fireplace. There he flung himself face down and wept unashamedly.

46

ON A GRAY MORNING A FEW DAYS LATER SENATOR
Wade faced a group of seven senators and five representatives he had
gathered together in his office at the Capitol.

Wade had been talking for an hour. His desk was piled high with
records and documents. He studied carefully the silent men around
the big oval table.

"I have explained why we must have the support of you gentlemen
to secure proper recognition for Miss Carroll."

He turned to the senator on his right.

"Browning, you've known the whole story for some time. You can
back up every word of it. Can we count on your support?"

"Without reservation, Ben. And I know Mr. Lincoln would have
wished it so."

"Good. Good." Wade seemed immensely relieved.

"And you, George?"

The white-haired man across the table shook his head.

"If you'll forgive me, I don't think the matter should be forced just
now. The assassination has shaken the town, the nation. Everyone
suspects treachery in high places. To bring out Miss Carroll's story
now—to refute military records—alter official judgments—revalue
reputations—with all the inferences to be made in this and other
matters that may have been engineered without the people's knowledge
—I don't think it wise. Later, when——"

Wade nodded. "And you, Edward?"

The representative from Illinois looked absently out the window,
then at Wade.

"Senator, we know your honesty. We have faith in you. But this—
this story, of which I never had an inkling, is well-nigh incredible.

380

What do you think is going to happen, sir, if, in a crisis like this, we toss such a bombshell in the faces of powerful followers of our military leaders? Already a secret caucus has been held to consider General Grant for some high office—perhaps the highest office in the land. You can't produce this woman at such a moment and reveal her as the author of Grant's greatest campaign, or publish her—her recommendations in regard to Vicksburg. Grant's supporters will wreck any such move. They'll be ruthless. You know that."

Wade glanced at a gentleman on his left.

"What do you think, Guv'nor?"

The former governor was a little man, a fighter, a political power in the Midwest. He stared broodingly at the green baize table cover.

"Ben," he said softly, "I'm a great admirer of yours. But in this instance I'm afraid I can't go along with you. In my state a determined move is already on to force this despicable campaign for female rights —for the right of females to vote, mind you!—and to wreck family safeguards reverenced for generations by our forefathers. To produce this woman now—to hand these females a figure they'd tie to, worship, and blazon across the country?" The governor shook his head. "My organization and I have no wish to commit political suicide, Ben. Even if all you claim for Miss Carroll were incontrovertible fact, which I——"

Wade raised his hand. He said wearily, "I understand, Guv'nor. Let's canvass the others."

Twenty minutes later, after a final word with Browning, Wade locked up his empty office, walked downstairs to the great rotunda, and stood there a moment alone, looking absently up at the huge paintings and portraits that rose in serried ranks into the dim light above him. Then he went out of the building, down the hill, and finally walked slowly and wearily westward along Pennsylvania Avenue, as if threading his way through thick fog.

A tall man hurried past him, halted abruptly, and then, with an expression of surprise, turned back and quickly overtook the senator.

"Hello, Wade. I didn't recognize you. Never saw you walk so slow. How are you?"

"Hello, Riddle."

Wade slowly lifted his clouded eyes and gazed dully at his astonished companion. Riddle's thin face showed quick anxiety as he saw the gray look of his friend.

"Ben, you look like the very devil. Are you ill?"

"No," said Wade wearily. "Not ill, Albert. Just tired, baffled, down in the mouth—and goddamn angry."

"Well," said Riddle sympathetically, "it's early in the day for such a mood. Where are you going? Did you know the conspirators have——"

Wade raised a protesting hand.

"I won't listen to any news, Albert, or discuss it. I just don't give a damn. I'm going home. For once I crave solitude. For once I intend to indulge that craving."

Riddle was baffled. He had seldom seen the senior senator from Ohio in such a mood.

"Ben," he said gently, "come into Willard's and have a drink with me. It'll do you good and I won't talk shop. The bar's almost empty. The noon crowd won't be along for an hour."

He spoke without much hope of Wade's assent and was astonished when the old senator nodded and said in a subdued voice, "All right, Albert, I will. And thank you kindly."

With glasses of straight bourbon before them, the two men stood by the long bar with its gleaming brass rail. Large spittoons placed on the floor at regular intervals stood like armored sentries. Only a handful of patrons lounged in the great room, talking in low voices. For some time Wade drank in silence, occasionally running his right hand through his thick thatch of bristling white hair. Riddle watched him attentively, baffled by a certain humility and unaccustomed gentleness in Wade.

"Ben, you're worried. What is it? I'm a good listener. Can't you talk about it?"

"I could—but I'd rather not," said Wade slowly. But immediately contradicting his decision, he remarked rather absently, "It's about Miss Carroll. I don't know what to do."

Riddle's sensitive face quickened with interest. In the uproar that followed the President's murder he had wondered more than once just how Wade would handle this matter. He drank slowly, waited for several moments, then asked with apparent casualness, "What about her? Tell me."

"I'm trying to get her off to Texas with Judge Evans at once. They're to be married—within a week, I hope. But that's not the point, Albert."

Wade paused, surveyed Riddle rather grimly, and then began to speak in quiet clipped sentences, in a monotone, with a weary indifference that might have been most convincing had not Riddle noticed the nostrils of the old war horse quiver a bit and dark patches of color appear in his rugged cheeks.

"You mean," said Riddle sharply when Wade had finished, "that the whole matter's to be dropped indefinitely?"

"It's deader than a doornail, deader than Marley's ghost. When

382

we find out who's running this damned country we'll try to bring it up again."

"Nonsense," said Riddle boldly. "There must be a way. It's too damned important, Ben. Never mind that group you just left. You and Chandler and Stanton alone can jam this through. The thing *has* to be cleared up. Not later—but *now.*"

Wade tossed off his drink, deftly slid the glass along the bar toward a distant bartender, and called out, "Fill it up again, Jim."

Then he turned about with great deliberation, his back to the bar, bracing himself against it. Riddle noted the rising glow in his eyes, the deepening flush in his cheeks, the deep furrows that ran up from each corner of his mouth to the powerful nose.

"All right, Albert," exclaimed Wade with unexpected harshness. "You've been on the floor. You've had the brains to get out of Congress and stay out when you didn't have to. You're a pretty able lawyer in this degenerate town. How would *you* go about it? I'll listen."

Riddle flashed an understanding smile at the grim old senator braced against the bar.

"Wade, you need a good rest and a sleep around the clock. We've all been overwhelmed these last terrible days. Wait a month—but no longer. Get your Committee on the Conduct of the War all primed. Call in Stanton, Colonel Scott, Grant, and Sherman. Take down their statements. Call together the chairmen of the House and the Senate Military Affairs Committees. Line up all the powerful support you command in both chambers. Then go to President Johnson and tell him what has happened. Tell him, with Stanton beside you, exactly what Mr. Lincoln had planned. And demand that this honorable procedure be gone through with at once. I suggest that it immediately precede the final review of the troops in this capital."

Riddle had caught fire from his own enthusiasm.

"You have the power, Ben. It's in your hands. You can demand this, force it through. Now, while the iron's hot. You can obtain at once for this woman all that——"

"Stop it! Stop it!" shouted Wade in a voice so hoarse one might have thought he was strangling. "In God's name, stop this damned nonsense! I intend to fight for Miss Carroll, Albert. I intend to fight for this as hard as ever I did in my life. But you don't understand. We are too late, I tell you! We are much too late! I told you what happened this morning. Yesterday I saw Stanton. He is a very sick man. Two attacks of vertigo this week. The man who raised and supplied the greatest armies ever known hasn't a dime. His fortune is gone. His health is broken. But his great spirit, thank God, is not. He told me he would hang onto the War Department until he is thrown out bodily.

383

He knows the havoc now being created behind the scenes. He knows the traitors creating it. He understands the battle now to be waged over the prostrate corpse of the Confederacy. Yesterday Stanton and I talked about Miss Carroll for an hour."

Wade studied the glass in his hand for a few moments. "We have plans for Miss Carroll, Albert. We made them. We will fight for them. But God in heaven—we're too late! I know it. I feel it. I finally saw it today. And I'll try to tell you why."

There was a note of renewed despair in Wade's voice which dismayed Riddle. Wade's face was now purple, and the veins of his powerful neck stood out like whipcord. As he continued to speak it occurred to Riddle that he had never seen him so angry.

"We have piled blunder on blunder, timidity on timidity! And God help me, I am to blame as much as any man. Every general in this land has his clique who will block Miss Carroll. The War Department, except for Stanton, will raise heaven and earth to obliterate her."

The old man was shouting.

"There are true gods in their rightful place, Albert. But the false gods, too, have been stuffed to bursting. And to pull that stuffing out now! It cannot be done, Riddle, it cannot be done! The false mold has been made. The false image has been cast. I saw that in every face about me this morning. And confronting all the powers arrayed against us, do we dare to shatter these false gods and raise up the images of a woman and a humble river pilot in their place; do we dare to presume that the prostrate worshipers will now get up, move over, transfer their blind and settled allegiance, and worship at a new and far humbler shrine that we deliberately concealed from them?"

The knuckles of Wade's left hand were white against the polished mahogany bar.

"We have all committed a crime, Albert, an outrageous crime, not alone against this woman but, by God, against the people themselves. The people fought this war. They died by the hundreds of thousands in it. They won it. And one of their own, a great and generous woman, provided the most powerful single weapon of their victory. And we hid it from them. We buried it, and a privileged few whispered and mumbled about it as if it were some dirty, shameful, backstairs secret that could not stand the light of day. After all, Miss Carroll is a civilian. *Above all, Miss Carroll is only a woman.* She can wait. That is what we said. I knew it was wrong at the time. Judge Evans knew it was wrong. And we continued to salve ourselves with sleek excuses, with the bloodguilt of others. We did nothing! God damn it, I am ashamed, Riddle. I'm ridden with guilt. I am as full of bitterness and rage at myself as at others."

384

The other man was shocked by this outburst. Wade's voice rolled out and filled the big room. The loungers had forgotten their drinks. They had crept closer, trying to fathom the mystery of why this distinguished old man was shouting. The two bartenders poised nervously over dark wood and gleaming glasses.

Riddle, his coat still gripped by Wade's right fist, attempted to lay a hand on Wade's shoulder and Wade roughly shook it off.

"Ben, try to calm yourself," said Riddle quietly. "Think, man, *think!* You can certainly get these claims of Miss Carroll's, this resolution passed by the committees you control in Congress."

"By God, I can, Albert. I can and I will," cried Wade. "But I know what is going to happen. And I saw it, I saw it with damnable clarity as I talked to Stanton and to those villains this morning. I think poor Stanton saw it, too, for he was white and shaken after we had canvassed the membership of House and Senate and faced the situation as we see it in this cesspool of double-dealing thieves.

"Do you know what Stanton said to me—an hour ago—the greatest war minister we have ever had, a man I love as a brother, a man with an unquenchable spirit, a man who had enough energy to fire a dozen armies? He came up to me when I left and pleaded with me. He said, 'Ben, we have helped to create a damnable injustice. You and I have got to fight for this.' And then he added with all the force of which he was capable, 'I owe my position to Miss Carroll. I came into the Cabinet on your demand and at Mr. Lincoln's request, pledged to execute her plan. Before God, Wade, and with all my knowledge of this conflict, I say to you now that hers was the greatest course in the war. She found herself, got no pay, and did the great work that made others famous.' "

Wade's voice was quieter now. He was speaking hoarsely and his tone was again sad.

"Let me tell you what is going to happen, Albert, as we develop this fight. The evidence will be acknowledged. It will have to be, for it is *there*. The statements will be accepted. The resolution—God in heaven, *any* resolutions we present—will be solemnly approved. We will win this fight, Albert—and we will lose it. The resolution will be carried. Oh, there's no doubt of that," he said with heavy irony, "no doubt at all. 'Wade can do it. Stanton will help.' You've said so yourself. But it will be carried over from committee to committee, and debated and tabled, and approved and tabled, and passed and tabled— and debated and *forgotten*—until the stink of delay and dishonor and futility fills our nostrils. For the Congress as a whole, Riddle, will never declare their convictions to the nation!

"And we will bring in Stanton and Tom Scott and Miss Carroll. We

385

will bring in Grant, perhaps, and Sherman, Cassius Clay, Senator Browning, and a host of able men. And in the last resort we will invoke the sacred shade of a murdered President—and all in vain!"

Wade tossed off almost half a tumblerful of bourbon.

"Riddle, Miss Carroll will be consigned to oblivion if Congress has its way. And why? Because, God help us, *she is a woman.* And they believe that to publish that fact would be to discredit all the generals and professionals in the Army. The 'good of the service,' the 'faith of the nation,' the prestige of the chosen, the honor of our omnipotent male oligarchy, the pride of men, the sacred shield of concealment that their self-appointed betters maintain over the people, the crushing idiocies of our ruling class, make it expedient, required, convenient, suitable, advisable, necessary—in fact, *demand* that Miss Carroll be suppressed. *And suppressed she will be!*

Wade slowly raised his glass and examined it for a moment, then slowly tilted it and allowed the rest of the liquor to spill on the floor. All at once he raised his arm still higher and suddenly hurled the glass with all his strength down at the gleaming tiles. And the glass crashed and splintered into sharp fragments that glittered and sparkled strangely in the light. The act seemed to calm him. His voice, when he spoke again, was slow, deliberate, reflective, and his eyes, burningly prophetic, held Riddle spellbound.

"This is what I believe," he said finally. "This is what I predict. We will fight hard. We will fight long for Miss Carroll. But in some distant day this resolution will drop unnoticed from the timid hands of cowards and small smug men with dulled consciences taken up with other issues of other days. There will be a new stage, a new cast of players. And we old meddlers, bent upon simple justice in some remote and forgotten matter, will be gone.

"There, Riddle, in the halls of Congress, the recognition and the secret of Miss Carroll will sleep.

"There, by God, it will die."

386

47

IN ALL HER LIFE ANNE HAD NEVER BEEN SO NUMBED
by shock, so worn with exhaustion as she was after that fateful Good
Friday. Apathetic, incredulous, rebellious against the inescapable
truth of Lincoln's death, she had gone to bed that night and for a week
had stayed there.

Milly, grief-stricken herself, had tried vainly to coax her into getting
up and going through the semblance of normal living. Caroline Wade
had come several times and begged her with no success to come for
tea, at least to go for a walk with her.

Her illness, thought Evans, was a measure of the role Lincoln had
come to play in her life, a role neither of them, nor many others,
he noted, had accurately measured until tragedy measured it for them.

But on the ninth morning her natural resiliency triumphed and she
astonished Milly by saying in her usual strong clear voice, "I'm going
to get up, Milly. And I want to know what's been happening. Please
go out and get the newspapers."

When he called a little later Lem was delighted to have her promise
to go for a short drive the next day. By the middle of the week Milly
had flung open all the windows and embarked on a vigorous spring
cleaning of Anne's crowded rooms, at Anne's suggestion.

On Thursday Evans came in again. His tall figure seemed to fill the
room with portents, his dark eyes were bright, and he was carrying a
packet of letters.

"How do you feel?" he asked, looking at her closely. "I have a
treat for you if you're up to it. And some news I can hardly wait
to share. Are you up to a drive over Arlington way? The Sewards,
who are all recovering, thank God, have been most anxious about
you. The Secretary has turned over his best carriage and two fine

387

Arabian horses to us for a week so I can get you out in the air and away from these rooms for a while. It's a beautiful day. Shall we go?"

"Yes—I'd love it, Lem," Anne said slowly. "It will do me good—and I must get back to work next week."

"We'll see about that in good time," he said with concern. "First of all, I want to get some color in those cheeks. Suppose I drive around in an hour."

The carriage was a luxurious affair, a low-slung phaeton with deep wine-colored cushions and arm rests, a wide top to shield them from the sun, and two magnificent horses that Evans managed with an expert hand.

They drove smartly over the Long Bridge, past half-masted flags and hundreds of yards of black bunting on the District side. He saw Anne bite her lips and tears come into her eyes. But on the Virginia shore, as he turned to the right, along the river road, they plunged into a mass of delicate green foliage with the fragrance and bloom of dogwood and wild flowers everywhere, and he saw with relief that she was beginning to relax.

Shortly before noon they came to the white-pillared portico of Arlington. A hundred yards from the handsome old Lee mansion Evans spread rugs and blankets and a basket lunch on the grass. He made Anne comfortable against a maple tree bursting with new leaves, and they ate and sat for a time looking at the graceful bends of the Potomac and the city spread before them.

At last he laid the letters before her. Her face was still pale and he watched it anxiously. It was not like Anne to be so lacking in curiosity.

"Anne," he began gently, "I wanted to wait a while longer about these until you have more strength. But certain matters won't wait, and I'm afraid I must talk about them now."

"Fiddlesticks about my strength, dearest," she said with some of her old spirit. "I'm quite all right. What is it?"

"Well," he said hesitantly, as if already regretting the need for this tête-à-tête, "it's about us." His hands pressed the letters on the rug.

"It's this," he went on quickly. "I have to go back to Texas almost immediately—in two weeks. I want you to go there with me. And I want you to understand why we have to leave so abruptly."

She looked at the letters almost absently.

"You mean—they want you out there at once. Is that it? I thought you'd go to Maryland with me . . . ." Her voice died away. Evans glanced at her quickly.

"I reckon that's what they're after. I thought I could stave off things awhile, until we could get everything lined up our own way and at our

388

leisure. But after what's happened——" His voice sharpened, developed the twang it always did when he became excited. "Anne, there aren't many Texas Unionists available for the job ahead. It's an enormous state and the old crowd will pour back into power with new labels in a minute if they aren't blocked. Frankly, I'm eager to get down to the job of blocking them too." His face was alight with enthusiasm as he went on:

"They're planning a constitutional convention already. Judge Ogden wants me to lead the fight in persuading Texas folks to support it and pave the way for re-entry into the Union based on popular support—and not engineered by a bunch of power-hungry ex-rebels. These are letters from Judge Walker, Wesley Ogden, A. M. Hamilton, and others. Hamilton wants to put me up as Chief Justice of the Texas Supreme Court as soon as an honest-to-God state constitution is ratified. It's going to be a fight," he finished, his eyes shining. "I can't refuse them."

"You shouldn't," Anne said, and for an instant Evans thought he saw an odd look in her eyes. Was it envy or wistfulness? "You want me to read all these?" she asked doubtfully.

"I wish you would," he said, ignoring the look, "so you'll see the picture whole. Stanton accepted my resignation, with some very kind remarks, several days ago. Sweetheart, I want to go to Baltimore tomorrow and talk with your father. We'll arrange for a family wedding at Trenthan or Cambridge, whichever you prefer. After all, we have two weeks. But we should be in Austin by the end of May."

He studied her closely a moment, hesitated, and then said very soberly, "I talked to Ben yesterday about the plans Mr. Lincoln had made for you. He——"

"Don't, Lem," she interrupted. "Please don't talk about it. I—it doesn't matter to me now. I mean that. Later I'm sure Senator Wade will do the proper thing. But let's not talk about it for a long time." Tears were in her eyes again and her voice was curiously humble.

She picked up his letters, read them carefully, and then looked up at him with much of her old ardor.

"They make me very proud of you, Lem," she said softly. "You deserve every word of them." Her face was open and loving as she added slowly, "Of course you must go."

His whole expression seemed to shout relief. The taut lines about his mouth relaxed and he smiled delightedly.

"Thank God! I knew you'd see it that way," he cried, and leaned over and kissed her. "Then I'll see your father tomorrow and arrange everything. Do you realize we can be married next week? Then it's a train to New Orleans together, a government packet to Galveston, a

389

stage drive to Austin—and all the West you love and the whole state of Texas for your back yard! Darling, it's freedom and a new lease of life for us both! A new country—a different and beautiful country, you'll find. You can be just a wife for a while," he said fondly. "We'll have the rest of our days together," he finished jubilantly.

She was looking at the winding Potomac below them. Her voice, when it reached him, sounded faint and far away.

"Darling," she said in a frightened whisper, "I don't know how to tell you." Her eyes were dark with conflict. "But—I'm not going to Texas with you just now. Oh, Lem——" She hesitated, for he did not appear to be listening. In a firmer voice, she hurried on, "I can't go with you now, Lem. Later—but not now, dearest."

It had taken time for the impact of her words to reach him. But now he turned to her and he seemed dazed.

"What are you saying? What do you mean?" Then a look of comprehension crossed his face. "You're overwrought," he said gently, "I shouldn't have brought this up today. You can't mean it."

She shook her head. "Yes, Lem, I do. It's hard for me to explain. Oh, darling, don't you see? After what's happened, I can't run away. I can't just leave everything I've fought for so long. In a way I have the same decision to make that you have made."

"Run away!" he exclaimed. "Who's asking you to run away? Good lord, we've been talking about this for years! Now we have the opportunity we've longed for—to live together, work together if you want, for the rest of our days, please God. Why do you——"

"But the world has changed, Lem—like that," she said, snapping a stalk of fresh weed between her fingers. "If Mr. Lincoln hadn't been murdered—if I hadn't made a promise to him—— Don't you see, Lem, I have work to do and it's important too? Wait, don't say it," she begged as he angrily began to protest. "I know everything you could say. That I could work as well, perhaps better, at your side in Texas; that we belong together, which we do, we profoundly and lovingly do. And that we have loved each other a long time and waited. Lem, I do love you, please believe me, and I'll come to you and marry you in Austin just as soon as I can. But I've got to stay here now until I've assured myself of something."

"And what is that something?" demanded Evans, his voice hard and hurt.

"Lem, a little while ago I said I had hoped you would come with me to Maryland. I thought we could be married and live there for a while and you could help me."

"In God's name, what are you talking about?"

"I'm talking about finishing something I've begun," she said with a flash of anger. "Surely you can understand that." Then she spoke more calmly. "Let's not quarrel, darling. Let me try to tell you in my own way.

"Mr. Lincoln's death has shocked me, that's true. Not just the loss of a man I had come to feel very close to, but the meaning of it. Something invaluable at this time was taken away—a quality of mercy, a measure of tolerance, a world of patience and understanding and insight into human beings." Her face was sad and there were tears in her eyes as she stared into the distance.

"There are so many men who stand for part of us, Lem. Mr. Lincoln changed me enormously. And now I know that he stood for the finest things in *all* of us. I've made many mistakes in my life, Lem, but I think the greatest of all has been my lack of understanding of human forces all about us. My lack of truly compassionate understanding. And that mistake Mr. Lincoln made most glaringly clear to me. All my life I've seen the horrors of slavery, the exploitation of the poor, the abuse of the ignorant—I knew they were wrong. When Negroes were sold or driven away I wept over them as individuals. But I would not go out and fight to destroy the damnable system that so enslaved them. I was blind and cautious and narrow. I thought all that could be ended if 'legality' and 'order' were first established. I was hypnotized by the letter of the law. I wanted reforms done legally, without violence. I am afraid there is no such way. There are so many slaveries all about us. Mr. Lincoln made me see that, and if knowing him has affected me so deeply, I can't help beginning to grasp what his death must mean to our whole nation."

"And because of that, you believe we must pursue separate paths, deliberately prolong the unhappy state we're in. Just what do you expect to accomplish by that?"

His words were bitter, mocking, full of pain.

"I expect to finish what I've started in Maryland," she answered quietly. "It won't take long. I'll be with you in only a few months, dearest. But you must see this, Lem. I could not bear it if I could not make *you* understand how I feel. The death of this man means that a great betrayal of this war is already planned, all he worked for, all that nearly a million men died for, even the little that we ourselves have done. If we loved him, if we believed in his magnificent spirit, we must not let what he died for perish."

"Wait a minute," said Evans with patient reasonableness. "Why can't you do whatever it is you plan to do, if you insist upon it, in Texas?"

"Because, Lem," she said simply, "right now I can do it better in Maryland. I know my people. And I made a promise."

"What promise was that?" Evans asked sharply. When she told him he was silent and shook his head slowly.

"Something very profound has happened to me, Lem. I feel I owe a debt to Mr. Lincoln, to others, and to myself to work in Maryland, at least for a time." She reached for his hand and took it in both of hers.

"Lem, I often think of Mingo, of Milly, Uncle Nathan, and of our house servants and slaves, many of whom I loved deeply. I admired Fred Douglass, who once lived and worked near us on Colonel Lloyd's place. Above all, I admired Harriet Tubman, from our own county, who led so many poor wretches to freedom. What bitter avengers of slavery the Eastern Shore has nourished! And what I fear now is a world that will slowly return to its old evil ways. That's something I cannot and will not endure. There is no reason to life if we have no firm belief in the future and what people can do with it. Those who killed Lincoln———"

"But that was the act of a madman," interrupted Evans somberly. "I don't believe it is significant of any great betrayal. . . ."

"John Wilkes Booth a madman? Nonsense! Listen to me, Lem. I, too, have worked in political life for years. I know something about the violent extremes to which men can go. For months, as far back as January, we knew plots were afoot against Mr. Lincoln and his Cabinet.

"I met Booth a number of times. He was a clever, brilliant, even dangerous man. But there was nothing mad about him. That is an idea that is being deliberately fostered. Booth was in touch with the Richmond people, with Davis even, during the last days of the war. Nothing will ever convince me that Mr. Lincoln and the Sewards, to say nothing of other Cabinet members, were not victims of a definite conspiracy plotted in the South. Look at the scope of it, the type of men marked for death, the cautious way an inquiry is being conducted, that cryptic note left at Johnson's hotel—the way people are being kept from talking.

"I know what certain men think about this crime. And I agree with them. But the truth will never be made known, for I honestly believe too many important men, South *and* North, were deeply implicated."

Evans had heard many shocking rumors and suggestions himself, most of which he did not believe. But after a single glance at her white face he dared not pursue the subject. He saw the tiny lines about her eyes, the violet shadows under them, a certain transparency in her skin —a look almost of dedication about her whole posture.

"Then, Anne," he said quietly, "tell me what it is you really wish to do."

"There isn't a great deal I can do," she said humbly, "and what I

392

can do shouldn't take long. I want to make sure that in Maryland, at least, the old bondage broken by this war will never be restored. That is what I promised Mr. Lincoln. I intend to work for and with the Negroes, to see their political rights assured, to work with the Maryland Republicans until this is done——"

"Good God, Anne! In a state like Maryland that's the task of a lifetime."

"No, it isn't," she contradicted him quickly. "I've already made a good start. You remember I told you that last month I secured five hundred signatures from the state's leading Republicans solemnly promising to have just those provisions legalizing Negro rights written into Maryland's civil law. Besides, those very Republican leaders assure me it can be done in a few months." She gave him no time to speak.

"Lem dear, as soon as that's done, I'll join you, with no strings, no reservations, and a clear conscience. When I've crossed that finish line—I'll come to you."

"And will you know when you've crossed that finish line?" he asked softly.

She looked away and caught her breath. He could not know his question had recalled instantly with terrible vividness the identical phrase of another man. A remote and distant day came to her mind. The dim face and figure of a man long dead rose up, and Henry Clay, one of the great men she had worshiped, was smiling at her and shaking his head in affectionate reproach. And his words came back to her.

"You always were a stubborn girl," he had said. "Well, go on, if you must—but don't look for a finish line, Anne. You'll never find it."

She was frightened. For a moment she wanted desperately to undo her decision, to go with Lem, to make sure of their happiness now.

"What is it?" he asked tensely.

"Dearest," she began, still trembling from the instant of apprehensiveness, and she spoke as though to herself as well as to him. "I love you completely, devotedly, with my whole heart. And side by side with that love is something equally important to me. Can you know what it means to me to have had you treat me as you have— treated me as a *person*, an equal, somebody in my own right? Do you think that in spite of all the work I did in Baltimore I didn't have the feelings of a woman; that I didn't long for real companionship, someone truly to share my life with me; that I didn't wish for a home and children of my own, and that I didn't long with my *whole* heart, not just part of it, for someone who might love me and take me as I am?"

She looked at him, her blue eyes wide and dark with intensity.

"And then, dearest, you came along. You paid me the highest

393

honor of loving me and of taking my thoughts, my ideas, my words, and my work as seriously as you would your own. Lem, you know how I feel about you. And that's why I expect you to understand me now and let me do what I feel I must."

Lem looked out over the far expanse of land shimmering in the April sunlight.

"I will," he said slowly, as if weighing exactly each word he spoke, "if I can be sure you really understand your decision. But I'm afraid —afraid this decision is partly made by forces within you of which you may not be aware. There is such a thing as habit, invincible habit, habit of mind as well as action. If I could be sure that this force of destiny you seem to feel is your slave, and not your master—if I could be sure of this, I could go to Texas with a light heart and wait for you to come to me at a time we both recognize as the right time."

He struck the palm of one hand with his fist and was silent.

"But I am afraid," he repeated almost in a whisper. "Because you have been following the same course all your life."

Her hand went out and found his. She moved close to him.

"I am aware of that, too, Lem, and now I do know where to stop," she said with quiet confidence. "I will know when to come to you. I promise you that. And it will be soon, my darling."

He held her in his arms for a long time. And then suddenly she looked up at him and smiled.

"You're to blame for all of this," she said, and laughed. "Perhaps if you hadn't treated me as an equal . . ."

"What do you mean?" he asked quickly. "Here I've finally come to believe that every person, of either sex, of every race, every color, every creed, was born free and equal and is to be respected and given the same rights and opportunities I enjoy. And now you blame me!"

"Forgive me, then, Lem, for asking you the question I am about to ask you. If you truly believe in that kind of equality"—she paused —"what would your answer be if I pleaded with *you* to stay here and work with *me,* to stay here in Washington where you've already worked, where you're respected, have friends, and there is so much to do? Tell me honestly, Lem, what would you say?"

"Damn it!" he said, and plucked a handful of fresh grass at his side and threw it from him. "Damn it, Anne, you're too good a lawyer —and a lovable one! You've broken me over the back of my own argument. I've got to go to Texas. I can't stay here."

"You see?" she said gently. He turned quickly, put his arms around her, and kissed her passionately. After a while she leaned back and looked at him tenderly.

"Lord help us, Lem, we're chips off the same block, and we'd both

394

better keep it in mind. You have to fight for a time in Texas and I in Maryland. But not too long. Then I'll come to you, dearest, that I promise you. After all, Lem, there's a time for every purpose——"

She gave him a startled look, as if she had quite unexpectedly found a comforting answer to a long-perplexing problem.

"I haven't thought of those words for years, Lem. And I've always loved that passage so much. Do you know it?"

Her voice was clear, calm, reflective, and carried like music on the fragrant air.

"To every thing there is a season, and a time to every purpose under the heaven:

"A time to be born, and a time to die; a time to plant, and a time to pluck up that which is planted . . .

"A time to weep, and a time to laugh; a time to mourn, and a time to dance . . .

"A time to embrace, and a time to refrain from embracing . . . a time to keep silence, and a time to speak;

"A time to love, and a time to hate; a time of war—and a time of peace."

Her voice died away and Evans held her close.

"A time of peace!" he exclaimed at last, and the words fell on the quiet air like a benediction.

But he said no more and they remained in one another's arms until the river lay in shadow.